fly away little bird

OBSESSION

gemma
weir

Amanda,

Birds fly free, unless they're chained in a pretty cage.
Be the bird, or embrace the cage if it includes a
big dick and an alphahole who knows how to use it.

#littlebird

WARNING

I didn't think this book was going to need a warning, but after writing the first few chapters, it looks like it is, so here goes.

This book contains elements of bullying, and at times skirts along the lines of dark romance with some scenes that could be considered as having dubious consent.

Sebastian Lockwood is controlling, manipulative, cruel and sometimes cold to the point of being glacial. Please do not let his age fool you, he is as alpha and dominant as all the other heroes I've written and if alphaholes are not your jam, then please stop reading now.

All of my heroes are over-the-top, jealous, unreasonable, possessive assholes.

If you consider unapologetic alphaholes unacceptable, or feel their behavior is in some way abusive, then this isn't the book or series for you.

If you're a naysayer who thinks what I write is romanticizing domestic violence and abuse then please, please stop reading now, you will not enjoy this book!

This book isn't a guide to dysfunctional relationships, it's fiction. My books are fantasy, this isn't real life, it's a romance novel and should be read as such.

Just because this book is based during the high school and college years, please do not mistake this as a young adult romance—it's not. This book is packed full of sexual scenes, dirty, filthy sex and some scenes that will make you slightly ashamed that you enjoyed them so much.

Nothing I write is based on real life, it's pure fantasy, so it's okay to agree that the dysfunctional relationships between my characters are incredibly sexy. Please do not kink shame me or my enthusiastic readers for finding these extreme alphahole behaviors hot, maybe if you read this book with the pinch of romantic salt it was intended to come with, you might like it too.

So if, like me, you love a guy who is so obsessively in love with his girl that he will manipulate, coerce, control and obsess over her until she gives herself to him completely, then read on and welcome to the world of the alphaholes ;)

OBSESSION

PROLOGUE

Firm, unyielding fingers roughly force their way between my thighs and cup my pussy tightly. "This cunt is mine, it's for my eyes, my fingers, my tongue and my cock only. I won't share, and that includes you suggesting this could ever belong to anyone else. The only things that will be inside your wetness will belong to me. You're mine, Starling, you always have been, so get used to it. I've owned you since the day I set eyes on you in high school and I'll always own you. You might have run from me, but I always knew where you were and I always will. You'll never be free of me."

Shaking my head, I yank my wrists from his hold, trying to free myself, but all I can move is my head, so I shake it, denying his words in the only way I can.

His laugh is menacing and full of confident promise. Leaning down, he presses a kiss to my lips, resting his nose against my cheek as he pulls in a deep inhale. "Try and run, little bird. I'll chase you to the ends of the earth. You don't get to leave this house unless I take you. The entire population of the campus knows you belong to me, and your mom would love to know you're under my care and protection. Behave and life can be good, fight me and I'll make the me you knew in high school seem like a walk in the park."

Tears spill from my eyes, rolling down my cheeks as I stare up at his excited eyes. He's enjoying this.

I hate him so much. But I've moved on, I've put high school behind me. I've forced myself to forget him, or at least I've done a really good job of pretending to forget about him.

I moved halfway across the country, and only came back because he wasn't meant to be here. But here he is, my tormentor, and the only guy my panties have ever gotten damp for. "I hate you," I whisper through my arid throat.

"Good, I hate you too."

PART ONE
THE BEGINNING

ONE

STARLING

"Starling."

"Yeah."

"Courtney's here," Mom yells from the bottom of the stairs.

I don't have to see her to know she's leaning against the stair rail, her hair still in a messy knot at the top of her head, her bathrobe open and revealing one of the massive oversize nightshirts she sleeps in.

"I'm coming," I yell, hurrying to finish braiding my hair that's in desperate need of a cut. It's so long now, the braid almost hits my butt when I finish twisting the band into the bottom and let it fall over my shoulder.

"Starling," Mom yells again. "You're going to be late unless you get your butt downstairs right now."

Shoving the tube of lip gloss in my hand into the pocket of my blazer, I grab my backpack from the floor and rush out of my room and downstairs. My ratty Chucks are still sitting by the door where I kicked them off after I got home from my late shift at the diner last night. I shove my feet into them while Mom waves a five-dollar bill in front of my face, her glasses balanced on the edge of her nose.

"I have money," I tell her.

"You shouldn't be spending your money on food, the money you earn is for you."

"No, the money I earn is for us. I live here, I'm more than capable of contributing. You won't take my wages toward the bills, so I can buy my own lunch."

"Honey, I can pay our bills. I'm the adult, you're the kid. My next book is ready to go to the editor, after that I'm going to take that gig writing instruction manuals for a while."

"No, you're not. You'll hate it, and you'll die a little more inside each time you have to explain how to insert a battery into a clock or whatever."

"It's regular money, a guaranteed salary each month instead of relying on my publisher to promote my back catalog."

Shaking my head, I lean in and press a kiss against her cheek. "I'll get a few extra shifts a week, I can help."

Smiling a sad smile, she lifts her hand and grabs my face, squeezing my chin and squishing my cheeks the same way she's been doing since I was a little kid. "I love you so much."

"Love you too, Mom."

She slaps her lips against mine in a quick, over-the-top smoochy kiss, then drops her hand and ushers me toward the door. "Go, or Courtney is going to start honking, I can't deal with Mr. Longstein coming over here to complain about the pitch of her horn again."

"Okay, okay, I'm going." Grabbing the door handle, I open it and wave absently behind me as I rush down the steps.

"Morning," Court sings, rolling down her window and almost falling out of the car as she enthusiastically dances in her seat to the terrible bouncy pop music she loves that's blaring from the stereo.

"Wow, how many cups of coffee have you had this morning?" I ask, sliding into the passenger seat and closing the door, shoving my backpack down between my feet.

"Only two and a couple of energy drinks."

"Jesus, Court, that's far too much caffeine before eight a.m."

"It's not even my record, the other week when you were sick I had three coffees and three Red Bulls before lunch. I swear I did all of my summer homework in less than an hour."

"You're going to give yourself a heart attack at sixteen, I'm cutting you off. I'm serious, one coffee before breakfast and no energy drinks until school finishes from now on."

Courtney giggles, settling back into her seat and pulling away from the curb. "So, you'll never guess who was at the party on Saturday night."

"What party?"

"Jennifer Houston's party, I told you about it."

"Oh yeah. I think I remember you mentioning it," I say, absentmindedly rooting through my backpack, trying to find my cell that I shoved in there before I started braiding my hair.

"So…" Court prompts.

"So what?" I ask, finally locating it at the bottom beneath a candy wrapper.

"So, guess who was there?"

"Where?"

"At the party."

"Oh, who?" I ask, not really caring, but trying to sound like I do. Court has never understood why I'm not more interested in the kids we go to school with, and it's too early to deal with her being pissy with me.

"Evan, Hunter, Clay and Sebastian."

"Oh, cool," I say, typing out a message to my boss to ask if there are any more shifts I can pick up this week.

"Are you even listening to me? The Acres Elite were all at Jennifer's party and they stayed for almost an hour."

"They only stayed for an hour? That seems kind of rude."

"Jennifer's only a sophomore like us, it's amazing that they showed up at all," Court gushes, animatedly talking with her hands until she has to grab the wheel as her car starts to drift across the road.

"Isn't it a bit sleazy for a group of seniors to go to a sophomore party?"

"Well, it was Jennifer's brother Justin's party really, he just let Jennifer invite some friends. Justin's a senior, but even he seemed shocked they turned up. He was trying to act all cool, getting them beers and chatting like they were besties or whatever, but everyone could see how excited he was that The Elite came to his party. Clay is gorgeous, so is Hunter, well they all are, but Evan is kind of a dick and Sebastian, well he's just scary. Scary hot, but still... scary."

"Having an attractive face doesn't make you less of a douche, and all four of them are douches. They're bullies and everyone knows bullies have small dicks. Their asshole behavior is just them trying to overcompensate for lacking in the trouser department. I bet all four of them have the worst case of little dick syndrome."

"Muffy Hamilton said she saw Evan screwing Amanda Collins in the science lab and that his dick was huge."

Cringing, I turn and look at Courtney. "Eww, he was having sex in the science lab? We have to sit at those tables, that's disgusting."

Courtney giggles. "God, Starling, you're such a prude. Muffy said Evan had his hand over Amanda's mouth because she was being so loud."

"She was probably just asking if he'd even got his microdick inside her yet." I laugh.

"Oh my god, can you even imagine if his dick was that small?" She cackles. "How gutted would you be if a boy that hot had a microwang?"

We're still laughing as we pull into the school parking lot. There're separate dedicated parking areas for sophomores, juniors and seniors. The sophomore spots are the farthest away, the juniors in the middle and seniors right outside the entrance doors. Courtney pulls her car into a spot and kills the engine, then turns to look at me. "First day of sophomore year."

I can hear the excitement in her voice; she loves this. Being at school, having a million friends, going to parties. She's been talking about what we'll do once we're in high school since the fourth grade when she moved into my class. Now we're finally here, the shine doesn't seem to be wearing off. Our freshman year, she calmed down a little bit. I guess it takes a while for everyone to find their place in the hierarchy, but once she officially settled into her role as cheerleader, she embraced it wholeheartedly. I, on the other hand, am still trying to figure out where I fit in.

The town of Green Acres where we live is split into two halves, the 'Haves' and the 'Have-nots'. The 'Haves' live in North Acres, which is where all the houses have electric gates, their own pools, and big enough plots that you can't see your neighbors' houses. South Acres is where the 'Have-nots' live. Run-down houses sit next to abandoned lots, beside drug dealers selling from street corners.

Courtney's family has a beautiful McMansion on a beautiful road in North Acres, her parents are lawyers and her family comes from money on both her mom and dad's sides. I live slap bang on the border of north and south, or no-man's-land as I like to call it. My house is small, just two beds, one and a half baths, and a yard full of flowers my mom bought at the grocery store when they were on offer. We're not rich like Courtney's family, but we're not poor either.

My mom is an author. She writes thrillers and has even hit the *New York Times* bestseller list a few times. What people don't realize is that even when an author sells a shit ton of books, they don't necessarily make a shit ton of money.

Some months she makes loads, other months she earns practically nothing, which means that although we almost always manage to pay the bills, we need the money I make working at the diner to bridge the gaps between the good months and the bad.

The only reason I can afford to attend Green Acres Academy—a classy private school in North Acres—is because my mom got a big advance from her publisher to write the next three books in her current series and she paid my tuition in advance for my freshman and sophomore years. If I'll be able to attend here for my junior and senior years is kind of up in the air at the moment.

Climbing out of the car, I smooth down my green-plaid skirt and hook the straps of my backpack over my shoulders. The kids at GAA are all rich, and even though they're not assholes to me, they know that I'm not one of them. Thank God the diner I work at is in South Acres, because if anyone here came to the place I work and I had to wait on them, they'd never let me forget it.

I'm not ashamed of having a job, I'm happy to contribute to take some of the pressure off my mom. But to the kids that go here, their idea of a part-time job is interning at their parents' Fortune 500 company, not serving burgers in a run-down diner in a rough part of town.

"I'm so excited for sophomore year," Court exclaims, hooking her arm through mine and marching us toward the school entrance.

"Really? Why?"

"Duh, because we're not the newbies anymore, select sophomores get invited to all the good parties, and we're going to be two of those people. We're both hot, maybe we could even get junior boyfriends and then we'd be a shoo-in to be Elite by the time we hit our senior year."

Green Acres Academy has a ridiculous tradition where instead of having prefects, they have The Elite, it's a group of seniors that basically constitute the most popular kids in school. Each year, the graduating seniors name The Elites for the following year, or at least that's how it normally goes. The reigning Elites weren't picked when they were juniors, they were picked when they were freshmen. From what I've been told, that's never happened before.

Evan Morris, Hunter Rossberg, Clay Jansen and the king himself, Sebastian Lockwood entered the school as rich nobodies and by the end of their freshmen year, they were running the place. According to Courtney, who actually pays attention to the social hierarchy at GAA, their uninterrupted reign of terror hasn't ever been challenged, because even as freshmenthe seniors all deferred to whatever the four of them said.

Normally The Elites are a mix of boys and girls, but the guys have never added any girls to their power foursome. Instead, they have a rotating harem of eager Elite bunnies who all think they have a shot at the crown if they spread their legs for one of the guys.

What makes no sense to me is that these girls all see fucking an Elite as a badge of honor, and if they manage to bag all four, then I think they get special privileges or something. In this day and age, surely we should all be aiming to get ahead with something more progressive than what's between our legs.

Courtney's chattering away as we walk, but I'm not really listening to her. The closer we get to the school the more tense I feel. My bestie spent all summer at pool parties or lounging on the beach at bonfires with our classmates. I spent my summer working every shift my boss Henry would give me. While she was getting tan in a bikini, I was sweating through my polyester waitress uniform.

I'm not jealous of the parties; they aren't really my scene

anyway, but I am jealous of the friendship and connections she made this summer. Before high school, the disparity between mine and Court's lifestyles didn't seem as wide as it does now, and I'm not sure I can survive this place without her if she starts to realize I'm not playing in the same league as her.

"Oh my god, look at them. I swear my panties almost melt off just from looking at them," Court says loudly, her grip on my arm tightening.

"Who?"

"Seriously," she huffs. "The Elite."

My eyes follow her line of sight and there they are, the four beautiful boys, Clay, Evan, Hunter and Sebastian. Even in their uniforms they look like they're posing for a Calvin Klein advertisement. GAA has a strict dress code, green-plaid skirts or pinafores, white blouses, green ties and blazers for the girls. Tan chinos, white shirts, green ties and green blazers for the boys. We basically all look like extras from *Gossip Girl*, but somehow The Elite boys make the forest-green jackets look good.

I'll never admit it to Court, but I don't know which boy is which. All four guys are over six feet tall, well built and muscular. GAA doesn't indulge in the classic high school sports so there's no football or basketball teams. Instead, the guys do lacrosse, rowing and fencing, and The Elite dominate in all three. Clay is the captain of the rowing team, Evan fencing and Sebastian lacrosse. They also hold the top four spots on the class list and have done since they started.

Now that I think about it, I suppose it makes sense that they became Elites so early on. Top of their class, captains of all the sports teams, good-looking, and of course, outrageously rich. Individually, perhaps they could have been toppled. Together, they're an unstoppable force.

"God, can you imagine getting one of them as your boyfriend?" Court says dreamily.

"No," I laugh. "They don't have girlfriends, they have bunnies who drop their panties the moment one of them clicks their fingers."

"Maybe if they met the right girl¾"

"Jesus, Court, get a grip," I snap. "Please don't get dragged into their web; they'd pass you around and then discard you. That's not what you want, is it?"

"I suppose not, although I bet it'd be fun," she sighs. "They're just so pretty."

Laughing, I shake my head and then pull her away, dragging her past The Elite and into the school.

TWO

SEBASTIAN

"**F**ly away, little bird," I mutter quietly as I watch her drag her friend across the parking lot and into the school building. Despite the dirty sneakers and messy braid, my little bird is just as beautiful as always. I noticed her the moment she walked through the doors the first day of term last year. So pretty, so sweet, so innocent.

I thought about taking her right then and there, separating her from her friend and making her mine for the whole school to see. But I didn't. I'm an Elite, I have a certain reputation to uphold, a legacy to protect, and there's no way I could risk it all by touching a freshman.

GAA has been providing an education to the youth of North Acres for over a hundred years. According to the records.

there's been Elites here since the very start and the tradition will continue long after we leave. With The Elite legacy comes rules, and one of those is that even *we* don't get to mess with the freshmen.

Everyone who enters these hallowed halls has a year to show the rest of the school who they are. A whole year to sink or swim. Those who swim survive, those who sink do not, but everyone gets their year.

Me and my friends are an exception. We didn't just swim after our arrival at the school, we soared, and The Elite at the time saw that. It pissed off a lot of people when Clay, Evan, Hunter and I were named as Elites at the end of our freshmen year. When we beat down anyone who thought to question our status, it soon became common knowledge to everyone that we are the kings of this school until the day we leave.

Sure, I could probably have broken the rules and claimed my girl, but I wanted to watch her, to see what she did, see the impact she'd make before I took her. For a whole year I've watched and waited, refusing to allow myself to become any more obsessed. I don't even know her name, all I know is that she's mine. Now her year is up, and it's time to elevate her to her rightful place at my side.

"You ready to know?" Clay asks from beside me.

It's rare I ever let anyone sneak up on me, my little bird is the only thing that distracts me enough that I stop paying attention to what's going on around me. "Let's go in," I tell him, not answering his question just in case anyone else is listening in.

Clay whistles, and both Evan and Hunter's heads turn in this direction.

"Let's go," I say, tipping my head toward the school building.

Standing, they brush off the bunnies that are crawling all over them and head over. Clay and I start to walk and a sudden hush falls over the students that are mulling around. The reverence and adulation should be cringeworthy, and it kind of is, but I'm not going to lie, it's good to be king.

Being Elite is more than just a status thing, we also have a role within the school we're expected to play. We maintain peace between the students, enforce the ancient GAA rules and mete out punishments when we have to. The faculty trust us to do what's expected and in repayment, they turn a blind eye to whatever we do to keep order.

When GAA originally opened it was a boarding school, but thirty years ago the last dorm shut down and the rooms were repurposed. The one room that remains intact and relatively unchanged from all those years ago, is The Elite common room. This room has belonged to the reigning Elites for nearly a hundred years. It's a sacred space that only The Elite can use.

The familiar smell of old leather, books and cinnamon hits me the moment I push through the door. For every other reigning Elite in the past, this room has only been theirs for a year. For us, this is our third, and as such we've left our mark more so than our predecessors. We've added a few updates, like a huge flat-screen TV, a PlayStation and a fancy coffee machine. But more than that, this is our private space where we can relax without the constant adoration and scrutiny of the rest of the school.

I wait for the others to enter the room and close the door before I speak. "Tell me everything."

THREE

STARLING

O kay, so maybe being a sophomore does come with a few perks. My locker is in a much better position and my homeroom is in the main building instead of being in the cold annex that used to be one of the dorms from back when the school had student housing.

Sophomores can use the coffee cart in the quad and we get to have lunch in the restaurant-style cafeteria complete with serving staff, instead of the freshmen one where you have to line up with your tray.

On the other side though, sophomores are fair game to the older kids. There's an unwritten rule at GAA that freshmen are off-limits. No one gets to bully them or do anything to them; they're basically ignored for the first year, but after that, all bets are off.

Our sophomore class is down ten people. Seven boys and three girls have apparently transferred to other schools, which is kind of weird considering the next closest private school is nearly an hour away, and there aren't any public schools in North Acres.

Now that everyone is fair game, I've already seen one kid in my class being dragged into an empty classroom by a bunch of juniors. I'd have intervened, but the kid, Elliot, is a grade *A* asshole who tried to shove his hand up my skirt this morning. Him getting his ass kicked kind of feels like karma.

Courtney and I are in different classes this year which sucks. She's super smart and her parents have her in all AP classes, I think they're hoping she'll be able to skip a grade and graduate early. I'm a middle-of-the-road, average student, and right now there are no AP classes in my future unless I want to fail them. So I've been friendless all morning while Court learns all the important stuff they teach to the brainiacs.

Heading to my locker, I twist the combination into my lock and pull it open, shoving my backpack inside and pulling my wallet and cell out. School rules say no cells, except at lunch. It drives my social-butterfly bestie crazy, but it doesn't bother me too much. I don't really have any friends here except for Court. I went to grade school with most of the kids in my class, but once they realized I wasn't one of them, I became a social pariah. Only Court stuck by me once she realized my family was just normal and not superrich.

"Hey, bestie," she singsongs as she skips down the hall toward me. Court has so much pep she could take on the entire cheer squad on her own. She's bouncy and enthusiastic and well, she just has an awful lot of school spirit. I'm the opposite, I go here because my mom spent a small fortune to send me here. I don't love the place, in fact I don't even particularly like the place. But the alternative is the public school in South Acres, where you have to go through metal detectors and have your bag checked for weapons before you can even get inside.

Court barely breathes as she talks at a hundred miles an hour, telling me about all the drama she's heard this morning. Someone's parents split up and are in the middle of a very nasty and very public divorce. Someone's dad got arrested for embezzlement, and someone else is fucking their pool boy. I listen and nod in all the right places. This stuff is important to Court because she's a part of their world, but I'm not. I have a job and bills and responsibilities; I don't care what the rich bitches of North Acres are doing.

"Are you listening to me?" she snaps.

"Emma Jerico's parents are fighting over the ski lodge in Canada, Hayden Long's dad stole ten million from his clients, and Jeff Winterborne is exploring his sexuality with his family's Puerto Rico pool boy," I repeat back to her, my voice monotone and bored.

"Did you hear that Elliot Williams got his ass kicked by

some juniors?"

"I actually did, I saw them dragging him into one of the science labs. He's an asshole, he tried to grope my vagina this morning, he deserves a beatdown," I say with a shrug.

"Oh my god, he tried to grope you?" She looks aghast, the other thing about Court is that despite the world she inhabits, and the fact that having endless amounts of money tends to give the kids we go to school with an unhealthy sense of entitlement, she isn't like that. In fact, she's almost naively innocent.

"I planned to knee him in the balls, but Logan saw him with his hand up my skirt and dragged him off me before I got a chance."

"Logan has the biggest crush on you," she smirks.

"He does not. He's just a nice guy. He saw Elliot being an asshole and stepped in."

"Would you date him, if he asked?"

"Logan? No, he's cute, but I'm not interested in dating anyone at GAA. Can you imagine their face if I took them back to my house? The kids that go here spontaneously combust if they step into South Acres," I laugh.

Rolling her eyes, she pushes open the door to the cafeteria and pulls me inside. "No one would care about where you live."

"No, *you* don't care about where I live and that's because you're the most amazing person I know, but the other kids that go here, they all care. That's why no one but you speaks to me. I'm inconsequential to them and that's okay, they're inconsequential to me too."

Stepping into the large open-plan dining area, the smell of garlic and tomato hits my nose and I inhale greedily. "Oh wow something smells good."

"I think I gained ten pounds just from the calories in the air, but it does smell amazing. You need to eat it for me."

"Come on, let's find a seat. I can't believe we order our food from an app instead of having to wait at the counter," I say, steering her toward an empty table.

"Being a sophomore rocks."

Sitting down, we both pull out our cells and order our food. I get the lasagna with a green salad and a bottle of water, my mouth already watering in anticipation.

"Skinless chicken breast salad, dressing on the side and a bottle of water," Court says aloud as she taps at the screen of her cell.

"You don't need to watch your weight, you're practically skin and bone as it is."

"If I want to fly this year, I can't gain even an ounce. Heidi is making us do a weigh-in each week on a Friday and if you gain, you don't get to cheer."

"Having cheerleaders at fencing competitions is ridiculous anyway, you should quit and then you can eat whatever you want," I scoff.

"Did you see how cute the new cheer uniforms are? There's no way I'm giving up the chance to wear one of those. And I'm a flyer, it's practically a one-way ticket to Elite status."

The uniforms are tiny fitted forest-green crop tops, with the school logo emblazoned across the front in gold, and an equally tiny green skirt with gold trim. I'm sure she's going to look fantastic in it, but there's no way I'd starve myself all year just to be able to wear it once a week to hop around cheering when one pretentious asshole stabs another pretentious asshole with a blunt sword.

Our food arrives and it looks as good as it smells. My mom is a quarter Italian. I'm not sure which quarter, because none of the relatives I know of on her side will admit to being a part of the Italian contingent. But her imagined heritage has given her a love for all things Italian cooking. Unfortunately, or fortunately, depending on how you look at it, this means that my house is always full of freshly made pasta for salads, sauces and lasagna. Cutting into the steaming square of tomatoey, creamy, cheesy goodness, I bring the forkful to my mouth and eat, it's delicious and I hum in approval as I chew.

"God, I hate you so much right now," Court says, glaring at me then down to the green leafy salad in front of her. "You sound like you're on the verge of a foodgasm."

"That's because I am," I say, my mouth full of my second bite of yumminess.

"How are you so skinny? You should be the size of a truck."

"Just lucky, I guess," I tell her, although the truth is, I work too much, sleep too little and most of the time I forget to eat.

The only time I had off this summer was the three weeks when I went to visit with my dad. He owns and runs a fishing boat in Maine so instead of relaxing, I spent my time with him helping out on the boat. It's hard work and long hours, but it's the only time I get to see him and I don't mind a little hard work. For once, hauling nets and lobster out of the sea has paid off. I have a layer of muscle that only comes from exercise and a diet that mainly consisted of things caught on a line from the sea.

The hair on the back of my neck prickles and the horrible sensation of being watched hits me. It's irrational, I'm in a roomful of people, no one is looking at me specifically, more than likely it's just kids scanning the surroundings, but I can't help feeling watched.

Surreptitiously, I take a moment and glance around the room, but it's packed and if someone is looking at me, they're not being obvious about it.

"Are you okay?" Court asks.

"Yeah, I just had that horrible feeling of being watched, do you know what I mean?" I wrinkle my nose, hating that I sound like an idiot.

"Oh my gosh, I get that all the time when I get out of the pool at night and have to walk back up to the house. It's creepy."

I can't help but smile at my sweet, ditsy friend. "Really creepy," I laugh, stabbing my fork into my lasagna and ignoring the lingering sensation of eyes on me.

FOUR

SEBASTIAN

The information Clay gave me about my little bird is running on a loop through my head.

Starling Kennedy, sixteen, born September 4 in Maine. Her mother's name is Cassidy Clark, thirty-two, author writing successful thriller novels. Father, Derek Kennedy, forty, lives in Maine, owns and runs a lobster fishing boat. Starling lives with her mother in a small house slap bang on the border between North and South Acres. Their mortgage is more than they can afford and Cassidy takes other writing jobs in between publishing novels to help pay the bills and her credit card debt. They don't own a car, although both mother and daughter have their driving permits. Starling works at the Yummy Tummy diner in South Acres and rides the bus to and from work. She works three or four nights a week and most weekends for minimum wage. She must give all her wages to her mom because she only has twenty-five dollars in her checking account.

Her parents divorced when she was two years old, around the time Cassidy published her first successful book and bought the house they currently live in when they moved to Green Acres. Starling only sees her father once a year for a couple of weeks during the summer break, when she works on his fishing boat.

She has one friend, Courtney Ortega, fifteen, daughter of Larrissa and Michael Ortega. Cheerleader. They live in a decent house in North Acres, and Courtney has a substantial trust fund which she will gain access to once she graduates from high school.

Courtney's family driver collected Starling from her home and drove her to and from school every day during their freshmen year. Now Courtney has her driver's license, she instead picked Starling up from her home this morning.

Starling is an average student, passing all of her classes with an average of a *B* on most assignments. Her mother paid two years tuition up front when she enrolled Starling in the school and if their financial situation does not improve, my little bird will have to transfer to the hellhole public school in South Acres for her junior and senior years.

All of these facts paint a picture of the girl I've been obsessing over for the last year, but even knowing all these things about her, I still don't know *her*.

I don't know if she keeps her hair long and wears it in a braid every day because she doesn't want to waste money on a haircut, or if she just likes it that way. I don't know if she resents her father for never coming here to visit her or if she's happy she's only forced to see him once a year. I don't know if her creamy thighs are as smooth as they appear, or how they'll look with bite marks all over from where I plan to bury my head between them and lick her virgin pussy.

I don't know enough, and I need to change that. The ban on her has been lifted and it's time to claim her, to make sure that the entire school knows she belongs to The Elite, to me. She's too beautiful to be left unprotected, that little fuckwit Elliot Williams already tried to touch what's mine today. He's lucky I only ordered an ass kicking, not for him to have his fucking hand removed.

The juniors and seniors already know that Starling is off-limits. They don't know why, but they were warned the moment she stepped onto my radar that she was untouchable, that she had The Elites' protection. Thank fuck Logan is in her homeroom, he saw Elliot shove his hand up *my* little bird's skirt and dragged the asshole off her. If he hadn't, if that fucker had touched her, had breached her or even got the scent of my little bird's pussy on his skin, I'd have killed him.

As it is, he'll probably be pissing blood for a few days and he's going to have to find a new school. Or maybe I'll let him stay so he can act as a warning to everyone else at GAA about what happens if you touch The Elites' property.

My body heats with awareness as she walks into the cafeteria, her arm looped through her friend's. She's so beautiful, so perfect, so utterly mine. Even though she doesn't know it yet.

I want to go and get her, to have her sit on my lap while I feed her, but instead I watch as they head to an empty table on the other side of the room. Last year she wasn't a temptation, because the freshmen eat in a different dining area, but now she's here, her cell in her hand, laughing, and I can't tear my eyes away.

Clay's research is always one-hundred-percent accurate. So when he told me she and her mother ate a lot of Italian food, I contacted the kitchens and made sure they altered the menu just for her. I'm pleased to see that he was right, as the server delivers the lasagna I arranged to her table. I watch as she cuts off a slice and eats it, her eyes closing, her smile wide. She likes it. I'm glad. She's skinny, but I don't think it's deliberate. Not like her friend who orders a salad and stares longingly at my little bird's lunch. According to Clay's research, she usually gets home late and gets up early, working as many hours as Henry, her boss, will give her.

She's exhausted, but I can fix that. I can look after her, take care of her. I'm only seventeen, but I know that Starling is mine, that our age is irrelevant. The way I feel about her might perhaps be called obsession, but I prefer to think of it as all-consuming desire. Whatever it is, it's time to make her understand she's mine.

When she stills and looks around, I know she can feel my eyes on her. I want her to know she's being watched, but I don't want her to know it's me who can't look away. Not yet. Lowering my gaze, I carefully keep her in my periphery until she goes back to eating. The moment I know she can't see me, I allow my gaze to lift to her again and I don't look away for the rest of lunch.

If I could, I'd have moved myself into her classes, or her into mine, but I can't. I'm still a senior and she's a sophomore, but just because I'm not in the room doesn't mean I don't have eyes on her. Being one of The Elite is like holding the keys to the kingdom and everybody wants to be us. It was almost too easy to recruit someone in each of her classes to surreptitiously keep watch over her. Of course, they don't actually know why they're watching. As far as they're concerned, they're just doing a task for me, like passing out assigned seating charts for each class so my little bird is exactly where I want her to be, in full view of the security cameras that are fitted in each classroom.

I'm not a complete psycho; I don't sit in a dark room watching her on a computer screen all day, I have my own classes to attend. But I do have access to all of the security recordings and livestream and if I wanted to peruse the footage of her English class, I could.

By the time the last bell of the day rings, I'm more than

ready to claim her and feel her full pouty lips against mine. I've been imagining how excited she'll be when I make her my queen for over a year, and today is finally the day. I've been patient, but I won't wait a moment longer.

Her friend has cheer practice after school today, which means my little bird is without a ride home. There isn't a school bus, GAA is more likely to offer a car service than a communal bus so without her ride, she's stranded here.

I want the whole school to see her with me, to truly understand how off-limits she is, but that can wait until tomorrow when I walk her into the school holding my hand. Taking my time, I stroll down the halls, my eyes constantly searching for her, my dick hard, eager to make her mine. She's sixteen, legal, but as far as Clay can find, she's never had a boyfriend before. I'm glad I'll get to be her first, her only.

By the time I reach the main doors, I'm concerned that I haven't found her yet. She could be in the library, or watching Courtney from the bleachers, but I assumed she'd wait out front for her. Pulling my cell from my pocket I type out a message into the group chat I share with the other Elites.

Me

Where is she?

Evan, Clay and Hunter are my brothers in every way except for blood. Our parents are friends, we grew up together, holidayed together, plan to go to college together. We're a team and although they don't really understand my obsession with my

40

little bird, after a year of watching, they feel almost as protective of her as I do.

Evan
She's not in the gym, the friend is at practice but theres no sign of starling.

Hunter
on my way to the libary.

Clay
She's not in the library and I can't find her on any of the cameras.

Annoyance barrels through me. Once I've claimed her, she'll learn the rules, and her place. Then I won't have to seek her out, she'll be where I tell her to be waiting for me.

A new message pings on my cell just as I'm shoving it into my pocket, and I quickly click into the screen.

Clay
Just checked the footage for the parking lot, she walked off the school grounds about five minutes ago.

Me
And went where???

Clay
No idea, she walked off the site and out of the camera's view.

Before I realize what I'm doing, I'm running out of the building and toward my car that's parked in the lot. We all drove together, but I don't care. I'm just starting the engine as the others appear and jump in, then we're careening out of the lot and down the street.

"Where the fuck would she go? There's nothing around here, no stores or restaurants, it's too far for her to walk back to her house, it's at least five miles," I mutter distractedly as I drive too fast, my eyes scanning the street for her.

"Could she be getting a ride with someone else?" Evan asks.

"I doubt it, she doesn't speak to anyone but the cheerleader," Hunter says.

"There," Clay shouts, leaning between the front seats to point ahead of us where Starling is climbing onto a Green Acres city bus.

The bus pulls away from the curb and into traffic before I can even process what I'm seeing. She rides the bus, of course she rides the bus, why didn't I consider that? She rides the bus everywhere else, it makes sense that she wouldn't hang out after school for an hour, when she has an alternative way to get home.

"I didn't even know the city bus stopped in North Acres," Evan says, his tone perturbed.

"The bus, huh," Clay mumbles, his voice that odd tone that means he's intrigued by something he wasn't expecting. Clay is a genius and not just someone who thinks they're smart, he's a legit genius. His IQ is off the charts high. He could have finished high school and probably be on his way to graduating college by now, but he didn't want to do it without the rest of us, so he's stayed in school and takes online college classes to keep his brain active.

"I'm going to her place, I'll drop you all off at home first."

"Do you think ambushing her at her house with her mom there is the right way to go?" Hunter cautions.

"I've been waiting a fucking year, I'm done waiting."

"Bro, you've never even spoken to her, turning up at her house and telling her she's yours is going to scare the shit out of her. You need to at least try to ease her into this."

"No," I growl, angry that he's suggesting I delay claiming her even a moment longer.

Evan sighs. "We'll come with you, just in case you lose your shit."

"I don't need a fucking babysitter," I snarl, shifting gear and accelerating down the street, passing the bus my girl is sitting on and barely managing to suppress the urge to force it to stop so I can drag her ass off it.

"Dude, you're doing nearly ninety miles an hour in a thirty zone, you definitely need us to come and keep you calm." Clay laughs.

Exhaling, I glance down at the speedometer and immediately lift my foot from the accelerator, watching the needle drop down to a more acceptable fifty miles an hour. Forcing myself to calm, I drive through North Acres and toward the no-man's-land where Starling's home is situated. The modest house is either the destitute relative of North Acres or The Elite of South Acres and I'm not sure which it is.

Not that it really matters, she won't be spending much time here once she's mine. My home is big enough to fit her whole house in just the kitchen and dining rooms. Her mom might not be okay with her moving in with me, but I'm sure I can make her understand I'm not really giving either of them much of a choice.

If I need to, I'll marry my little bird right now, then she'll be mine legally and her mother won't be able to stop me doing whatever I want to my wife. I like the way that sounds. My wife. I'm only seventeen, far too young to be thinking about getting married, but I'll do whatever I have to do to get my way, and if that means putting a ring on Starling's finger, then that's what I'll do.

Reaching her house, I pull up at the curb outside. There's no way that the bus made it back here before we did, so I don't bother getting out and going to the door. Now that I'm here, I might as well tell my little bird that she's mine before she goes inside and informs her mother, then she can pack a bag for tonight and we can go back to my place.

"Dude, you have that scary look on your face again, what the hell is going on in that psycho head of yours?" Hunter asks with a smirk.

"I'm just considering what I'll do if her mother decides to be a problem."

"Starling's sixteen, I think we can all agree that her mom is probably going to have a problem with you basically wanting to kidnap her daughter and keep her prisoner on your dick," Evan laughs.

"She's mine and I don't plan to get her pregnant yet, what we do is none of her mother's business."

"Jesus, Bastian, please don't say that to the girl or her mother, you really do sound like a fucking psycho," Evan laughs.

The scary thing is that I feel psychotic, I have since the moment I laid eyes on her. I don't know what it is about Starling that drives this urge to own, control and consume her, but the longer I've waited the more intense it's become. I don't just want to date her, I want to lock her in a gilded cage and keep her all to myself, my perfect little bird.

Ten minutes pass and there's still no sign of her.

"Do you want to go and knock? Could the bus have taken a shortcut?" Hunter asks.

"It didn't, I'm on their website and the bus route takes a pretty direct path through North Acres, only stopping twice until it passes into South Acres where it stops ten more times before it hits the bus depot. Assuming the bus she was on didn't encounter a delay, which is unlikely, she should have been home by now," Clay tells us.

No one disagrees or questions him, like I mentioned, he's a genius and if he says she should be home by now, then she should be home.

"Could she have stopped to get groceries or something?"

Evan suggests

"She shops at the grocery store in South Acres, and she only went yesterday," Clay tells us matter-of-factly.

"You're such a good little stalker," Hunter laughs.

"Could she have gone to work?" Clay suggests.

"I thought you said she doesn't normally work on Mondays, or this early," I say, panic rising in my chest. Unclipping my seat belt I open my door, climb out and stride up the path to her house, ringing her doorbell.

When the door hasn't been opened a minute later, I press the doorbell again and then once more just for good measure. Waiting impatiently, I tap my finger against the doorframe, until the sound of someone descending the stairs comes from inside.

"I'm coming, I'm coming," her mother calls, a moment before the door is thrown open and an older version of Starling looks up at me.

"Hello, Ms. Clarke. Is Starling home?"

The woman in front of me assesses me for a moment, her eyes narrowing slightly as she looks me over. "And you are?" she asks me coolly.

"I'm one of Starling's classmates, I was hoping I could speak to her about a school project, but we forgot to exchange cell phone numbers earlier," I tell her, using the polished, cajoling tone I use whenever I'm around my parents' obnoxious friends.

"Oh," Cassidy says, exhaling a shaky breath as she smiles up at me, like somehow me going to GAA makes me less threatening. "I'm sorry, she's not back from school yet, would you like to leave a message for her?"

Furrowing my brow, I grit my teeth and try not to let my frustration show. This is my little bird's mother, why the fuck doesn't she know where her daughter is? Why isn't she concerned that she's late getting home? "No that's fine, I'll speak to her tomorrow in class."

Turning, I stride down the path back toward my car as she calls. "I'm sorry, I didn't get your name."

Ignoring her, I climb back into the car, turn on the engine and pull away from the curb. "Track her cell," I snarl to Clay, who shakes his head, but immediately starts pressing the screen on the tablet he has on his lap.

In the year since I first laid eyes on Starling, I've had the ability to track her cell phone and find out her whereabouts, but I've refrained, for the most part, just like I didn't allow myself to know her name or anything about her. But everything's changed now and I won't hold back anymore.

"She's at the diner," Clay announces, lowering the tablet to his lap, a map with a flashing dot visible on the screen.

Without saying a word, I turn my car in the direction of the shitty diner my little bird works at, and race through the streets of South Acres until I park in the lot outside a crumbling-looking building. The sign above the door—that might have had neon lights attached to it in its heyday—welcomes us to the Yummy Tummy diner, and I feel my nose wrinkle as I think about her working in this shithole.

"Jesus, this is a cesspit," Evan says, pushing open his door and grimacing at the diner, like he can sense the salmonella from outside.

"Please tell me you don't plan to actually eat here," Hunter laughs.

Rolling my eyes, I ignore my friends as I climb out of my car, wait for them all to follow suit then lock it behind me. This is a shitty neighborhood and if I'd have known we were coming here, I'd have had one of The Elite wannabe's follow us to keep watch over my car. My Mercedes isn't particularly flashy, but it's an eighty-thousand-dollar vehicle and I'd rather the wheels were still on it once I've collected my girl.

The bell above the door buzzes brokenly as I push it open and make my way into the run down, but surprisingly clean-looking restaurant. A harried-looking middle-aged woman wearing a pink-and-red waitress dress smiles at us from behind the counter. Grabbing menus, she strides over. "Hey there, boys, my name is Darlene, why don't you follow me and I'll get you set up."

"We're looking for Starling," I tell her simply.

Her step falters and she glances nervously over her shoulder at us. "Her shift doesn't start for another fifteen minutes, what do you want with her?"

My jaw clenches, and I open my mouth to demand that she get Starling out here right this fucking minute or I'll get this health hazard of a diner shut down within the hour, but Hunter speaks before I can utter a word.

"We're friends of hers from school, could we sit in her section and we'll order some drinks while we wait?"

His voice is pure seduction and Darlene, who is easily old enough to be his mother, actually blushes. "Oh, you go to that fancy school over in North Acres?"

"Yes, ma'am," Hunter winks.

"I should have guessed that from the uniforms." She's smiling now, all of the concern gone as she leads us to a different table from the one she was originally taking us to. "What can I get you to drink?"

"I'll have root beer if you have it," Hunter smiles, charming the older woman as easily as if she was one of his teenage fangirls at school.

"What about for you?" she asks me.

"Coffee, black, please."

Clay and Evan order Cokes and she disappears into the back, returning a couple of minutes later with our drinks on a tray. "Here you go, Starling is just getting changed into her uniform, she'll be out soon."

Knowing she's getting undressed makes me want to storm back there and drag her out by her hair. It's so long, I could use it as a leash when she has it in a braid. Instead, I sit in the booth, my eyes fixed on the swinging door that leads into the kitchen until it opens and my little bird walks into the diner.

She immediately spots us and as if she already understands

she belongs to me, her gaze locks with mine. This is the first time I've allowed my eyes to really find hers, the first time I've been this close. From a distance she's beautiful, but this close, she's stunning. Her features are petite and there's a sprinkling of freckles across her nose that I can see now she's only a few feet away from me. Her breasts are small, high and perky, her hips narrow, her body a little too thin.

She's perfect, even in the ugly uniform that hides her barely there curves.

"Er, hi," she says as she approaches our table, her expression confused. "Are you ready to order?"

Evan snickers and I flash a glare at him before I turn back to my little bird. "We're not here to eat."

"Okay," she says slowly, elongating the word as she slides her pad into the pocket of her dress and waits for me to explain why I'm here. A long second passes while no one speaks. "Shall I give you a minute, or should I get your check?"

"I'm here for you," I tell her succinctly, there's no point beating around the bush.

"I'm sorry, what?"

"I'm here for you."

"Yeah, that's the bit I'm having difficulty with," she laughs, sighing like I'm inconveniencing her. "Who are you? Do we know each other?"

"You know who we are," Evan says with an exaggerated laugh.

Her brows lift and she looks at us each in turn. "I mean, obviously you go to my school, but other than that I'm sorry, I'm drawing a blank." She shrugs.

"You know who I am," I tell her, staring at her intently, looking for her twitch, her tell that proves she's lying, that she recognizes us, but there's nothing.

"We're The Elite," Clay says simply.

Her eyes widen and her lips form a perfect *O* as she looks between the four of us again.

"I'm Sebastian."

FIVE

STARLING

"I'm Sebastian." His lips twitch into a charming smile as he speaks, and I just stare at him.

Sebastian Lockwood, Evan Morris, Hunter Rossberg and Clay Jansen are here, all four of them, in my section in the diner I work in. I'm fucked. Nothing good can come of them seeking me out in my place of work. Especially when that place is in South Acres, the side of town that to my knowledge The Elite never set foot in. Not that I know anything about them really, except what Courtney has told me.

Truthfully, before I started GAA, I didn't believe that the stupid stories about The Elite were even true. It just seems too far fetched that the school would have kids that play kings and queens and literally rule over the place with an iron fist. But it's true and the four boys—or should I say men because they don't look anything like boys—are the rulers of our school and if they're here, I must have done something to really, really piss them off.

Sebastian is staring at me, with this intense expression across his face that kind of makes me want to pee myself. I try to think about what I could have done to warrant them searching me out, but I really can't think of anything. Letting my gaze move from Sebastian to the others, I try to figure out which boy is which. Courtney talks about the four of them all the time, but apart from seeing them from a distance, I've never paid any attention to the kings of GAA.

"I didn't think you guys came to this side of town?" I say, wondering if they're just here to scare the shit out of me.

"Why?" one of them asks.

"Sit," Sebastian says, motioning for me to take the spot next to him.

"I'm working."

"How much do you earn per shift?"

"I'm really not sure how that's any of your business," I snark, clamping my mouth shut the moment the words are out there. Fuck, being bitchy to them isn't going to help things, but if they've come all the way to South Acres, whatever I did, it's bad, and they're probably here to tell me not to bother coming to school in the morning. I may not have recognized them personally, but I'm familiar with the power The Elite hold. They can get me expelled from GAA just by clicking their fingers. I wonder if we get a refund on my tuition if they do kick me out. Mom and I could sure use the money.

"Little bird, are you listening?" Sebastian says, demanding my attention when I was daydreaming about the thousands of dollars my mom gave to the school for my education.

Little bird? Did he call me little bird? "Seriously, why are you here, if I'm expelled that's fine, but my mom should get a refund on my tuition, especially seeing as I have no idea what I've done to warrant getting kicked out."

I don't realize that I'm waving my arms around until his hot grip on my wrist stops me from gesticulating. "Sit," he growls, dragging me down and into the spot next to him as one of the others shuffles out of the circular booth and climbs in on the other side of me, trapping me between them.

"What are you doing? My boss will fire me if he comes out and sees me sitting here instead of working."

"That's okay, you won't be working here after tonight anyway," Sebastian informs me calmly.

I feel my eyes widen, then narrow. "What? Seriously, this is insane, why are you all here?"

"I'm here to tell you that you're mine, and to take you home." Sebastian grins.

I laugh. I can't help it. I throw my head back and laugh so loudly I probably sound like I'm losing my mind.

"What's funny?" he demands, his grip on my wrist tightening

until it's just shy of painful.

"Are you serious?" I chuckle. "You're mine and I'm taking you home," I mimic, attempting to replicate his gruff tone.

"Starling, you belong to The Elite now, it's an honor," one of the others says, his expression so solemn I almost take him seriously.

"The Elite. Yeah, sure," I smile sardonically. "Which one are you again?"

"Evan," he smirks.

"Ahhh yeah, you're the science lab defiler."

"Excuse me," he chokes out a laugh.

I wave my hand dismissively. "You were spotted having sex in one of the science labs. Look, I really need to get back to work."

"Clay," Sebastian says, looking to the guy who is sitting on the other side of the table.

"Got it," Clay nods, rising from his seat and striding toward the door into the kitchen and staff area.

"What's he doing? Why is he going back there?"

"He's advising your boss that you no longer work here."

Panic swells in my throat. "He can't do that. I don't understand, what did I do? It's the first day of school."

The hand that's holding my wrist loosens and he moves to cup my cheek, his thumb rubbing gently back and forth. "You didn't do anything, little bird, but you're mine now and I want you with me, not working here in this hovel."

His voice is so calm, so reasonable, even as he's telling me that I'm his now. I mean, what does that even mean? His?

"I don't know you," I breathe.

"That's okay, I know you and we have time for you to learn all you need to know about me."

The door to the back of the restaurant swings open and Clay strides through, smiling widely with my backpack in his hand.

His reappearance drags me from the haze Sebastian's touch has put me under and I turn away from his hand, forcing him to move. "He has my stuff. Why does he have my stuff?"

"Because we're leaving," he says simply, gesturing to the guy who's blocking my exit from the booth.

The guy—Hunter, I'm assuming as apparently the other two are Clay and Evan—slides out and I quickly follow him, rushing to grab my backpack from Clay and pulling it tightly into my chest.

"Here's your final check, your boss added a month's pay as severance," Clay smiles.

Breathing becomes hard as the air around me seems to become thinner and less effective. I need this job; my mom and I need this money. She doesn't even realize she's taking it from me, but at least with me contributing, the lights don't get turned off and there's food in the cupboards.

Eyeing these awful boys who have come in here and turned my life upside down, I dart past them and into the kitchen, ignoring Esteban, the chef, who calls to me as I head for the manager's office. The door is open and Henry is sitting behind his worn, chipped, wooden desk.

"Henry, what's going on? I need this job."

His face is pale, his normally sallow skin almost white as his eyes stare unseeingly at the wall.

"Henry," I call his name again.

"I'm sorry, Starling," he says, turning his sad gaze on me.

"What's going on?" I beg. "Why?"

"Because if I continue to allow you to work here, they'll have this place shut down."

Scoffing, I shake my head. "They're kids, they're in high school for god's sake."

"The Lockwoods, Jansens, Morrises and Rossbergs run this town, even the shitty parts of it. I can't risk this place getting on their radar over a sixteen-year-old waitress. I'm sorry, Starling, but you need to leave. I've given you a month's wages, I know you need the money to help out your mom. But don't come back here, you belong to them now."

I'm gaping, my bottom lip trembling as I take in what he's saying. I've just lost my job, he's fired me because a rich kid wearing his school uniform threatened him. I shake my head. "I'm sorry too," I whisper, turning and leaving his office.

Sebastian is waiting for me in the cramped corridor, his arms folded across his chest, his gaze imperious. He's taller than I realized, towering over my diminutive five-foot-two height so I have to tip my head back to glare at him. His hair is a dirty blond, shaved close to his head at the sides, but long enough to style into a floppy mess on the top. Piercing green eyes watch me closely, like he's taking in every detail and cataloging it. His expression is fire and ice all at once, and I shiver beneath his penetrating gaze. His arms are straining a little at the sleeves of his school blazer, the green color complementing his olive-toned tan skin. I don't allow my eyes to venture farther down than his chest, although I'm sure his legs are muscled from all the sports I know The Elites are involved in.

Being this close to him is stifling. Everyone at GAA is aware of The Elite, their legacy is omnipresent everywhere at school. It's like royalty or the president, you know who they are but you don't *know who they are*.

I've never spoken to them, never seen them up close, never considered them as more than a high school staple that wouldn't have an impact on me. I'm not one of the kids that wants to be popular, I'm the polar opposite, I just want to make it through my sophomore year with as little drama and involvement as possible.

"Let's go," Sebastian orders.

"Go where?" I ask, shell-shocked.

"Home."

"I can get the bus."

"That won't be happening again, the bus isn't safe."

"I've been riding the bus on my own for years, it's perfectly safe."

"It won't happen again," he tells me, and there's no mistaking the order in his tone. His expression and his voice say he's not used to being disobeyed, and yet I don't seem to be able to heed the silent warning.

"You can't tell me what to do."

"I can and I am. You won't ride the bus again. Either I or one of the others will take you anywhere you need to go from now on." He's so calm, because he expects to be obeyed and the thought of me not doing what he wants is completely out of the question.

I laugh again, I just can't help it. "What the hell is going on? Who do you think you are to tell me what I can and can't do? This isn't school."

"I won't allow you to put your safety at risk just for the sake of being stubborn." His fingers trace a line across my cheek and I flinch, recoiling from his unfamiliar touch.

His expression darkens and he closes in on me, backing me against the wall and keeping me prisoner with his body. "You flinched. Why? I'd never hurt you. You're mine, I'll only ever protect you."

My lips part to speak, but I have to swallow several times before my mouth is moist enough to make a sound. "What if you're the thing I need protecting from?" I whisper.

A soft smile graces his lips, showcasing how full they are. "No one can protect you from me, little bird."

A shudder racks through me at the threat and promise in his

GEMMA WEIR

words. He's telling the truth, or at least he believes what he's saying is the truth. This time when he reaches out to touch me, he does it slowly, making sure I know it's coming. His palm strokes over my head, trailing his fingers over my braid before giving it a gentle tug and smiling to himself.

"We should go. I take it you haven't eaten yet?"

Blinking up at him, I shake my head. "Esteban makes me something on my break."

"Who the fuck is Esteban?"

"The chef," I whisper, fear roiling to life in my stomach. For the first time since I found them sitting in my section, I'm starting to sense the danger I'm in. Sebastian is an Elite, they see themselves as untouchable, above the law. His family is powerful old money, and just the mention of their name and the potential reach they have was enough to make my boss fire me. I'm out of my depth. I'm sixteen, a virgin and although not poverty stricken, my family is basically destitute in comparison to his wealth.

In the space of an hour, I've walked headlong into a cautionary tale, the kind you see on after-school specials, that warn about rich older boys preying on girls like me. They spoil them with money, treat them like they're special, then rape and murder them, discarding their bodies on the side of the road or in trash cans like they mean less than nothing.

Lost in my own thoughts, I startle, flinching again when he presses his lips to my cheek, kissing me as he takes my hand in his. Twining my fingers with his, he half leads, half drags me out of the dingy corridor and into the restaurant where the other three boys are waiting for me.

Three matching smirks stare back at me when I take in the other Elites. Clay is all classic blond surfer, messy hair, his tie loosened and askew. Evan is polished, his hair combed into a side part, black-framed glasses giving him a Clark Kent vibe that I'm sure makes even the smart girls swoon. Hunter, the only one who I haven't been directly introduced to, is by far the biggest. With broad shoulders, he's the tallest of the four, and his sheer size is intimidating even though his face is angular and beautiful, almost in spite of his behemoth frame.

Evan heads for the exit and Sebastian moves after him, towing me along behind as Clay follows and Hunter takes up the rear. The movement feels practiced, like this is the order they always move in, and I wonder if they do this at school.

It isn't until we get to a car at the curb that I start to panic. What do they plan to do with me? I can't get in that car; something tells me if I do then it'll only end badly for me. "Let go of me," I say, dragging my hand back in an attempt to free myself from Sebastian's grip.

Ignoring me, he hands my backpack off to Hunter, who opens the trunk and drops it inside, then throws his keys to Evan, who smirks as he opens the driver's door and climbs inside.

"I'm not getting in there, I don't know you," I tell him, yanking and fighting to get away.

"Get in the car, little bird," Sebastian says calmly.

"Stop calling me that. Let me go or I'll scream."

Stopping, he turns to look at me, not releasing his hold on my hand as he closes the distance between us, wraps his other hand around the back of my neck and yanks me in for a hard kiss. Gasping in shock at his unexpected assault, my lips part and he takes advantage, shoving his tongue into my mouth.

I've never been kissed before. I feel pathetic even admitting that inside my own mind. Who gets to sixteen without kissing someone? Well, me, the nobody from the wrong side of the border, that's who. Turns out it's pretty easy to never play seven minutes in heaven when you're not invited to the party. The only person who ever invites me anywhere is Courtney and as much as I love her, I have no interest in making out with her.

I don't kiss him back, and I'm pretty sure he growls before he pulls his lips from mine, but stays close enough that our foreheads are touching. I can feel his hot breath against my mouth. "Scream all you want, no one will come, no one will intervene and no one will take you from me. You're mine now, my little bird, and I'll clip your wings if I have to, just to make sure you can never fly away."

His words are soft and almost romantic in tone, but there's no mistaking the threat in them. He's a psycho, completely insane and dangerous, and for some reason he's noticed me. I want to run, to fly away if I am the little bird he keeps calling me, but before I get a chance to try to escape, he lifts me and puts me in the car. Clay is blocking the door on one side, I'm stuck in the middle with Sebastian on the other side. I'm caged in, imprisoned, and I have no idea how I'm going to get free now that he has me in his clutches.

Frozen in fear, I try not to move or allow myself to touch either of the boys beside me, despite how cramped it is in the back seat.

"Text your mother and tell her you won't be coming home tonight," Sebastian tells me softly.

"I can't do that."

"Why?"

"Because I'm sixteen, if I don't come home she'll call the cops," I snap, not caring how angry the terror I'm feeling is making me sound. I should probably try to be nice, to charm these scary boys into letting me go, but with all the crazy things he's told me so far, I don't think it'll work.

"Tell her you're sleeping at Courtney's house then," he says, reaching out and cradling my jaw again.

"She won't believe me."

"Why not?" he snaps, his grip tightening.

"Because I don't stay over at her house, I've never stayed there because her parents don't like me. If we have a sleepover, it's always at my house."

Tutting like the truth is incredibly inconvenient, he sighs. "Fine, tonight, I'll return you to your home, we'll have to come to some arrangement for the future."

Relief at the fact that apparently they don't plan to kill me and dump my body tonight makes another bout of tremors ricochet through my body.

"Are you cold? Why are you shaking?" Sebastian asks, taking off his blazer and draping it over my shoulders before he clicks my seat belt into place.

"I'm shaking because I'm scared," I admit, the words falling from my lips before I can swallow them back.

"Scared of what?"

"You," I say, incredulous.

His eyebrows arch and he looks down on me with shock etched across his expression. "You're scared of me, even though I've told you not to be?"

"You have basically kind of kidnapped her, bro," Hunter says, looking over at us from the front seat.

"She's my girlfriend, you can't kidnap your own girlfriend," Sebastian declares passionately.

A lump fills my throat and I can't breathe. Girlfriend. He thinks I'm his girlfriend. "I'm n-not your gir-girlfriend," I stammer out through my tight throat.

"Would fiancée make you feel better? We can't get married until you turn seventeen, but I'm more than happy to make it official now and then you can take the time to plan the wedding of your dreams."

My mouth parts and a helpless gasp falls from my lips. I try to make more noise to argue, to try to escape, but blackness starts to filter into my vision as it gets harder and harder to breathe. Lifting my hand I claw at my throat, but my limbs feel heavy right before the darkness overwhelms me and I descend into silence.

SIX

SEBASTIAN

The hand I'm not holding lifts into the air, flops about uncoordinatedly, before it falls back to her lap. Her eyes widen manically and her mouth opens, but no sound comes out. Her eyes roll all the way back and she slumps down to the seat, her head rolling to the side and resting against Clay's arm.

"What the fuck!" I shout, grappling for her face, turning it toward me.

"I think she just passed out," Clay says, a hint of concern lacing his words.

"Starling. Starling." I call, tapping at her cheek carefully as I pull her lax body away from my friend and into me instead. If it wasn't dangerous, I'd unclip her seat belt and drag her into my lap, but I won't risk her safety no matter how much I want to feel her luscious body against mine.

"Call Dr. Harris, have him meet us at home," I shout, knowing one of my friends will do as I ask as I rest my fingers against her wrist, feeling her pulse beat steadily.

Exhaling shakily, I curl my arm around her, wrapping my blazer a little tighter around her shoulders, enjoying seeing her in my clothes despite the circumstances.

"Is she okay?" Evan asks, glancing quickly over his shoulder at us before he turns his attention back on to the road.

"You need to tone down the crazy, bro. You're freaking me out and I know you," Hunter warns.

"I don't need you to tell me how to deal with my girlfriend."

"We care about her too, Bastian," he snaps. "We're the ones who've been keeping an eye on her for the last year while you stopped yourself from going near her."

"She's mine," I growl animalistically.

"Chill, no one's trying to take her from you," Clay says, ever the peacekeeper of our group. "She's yours, we all get that, but you're scaring her. She freaked out so much she passed the fuck out from fear. You need to dial it back and find some of that charm you're famous for."

Inhaling sharply, I nod, my fingers still at her pulse, the steady beat of her heart the only reason I'm not completely losing my shit right now.

"Doc's on his way. Not going to be easy to explain why you have an unconscious sixteen-year-old girl at your place though," Hunter warns.

"My parents know about her."

"They do?" Evan asks, shocked.

"Of course they do. If she was eighteen I'd be moving her in tonight. Unfortunately she's not, but I thought it best to warn them that they'd be meeting their future daughter-in-law. They looked into her too, they probably know as much about her as I do," I say with a shrug.

"Fuck me, no doubt they've told my mom and dad. They'll be expecting me to lose my shit and bring home a girl too now," Hunter sighs dramatically.

"My dad will be giving me the lecture about how women are only useful on their backs again," Evan laughs.

Ignoring them, I focus all of my attention on the girl in my arms. I never intended to scare her, I'd never hurt her and I told her that. I assumed she'd be excited to be mine, any other girl at school would be. Her body trembles, even in her unconscious state and I scowl, wondering what I need to do to make her understand. When the gates to my house come into view I allow myself to relax a little. Perhaps this has all just been a little too much for her tonight. A lot has happened in a short amount of time and she's so sweet and innocent.

I don't want to take her home, I want her in my house, even if I can't have her in my bed. A plan starts to form, how I can keep her. She's right, her mother would, I'm sure, call the police if she failed to return home as expected, but what about if she wasn't expecting her?

Evan slows to a stop outside the front door to my house and I don't waste any time, unclipping my own seat belt and then hers before I lift her into my arms and out of the car. Richard, our house manager, opens the door before I reach it and his brow arches in concern at Starling's prone body. "Could you please show Dr. Harris straight up to Starling's room when he gets here, please?"

"Of course, shall I inform your parents that you're home?"

"Yes, please, let them know Starling got a little overwhelmed in the car and fainted. Assure them that I'm having her checked over, but both her and her mother will be staying here tonight."

"Very good, sir," Richard says, his old-fashioned, courtly manners making me smile.

"You're going to bring her mom here?" Clay asks on a laugh as he follows me up the stairs and to the bedroom beside mine that I had decorated for Starling this summer.

"I want her here, and if having her mother here is how I achieve that, then so be it."

Opening the door to her bedroom, I carry her inside, then close it behind me, shutting my friends outside. Crossing to the bed, I carefully lay her down onto the comforter, pulling her sneakers off her feet and placing them on the floor. I debate stripping her out of the ugly waitress uniform, but decide against it. That wouldn't be easy to explain to her mother.

Sinking down onto the bed beside her, I run my fingers

through her hair. Her eyes flutter open and she blinks, looking up at me as her full lips form an *O* shape. She stares at me for a long moment, before her eyes roll back and she slumps back into unconsciousness again. My heart starts to beat at a frantic rate, just as there's a knock at the door. "Dr. Harris, thank you for coming on such short notice." I greet him, opening the door wider and allowing him to enter. "This is my fiancée, Starling, she got a little flustered in the car and passed out. I've been monitoring her pulse, which is steady and strong, but she's been in and out for a little over five minutes now."

"Has she come round at all?"

"Briefly for a few moments, then she passed out again," I tell him.

"Starling, can you hear me?"

Her eyelids start to flutter and she looks up from her position on the bed. As she comes to, she blinks, looking around in shock before her eyes land on me then the doctor. Bolting upright, she wildly surveys the room, trying to figure out where she is.

"Little bird, you passed out in the car, this is Dr. Harris, he's here to check you're okay. Your mom's on her way."

"My mom?" she asks, pausing frantic eyes on me.

"I called her, she wanted me to bring you home, but when I explained Dr. Harris was on his way, I suggested she come here instead," I lie. I do plan to call her mom, but not until Starling is settled and the doctor's done all that he needs to do.

"Where am I?" she asks frantically.

"My house, sweetheart, just stay calm and let the doctor examine you."

Turning to look at the doctor again, her brow furrows. "You're a doctor?" He nods and she glances at me warily, before turning back to him. "He's kidnapped me, please help me."

Dr. Harris turns his head and eyes me cautiously before looking back to Starling. "Let me examine you first, fainting can be scary and a little disorienting."

Her eyes keep warily glancing at me, but she nods and her body relaxes a little as she leans back into the mountain of pale-blue-and-white cushions I picked out for her.

Dr. Harris is quick and efficient as he checks Starling's pulse, takes her blood pressure, then shines a light into her eyes to check her reactions. Draping his stethoscope around his neck, he walks over to where his bag is sitting on top of a console table and I quickly follow.

"Is she okay?" I ask quietly.

"Her pulse and blood pressure are a little elevated, but not to a concerning level. What happened before she fainted?"

"It's taking her a little time to adjust to being my fiancée and all that entails. We were having a heated discussion when her eyes rolled into the back of her head and she slumped down into the seat."

"I see," Dr. Harris says, his tone almost snippy. "How old is she?"

"Sixteen."

"Sebastian, I've been your family's doctor for thirty years, but I feel in good conscience that I need to remind you that the legal age of consent in Florida is eighteen. You're young, in love and engaged, but if someone were to report you…" he trails off and I smile reassuringly at him.

"I appreciate your concern, but I am more than aware that Starling is younger than me. We're taking things slowly on that front and I have no intention of compromising either her or myself. Right now, I'm more concerned about her immediate health. Will she be okay? Does she need bed rest, more tests?"

"She needs to rest tonight, but she should be fine in the morning. Her mother is on her way over?"

"Yes," I lie, not allowing any doubt to cross my expression. "Perhaps you could administer a mild sedative to make her more comfortable for the night?" I suggest, forcefully.

His eyes widen a little and I can sense a hint of reluctance, but in the end he nods. "That might be a good idea, a restful night's sleep can do wonders."

"She can't swallow tablets, perhaps you have something that could dissolve in water so she can drink it?"

This time his reluctance is more obvious and he starts to shake his head, but I speak before he can say anything to piss me off, like tell me no. "How is your granddaughter Amelia? Is she still hoping to attend GAA next year?"

Heat fills his cheeks, but he nods. "Yes, she's hoping to get a partial scholarship."

"A partial scholarship? Wouldn't she be better applying for the Hayes Millard award, that's a full scholarship for all four years. Do you remember my friend Clay Janson? His mom is the one in charge of picking the recipient, I'm sure I could ask her to have a second look at Amelia's application, ensure she's aware of how splendid a choice she'd be for GAA."

This is complete coercion. I know it and so does he, but we both know that a full scholarship is worth tens of thousands of dollars, and that kind of motivation is enough to have him walk into the bathroom, fill a glass with water and add a sachet of white powder that instantly dissolves.

With a smile I take the glass from him and cross the room to Starling, sitting down beside her and handing her the glass. "Here you go, little bird. The doctor says you're fine, but that you need a good night's sleep. Drink this and then lie down and take a nap until your mom gets here."

Starling looks dubiously from me to the doctor. When he smiles and nods at her, she lifts the glass to her lips and takes a deep pull. She goes to put the glass down on the nightstand, but I push it back into her hand. "You should drink that, you look a little flushed. Are you hungry? I can go and get you something to eat."

She shakes her head. "I'm fine, I'll have something to eat when I get home."

I don't agree or disagree, instead I nod my head toward the glass in her hand and watch as she brings it to her lips and drinks the rest of it. Smiling, I take the glass from her and place it on the nightstand beside me, then I lift my hand and slowly and carefully smooth my fingers over her hair. "Why don't you lie down and close your eyes. Dr. Harris will stay with you while I go and keep a look out for your mom."

Warily she nods, shuffling down the bed a little and exhaling into the cushions as I stand up and move away. The farther away from her I get, the more she relaxes. I fucking hate it, but I don't want to risk her passing out again if she gets too riled up.

"Could you stay with her for a little while? I want to get her a sandwich in case she gets hungry."

Dr. Harris nods, then busies himself packing up his supplies into his bag as I step to the door and move out of the room.

"How is she?" Hunter asks as I close the door quietly behind me.

"She's fine, the doctor gave her a sedative to help her sleep."

My friends all fall in step with me as I stride away from Starling's room and head downstairs to my father's office. The door's closed when I reach it and I lift my fist and knock, waiting for my father's voice to invite me in.

"Come," he booms.

Pushing open the door, I step into the room, Clay, Evan and Hunter trailing behind me.

"Sebastian, how did it go? Can we meet her? Your mother is very excited," he says, standing from his seat behind his desk and moving toward me.

"She's okay, she fainted in the car on the way over here, so Dr. Harris is just checking her over. He suggested it might be a good time to fit her nano."

Dad's smile broadens. "Good thinking, saves him having to visit again. I have hers in the safe, let me just get it for you," he says, pushing a large picture on the wall to one side and revealing a modern-looking safe.

Typing in the code, the safe beeps a moment before the door springs open. I don't know exactly all that's inside, but I can guess. Probably some deeds, confidential documents pertaining to some of his more lucrative business deals and a pile of cash, just in case we need it. There's also a stack of nano tracking devices. We all have one, me and my friends, our parents too, this is just a part of being one of us, and now Starling will too.

Dad offers the small black case out to me and I smile, taking it from him and gripping it tightly. "Thanks, I'll take this up to the doc. Starling's mother Cassidy will be here shortly, perhaps you should gather all the parents so she can meet everyone in one go," I suggest.

Dad's eyes light up and he smiles widely. "I'll go and tell your mother, she'll be so excited." My dad's a great guy, he's not what I'd consider your classic, powerful, rich dude. In fact, in person he appears to be the opposite of the stereotype he's usually cast in. He's warm, friendly, inclusive and a great dad. He's also ruthless, incredibly intelligent and morally ambiguous when he needs to be.

The apple didn't fall that far from the tree, I'm just like him. That's why I don't have even a moment of doubt as I head back up the stairs and into Starling's room.

My eyes search her out the moment I enter the space. She's on the bed, her eyes closed, her chest moving up and down in a rhythmic pattern. In sleep she's almost as stunning as she is in motion, and I sit beside her on the bed and brush the hair that's fallen over her face back behind her ear.

"Our parents think this might be a good time to get her nano in place," I tell the doctor, holding out the black case in my hands in his direction.

"But she's asleep," he says suspiciously.

"Then she won't feel any pain, will she?" I tell him with a smile.

"Her mother agrees with your parents about this?" he asks, his tone dubious.

"We all just want to keep her safe," I say, avoiding his question. "You understand the pressure of being who we are."

Sighing, he nods then takes the case and places it onto the mattress beside me. Opening the lid, he pulls on a pair of latex gloves, lifts out the sealed sterile syringe and removes the packaging. "Same place as you have yours?" he asks.

I nod, pulling her hair up off her neck and moving to the side as Dr. Harris steps closer to her. He wipes a patch of skin right at the base of her hairline with an alcohol wipe, before bringing the syringe to her skin and carefully inserting the needle into her. She grimaces a little in her sleep, but doesn't wake as he depresses the plunger and the nano is planted beneath her skin.

Carefully, he pulls the needle from her neck and then puts the syringe, wipe and glove into a disposable waste box he has in his bag. Returning to the bed, he picks up the scanner from the box, turns it on and runs it over her neck. When the scanner beeps, he turns it in my direction, showing me the screen that confirms the chip is active and working.

"Thank you, Dr. Harris," I tell him. "Please make sure you send your bill to my father's secretary and wish Amelia good luck with her scholarship application."

The older man smiles, then packs up his bag and leaves without another word.

Smiling down at my beautiful little bird, I run my finger over the patch of skin on her neck, feeling the tracking chip that's barely the size of a single grain of rice. We were all fitted with one when a plot was discovered to kidnap me, Clay, Evan and Hunter when we were ten.

Our families are rich and powerful, a combination that attracts those who seek to take advantage of what they thought were our parents' weak links. The one beneath my skin has never been activated, it's only there in case of an emergency. Little Bird is mine and the nano in her neck will ensure that even though she might think she can fly free, she'll always be tethered to me. I'm her gilded cage, the lock and the key all at once and no matter how far she tries to run, she'll never be able to hide.

I sit with her for a while, stroking her hair and watching as her chest moves up and down as she breathes. Eventually, I reluctantly get up and leave, pulling the door to her room closed behind me as I step into the hallway. Taking my cell from my pocket, I dial her mother's cell number that Clay gave me as part of the information he'd found out about her.

"Hello," Cassidy answers.

"Ms. Clark, my name is Sebastian Lockwood, I'm Starling's boyfriend, we met earlier."

"Her boyfriend?" Cassidy says, laughter lacing her voice. "I thought you said you needed to speak to her about an assignment?"

"I'm sorry about the subterfuge, ma'am, Starling wanted to wait until tonight to introduce me. I'm calling because she passed out earlier and¾"

"She what?" she interrupts. "Is she okay? Where is she? What hospital?"

"She's fine, she's not at the hospital, she's at my house. I've just texted you the address. Our family doctor was here so he checked her over, and he says she's absolutely fine. He said it was more than likely exhaustion, which is probably from all the shifts she worked at the diner recently."

"She works too much, I told her she works too much," Cassidy mumbles, her voice cracking.

"I agree, which is why she quit her job tonight."

"Good," she agrees.

"I think so too."

"I'll come and get her. Thank you for calling, Sebastian."

"She's sleeping and honestly I think it might be better just to let her get a good night's rest."

"Sebastian, I don't know you, or your family, hell, tonight's the first thing I've heard about my daughter having a boyfriend. I'm not going¾"

"Ms. Clark," I interrupt her tirade. "I was only going to suggest you bring an overnight bag and stay here too, so we don't have to wake her."

"Oh," Cassidy gasps.

"There's plenty of room and my parents would love to meet you."

"Your parents? What did you say your last name was?"

"Lockwood, ma'am."

There's silence on her end of the call and I smile, knowing she recognizes who my family is.

"I wouldn't want to impose."

"There's no imposition. Starling's asleep and with how tired she was, I'm sure you'd agree it's best not to wake her if we don't have to. Since we haven't gotten to know each other yet, it would be best all around if you just stay here tonight, that way if we need to call the doctor again, he can come straight over."

She pauses again, but I know I've got her. She has no idea that I'm manipulating her, and that's just the way I want it. Starling is mine and regardless of what her mother thinks, nothing will change that, but if I can get Cassidy to agree to my way of thinking, it'll make it so much easier to get Starling to agree to the things I want too.

"If your parents are sure."

"They are, I want to get back and check on Starling, so I'll see you when you get here, just buzz the gate and someone will let you straight in."

"Okay, I'll see you soon, Sebastian."

Ending the call, I slide my cell into my pocket and head back into Starling's room. I know Clay, Evan and Hunter are somewhere in the house, but I don't want them in here with her when she's like this.

Her eyes are closed, and her hair is pulled to the side revealing her slender neck. My dick twitches in my pants, but I ignore it. As much as I wish I could strip her naked and slide under the covers with her, I won't, at least not right now. She's mine, and I'll be the one and only man to ever get my dick inside of her, but not tonight.

Her brow furrows and I reach out and run my finger over it, smoothing it as I try to imagine what she's dreaming about. I've no idea what haunts her sleeping thoughts, but I will. Soon I'll know her so well I'll be able to know what she's thinking before she speaks.

I know the way I feel about her isn't normal, she's consumed me completely since I first laid eyes on her. She's my obsession, but surely obsession is just the basis that love is built on? I'm not in love with her yet, I don't know her well enough, but soon that'll change. Soon I'll be the reason she smiles, the reason her panties are damp, the reason she can't wait to wake up every morning.

She's my obsession, but I'm going to make myself her world. I'll protect her from everything but me.

Pulling my cell from my pocket, I turn on the camera and take a photo, then switch it to video mode and record a few moments of her sleeping peacefully, then of me brushing the hair from her cheek, my hand trailing a path down her neck. "My perfect little bird," I whisper, ending the recording and sliding my cell into my pocket without watching it. That will be my reward later when I'm lying in bed next door, only a wall separating us. I'll watch the video while I take my dick in hand and wish it were her fingers instead of my own wrapped around it and covered in cum when I find my release.

A knock at the door banishes my filthy thoughts and I get up and cross the room, opening the door and peering around the frame.

"Sebastian darling, Starling's mother is here," my mom says, smiling widely.

"Ms. Clark," I say, greeting her with my most charming smile as I push the door open wide and step back to allow them entry into the room.

Cassidy Clark is only slightly taller than Starling is and she has to tip her head back to look up at me.

"It's lovely to meet you properly, I'm just sorry it has to be under these circumstances," I tell her, crossing the room and sitting down on the edge of the bed beside my girl.

Cassidy rushes to Starling, leaning down and running her palms over her daughter's face. "Oh, baby," she croons.

"Dr. Harris said she was fine, just tired," I tell her again, glancing up and smiling at my mom, who is still standing beside the door. "We'd planned to do a whole meet-the-parents thing tonight," I say with an ah-shucks smile and then watch as both my mom and Starling's mom visibly sigh at just how adorable and cute I am.

I don't normally enjoy manipulating my mom, but right now I need her to be completely on board with the whole Starling situation. My parents know she's mine, I told them about her, I just never mentioned that I hadn't told Starling at that point. Not that it matters now. I hate that she fainted, even more so because I'm ninety percent sure it happened because she was freaked out and a little scared of me.

But ultimately, I wanted her here in my house and here she is. I wanted my parents and her mom to understand how serious I was about her, now they do. I wanted to capture and cage her and make her mine, and now she is.

"Ms. Clark, I hope you'll help me convince Starling that she doesn't need to look for another job. GAA is a serious school and if she tries to work and keep up with her homework and studying, I'm worried she's going to make herself even more sick than just fainting from exhaustion." I pause, then offer Cassidy a sad, understanding smile. "I know she wants to help out and that money is an issue, but…" I trail off, waiting for Cassidy to fill the silence.

"I don't need her to help out with money, I've told her this a hundred times. I'm not sure what she's told you about my job, but I'm an author, I write thrillers and with publishing there are peaks and troughs in sales. Starling panics, but she really doesn't need to."

I nod, agreeing with her, even though I know she's lying. I'm completely apprised of Starling's family's financial situation. The money Starling was earning was paying the bills her mother's royalties weren't covering, but that stops now. I want all of her spare time and so her mother will have to make alternate plans to cover the loss of Starling's income.

"She's so still. Normally she's a light sleeper."

"Poor dear, she must have been exhausted. Let's leave her to sleep and we can get you set up in a guest room, Cassidy," My mom suggests.

"I should just take her home," Cassidy starts.

"Nonsense, what's the point of having guest rooms if people don't use them?" Mom says, waving away Cassidy's concerns and ushering her out of the room and down the hallway to the spare room on the other side. "Sebastian, dinner's going to be ready in ten minutes, the boys are all downstairs in the den, leave Starling to sleep, you can check on her later."

"Cassidy, let's get you settled and then I'll introduce you to my husband and our good friends and neighbors who happen to be the parents of Sebastian and Starling's friends."

Mom's voice trails off as she leads Cassidy away and I smile to myself, then down at the girl on the bed beside me. I've waited a year for this moment, and now she's here in my house, in the room I had decorated just for her, my little bird is finally mine, and I can't wait to make sure the rest of the world knows it too.

SEVEN

STARLING

"Time to wake up, little bird," a low, somewhat familiar voice says, dragging me from sleep.

Blinking my eyes, I stare up at an unfamiliar high ceiling, a modern chandelier hanging from the center. The bed moves beside me and I jolt all the way awake, snapping my head to the side and finding a very smug-looking Sebastian smiling down at me.

"Where am I?" I ask, my voice shrill.

"My house."

"What? Why? Oh my god, what time is it? My mom is going to kill me," I blurt, speaking so fast I can barely understand myself.

"Calm down, little bird, your mom is here, remember? She's

downstairs drinking coffee with my parents."

"Am I dead?" I blurt.

His laugh is loud and warm, the audible equivalent of a mug of hot cocoa on a cold day. "No, baby, you're not dead."

"I must be, there's no way in real life I'd be in bed, in your house while my mom is downstairs having coffee with your parents. Oh god, this isn't your bed, is it?" I gasp.

"No, this isn't my bed, the first time I get you in my bed, I want to be in it with you and for you to be fully conscious." He smirks.

"Why am I here? What happened? Why is my neck sore?" I demand, anger bleeding into my words, now that the initial shock has started to wear off.

"What do you remember about last night? Dr. Harris never mentioned you'd have any issues with your memory."

A barrage of memories hits me as I think back on everything that happened after I got to work. "You got me fired, and you were spouting all this bullshit about me belonging to the freaking Elite."

"You belong to me," he snarls, then smooths out his expression and smiles again. "But you're part of The Elite now, and if you're working every night, when will we get a chance to see each other? I'd assume your neck hurts because you slumped over in the back of the car when you passed out, and I didn't want to risk your safety by removing your seat belt to put you in a more comfortable position," he says simply, taking my hand in his and twining our fingers together.

I try to yank my hand free, but he just tightens his grip, refusing to allow me. "I don't want to see you, I don't know you," I shout, feeling a pulsing headache building at the back of my head.

Strong hands curl around my waist and then I'm being lifted from beneath the covers and lowered down into Sebastian's lap. "Shhhh, little bird, it's okay. It's all going to be okay. I know this feels like a lot right now, but this is all meant to be. The moment I saw you for the first time last year, I knew you were mine, but you were a freshman and completely off-limits. I've stayed away, but I can't do that anymore. I'm going to take such good care of you, I promise. I'm obsessed with you, my little bird; I'd give you the entire world to make you happy."

I don't mean to, but for a moment I rest my cheek on the fabric of his blazer and let him soothe me. I shouldn't be calming down right now, but somehow the smooth timbre of his voice and the sweet, terrifyingly overwhelming words he's saying calm my erratically beating heart, and I feel my tense muscles start to relax against him.

"Sebastian?"

"Yeah, baby?"

"Why do you keep calling me little bird?"

His hand curves up my spine and beneath my hair, resting against my neck and rubbing soft fingers over the skin. "Because your name is Starling, and because you're beautiful and wild like a bird, and because I want to clip your wings and tie you to me almost as much as I want to watch you soar."

His honesty is almost as disconcerting as his regal beauty. The things he's saying are making goose bumps prickle along my skin and a cold chill waft over me. But no matter how much I know I should be running from him, there's a lethargy in my muscles that won't let my natural flight instinct kick in. I should be fighting free of his disarming hold, but instead I'm sitting placidly in his lap, like this is where I want to be.

Confusion over my reaction to him consumes me. Boys have never really been on my radar. Of course I've had crushes, but they've all been unrequited and unmentioned. The middle school Courtney and I attended was in North Acres but even at the ages of nine and ten, the kids in my grade knew my house was smaller than theirs, my clothes were from Target not Ralph Lauren, and my summers were spent in Maine, not Mauritius. Nothing in my life so far has prepared me for Sebastian Lockwood. He looks like a man, sounds much older than his years and is so far out of my depth I'm already drowning, and only my toes are in the water.

"What time is it? I need to go home and get ready for school," I say, forcing my arms to life and pushing away from his chest, struggling to free myself from his hold.

"Relax," he coos, curling his hand around my ribs and stroking the underside of my boob with his thumb.

I freeze beneath his touch. "It's a little after seven. Your uniform is washed and pressed and your mom brought you some underwear last night."

His thumb lifts a little higher. "There's the shampoo, conditioner and body wash you like in the shower, but if you're still feeling unwell, I'm sure your mom wouldn't mind calling in for you."

At the first swipe across my nipple I feel myself go completely tense, it's barely second base, but it's the most provocative way I've ever been touched by a boy.

"We could spend the day relaxing and getting to know each other better," he suggests as he cups the weight of my breast in his hand.

"I'm not having sex with you," I blurt, trying to release myself from his hold.

"I'm not trying to have sex with you," he says as he pinches my nipple between his finger and thumb.

"Oww," I gasp, reaching for his hand to push him away.

Grabbing first one wrist, then the other, he clamps them at my sides with the arm that's now banded painfully tightly around my waist. "I'm going to fuck you, Starling, soon, but not today," he warns, pushing the nightshirt I'm wearing up my thighs, revealing my panties as he works his hand back to my breast, caressing it lightly, then pinching my nipple again, twisting it and plucking at it.

"Stop, you're hurting me," I cry, wiggling in his lap in an effort to evade him.

"The wet patch on the front of your panties disagrees, little bird," he mocks, alternating between pinching my nipple and soothing it.

"Imagine how good it'll feel when I'm sucking your pink little nipples between my teeth, a hint of pain to create limitless pleasure." His voice is sex incarnate and I close my eyes as heat pools between my thighs.

Releasing my breast he pushes his palm between my legs, rubbing my pussy with the heel of his hand through the fabric of my panties. I don't need to look to know that the fabric is damp and sticking to my folds.

"I love knowing your panties are wet because of me, I might jack off into a pair for you to wear to school."

My brows lift so high I swear they almost jump all the way off my face, and my shocked gasp is so loud it seems to fill the empty air.

"Which is the shocking part, baby? That I know how wet I'm making you or that I want your hot little virgin pussy soaked in my cum all day?"

"Both," I croak.

Cupping my cheek, he leans into me. "This virgin cunt's mine, little bird, your sexy legs are mine, your perky little tits are mine. Your tight asshole and hot mouth are mine. You belong to me and make no mistake, soon I'll be coating my dick in your blood as I break through your barrier and coat you with my cum. You should get used to wearing wet panties, Starling, because once I get inside of you, you'll be taking all of my cum. I won't jerk off unless it's over your tits, pussy or ass. I'll save it all up and you'll take it all while you scream my name and beg for more."

With each dirty word that slips from his mouth he grinds his hand against my clit, arousing me more and more as he works my clit until I'm pushing into his touch, my breath becoming ragged.

"That's it, baby, let go. I want to hear you come for me," he coaxes, pressing down a little harder against me until I'm writhing and panting. When I come, it's with a startled cry that falls from my dry lips and seems to ricochet around the room.

I shudder as waves of pleasure roll through me. "Good girl, you're so fucking beautiful. Lift your butt," he directs me.

Doing as he asks, I lift up and he slides my underwear over my hips, pulling them down my legs and off my ankles. "What…?" I question as he balls them in his hand and then lifts them to his nose, inhaling deeply.

"You smell delicious."

Before I have a chance to protest, his lips are against mine and he kisses me, sliding his tongue between my lips and exploring my mouth. His kiss is elegantly forceful with single-minded intent. "My pretty little bird," he whispers against my lips as he pulls back.

"Sebastian."

"Bastian, my friends call me Bastian."

"We're not friends," I pant shakily.

"No, we're so much more. Go take a shower, before I spread your legs and shove my cock inside you. I'll come back and take you down for breakfast once you're dressed."

When he leaves the room, shutting the door behind him, I jump up from the bed and slide the lock into place, resting my back against the wood and exhaling shakily. Bastian is intense. His presence sucks all of the air from the room, until all I can see and focus on is him. The orgasm he gave me is nothing like the ones I've given myself. If that's the way it feels when one of The Elite touches you, it suddenly makes sense why the girls at school will literally do anything to get a moment of their attention.

When he calls me little bird, goose bumps pebble over my skin, but I'm not sure if that's because I like it, or because he scares the hell out of me. Maybe both. He wants to fuck me. It's not like I've never thought about sex, of course I have. I'm sixteen, I have fantasies and I've explored my own body to see what feels good, but I have zero real-world experience.

I don't even know if I find Bastian attractive. Who am I kidding? He's gorgeous, but he's also high handed, obnoxious, terrifying and an Elite. That's not me. I'm not motivated by power or popularity. I would rather be invisible than be one of them, but I doubt that's something he could ever understand. When you look like he does, with a name like Lockwood, invisibility isn't an option.

The door to the bathroom is ajar and I pad over to it on bare feet, realizing that at some point someone changed me out of my diner uniform and into the soft nightshirt I'm wearing. I'm really hoping it was my mom, the shirt looks vaguely familiar so I think it's one of hers.

White tile and black marble fittings assault my eyes when I step into the palatial room. It's huge, bigger than my bedroom at home, and so fancy if I didn't know I was in his house I'd assume I was at an expensive hotel. A claw-foot tub calls to me, but I don't have time for a soak, no matter how much I wish I did. If my mom really is downstairs, like he said she was, then I need to get to her and get away from this house and the crazy boy who lives here as quickly as possible.

Stripping out of the sleep shirt and my underwear, I step into the shower and search for the controls, only there aren't any. It takes me far longer than it should to figure out the water is controlled by a touch screen and once I make it work, the jets are like getting an hour-long massage in an instant.

I linger beneath the water for longer than I should, but the comforting heat combined with all my favorite products makes me want to indulge, even though I shouldn't. Once I'm done, I wrap myself in the softest, fluffiest towel I've ever touched and step back into the bedroom.

Now that I'm fully awake I take a moment to look around. The walls are painted an off-white, except for the one behind the bed that's covered in patterned wallpaper. The bed is massive and made of dark wood and there're matching nightstands on either side. All of the soft furnishings are a mix of blues with the odd hint of gold dotted here and there. It's beautiful and incredibly classy, like it was put together by a designer—which it probably was.

I search the floor for my backpack, hoping that my uniform isn't too creased from where I folded it into my bag last night after I got changed at the diner. There's a door next to the bathroom that I'm assuming leads to a closet, so I open it and find my backpack on the floor and my uniform hanging on the rod. There's a second bag beside the first and I recognize it as mine.

Shock hits me and I stumble back from the force. My mom is here, she stayed here last night, she's having coffee with Bastian's parents downstairs right now. What the hell did he tell her to have her agree to all this? I've never mentioned him to her, we're not friends, I'd never even spoken to him myself before yesterday. But he must have told her something that convinced her to believe him, or else she wouldn't be here and she wouldn't have allowed me to stay here either. I wonder if he's told her the things he's been saying to me? That I'm his, that we're together, a real couple.

Rushing to get ready, I pull on fresh underwear from the bag Mom must have brought for me and quickly dress in my uniform. My hair is too long and too wet to leave loose, so I brush it quickly then twist it into two thick braids that sit flat to my head on either side, trailing down over my shoulders to the middle of my back.

I never usually wear makeup but right now I wish I did, because I could do with something to help give me a little armor against whatever I'm going to find when I go downstairs. I've never found myself in such a fucked-up position before, but as a general rule I always think honesty is the best policy. But how the hell would I even start to explain this? I doubt either his parents or my mom would appreciate me screaming that Bastian is infatuated with me and thinks this gives him some moronic claim on me. It sounds insane even to my own ears.

Smoothing my hands down the front of my blazer, I pull in a deep breath and glance around the room. I quickly give up hope on finding a portal back to my house or an excuse so that I can abandon my mom and leave without having to go downstairs and face whatever the hell is happening down there. My eyes snag on the pictures on the wallpaper. Stepping closer, I lift my hand and trail my fingers across the images. It's a tiny pale-brown bird—a starling in a beautiful, ornate gold cage.

A shudder runs through me. It's a coincidence, it has to be, but the imagery still disturbs me. He calls me little bird. He says I'm his. He said he wanted me in his house and here I am, in his home, in a room with caged birds all over the walls.

I need to leave. The best thing I can do is to go downstairs, find my mom and get us out of here as quickly as possible, then do whatever I have to do to avoid Bastian until he forgets all about me.

Nodding to myself, I slide my feet into my shoes, remake the bed, pick up my bags and unlock the bedroom door. Pushing it open, I step into a hallway and glance from left to right. To the left, there're two doors, one on either side of the hall, to the right, two more doors. Stepping cautiously out, I strain, listening for some clue that might guide me to my mom, but the house is silent.

Cautiously, I walk to the right and find myself at the top of a movieworthy double staircase that curves around, ending in a marble foyer at its base. My steps sound loud once I descend, but I'm still none the wiser as to where I need to go.

"Starling, sweetheart," a female voice calls, and I turn to find a beautiful woman striding toward me. She's dressed casually, in jeans and a sweater, but everything about her screams money, from the diamond earrings in her ears to the way her hair sits just so, the natural-blonde color accentuated with artfully applied highlights.

"Hi," I wave awkwardly.

"How are you feeling? You shouldn't have carried those bags down, one of the boys would have gotten them for you. You must be starving, let's get you something to eat."

"Er," I mumble.

"Oh, where are my manners," she laughs. "I'm Miranda, Bastian's mom."

"Nice to meet you, Mrs. Lockwood, I wasn't sure…" I trail

off, not sure what to say. "I'm so sorry we've invaded your home, which is beautiful by the way. Sebastian should have taken me home."

"Nonsense," she chides, dropping her arm around me affectionately. "He did the absolute right thing bringing you here. Dr. Harris was on a call just a few houses down and he rushed right over to check you last night, if he'd have taken you home you'd have had to go to the ER. Drop your bags and let's get you something to eat. Chef made croissants this morning and they're to die for."

Before I get a chance to protest, or suggest I just find my mom and go, my bags are out of my hands and she's herding me down a hallway and into a bright, airy dining room that's full of people.

Sebastian is out of his chair and at my side in an instant, pulling me from his mom and into his arms as his lips descend to mine. He kisses me like there's no one else in the room and when he finally lets me go and leans back, my lips feel kiss swollen and I'm shell-shocked. "Little bird, I was just coming up to fetch you." The way he uses the nickname he's given me like an endearment confuses me, then frightens me when I think about all the gilded cages on the wall upstairs.

"Let me introduce you to everyone, then you need to eat," he tells me warmly, curling his arm around my back and pulling me into his side as he turns us to look at the curious faces sitting at the table. "Obviously you already know Evan, Clay and Hunter.

Then this is my dad, Richard, beside him is Clay's mom Heather and his dad Eric. Hunter's dad Vance, his mom Mary, and then beside your mom is Evan's dad Harry."

I smile politely, offering them all an awkward wave as Sebastian leads me to the chair beside my mom and pulls it out for me. Waiting for me to sit, before he takes the seat beside me, he immediately starts to play with the bottom of one of my braids, lifting it to his face and rubbing the end over his lips.

"Honey, how are you feeling? You were dead to the world last night when I got here. I'm so glad you've quit your job, look what happens to you when you allow yourself to get so exhausted," my mom chides, not saying a thing about the fact that the guy beside me just kissed me senseless, or that we're in his house eating breakfast with his family right now.

"I didn't quit, Sebastian got me fired," I snap a little too loudly.

Mom tuts and purses her lips. "He was worried about you, honey, and I agree, you work too hard and with you being a sophomore now, you need to focus on your studies."

My mouth falls open and I turn from her to glare at Sebastian. He's smirking at me and I feel instantly aggravated. "Mom, we should get going, Courtney's picking me up this morning."

Dropping my braid, Sebastian places his hand on my thigh and squeezes. "She's already been informed you don't need a ride this morning."

"What do you mean?" I ask slowly.

"I'm taking you to school."

"I don't need you to take me, I get a ride with my friend."

Leaning in, he presses his lips to my ear. "From now on, I'm taking you to school and bringing you home afterward. Your friend has been advised."

"What if I don't want to ride with you?" I whisper.

"You misunderstand me, little bird. I'm not asking you, I'm telling you." Pulling back, he presses a kiss to my cheek and then lifts the empty plate from in front of me. "What would you like for breakfast?"

I want to rail at him, to tell him to go fuck himself but we're not alone, we're in a room full of my mom, his parents and all of his friends' parents too, so I bite the inside of my cheek and swallow my words.

"Try the French toast, honey, it's unbelievable," Mom gushes.

I open my mouth to suggest it was probably about time we left, when her attention is pulled away by the man sitting on her other side. Sebastian mentioned it was Evan's dad, but I wouldn't have needed to be told that because he's very clearly an older version of his son.

Laughter lines crinkle at the corners of his eyes, but he's still handsome, even though his hair is peppered with grays. Within seconds of him engaging my mom in conversation, both of them are laughing and talking animatedly while I look on. My mom is an introvert, she's a writer who is happier living in the fantasy world she brings to life on paper than in the real world that's going on around her. When she's forced to interact with humans other than me, she's normally quiet and awkward, but right now she's bright and vivacious and fitting right in with the other adults in the room.

I want to ask her what the hell is going on right now, but instead I take the plate of French toast Sebastian has made for me and thank him when he hands me a cup of coffee made just the way I like. I should ask him how he knows, but I'm starting to understand that he's taken the time to find out. I wonder what else he knows about me, or more appropriately, if there's anything he doesn't know.

"It's so lovely to finally meet you, Starling, we've heard so much about you," Mr. Lockwood says.

Almost choking on the bite of toast I'm eating, I try to force a smile to my lips but it comes out as more of a grimace.

"Dad, you're embarrassing her," Sebastian smirks, resting his arm on the back of my seat, watching me eat while he sips at a glass of juice.

"I'm sorry, sweetheart, it's just that Bastian's never brought a girlfriend home to meet us before. You must be very special and I'm excited to get to know you and your mom better."

"Cassidy, we're having a girls' night on Saturday, you must come with us," Mrs. Lockwood says excitedly.

I expect my mom to turn her down and when she parts her lips, I anticipate her awkward excuse, but instead she smiles.

"Oh a girls' night sounds wonderful, I've been so busy finishing my most recent novel it feels like I've barely left the house in a year," Mom laughs. "I tend to get a little absorbed in my work."

"I'm guilty of getting a little consumed with things I'm passionate about too," Evan's dad says flirtily.

Oh my god, Evan Morris's dad is flirting with my mom. I've heard of Morris enterprises, the company Evan's family owns, I doubt there's anyone in the state who hasn't, but I've no idea what the company does, or where Evan's mom is. What I do know is that my mom has no business flirting with a man like Mr. Morris, just like I have no business playing these weird games with Sebastian. These people are out of my and my mom's league and the sooner we can get away from them, the better.

I open my mouth to suggest an excuse to extricate us both from this house, but a loud whistle from the other side of the table has me snapping my lips back together.

"Time to go," Hunter says, pushing up from his chair while Clay and Evan follow suit.

"Come on, little bird, we don't want to be late," Sebastian drawls, taking my hand and tugging me up.

"I should—"

"Thank you so much for allowing Starling to stay here last night, Ms. Clarke," Sebastian says to my mother, preventing me again from trying to encourage my mom to leave.

"Sebastian, please call me Cassidy. I'm happy to know

Starling has found a boy who takes such good care of her. Miranda, Richard, your son is an absolute credit to you."

Sebastian's parents preen under my mom's praise of him and I roll my eyes. I wonder how they'd feel about him if they knew he'd announced I was his the very first time I met him, got me fired from my job by threatening my boss and then coerced me to get into his car with threats and manipulation.

"Baby, we're going to be late," he croons, wrapping his arm around my waist and guiding me out of the room, his grip firm and unyielding.

The good boy grin he's been using on my mom and his parents morphs into a conniving smirk the moment we're out of the dining room, but his hold doesn't loosen as he frog marches me down a hallway and into a garage filled with at least a dozen cars.

"I'm not getting in that car again," I snap, spotting the Mercedes I was herded into last night parked in the space closest to the shutter doors.

Sebastian laughs and after a moment, the others, who I hadn't noticed were beside the car, join in. The sound of the four cruel boys mocking me is chilling and a slight tremor runs along my skin, leaving goose bumps in its wake.

"How are you planning on getting away, little bird?" he taunts. "Are you going to run? Scream? Fight?"

"Which option will get you to leave me alone?" I ask, my voice shaking and betraying the strength I want him to hear.

He laughs again, then moves so fast I don't have a chance to contemplate running before I'm off the ground and hanging upside down over his shoulder.

"Let me go," I shriek, pounding my fists against his back.

"Bro, eventually she's going to have access to your dick, women have long memories, just saying," Clay chuckles.

"She likes it really. Open the door, asshole," Sebastian orders.

I'm swung the right way up and placed surprisingly carefully into the back seat, Hunter beside me, Sebastian blocking the other side while Clay drives and Evan takes the passenger seat.

"You're all assholes," I hiss, crossing my arms over my chest and trying to find enough space to not be touching either of the guys keeping me prisoner in the back seat.

"We're actually pretty nice once you get to know us," Hunter says from beside me, his voice soft and kind.

"I don't want to know you. You guys have your whole Elite thing going on and I just want to keep my head down and get through this year, then next year I'll be gone."

"Gone where?" Sebastian growls.

"Public school."

"No."

I laugh. "Okay, oh lord and master, you said no so the whole world must obey. What does it matter anyway? You guys will be at college next year."

"I'm not having my girl at that hellhole of a school in South

Acres. You'll stay at GAA." His brows are furrowed and his tone and expression are so serious that I feel myself soften a little toward him. Poor little rich boy, he literally has no idea about how the real world works.

"I'm not your girl, Sebastian, and South Acres High isn't that bad. I'm a mediocre student at best, I was never headed for an Ivy League, my aspirations are ambitiously aimed at middle-of-the-road party schools."

The guys seem to have a silent conversation, exchanging glances that make me want to huff in annoyance at not being included. But then I internally roll my eyes at myself. I don't want to be part of their little gang, and them having private little discussions that don't involve me is for the best.

The ride to school from Sebastian's house is much shorter than it is from mine and before long, we're pulling into the school gates and Clay is parking in The Elite spots right outside the doors. The groups of kids milling around all stop and turn toward the car and I swallow down the lump that's formed in my throat.

"I shouldn't be here," I mumble.

"This is exactly where you should be," Sebastian smiles, sliding his hand over my thigh and squeezing.

"Everyone is going to see me getting out of this car with you."

"Good, I want them to."

"I don't," I gasp.

Before I have a chance to formulate a good argument as to why no one should see me with The Elite, Sebastian is opening his door and climbing out. Turning, he reaches a hand out to me, but I keep my arms folded firmly across my chest.

Sebastian scowls, then looks past me. Hunter's hands circle my waist and he lifts me off the seat and sort of throws me to Sebastian, who plucks me out of the car like I weigh nothing at all.

"Please don't do this," I beg, but he ignores me, curling his arm around my shoulders and clamping me to his side.

The other guys surround us, and I swear the noise of kids and cars and life fades away and instead, everyone is silently staring at us.

"Smile, little bird, we're kings and we just made you a queen."

Closing my eyes, I force back the tears that are trying to break free. This isn't the moment to be weak. "I hate you," I whisper.

Strong arms turn me until I'm face to face with an angry-looking Sebastian. His fingers grab my chin and he forces my head back so I can't look away. Then he leans down and kisses me, keeping me in place while he plunders my mouth, his free hand grabbing my ass and showing everyone who's watching that I belong to him.

He keeps his hold on me when he pulls his lips from mine. "Hate me all you want, it won't make you any less mine."

This time my tears really do break free and his lips purse as the first one rolls down my cheek. Releasing my chin, he stops the tear with his finger, then sucks it into his mouth. "I don't want your tears, but for now if that's all you'll give me, I'll take them, because everything you are belongs to me."

The next ten minutes are a blur. Sebastian takes my hand and forces me to stay by his side as he parades me through the hallways, smiling and speaking to every single curious student who worships at the stupid fucking Elites' feet. He introduces me to everyone as his girlfriend and by the time I'm at the door to my homeroom, I doubt there's a single person who doesn't know we're apparently a couple.

The only person I was hoping to see is Courtney and she's concerningly absent. I don't know what Sebastian said to her when he told her not to pick me up, but she's the only person here who knows that he and I are not really a couple and I need her. I need someone who cares more about me than they do about status and hierarchy, I need my bestie.

By the end of first period, I'm ready to go home and hide beneath my comforter. The blissful anonymity I had here is officially gone. When Sebastian kissed me, he might as well have put a target on my back because it seems every kid in my class either witnessed him trying to eat me alive, or knows someone who witnessed it. There's even a video of it on Instagram and TikTok. Great.

People I've never spoken to want to be my friend, and the

kids who have refused to acknowledge my existence since middle school suddenly want to reminisce about all the good times we never had. I hate it and I hate Sebastian for causing it.

I've lost count of how many times I've told people he's not my boyfriend, but they don't want to hear it. What I have to say doesn't matter when the mighty Elite have spoken. When lunchtime rolls around, I'm desperate to escape to a quiet corner with Court and hide from all the curious stares and jealous daggers.

Grabbing my backpack I rush to the door, eager to find my friend, except Clay is leaning up against the wall outside my classroom, a knowing smirk stretched across his annoying mouth. "He said you'd try to hide."

Ignoring him, I drag my bag onto my back and step past him, but my forward movement is halted when he grabs hold of the straps on my backpack and drags me backward.

"Come eat with us, you'll only piss him off if he has to hunt you down," he warns, his voice friendly.

"I don't want to have lunch with him, I want to eat with my friend."

"She can eat with us too. We don't normally allow outsiders in, but if you ask him, he'll make an exception for you."

"Why is he doing this? He doesn't even know me. He's ruining my life," I whisper-yell.

Rolling his eyes, he sighs. "Dramatic much?" Taking my bag from my shoulders, he holds it in his hand and then places his other palm high on my back and guides me away from the classroom and all the people who are pretending not to watch us.

"I was invisible, no one saw me and I liked it that way," I say petulantly.

"He saw you."

"Fucking great, I'm not invisible to stalkers, good to know," I hiss beneath my breath.

We round the corner and Sebastian is striding toward us. His eyes narrow when he sees Clay has his hand on me. "You touching my girl?" he growls angrily.

"Just making sure she's where you told me to bring her. Starling has something she wants to ask you," Clay says, moving his hand away from me as he passes my bag to Sebastian.

"Is that right, little bird?" he purrs, stepping into my personal space until our chests are touching.

"I want to eat with my friend."

"She can sit with us."

"Alone, I want to eat with my friend alone, like we normally do."

"No," he says harshly, smashing his lips against mine punishingly hard, dominating me with his touch, like he thinks he can bend me to his will with a kiss.

"I'll text Evan to find the friend," Clay says from beside us.

At the sound of his voice Sebastian relaxes his hold on me, running a soft fingertip over my cheek. Discombobulated, I stumble a little and Sebastian carefully wraps his arm around my waist, his gentle touch in complete opposition to the way he just punished me with his kiss.

"I'll text her, I just need to find my cell," I say, reaching for my backpack.

"I have your cell," he smiles, pulling my old model cell phone from his blazer and handing it to me.

"Why do you have my cell phone?" I demand.

"I charged it for you. I also programmed mine, Clay, Evan and Hunter's numbers in there too. That way if you can't reach me, you can contact them instead."

"Why would I need to contact any of you?" I protest.

Taking my hand in his, he tugs me behind him, leading me toward the cafeteria. "I've never had a girlfriend before, but I understand it's customary to speak to one another while you're not together. Judging by the lack of texts and calls on your cell I can see you don't adhere to this with your other loved ones, but if we're not together, Starling, I expect you to text me and tell me where you are, who you're with and what you're doing."

"You went through my phone?" I gasp.

"I did," he says, not a hint of apology in his tone.

"And you think that's okay?" I admonish.

"You're my girlfriend, there won't be any secrets between us."

"Firstly, I'm not your girlfriend and secondly, even if I was, going through my cell phone is completely not okay," I say through gritted teeth.

"Hmm." That's it, no apology, no admission that he understands being a controlling asshole is not okay, just hmm. God, he's such an asshole.

We reach the cafeteria doors and I yank at my hand, trying to free myself from his hold. "I don't want to go in there with you."

"Little bird." It's a warning, not an endearment, but I don't heed him.

"Everyone will see me with you."

"Good, now march your cute butt in there, or I'll put you over my shoulder and carry you in."

"I don't want this," I tell him, my voice taking on a pleading note that I despise myself for.

"This isn't about what you want, this is about making sure that everyone in this school knows you're mine," he growls, dropping my hand and wrapping his arm around my waist, holding my hip in a just shy of punishing grip. It's a warning that he can and will hurt me if I don't do as he says, and I'm helpless but to comply.

The room doesn't fall silent like I expect it to, but I doubt there's a single person who isn't watching Sebastian touch me. They don't see the fact that I'll no doubt have a bruise from the strength of his grip, all they know is that one of their kings is with a girl. A girl he's leading to their table, a girl that he's placing in his lap and whispering in her ear.

Another tear tries to break free from my eyes, but I don't let it. Being here, being seen like this by all these people who know I'm not like them, who know I'm below them, makes me want to curl up in a ball and disappear. I'm not Elite, I'm not popular, or even well liked, and I know what they'll be saying the moment The Elite are out of earshot. They'll be calling me a gold digger, a slut who's getting on her knees to keep one of the kings.

They'd never imagine I don't want to be here, that there's blood in my mouth from how hard I'm biting my tongue to stop myself from crying. No, all they see is the poor girl from the wrong side of town, sitting in the rich guy's lap.

I swallow down a sob when the doors to the cafeteria open, and an excited-looking Courtney bounces into the room with Evan beside her. Unlike me, she seems exuberant to be speaking to one of The Elite. She should be here, not me. She'd love to have Sebastian's attention, to be the one on his lap while the entire school looks on wondering what she did to be picked. The skirt of her cheer uniform is bouncing with her as she moves, giving everyone a peekaboo to the booty shorts she's wearing beneath.

Everything about her is quintessential all-American, apple pie and white picket fence. I wonder if I could convince Sebastian she'd be a better choice for him, would he treat her the same way he does me? No, she'd want him, this notoriety, she wouldn't fight him, she'd love it.

"Starling," she shrieks, literally running across the cafeteria until she reaches The Elites' table and plops down in the chair beside us. "Bitch, why didn't you tell me?"

"Are you serious?" I gasp. "There's nothing to tell."

"Babe, you're sitting in Sebastian Lockwood's lap and there's a video going around of you getting out of his car this morning and him dry humping you in the parking lot. I'd say there's plenty to tell and I want *all* the details."

Sebastian chuckles and pulls me back onto his lap a little deeper. I freeze when I feel his hard dick beneath my butt. I may be a virgin, but thanks to Courtney insisting we educate ourselves with an afternoon of truly awful porn, I know what a dick looks like and that they get hard at the strangest things. Apparently one of those things for Sebastian, is having an unwilling girl sitting on him.

"Courtney, I'm sure Starling will fill you in on the details later, but first we should order," he tells her as Hunter appears at the table and sits down in the chair opposite mine.

"Little bird, what do you want?"

"I'm not hungry."

"You need to eat, you didn't have dinner last night, or that much at breakfast this morning," Sebastian scolds

"Did you stay at his house last night? Is that why you didn't need me to pick you up today?" Courtney yells. She's so loud that the whole room really does stop talking and turns to look at us.

"Court," I hiss.

"Oh. My. God. You had sex with Sebastian Lockwood?" She's getting louder and louder so I reach over and slap my hand over her mouth, silencing her.

"Shut up. I haven't had sex with him, I don't even know him. They turned up at the diner last night, got me fired and scared the crap out of me. I passed out and he took me back to his place," I tell her quietly, glancing at the other boys at the table who are stifling chuckles of amusement.

"What do you mean you don't know him? You made out with him this morning, you're sitting in his lap." Her arms flail toward me, gesturing to the position I've been forced into.

"I wasn't given much of a choice about this." I tip my head back to Sebastian behind me.

"Little bird, you practically begged me to sit on my dick," he laughs, his tone the warm, amiable one he uses with everyone except me.

"Are you kidding me?" I bark. "You threatened me."

"Baby, you're so dramatic," he laughs again, releasing his hold on my waist for the first time since he dragged me in here.

Making the most of the opportunity, I jump up from his lap and scoot around into the seat beside Court, letting her act as a buffer between the two of us. Risking a glance at Sebastian, I'm not at all surprised to find the cordiality he's been showing Court completely gone, replaced by a dark anger that has fear skittering along my skin.

This beautiful boy has two completely different faces, the one he shows to his parents, his friends, and the kids who worship him at GAA is confident, calm, kind and nice. Then there's the one he only seems to show to me. That face is angry, consumed, obsessed and I don't know which is the real him.

"Starling, are you listening to me?" Court asks, tugging on my uniform and forcing my attention to her. "Stop staring at your hot boyfriend and listen."

"Oh, er, I wasn't."

"You were totally staring at him, but that's okay if I had a boyfriend as hot as him, I'd stare too," she giggles.

For the next five minutes, Court talks at me in between talking at Sebastian, Clay, Evan and Hunter. She single-handedly keeps the conversation going as Sebastian watches me with an intensity that has all the hairs on the back of my neck standing to attention.

When my cell phone buzzes with a text, I ignore it, the only people who text me are Court and my dad. Court's talking with her hands so it's not her and if it's my dad, it'll be because he's lost something and thinks I might know where it is.

When it buzzes again, I reluctantly pull it from my blazer and check it.

Bastian
Your friend talks too much.

I don't want to chat with him, so I slide my cell back into my pocket, only to have it buzz again almost immediately. I pull it back out, inhaling slowly as I read the messages.

Bastian
It's rude to ignore me.

Bastian
Come and sit back in my lap.

Unable to resist I type out a reply.

Me
It's rude to get people fired and kidnap them.

His reply is instantaneous.

Bastian
You having a job was unacceptable. And it hardly classes as kidnapping when I took care of you when you were sick, had you checked by a doctor and then contacted your mother and invited her to come and check on you.

Me
I wouldn't have been sick if you hadn't been there getting me fired from a job I need.

Bastian
My lap...

Me
What about it?

Bastian
Come sit in it.

Me

No.

Bastian

Now!

Me

No.

Bastian

If you continue to defy me, I'll happily make a scene and ultimately, you'll end up doing as I please and sitting in my lap. Or you can come and willingly sit your ass on my dick and I'll reward your obedience.

Me

I'm not a dog!

Bastian

I never insinuated that you were. I merely suggested that you behaving would mean me rewarding you.

Me

Will this reward involve you leaving me alone and never speaking to me again?

Bastian

No.

Me

Then I don't see what's in it for me.

Bastian

I will allow you to go home
with your friend after
school, instead of me
driving you back to my
place

I freeze as I read the words. He wasn't planning on letting me go home after school? This is the first I've heard of this plan, but now that I know, I'm positive I don't want to go anywhere with him. I need space and time and possibly a continent or two between us.

With my legs shaking and my heart racing I push up from my seat, take the two steps to Sebastian and then carefully lower myself back down into his lap.

"Good choice," he breathes against my ear as his arm bands around my waist. His grip is tight and I realize I've walked straight into his trap. Not only am I exactly where he wants me to be, but I willingly put myself in this position.

Soft lips find my neck and I flinch. His body tenses beneath me and I know I've pissed him off, but he remains silent while Court keeps talking. His arm around my waist might as well be made of steel because he doesn't allow me even an ounce of wiggle room as he keeps nipping and kissing my neck, even going so far as to pull my braid out of the way to give him more room.

His teeth clamp down on my skin and I let out a whimper as he bites me and sucks, deliberately marking me on the back of my neck in a place that I can't see, but will be clearly visible to everyone else.

I try to squirm away from his punishing touch, but he just wraps his other arm around me, keeping me completely immobile while he brands me. It's barbaric and cruel and a message. A warning that if I don't do as I'm told or act how he wants, he'll punish me.

The urge to claw, slap and fight flashes through my head, but I push it away. Sebastian is bigger and stronger than me. Physically, he's more than capable of overpowering me and he's proved that he's not above using others to manipulate me into getting what he wants.

The best thing I can do right now is to just acquiesce and accept my fate, at least for the rest of lunch break. I do my best to relax and the moment I do, he releases his teeth and replaces the pain with a tingling kiss as he gently licks and soothes the place he just hurt.

"I like seeing my mark on your neck, I might keep it there so everyone else can see it too. Once I've taken your virginity, I'll finger your pussy while I bite down on my mark until you come, then I'll do it over and over so often that the moment my teeth scrape across that spot, your body will spontaneously orgasm."

His voice is barely above a whisper, so no one but me and him can hear what he's saying to me. I shudder in response, revulsion with the tiniest hint of desire. Nothing he's said or done should appeal to me and mostly it doesn't. Except there's a little tiny part of me, a part so small I might have gone my whole life without ever knowing it exists that preens at his words.

I might only be sixteen years old, but I understand feminism. I was raised by a badass, albeit slightly erratic single mother. I'm more than aware that I don't need a man and that I never want to be in a position where I'm beholden to one.

If I ever have a long-term partner or get married, I want my relationship to be equal and balanced by mutual respect and love. But there's also that hidden fantasy perpetuated by fairy tales and *Fifty Shades of Grey* that makes me crave a man to sweep me off my feet, to look after me and save me from anything, from puddles to big bad monsters. That's the part of me that's a little excited by his dominance and the way he's managing me.

I'm grateful for the distraction when a server arrives at our table, placing a plate of food at each place setting and two in front of me and Sebastian. "I didn't order anything?"

"I ordered for you," Sebastian says.

Scowling, I turn to glare at him, all my resolve to just behave and get away from him as soon as possible gone in an instant. "I told you I wasn't hungry."

"And I told you, you need to eat, you don't take good enough care of yourself."

"That's—"

Sebastian shuts me up by grabbing my chin, turning me toward him and slamming his lips to mine. His tongue forces its way into my mouth while his fingers tease at the underside of my breast. I wish I could say I don't respond, that I sit there like a wet fish refusing to participate, but that would be a lie and by the time he leans back, separating us, I'm panting and squeezing my thighs together to quell the ache that's formed between my thighs.

"Eat," he orders, pressing a soft peck against my lips and dragging the plate containing a delicious-looking deli sandwich toward me.

EIGHT

SEBASTIAN

She's perfect. Even when she's fighting me, she's still everything I've ever wanted. She's feisty and high strung, she's a challenge that I can't wait to conquer. She thinks she won a battle with me at lunch, but what she doesn't realize is that I don't mind negotiating with her to ensure she does as I ask. Letting her ride home with her friend was an easy concession, especially because I plan to follow her home, wait for her to change and then bring her back to my place again anyway. Not that I told her that, I gave her something she wanted and I got what I wanted. Everyone's happy.

When lunch is over, I reluctantly let her go to class. Clay put an app on my cell so I can access the security cameras and watch her whenever I want, but I resist. She's already my obsession, if

I allow myself to watch her more than I already do I'll fail every single one of my classes.

The afternoon drags, the weight of my cell in my pocket taunting me. My last period is in the classroom opposite hers and the moment the bell sounds, I leave, settling my back against the wall to wait for her.

The other kids pour out of the room, but she's slower to leave. She's not looking where she's going, her backpack in her hands, her gaze fixed on it as she slides something inside, then concentrates on fastening it up. All eyes are on her, but she's completely unaware. I don't know if that's because she doesn't know that they can't keep their eyes off her or if she just doesn't care.

No one has dared to ask why her, but I can see the unspoken question on all of their lips. In terms of GAA hierarchy, she's at the bottom. Her family's not rich or powerful, she's not slutty or infamous. To the other students she's a nobody, or at least she was until I made her mine. Now she's a curiosity, someone to study, to emulate, because she's done what no one else has in the three years we've held our positions as The Elite, she's caught our attention.

Don't get me wrong, we've hardly been celibate since we took over from the seniors, in fact we've fucked more than our fair share of girls. There's even some kind of club for girls who have fucked all four of us, but none of us have ever had more than a passing fancy.

The Lockwoods, Jansens, Morrises and Rossbergs all have legacies to protect, we all know what's expected of us and that means we don't have the luxury of dating indiscriminately. The women we ultimately marry will either have to bring an alliance, or have a pedigree that makes them an asset.

Starling has neither of those things, but my parents are romantics and when I realized my obsession with her wasn't going away, I told them about her. If I was in my senior year at college they probably would have told me she wasn't an option, but claiming her now when she's only sixteen gives me and them time to shape her and our future together into something they deem worthy.

"Little bird, if you don't pay better attention to what's going on around you, you'll end up falling over someone or something and getting hurt," I say, curling my palm possessively around her neck, stroking my thumb over the purpling bruised bite mark I put on her.

"Oh god," she gasps, startled. "Jesus, you again. You need a bell or something, you scared me."

"Sorry, baby," I coo, laughing as I turn her into my arms, lean down and kiss her.

"You need to stop kissing me," she whispers breathlessly when I release her.

Draping my arm across her shoulders, I urge her to start walking again. "Until I can get my dick inside of you, kissing you and touching you is all we've got. I plan to use your lips as much as I can. Unless you'd prefer I lift up your skirt and play with your pussy again, like I did this morning?"

Her cheeks heat to a light-pink color and I smile to myself. She likes me kissing her, she likes it when I tell her all the dirty things I plan to do to her. She can deny wanting me as much as she likes, but I saw and felt how wet she was this morning. I kept her panties as a fucking souvenir. She's the most tempting kind of jailbait, and I'll take her and own her, but not yet, not until she's begging for it. I can wait, because the moment she's ready I'll make her mine in every way possible; until then my balls will be bluer than a fucking Smurf's and my dick will be chaffed from all the whacking off I'll be doing.

"What's up anyway?" she asks.

"Nothing."

"Then why are you here? I'm riding home with Court. You said."

"I know, although you could both ride with me."

"I want to ride with my friend." Her tone becomes defiant and I grip her a little tighter.

"I said you could ride with your friend; I didn't say you could be a bitch to me. You're my fucking girlfriend, if I want to meet you after class, I will. And you'll smile and kiss me and be fucking pleased to see me."

"God, Sebastian, hasn't this game gone on for long enough already? I'm not sure what you win or whatever, but you've belittled me, embarrassed me, ruined at least the next couple of months at school until people forget about this, and got me fired from a job I liked. Isn't that enough? Whatever I did to piss you guys off, I'm sorry, I won't do it again, just please, please leave me alone."

She's pleading, begging, and all I feel is anger. I want to brand my name on her ass, put a ring on her finger and have her ride my dick twenty-four seven until she understands this isn't make believe, it isn't a game or a punishment or any kind of childish folly. "You think being my girlfriend is a punishment?"

"I think this is all just a cruel game, The Elite dishing out an outlandish punishment, like you do to the other kids who do something to piss you off."

She's not wrong about us being creative in the ways we punish those who step out against us, or break the rules we have set in place to keep order at GAA. I suppose it's not entirely out of the realm of possibility that we could pretend to claim a girl, get her caught up in our web and dump her. It's not something we've done before, but then penance is rarely doled out in the same manner twice.

"Our punishments aren't cruel; we mete out justice in equal measure to suit the crime. Have you done something that would warrant being punished by The Elite?" I ask.

"No," she cries. "I haven't done anything. The school year only started yesterday and I didn't see anyone but Court all summer."

"If you haven't done anything to break the rules, why would

you think I'm punishing you?" I ask, genuinely curious why she's so determined not to believe this is real.

"Seriously," she deadpans. "I'm me and you're you. Even if we disregard the differences in our socioeconomic status, before yesterday we'd never spoken to one another, I'd never even glanced in your direction for longer than a second. You're an Elite and a senior, and I'm an antisocial outcast sophomore. This," she motions between the two of us, "Doesn't make any sense, ergo, this must be a trick, or a punishment, or hell, maybe it's a bet. Whatever. I just think that enough is enough; you've had your fun, I'm thoroughly humiliated and humbled."

"I'm not punishing you, little bird."

We're outside now and her friend is waiting with Evan, but I ignore them, taking Starling's chin between my fingers and lifting it up, forcing her to look at me. "This isn't a trick, a game, a bet or a punishment. I've wanted you since I saw you last year, but you were a freshman and completely off-limits, even to me. I've waited a full year to touch you, kiss you and tell the whole fucking world you're mine. I won't ever be cruel to you, unless you force my hand. You're mine and when we graduate, we'll name you Elite so you'll be protected, I look after the things that belong to me."

Her pupils are blown wide and her full pouty lips are damp, the bottom red from the way she's nibbling at it as she stares at me. "I just want to be invisible; I don't want to be seen or protected, I'm happy just being ignored."

"The time for hiding has passed, you're a queen now, better get used to it." I smile, turning her toward Courtney and slapping her ass hard, propelling her forward as Clay saunters over to me, staying at my side as I watch Starling and Courtney walk away.

"Hate to see them go, love to watch them walk away," Clay whistles.

"You better not be looking at my woman's ass," I spit.

"Nah, bro, my eyes are on the talkative cheerleader's ass. That fucking uniform never looked so good before. If I could gag her to shut her up, she'd be the perfect fucking woman."

"I thought you preferred feisty Latina girls? Courtney couldn't be any more WASP if she tried."

"She's a cheerleader, she can bend like a fucking pretzel, imagine all the possibilities," Clay says with a wistful sigh.

"You can do whatever the fuck you want to her now she's a sophomore, you know the rules as well as I do. But she's not sixteen for a couple of months and you'll be eighteen soon, you know your parents would kill you if there was a scandal about you fucking an underage girl."

"I know, I know," he says, waving me off. "I've heard the talk about family expectations and keeping up appearances just as many times as you have, it's why we've been screwing seniors since we were freshmen. Gotta say, I'm surprised you're letting Starling go with blondie, I figured you'd want eyes on her."

A low, dry laugh falls from my lips as I move toward my

Mercedes. "I said she could ride with her; I didn't say we wouldn't be following. Find out where Evan and Hunter are, we're leaving the moment little bird leaves, whether they're here or not."

"Dude, you are so whipped," he laughs.

"Just thoroughly obsessed."

By the time Courtney's car drives out the school gates, we're behind her, staying on her tail the entire way back to Starling's place despite their attempt to lose us by taking several random detours and attempting to outrun us on a stretch of quiet road.

"What the hell, Sebastian? Why are you here?" Starling demands the moment she barrels out of Courtney's car.

"We're eating at my place," I tell her calmly, grabbing her wrist when she's close enough and pulling her into my chest.

Fighting me, she slams her fists against my pecs, but I just hold her tighter, immobilizing her. "Behave, little bird, go and say goodbye to your friend."

"I'd rather say goodbye to you. I've spent the last twenty-four hours dealing with you and all your bullshit, I just want to go in my house, get into my comfy clothes and search for a new job while I try to pretend you don't exist," she says, exhaling tiredly.

"Say goodbye to your friend," I snarl as calmly as I can muster.

Her eyes close and she exhales, her shoulders slumping as she turns and pads resignedly to Courtney's car. I'm not sure exactly what she says to the cheerleader, but they embrace through the window before Courtney backs the car down onto the street and waves gleefully to me as she speeds off back toward North Acres.

Without saying a word, Starling wraps her fingers around the straps of her backpack, climbs the steps to her door, opens it and walks inside without even a backward glance. Watching it swing shut, I smile to myself, then turn back to the car and my friends who are waiting inside.

"I have to go and deal with my girl. Go home, grab the Lambo, then drop it off back here for me in an hour or so. I'll negotiate with my angry little bird, then bring her home to hang out later."

"Let's watch a movie at mine, the media room refurb is finally finished and we can chill," Hunter suggests.

"Sounds good, can someone let my mom know I'm eating dinner with Starling?"

"Sure, dude, have fun." Clay laughs.

Flicking him the bird, I head for the front door, open it and let myself in. I can hear Starling talking to her mom on one side of the house, so I follow the sound and find myself outside a tiny, and what appears to be a very cluttered office space. Cassidy is behind a small desk, the wall behind it is covered in Post-it notes with strings connecting one note to the next. It's like a serial killer lair, which is kind of apt considering Cassidy writes books about murderers.

"It's not true, Mom," Starling says, her voice imploring.

"Oh, sweetheart, you don't need to pretend. I've met him now, he's a lovely boy and his family was so kind and gracious to me last night. I don't know why you thought you had to hide him from me, you know you can tell me anything."

Starling tips her head back and groans. "It's all bullshit, the first time I ever spoke to him was yesterday, I haven't hidden anything from you, because there's nothing to hide. He's an asshole and he's playing you; he's playing everyone as part of some fucked-up, malicious game."

"Baby," I coo, stepping out of my spot outside the door and into Cassidy's office, sliding my arm around Starling's waist. "There's no need to be embarrassed. I'm your boyfriend, your mom understands young love, and we agreed now summer's over we need your mom to get to know me, so we can spend as much time together as we can now that we're back at school."

Starling's mouth gapes open like a fish, but I don't give her a second, pressing a kiss to her cheek as I stare lovingly at her for a moment, then look to her mom. "Cassidy, Starling has been so worried to tell you about us. I told her you wouldn't be mad, I know I'm a little older than her, but I was raised to respect women and I promise I'll only ever behave appropriately toward your daughter. I love her, she's my world and I just want to be with her. Please give us your blessing, I know it would mean the world to Starling."

Cassidy's eyes soften and she smiles at us wistfully, like

she's remembering what it's like to be young and in love. "Starling, baby, you should have just told me, I only ever want you to be happy and loved and I think it's obvious to anyone who looks at the two of you together how much Sebastian loves you. You're young, it's the time to love big, so of course you have my blessing. Enjoy one another, just not too much, doors stay open, because I don't want to be a nana until you're at least thirty."

"Mom," Starling gasps. "How¾"

Before she can say anything, I interrupt. "Don't worry, Cassidy, I promise to take the very best care of her. Thank you so much for being so wonderful about this. My parents are having a pool party this weekend, of course Starling will be coming, but we'd love for you to come too. Family is so important to my parents and they don't just want to get to know Starling, they want you to feel comfortable with them too."

"Oh that would be so lovely, your parents made me feel so welcome last night, I'd love to join you. Your mom and I exchanged cell numbers, so please have her call me with the details."

"Perfect," I smile. "We are going to order pizza for dinner, are you joining us? Is there anything specific you like?" I ask her, while Starling just gapes at me.

Cassidy waves her hand in the air, "No, you kids just feed yourselves, I have so much to do to get this book finished, I'm planning to just hole up in here for the rest of the night."

"We're going over to Hunter's place to watch a movie once we've eaten, so we won't be here to disturb you."

"Sebastian, that is so sweet of you to think of me, but you don't need to worry, my office is soundproofed. I'm always telling Starling she can bring her friends around, but it's usually just Courtney."

"I need to find a new job," Starling says loudly.

"We talked about that, baby," I say through gritted teeth.

"Starling, I agree with Sebastian, you need to concentrate on your schoolwork and having a job in the evenings and weekends just isn't appropriate now you're back at GAA."

"But spending the evening watching movies with Hunter is?" Starling spits.

"As long as you've finished all of your homework, then yes it is," Cassidy says, straightening her spine and steeling her voice. "I'm not going to argue with you about this, high school is important, so is making friends and being a kid. I've talked to my publisher's PR people today and we've worked out a plan to market my back catalog better. I know you think you need to act like an adult, but you don't. I'm the parent, so no job, more focus on being sixteen."

"But, Mom¾" Starling starts.

"Enough Starling. Now scoot, I have work to do and you have pizza to eat and a cute boy to make out with. With the door open," Cassidy laughs, dismissing us as she turns her attention to the screen in front of her.

Starling starts to protest, so I grab her hand and tug her from the room, closing the door behind us.

"What the hell are you doing?" she shrieks, all of the stunned silence from a few moments ago gone and replaced with indignant outrage.

"Letting your mom know what my intentions are," I smirk.

"You're an asshole."

"Little bird, you haven't seen anything yet, there isn't a limit to what I'd do to keep you."

"You can't keep something that isn't yours in the first place."

Turning her, I press her against the wall, collaring her throat with my hand as I lean in and kiss her. Sliding my tongue into her mouth, I barely repress a smile when her own tongue immediately tangles with mine. There's no hesitation, she's kissing me with just as much fervor as I'm kissing her. Her hands are gripping my blazer, and despite what she might try to say later, she's not trying to push me away.

Sliding my leg between hers, I use my free hand to push her skirt up and palm her ass, tilting her forward until her cunt is pressed against my thigh. Rolling my hips, I grind against her core and she moans, arching into my touch, not away from it.

She can deny the connection between us as much as she wants, but her body is betraying her, it knows that she belongs to me, and that the only person who can give her the pleasure and release she needs, is me.

In time she'll learn that only my touch will satisfy her and

I crave that, crave her needing me to feel good. Not that she'll ever have the chance to know what it feels like to be touched by anyone but me. Most of what I said to Cassidy might have been bullshit to get her on board with my plans for her daughter, but Starling being my world was one-hundred-percent true. She's who I wake up thinking about and the image that chases me into my dreams. She's everything, and I'll do whatever it takes to tie her to me.

Tightening my hold on her throat, I grind my leg a little more vigorously against her cunt and she pants, a cry falling from her lips as I fuck her mouth with my tongue, squeezing her ass and guiding her to roll her hips.

She comes on a startled cry, her grip on my blazer tightening as her body jerks and shudders as she comes all over my pants.

"If you're not mine, why was your tongue in my mouth? If you're not mine, why is your skirt around your waist and my hand on your ass? If you're not mine, why are my pants wet from where your pussy has soaked them with your cum?"

Pulling her head away she closes her eyes, trying to hide from me and the truth of my words, but I release her throat and grab her chin instead, squeezing. "Open your eyes, you don't get to lie to me and hide from me. Look me in the face and tell me how I've given you two orgasms today but I don't fucking own you."

I force her gaze to lock with mine, refusing to allow her to deny this for a second longer. Her silence is more telling than any words. I let her sulk as I order pizza and we sit together in her bedroom, eating and doing homework. It's a strangely nice and domestic moment but she's tense, waiting for me to do something or say something.

When the pizza boxes are finished, I collect all the trash and stand. "You need to get changed, we're going to Hunter's."

"I don't want to go to Hunter's, I don't like Hunter," she whines.

"Why don't you like Hunter?"

"I don't like any of you. You're all elitist assholes."

"Cute," I smirk. "I'll take these, you find something comfy, we're watching a movie in his new media room."

"His media room," she scoffs.

Rolling my eyes, I take the pizza boxes outside to the trash can, then walk back into her room, finding her in nothing but her bra and panties.

"Get out," she yells.

"Hell no." Crossing to her bed, I sink down onto it and lift my hands behind my head, settling in to admire the view.

Grabbing her uniform from the floor, she scrambles to cover herself and I laugh. "Drop the clothes, little bird, let me see."

"Fuck you, get out of my room."

Tutting softly, I let my gaze roam over her body. She's soft in all the right places, despite how skinny she is, and I can't wait to see how lush her curves get when she's eating properly and not exhausted and running on fumes.

"Perhaps we can make a deal."

"What deal?" she asks slowly.

"Quid pro quo, you do something for me and I'll do something for you."

"All I want from you is for you to leave me alone."

"Never going to happen, but how about you drop the clothes and let me look at you, and I'll allow you to ride to school with Courtney in the morning."

Scoffing dismissively, she tightens her grip on the shirt that's barely covering her tits. "I don't need your permission to ride with her."

"She's been advised not to collect you anymore and she was only too happy to oblige, she's over the moon that you're my girlfriend," I say smugly.

"I'm not your girlfriend."

"Considering you were coming on my leg less than an hour ago, I beg to differ."

"You're an asshole."

"So you've said," I smirk.

"I hate you," she hisses, then glances down at the clothes she's using to hide herself from me, a conniving look shining in her expressive eyes. "I'll let you see me, but I want to ride to and from school with Courtney permanently."

"No deal. If you want that, then I want your virgin cunt riding my dick."

"What? No!" she gasps, shocked.

"That's okay, I can wait till the next time I make you come, then I'll strip you out of your clothes and lick you from head to toe."

A flash of panic, laced with desire darts across her face. "Courtney picks me up and drives me home from school all week and we eat lunch at our own table."

I pause, making her think I'm considering her offer. I'm not. She may think she's in charge right now, but this is all just a game and I'm the one moving the pieces. "Very well. Strip. Slowly, I want to savor my first view of you bare to me."

Closing her eyes, she drops her chin to her chest and inhales. After a long moment, she lifts her head and then drops the shirt she's been using to hide herself to the floor.

My dick surges to life. She's perfect. "The bra first," I prompt.

Reaching behind her, she unfastens her bra, then freezes, her elbows clamped to her sides keeping her bra in place.

I could demand she drop it, but I don't want that, instead I keep my steady gaze on her and wait. It only takes a couple of minutes and then she drops the bra, forcing her arms to stay at her sides, her hands clenched into fists.

"Now the panties." I want to say more, but my throat is tight, her breasts are perfect, small, but perky, her nipples are a rosy-pink color, the peak pebbled and begging to be sucked.

Her fingers dip to her panties and instead of delaying, she closes her eyes and pushes them down, kicking them free of her feet. Taking advantage of her eyes being closed, I run my gaze lasciviously over her naked skin.

There's a small, neat patch of hair coating her pussy lips that's wet with the arousal I know she'll deny if I point it out. Moving silently, I get up from her bed and step toward her, reaching out, but stopping myself an inch from her skin. She looks so innocent, even though she's standing here naked for me, and my dick twitches in my pants ready to steal that purity from her and dirty her up.

"Beautiful," I whisper against her neck, pressing a soft kiss against her fluttering pulse.

Snapping her eyes open, she lifts her hands to cover herself, but I bat them away, biting my bottom lip as I blatantly peruse her, wanting her to feel what it's like for me to have my eyes all over her.

"Sebastian," she says, my name on her lips a warning we both know I won't heed. She's mine, I can do whatever I please. I'm only allowing her a sense of control while I want her to have it.

Glancing to the partially open door, I peek out to check her mom isn't upstairs before I circle her, stroking my fingers over her luscious ass. Slapping it once, I watch it jiggle, then curl my arm around her waist and pull her into me, my dick pressed up against her back.

"You're utterly perfect, little bird. I'm a lucky man."

"You've looked your fill, I need to get dressed."

"Not yet, it's time for your reward."

"I don't need a reward, I just need to put some clothes on," she argues.

Moving the hand around her waist lower, she jolts when I slide my fingers through her damp folds. "You're such a good little bird, but I'm going to make you feel even better."

"No," she protests.

Dipping a single finger into her tight pussy, I wrap my other arm around her and press my thumb against her clit.

"Sebastian."

"I can feel how wet you are, Starling, your lips might be saying no, but your body is saying yes." Slowly I start to slide my finger in and out of her, rubbing circles on her clit, teasing her and coaxing her pleasure.

Slick arousal drips down my fingers, she's soaked. I add a second finger, pushing it inside of her and smiling when she clenches her pussy around them, a moan falling from her parted lips. Carefully I fuck her pussy and rub her clit until she's moaning my name and grinding her hips, moving into my touch, trying to force me to move quicker, fuck her harder with my hand. But she's not in control and instead of doing what she's begging for, I pull my fingers from her and move my thumb from her swollen clit.

"What?" she pants.

"I thought you wanted me to stop?"

"Sebastian." Her voice is desperate and I smile, this is how

I want her to always be, panting and writhing for my touch, for the pleasure only I will ever give her.

"Do you want me to touch you? To make you come?"

"Yes, yes," she whines.

"Say it, ask me for what you need."

"Touch me, make me come."

"You want me to put my fingers into your dripping cunt?"

"Yes, please," she begs.

"Say, please Bastian, fuck my dripping cunt with your fingers until I come all over your hand."

She's silent, so I use two fingers and tap twice over her swollen clit.

"The only way you get to come is by asking me."

Her hips roll and a soft moan falls from her parted lips. "Please, Bastian, fuck my dripping cunt with your fingers until I come all over your hand."

"Of course, little bird, you only ever need to ask," I say, smirking as I force my fingers back into her soaked core, fucking her hard and fast as I rub her clit until her knees give way and she cries out, her internal muscles fluttering and clenching around my fingers.

"I hate you," she whispers as soon as her body calms and she can stand on her own.

"No you don't, little bird, you just wish you did."

NINE

STARLING

Hunter's house is huge, not quite as big as Sebastian's, but still ridiculous for just him and his parents to live in. If he has any siblings, I've never heard of them or seen them at school. After Sebastian made me orgasm with his fingers; he insisted on watching while I showered and redressed, his eyes fixed on me as if I'd make a run for it if he glanced away. I didn't speak a single word to him and he didn't try to make me, it was a refreshing change.

The media room is ridiculous, with a huge screen almost as big as the ones you get at the movies. Huge navy-blue velvet couches are built into the tiered steps, allowing you to sit on three different levels depending on how far away from the screen you want to be. But despite how big the room is and how many couches there are to pick from, the guys all pile onto a single couch. Their actions are familiar and practiced. Hunter grabs sodas from a refrigerator and what looks to be a movie snacks station at the back of the room. Clay scoops freshly popped popcorn from an honest-to-goodness popcorn machine. Evan selects several boxes of candy while Sebastian grabs extra pillows and blankets. I'm the odd man out and I find myself almost grateful when Sebastian takes my hand and pulls me down onto his lap.

Being around him is exhausting, he makes me feel on edge and jumpy because his mercurial moods swing from coaxing to cruel. I'm actually starting to believe this is more than just an elaborate game. The way he touches me, the things he says and the look on his face, it all seems too real, too raw and intense to be make believe.

If he'd approached me, been nice to me and then asked me out, I might not have said no. But that's not how it happened and I can't forget the glint in his eye when he forces me to behave a certain way. He enjoys it. He likes his control over me, just like he enjoys being an Elite and having power over a whole school full of kids.

What is it they say? That power corrupts? In Sebastian's case, I'm sure it's true. He's rich, confident, revered, beautiful. Anything he wants he gets, but I can't allow myself to be just another thing that belongs to him. I refused to be owned.

The guys chat between themselves, but I don't try to insert

myself into their conversation, I don't want to be a part of their world. Instead, I fidget in Sebastian's lap, trying to get comfortable, knowing that getting him to allow me to move will mean selling even more of my soul to the devil.

Earlier when I stripped for him, I thought I was winning. For a short moment I honestly thought I held the upper hand, after all, what could he do just looking at me? But when I was naked and his eyes were on me, I finally started to understand where the power lay—solely at his feet.

Everything he's done, the way he's behaved, has all been about him toying with me. We're playing a game that I don't know the rules to, and I need to figure out how I end the game without losing to him.

Maybe if the only players were him and me, I might stand a chance, but after only two days he's already got my mom and my bestie on his team. I'm outgunned by him and I have no idea what to do to try and free myself of his obsessive hold.

Someone dims the lights and a movie starts to play on the huge screen. It's vaguely familiar, a new release that Court suggested we go to the movies to watch. A sudden wave of exhaustion washes over me and I yawn, settling back against Sebastian. I want to leave, to go home and just sleep in my own bed, but I know if I suggest it he'll refuse.

"You okay?" he asks, his warm breath against my ear.

"Tired," I say wearily.

"Sleep then, little bird." Pulling a blanket over us, he turns me slightly and encourages me to rest my head against his shoulder. I know I should fight it, but I've tried to fight today, I've tried to negotiate. All it's gotten me is kissed in front of the whole school, a purple claiming bite on the back of my neck and naked while he touched me. So far I'm losing both the battle and the war; it's time to regroup and figure out a new plan.

I must fall asleep, because when I wake up, I'm being carried in Sebastian's arms. "I want to go home," I mumble sleepily.

"I am your home."

Vague memories of getting home and getting into bed, of Sebastian crawling in with me, his warmth pressed against my back, and his arm wrapped around my waist fill my dreams. But I wake up alone, in my own bed, wearing nothing but my bra and panties. Rolling to my back, I stare up at the ceiling. A plan came to me at some point last night, it's risky, but it might work. Sebastian is all about reputation. His family name is powerful, he's a force to be reckoned with at school and even at seventeen he's a formidable opponent.

He's acting like an adult, so maybe it's time to revert to a more playground-like defense. I'm going to make a scene. I'm going to wait for the perfect moment and I'm going to call him out, shout and scream and call him names. It's childish and juvenile, but right about now it's the only idea I have. If it works, he'll be embarrassed for himself and of me and he'll have to leave me alone because it will ruin his reputation to have a crazy girlfriend who acts like a ten-year-old. If it doesn't work, then...

well honestly, I'm not sure, but I have a feeling him taking over my life and bartering to get me naked will feel like a walk in the park compared to what he'll have in store for me.

Dragging myself out of bed I get ready for school, and then head downstairs in search of my mom. I expect to find her in her office still in her sleep shirt, her hair mussed, her glasses askew, but instead she's up, dressed and looking... good.

"Good morning, sweetheart," she says in an upbeat singsong voice.

"You look nice," I tell her, taking in her slim-fitted jeans, pale-pink silk blouse and low-heeled black ankle boots. She's even styled her normally crazy hair into sleek curls.

"Thanks, sweetie. Miranda, Mary, Heather and I are going shopping, then out for lunch. They're not picking me up for a couple of hours, but I was just so excited I couldn't wait, so I got ready."

"Mom, we can't afford to shop at the same places as them."

Mom's lips purse together. "Starling, I'm getting a little annoyed with you trying to be the parent out of the two of us."

"Well one of us has to be the grown-up," I snap, then instantly regret it.

"Young lady, I have kept a roof over our heads, clothes on our backs and food in the cupboards your entire life. You go to an expensive private school, we live in a nice house in a nice area, I suggest you check your attitude right now."

This is what drives me crazy about my mom. Yes, we have

all those things, but for the last few years, I've been the one reminding my mom to pay the bills and covering the difference with my wages if there's not enough in her checking account. I've been the one saying I don't need to go to an expensive private school. I've been the one working every shift that's been available to cover the deficit in our income when her books have had a bad sales month. She may be the parent, but I'm hardly a child.

"Are you serious right now? Do you know who paid the electric bill last month? Me. Do you know who deposited money into your account to cover the mortgage every month for the last six months? Me. I don't know if you're really this clueless, or if you're just so far in your own head that you have no idea what's happening in real life, but without me putting all my wages into your bank account, we would have lost the house months ago. You think it's a fun game to play with the rich folks, have at it, but don't forget that they're them and we're us. Sebastian flashed his winning smile and his parents' money at you and you're basically handing him my virginity on a platter, even though I've told you over and over that he isn't my boyfriend, that he thinks he owns me and he's not giving me a choice."

Mom's lips part and for a minute I think she's actually heard me, that she's listening to what I'm saying, but then she scoffs and rolls her eyes. "Wow, whatever you pair are arguing about must be quite the teen lovers tiff for you to be so dramatic this early in the morning. Sebastian is smitten with you and you're smitten with him, I was young and in love once, I recognize the look. Go to school and make up, hopefully you'll be in a better mood when you get home later, because Miranda has invited us for dinner."

Tears well in my eyes, but I blink them away. What use are they when my mom, the woman who's supposed to be my biggest supporter, is so blinded by him, his family and the wealth that surrounds them? "Have a nice day," I say quietly, grabbing a bottle of water from the refrigerator and a granola bar from the cupboard. "I'm going to look out for Court."

"Have a good day, honey," Mom calls, but I ignore her, hoisting my backpack over my shoulders, stepping outside and then sitting down on the front steps to wait for my friend.

I'm early and she won't be here for at least ten minutes, so I pull my cell from the bottom of my backpack and call my dad. His day starts about three a.m., so I know he'll be awake, hopefully he'll be at the helm and not pulling in pots.

"Starling, is everything okay?" he asks immediately when he answers.

"Hey, Dad, everything's fine, I just had a little time to spare."

"Oh well that's nice, darlin', how's school?"

I contemplate telling him about Sebastian, but decide against it when he's a three-hour flight or a twenty-five-hour drive away. There's nothing he can do. Hell, he might end up taken in by him and his family as Mom and Court are, and right now I don't think I could cope with losing him as well.

"Same old, same old. A bunch of rich kids all talking about their summer in the Hamptons or the Caribbean. Hopefully I can go to public school next year and be around normal people." Dad knows I don't love GAA, but he also knows it's paid for and that it would be wasteful to attend a run-down, no-opportunity public school while my tuition to GAA is there.

"Just make the most of the education that place can give you, work hard to give yourself a good foundation, so you're ahead of the curve if your mama can't afford to keep you there. You know I'd help her out if I could."

"I know you would, but there's no point you having to work any harder to send me to a school I don't want to be at in the first place. I'm the poor relation to these kids, apart from Court."

"Your mama told me you'd quit your job, so you could always come out and visit me during winter break, maybe even for Christmas, if you wanted?"

I haven't had Christmas with my dad since he and my mom split up. Once a year during the summer we spend three weeks together and we talk on the phone every Wednesday. He's never suggested I come during any other holiday.

"Wouldn't you have to work?"

"No, Christmas is the only holiday we have more than a day off for. There's always something to fish, catch or bait, but the whole crew has a week with their families over Christmas and New Year's."

Suddenly I feel five years old again, missing my dad and

148

just wanting to see him. "I'd love to spend Christmas with you, Daddy."

"Well that's just made my day, darlin'. I'll text your mama and let her know, then I'll get some flights booked. I got to get back to it, I love you."

"Love you too, Dad."

Ending the call, I slide my cell back into my blazer and exhale. The melancholy I'd felt since I woke up this morning fades and a feeling of hope settles in its place. My mom might be caught up in the Lockwood hype, but I'm not and neither is my dad. I need this, I need to be away from this town and Sebastian and even my mom and Court too, I need to be somewhere where no one cares who Sebastian is, where he has no power.

An unfamiliar car slows to a stop at the end of the driveway and I watch, waiting to see if someone will get out. No one does, then the rear window rolls down and Court appears. "Morning babe, how cool is this Tesla?" she shrieks excitedly.

My brows furrow in confusion when Sebastian steps from the other side of the car a smug expression etched across his beautiful face. "Good morning, little bird."

I shake my head and point at him angrily. "We had a deal, I get to ride with Court."

His smile is pure evil, sin in human form. "We agreed that Courtney would collect you from your house and take you to school and return you home at the end of the day." He gestures to the car. "Courtney is here, collecting you for school, you never specified that she had to be in her own vehicle, or that you two be the only people present. First rule of business, always read the small print."

Angry, frustrated tears pool in my eyes, but I blink them away. There's no point making a scene, fighting one-on-one isn't how I'll extract myself from his hold. Instead, I stand up and follow him to the car, climbing into the back row of seats with Sebastian next to me. Court is talking a mile a minute at Clay in the row ahead of us and Hunter and Evan are up front.

"No fighting?" he asks.

I shake my head, rest my cheek against the window and close my eyes.

The morning passes in a haze of covert glances and hostile glares. Arriving at school for a second day with The Elite and having Sebastian plaster himself to me as he walks me through the halls to my homeroom has everyone even more interested in me and why I've been chosen. I hate the notoriety it's giving me, but Court on the other hand is loving it. I saw the way her eyes lit up when everyone saw her get out of Evan's car and honestly, it worries me how much she's enjoying all the attention.

Sebastian is waiting outside my classroom the moment the bell rings. Sighing, I walk to him and hand him my backpack when he offers to carry it. His expression is confused and there's a furrow in his brow as he looks me over expectantly, trying to find something, but I'm not sure what.

When we reach the main hallway that holds the cafeteria,

there's a crowd of people surrounding something that's happening up ahead. Sebastian grips my hand a little tighter, guiding us through as the kids part to give him a clear path. When we reach the reason for all the onlookers, I'm shocked to find a boy being held by Hunter, with Evan and Clay standing intimidatingly on either side.

"Stay here, little bird," Sebastian orders, handing me back my bag and stepping forward toward the scared-looking boy and the rest of The Elite.

"On your knees, Adrian," Sebastian orders, his voice firm and low.

"Please, please, I'm sorry, it was a mistake," the boy pleads, in a reedy whine.

I've spent plenty of time with the GAA Elite in the last couple of days, they're intense and commanding, but I've never seen this side of them before. Right now they're formidable, hard and intimidating and I'm not going to lie, I'm a little scared of them all. By the looks of it, so is Adrian.

The kids that are crowded around the scene shuffle nervously as we wait to see what will happen. I understand the role The Elite play at the school, but this is the first time I've seen them mete out punishment in such a public way.

Sebastian points to a spot on the floor in front of the guys and a trembling Adrian slowly sinks to his knees.

"It was a mistake, it won't happen again," Adrian gasps.

"You're right, bringing drugs to a fucking party was a

mistake, so was bringing a fifteen-year-old date and fucking her in one of my guest rooms after you fed her several lines of coke," Clay hisses

"I—" Adrian chokes.

"I'm not interested in your excuses," Clay growls, pulling back his foot and then swinging it forward, kicking Adrian and sending him flying onto his back. "That girl was a fucking mess, high as a fucking kite and throwing up everywhere when the staff found her, and now my asshole parents are getting shit from her family because she was at my party."

"She wanted it, man," Adrian protests.

"She's fifteen," Hunter hisses, kicking Adrian again.

"Okay, okay, so what do I have to do?" Adrian begs.

"You're now our bitch." Evan laughs.

"What?" It sounds like Adrian's crying now.

"You heard him, from now until graduation, you're our bitch. You'll do our washing, carry our shit. Wipe our fucking ass if that's what we tell you to do. You're a social outcast, no one here will talk to you, no one anywhere will sell to you, buy from you, or associate with you. We've blacklisted you and your entire family to everyone in the tristate area," Sebastian says, his voice low and sinister.

"You. You can't do that," he whimpers.

"Sure we can. We can do whatever we want. Your parents are rich because of our parents. Our families give and they can just as easily take away," Evan says in his superior drawl that somehow doesn't make him sound like as much of an asshole as it should.

"I won't do it. I don't believe you," Adrian says, trying to force some strength into his voice and failing.

"Your choice. Alternatively, the video of you selling pills and coke at my party will be released to both the police and the media. We also have the name of your supplier which we'll release along with the pictures of you and him meeting so you could buy drugs. Then if that's not enough, we have video of you practically forcing coke on a fifteen-year-old girl and then fucking her. That's statutory rape and probably child abuse. You'll be on the sex offender's registry for the rest of your fucking life." Clay laughs lowly.

"I didn't know she was fifteen, she said she was legal."

"You're eighteen, asshat; legal or not, she's still too fucking young for you to be feeding her coke and fucking her at a party. Get some self-respect, you pedo." Hunter cries, kicking the stooped figure again.

"Okay, okay, I'll do whatever you want," a broken voice says.

"We figured as much. Come on then, bitch, it's time for lunch." Clay laughs.

I watch as Adrian starts to claw his way to his feet, only to be knocked back down by Hunter. His sheer size and the scowl on his face makes him much more intimidating in this moment than he's ever seemed before. "You crawl on your hands and knees behind us."

"What?" Adrian chokes.

"You're our bitch, and where should little bitches be?" Sebastian asks with a sinister laugh. "On their knees, so that's where you'll be from now on. On your knees either behind us, or at our feet."

All four men laugh as they walk away, pausing a few steps ahead to turn and wait for Adrian to follow. I expect him to argue, to fight, not that he deserves an ounce of leniency if what they said he did is true. But instead, he pushes up onto his hands and knees, lowers his head and moves forward, crawling along the floor like a dog behind his masters.

The congregation around me all watch in a state of utter shock as The Elite leave with Adrian following behind them. No one dares to say a word, the entire school has been stunned to silence.

"Oh my god, look at them," Courtney whispers excitedly from beside me.

I jolt, unaware she was even there, consumed by the scene happening in front of us. "It's barbaric."

"They're The Elite, he broke the rules."

"What he did was illegal, they should turn him over to the police. They're kids, not gods, they don't get to allow people to break the law," I blurt.

"They are gods, look at them, look at the power they have, the way everyone wants them, wants to be them," she says, her voice breathy and reverent.

"It's wrong."

"Stop being such a little bitch, Starling, they're the kings of the school and we're their queens. We're untouchable now, next year we'll be Elite. Stop being such a brat and suck his dick, fuck him, let him do whatever the hell he wants to do. God, I've already sucked off Evan, I'll do them all if that's what they want. This is the dream."

Wide eyed and appalled, I stare at the girl I thought I knew so well. I know she wants to be popular, but to condone this, to tell me to offer myself to these cruel boys for status is baffling to me.

"Starling," Sebastian calls, snapping my attention off Courtney. "Let's go get lunch."

My feet feel frozen to the ground, and I know my eyes are wide and full of fear, shock and realization. My plan to embarrass Sebastian and force him to distance himself from me suddenly feels pathetic. It wouldn't work, because Sebastian and The Elite are too powerful, too popular for anything I could say to have an impact. He wants me and until he stops wanting me there's nothing I can do, other than hope I survive.

Hopelessness consumes me as I step forward and take Sebastian's outstretched hand. "Don't look at him," he demands, tipping my chin up with his finger when my eyes go to Adrian. He's still on the floor on his hands and knees, his head lowered, despite the fact that the whole convoy has stopped and is waiting for me.

Leaning into me, Sebastian presses his lips against my cheek, before sliding his mouth to my ear. "He gave drugs to an underage girl, then had sex with her when she was so high on coke she couldn't say no. This, what we're doing to him, is only the start of his punishment. The only reason he's not in the hands of the cops is because the girl doesn't want her name released to the media, which it would be if she were to press charges. His family has enough money to buy him off any charges they could make stick, but they're not rich enough or powerful enough to defy us."

I feel myself nod, but I'm not sure if I'm agreeing with him or just doing what I need to do. Either way, it seems to appease him, because he presses a kiss to my lips, then leads me to the front of the group as the guys all start to move again.

When we enter the cafeteria, Sebastian turns to lead me to the table Court and I sat at on the first day of term, but I tug on his hand and shake my head. "It's okay, we can all sit together."

His brow furrows in confusion. "Sitting at *your* table with Courtney was part of our deal."

"Were you going to let me sit there alone with her?"

"No," he smiles mischievously, all of his anger from the scene with Adrian gone.

"So there's no point is there? Let's just sit at your usual table," I shrug, turning toward The Elites' table in the prime location in the center of the room.

"Hey," he says, grabbing my arm and turning me to face him.

"I'm hungry, can we just eat?"

His eyes narrow and he stares at me as if he's trying to figure out what I'm thinking. "Kiss me."

I should argue, but what's the point? After what he just did to that boy and Court's reaction to it, it's even more obvious how powerless I am against him. Instead of fighting, I push up onto my tiptoes and press my lips to his.

***

The next two and a half months are crazy. Sebastian has ingratiated himself into every aspect of my life and the only person who seems to think this is an issue, is me. My mom adores him. She's even started asking me what Sebastian thinks every time she and I have an argument, and she's even started hinting that it would be okay if I stayed overnight at his house as long as we slept in separate rooms. Courtney is so caught up in the world of The Elites, she's strutting around school like she's the queen bee, hanging off Evan and Clay's arms every moment she gets the chance. The sweet girl who stayed friends with me even though I was poor is nowhere to be seen. Sebastian, The Elites and a shot at being the most powerful girl in school has stolen her from me.

Even in all the time I've been ignored by my peers and

treated like I was beneath them, I've never felt as isolated and alone as I am now. Sebastian has somehow created a world where my life revolves around him. He's taken my best friend and even my mom from me, and now all that's left is him.

The hardest thing is that Sebastian isn't treating me badly, he isn't abusive per se, he isn't forcing me to have sex with him, or being physically violent toward me. Honestly if we'd gotten together under different circumstances, I think I could actually like him. He's beautiful, popular, powerful and rich. But the moment I start to soften toward him I remember that none of this is my choice. He didn't ask me out and I chose to say yes, he told me I was his and forced me to go along with it.

In a matter of weeks, he's taken over my life and stolen every ounce of control from me and I hate it. I hate that all of my choices have been taken from me and no matter how many times I tell him or my mom or my supposed best friend that this isn't what I want no one cares. I'm impotent, silenced and ignored and instead of growing accustomed to the feelings there's a simmering melancholic rage that's building and festering inside of me, I'm as angry as I am hopeless and I don't know what to do to make me feel normal again.

Everything that's happening to me is his choice. He wants me to be his, so I am. He wants me to go places and do things, so he insists I do it and when I argue he manipulates my mom or my only friend to coerce me to do what he wants.

I'm a prisoner in my own life and no matter how loud I shout or how honest I am, he's stolen my voice. Day by day it feels like I'm becoming more and more brittle, that constantly being forced to bend to his will is slowly snapping me in two. Winter break and Christmas with my dad is the only bright spot on my horizon. Mom lost her shit when I told her I planned to go to Maine for the holidays, telling me I was selfish and childish and mean for leaving her alone at Christmas. Miranda swooped in and saved the day when she invited my mom to have Christmas at their house with Clay, Evan and Hunter's families too.

Sebastian was beyond pissed when he found out I was going to visit with my dad, he even tried to invite himself on the trip, but my dad shot him down. He said that as much as he'd love to meet my boyfriend, this was our first Christmas together in fourteen years and he wanted it to just be the two of us.

Because winter break isn't that long, Dad convinced my mom to allow me to miss the last week of school so I could spend more time with him. Today is my last day of suffering, then tomorrow it's sayonara Green Acres and hello two weeks of blissful Sebastian-free time.

"Are you all packed?" Mom asks, her lips pressed into a flat line as she leans against the doorframe in my room.

"Yep," I say, nodding my head in the direction of my case leaning against my closet door.

"Have you got your thermals, it's probably going to be snowing and below zero, you'll freeze."

"I'm looking forward to seeing the snow. I have plenty of

layers and Dad said he's taking me to get a winter jacket and anything else I need when I get there."

"You know you could have just gone to Vail with Sebastian if you wanted to see the snow, the Lockwoods offered to have the holidays in the mountains if that's what you wanted."

"That was very kind of them," I say through gritted teeth. "But I'm not going to Maine for the snow, I'm going to spend time with Dad."

Mom rolls her eyes in a way I never saw her do before she started spending time with Sebastian's mom and her friends. "Why would you want to spend the holidays with your father in his tiny apartment, when you could be in the Lockwoods' beautiful home? Did you see how gorgeous their Christmas tree is? I swear it's got to be at least fifteen feet tall, it's just stunning. Sebastian is absolutely heartbroken that you won't be spending the holidays together, Miranda told me he'd planned to use their jet to come and surprise you on Christmas, until your father refused."

Closing my eyes and stretching my neck from one side to the other, I hold in the words that are dying to fall from my lips, but I know there's no point. Mom won't tolerate me saying anything bad about Sebastian or any of his family or friends. She's completely brainwashed, to the point that when Miranda suggested I only apply to the college Sebastian is attending next year, my mom nodded and agreed.

"Their tree is beautiful, Mom, but I already explained that

I'm looking forward to spending some quality time with Dad. When I visit in the summer he has to work, but he's on vacation during the holidays and it'll give us some real time together."

The front door opens and my mom literally leaps with excitement, preening slightly as she smooths down her now permanently straight hair and locks a wide smile on her face. "That'll be Sebastian here to pick you up for your date," she singsongs.

"Hey, little bird, hey Cassidy," Sebastian croons, giving my mom a hug as he passes her on his way into my room. Yep, you heard right, he just walks straight into our house now without knocking, because according to my mom, our casa is his casa and he can just treat this place like a home away from home. "You ready, baby? I made reservations for seven."

"Oh my goodness, I've made you late. Starling, you should have said something. I'm sorry, Sebastian, I was just trying to convince her that we should accept your mom and dad's kind offer to have the holidays in Vail, instead of her running off to Maine and leaving me all alone," Mom says, winking at Sebastian.

"I think that's a great idea, we could go shopping for ski stuff after dinner if you want?" Sebastian smiles.

"That's okay, I won't need ski equipment in Maine where I'm spending Christmas."

His scowl is glacial, but even though I've stopped trying to prevent him from asserting his will on every other aspect of my life, there's no way I'm giving up the opportunity to get away from him for two weeks. Mom pouts, yes, pouts her annoyance and then waves to Sebastian and leaves.

"This is our first Christmas together; I want you to be here with me. You and your mom can stay at my place and we can wake up together on Christmas morning," he coaxes.

"No, this is the first time my dad has ever asked me to spend Christmas with him."

"Then I'll come too," he says from behind gritted teeth.

"He has a two-bedroom apartment, there's no room for you to come."

"We can stay in a hotel, and you can spend your days with him and your nights with me."

"My dad would not be okay with me staying in a hotel with you, Sebastian. Plus he lives in a really small town, and the only hotel closes for the holidays. You know this, because you suggested it yesterday and the day before that." I've never been more grateful that my dad lives in the smallest, ugliest place in Maine, because I'm sure Sebastian would have followed me regardless of me telling him not to, if there was a decent hotel for him to stay in. Luckily my stalker isn't down for spending Christmas alone in a roadside motel, which is the only place still open within thirty miles of my dad's house.

"You're not going," he snaps, his voice laced with steel and unwavering determination.

"Yes I am."

"No, you're not. I fucking forbid it, Starling, you aren't going to fucking Maine."

"You can't forbid me from going to see my dad," I say as calmly as I can muster, my voice only cracking slightly as nerves pool low in my stomach.

"I'll convince your mom to make you stay, she's on the verge of doing it anyway."

"My dad has joint custody of me, my mom can't stop him from seeing me and neither can you. Why are you doing this?"

"Because you're mine," he roars angrily.

Every single one of my muscles tenses in response to his anger. I don't think he'd physically hurt me, despite his manipulating and coercing, he's never used his physicality to get me to do what he wants. Adrian crawling through the halls of GAA is enough of a reminder that Sebastian and the other Elites are ruthless rulers, and submitting to them is the only way.

"Sebastian," I say calmly.

"I don't want you to go," he admits, his voice softening.

"It's only for two weeks. Some downtime will be good for us both, and you can spend time with your friends and your family over the holidays. I'll be back before you know it."

PART TWO

THE BEGINNING
OF THE END

TEN

STARLING

"**A**re you sure about this, honey?" Dad asks me for the hundredth time this morning as I pull the zip closed on my case.

"It's my only option, Dad, you know that," I reply with a sigh. I've lost count of the number of times we've had this conversation in the last five months. "Not only is it the only school I got accepted to, but I got a full scholarship too."

"I just worry about you, honey."

Exhaling softly, I turn and look at my dad. "I know you do, Dad, but Sebastian isn't going to be there and Evan and I can tolerate each other from a distance. It's a big campus and I doubt we'll even see each other. I'm going to be a freshman and he's a junior, there's literally no reason for our paths to cross."

Dad nods, but from the furrow in his brow I can tell he doesn't believe the bullshit coming out of my mouth any more than I do.

A little over two and a half years ago when I boarded the plane to Maine to visit Dad, everyone—including me—assumed I'd be back in Green Acres after New Year's. But then I stepped off the plane in a different state and breathed in the first full breath I'd taken since the first day of school when Sebastian told me I was his.

For the first time in months, I kept my own schedule and relaxed. The more I relaxed the less I wanted to go home. The first few days, Sebastian rang and video called me relentlessly but the cell phone signal here is awful when the weather gets bad and suddenly I was completely out of his reach and it was awesome.

Spending time with my dad was great, Christmas was a chilled-out day spent in our pj's watching Christmas movies and eating a turkey dinner off trays on our laps. It wasn't until a couple of days before I was due to fly home that I realized I didn't want to leave, I didn't want to go home. The first panic attack took both me and my dad by surprise. When he took me to the emergency room and the doctor suggested he thought I was suffering with anxiety, I used it as an excuse to extend my trip by a couple of days. My plane tickets were transferable and school didn't start for a couple of days anyway.

The second panic attack came when Dad asked me if I was looking forward to seeing my boyfriend. That was the day I told him everything about Sebastian, about my mom and Courtney. When he suggested I could move to Maine permanently and live with him, I cried happy tears.

Mom lost her shit. She flew out to Maine, screaming and shouting, yelling at me, yelling at Dad, it was a mess. When I sat her down and told her I didn't want to live with her anymore, she told me I was behaving like a child and that until I learned to grow up, I shouldn't bother to call her. It was over a year before we spoke again.

Sebastian came to see me several times, he told me if I refused to come back he'd take away everything I loved. I believed him, but what he didn't realize was that he'd done that already when he stole my mom and my best friend from me. After six months and several changes of cell phone numbers, he gave up. But he did what he said he would, my relationship with my mom is broken beyond repair and no matter how many times I reach out to Courtney she's never called or texted even once.

To make matters worse, six months ago, my mom got remarried, to Evan's dad, so now one of Sebastian's best friends is my stepbrother. Harry, Evan's dad flew him, Mom and Evan out here for a visit so they could let me know about the engagement and I managed to be cordial to all of them, but the ghost of Sebastian has tainted any kind of relationship I could have with my new stepfather and stepbrother. I went to the wedding, so did Sebastian, he brought Courtney as his date. I managed to avoid speaking to both of them, by only flying in an hour before the ceremony and leaving right after the meal.

When it came time for me to apply to colleges, I planned to stay near home in Maine, but Mom begged me to apply to a couple of schools in Florida and because I'm a sucker, and because I genuinely hate the fact that I only speak to her on my birthday and Christmas, I did.

What I wasn't expecting was to be rejected by every school I applied to, even my safety schools. The only school that did accept me was Kingsacre college, a private school about an hour from Green Acres, and the one Evan has been attending for the last two years. Not only did they offer me a place at the school, but they also offered me a full scholarship.

I'm pretty sure me sort of being a Morris—even if it's only by marriage—is the reason I got in, and the scholarship is probably being entirely funded by Harry, considering there was nothing spectacular about the solid B grades across the board on my high school transcripts. But when my only choice is Kingsacre or community college, Kingsacre won out.

"There's nothing wrong with community college, you could stay home for the next year, go to school here, take some classes and then transfer to a four-year school next year," Dad says, desperately.

"I'm not a sixteen-year-old girl anymore, Dad. I'm going

to be nineteen soon, and I'm not going to be forced into close proximity or have to have anything to do with Sebastian. He was in a unique position of power at GAA so I had no way of sidestepping him and honestly, maybe it wasn't as bad as I remember. Sure he was controlling, but he never hurt me or pressured me into doing anything I wasn't comfortable with." Except that one time where we bartered over him seeing me naked, I think, but don't say aloud. Dad and I are insanely close now, but there was no way I was going to tell him about Sebastian giving me orgasms. In the most uncomfortable conversation in the world he asked me if Sebastian had raped me and I told him nothing like that had happened, that was the one and only time we discussed it.

"What school did your mother say Sebastian was at?"

"Harvard, I think," I tell him, then clear my throat. My mom is still firmly team Sebastian, and on the rare occasion I speak to her, she makes sure to always talk about him. I usually wind the conversation up at that point, but she takes pleasure in telling me all about how well he's doing and reminding me that I missed my chance with him. He really did take her from me, just like he said he would.

"That's good," Dad nods, and I nod back at him. "And your mom is meeting you at the airport to drive you to school?"

"She offered, but I told her I was fine just to go straight to Kingsacre."

"Oh honey, I don't want you moving in to your college

dorm alone, let me book a flight and I'll come with you and help you settle in."

"It's fine, Dad, I promise. You can't take time off the boat at this time of year and I can carry my own shit, I'm only taking one case with me anyway."

"I'm worried about you, honey," he says solemnly. "Remember there's an open-ended return ticket in your name saved on the airline account, all you have to do is pick a flight and you can come on home whenever you need to. You don't need to wait for the holidays, you can just come home, because this is your home and it always will be."

Tears fill my eyes and I launch myself at my dad, throwing my arms around his neck and clinging to him. "I love you, Daddy."

"I love you too, honey."

In the years I've been living in Maine, my dad has become my rock. He never once doubted my feelings or actions, his belief in me is unyielding, and that means more to me than he could ever understand. Living here has been great. We moved to a cute two-bedroom apartment overlooking the harbor about six months after I decided I was staying, and I spent the remainder of my high school years at the local public school.

The kids here are nice, and for the first few months I tried to make friends, but when the girls I started to get close to suddenly got friend requests from The Elite, and expensive gifts through the post, I gave up. The fear that Sebastian would swoop in and take away any friendships I made kept me from forming any real bonds with anyone. In the grand scale of things, the short time I spent as Sebastian's unwilling girlfriend shouldn't have impacted me as much as it has. But he fundamentally changed me, shattered my trust in the people who were closest to me and morphed me into the closed-off, emotional cacti that I am now.

The only important person in my life is my dad, because despite Sebastian's best attempts, whenever he turned up to lure me back to Green Acres, he could never influence my salt-of-the-earth working-class fisherman father.

It may sound lonely to never make friends or have a boyfriend at my age, but I'd rather be alone than have to watch my family or friends abandon me in favor of a pretty rich boy with a winning smile and a golden tongue. What hurts the most is that he didn't even have to try that hard to steal Mom or Court from me. Mom switched from team Starling, to team Sebastian the moment she stepped into his family's massive house, and Court was gone with a hint at the popularity I had no idea she was coveting so hard. I'd rather be alone than constantly worry that the people around me are just waiting to betray me.

"Right, come on then, honey, let's get you to the airport," Dad says, coughing to disguise the emotion that's filling his eyes with tears and reluctantly releasing me to grab my case.

A shudder of fear rolls through me the moment I step off the plane and into the Florida sunshine. Coming back here was awful last time, but at least then I knew it was only for a couple of hours. Now, I'm here to stay and it's unlikely I'll get a chance to go home until Thanksgiving.

Closing my eyes for a moment, I inhale a deep, affirming breath, then roll back my shoulders, pick up my case and move to the line of people all waiting for cabs. Mom wanted to pick me up, she kept saying that she deserved to be able to take her only child to college. I almost agreed, until she told me that Harry and Evan were looking forward to helping me get settled. Hell no, I'd rather Evan have no idea where my dorm room is. Not that I think my stepbrother will want to have anything to do with me.

Evan, Clay and Hunter were all nice enough to me, but they're his, and I don't want to be a part of anything that will bring him back into my world. The cab drops me at the bus station and I thank the driver and grab my case from the trunk. It takes an hour to get to the closest bus stop to Kingsacre, and then it'll be about a ten-minute walk dragging my case to the college campus.

Being a private college, I can pretty much guarantee I'm the only freshman who'll be arriving by bus and the closer I get to the place, the more worried I feel. I hate this world. I hate the rich and elitist, and here I am again, putting myself into a position where I'm going to be forced to interact with them and live with them for the next four years.

Of course, in a place like Kingsacre, there's no way any of the rich kids that attend could imagine sharing a bathroom with thirty others, so instead of shared dorms, the kids live in houses on campus, where each room has its own bathroom. It's pretentious as hell, but I wasn't exactly going to say no to a private living space rather than having to share air with a stranger. My dad offered to pay for an off-campus apartment, but with no car and the campus being twenty minutes away from the closest apartment up for rent, it didn't make sense for me not to take advantage of the free room and meal plan that was part of my scholarship.

My cheeks are red and there's a fine layer of sweat coating my skin when I finally arrive at the huge arched gates that signal the entrance. Like I expected, there's not another person on foot in sight apart from the ones climbing out of Ferrari's, Porsche's, and I think that might be a Bugatti. I'm stepping back into rich-kid hell and for the hundredth time since I got off the plane, I consider using my return ticket and just going back home. There's nothing wrong with community college... right?

The honking of a car horn behind me startles me, and I realize I'm literally standing in the middle of the road. Hauling my case off the street and onto the path, I lift my hand in a silent apology to the car whose path I was obstructing as I turn and start to walk to where the valet—of course this place has valet parking—is pointing people in the direction of student registration. The megarich can't park their supercars just anywhere, obviously.

"Hi," I say to a guy around my age wearing a white shirt and a navy-blue vest with Kingsacre university embroidered in gold thread on the pocket.

"Good morning, miss, let me take your keys and I'll give you a ticket. When you need your car again you can take the ticket to any of the valet points around campus and someone will collect your vehicle and bring it to you."

"Oh, er, I don't have a car, I was just hoping you could point me in the direction of freshmen registration."

The guy stops, stares and then blinks at me. "You don't have a car?"

"Nope."

"Did you come in a car service?"

"Er, no," I laugh awkwardly, furrowing my brow.

"Then how did you get here?" He sounds baffled, like he has literally no idea how anyone could possibly get through the gates without a car or a car service.

"The bus."

"The closest bus stop is like twenty minutes away."

"I thought it was only about ten minutes, but I'd say it took me closer to fifteen. Although I was kind of power walking so I didn't just turn around and go back to the airport." I have no idea why I've got verbal diarrhea with this guy. Normally I limit my conversations with people to polite and concise, but something about his sheer shock is keeping me from shutting up.

"You caught the bus and then walked here alone, with your case?" he says slowly.

"Yep," I nod.

Scoffing lightly, his lips tip up into a smile. "I'm Angelo," he says, holding his hand out for me to shake.

"Starling." I take his hand and shake it briefly, releasing it quickly and pushing my hand into the back pocket of my jean shorts.

"You're not like the other kids that go here, are you?"

"No, I'm not," I agree, dropping my chin to my chest and staring down at my feet.

A honking horn interrupts what has turned into an uncomfortable conversation. "I've got to get back to work, but I work at the valet booth over by the cafeteria full time, you should come see me one day, we could get coffee or something."

"Maybe," I say as noncommittally as I can.

"Registration is on the lawn outside the administration building, head on down this path and then swing a right, you can't miss it."

"Thanks, nice to meet you, Angelo."

"You too, Starling. You take care, you hear me? The kids that go here can be sharks," he warns with a warm smile etched across his lips.

"Don't worry, I know exactly how bad these types of people can get," I tell him sadly, gripping the handle of my case and walking away.

"Welcome to Kingsacre University, freshman," an overly bright girl says from her seat behind a desk situated out on the lawn under a gazebo.

"Hi."

"Can I take your name please?"

"Starling Kennedy."

Her brow furrows as she taps away at her keyboard. "Hmm, when's your birthday?"

"It's September 4th."

"I have a Starling Lockwood, birthday September 4th. Have you changed your name recently?"

My blood turns cold and I freeze, all the breath in my lungs suddenly evaporating. "My surname is Kennedy, there must be some mistake."

"Is Lockwood your husband's name? It says here you're Mrs. Starling Lockwood." Her chuckle is forced and uncomfortable.

This must be some kind of fucked-up joke. Is this Evan's doing, messing with me on my first day? It's been years, and apart from the wedding I haven't seen or spoken to any of The Elite since the day before I left town. Why would he do this now? It's not like Sebastian was genuinely hurt by me leaving, he was just angry to lose his control over me.

"I'm one-hundred-percent single, I'm eighteen," I say with a forced giggle.

"Wow, thank god. I was worried you were like Amish or something. Give me one minute, I'll just call down to administration and have them double-check I'm giving you the right house number. You want to let your parents know it's going to be a short wait?"

"I'm not with my parents, it's just me."

"Oh," her brows lift almost all the way up to her hairline. "Okay, I'll just make that call."

I nod, waiting awkwardly as she stands up, takes a few steps away from the desk and lifts her cell phone to her ear. She returns five minutes later, smiling. "All sorted, must have been an admin error. You are most definitely the only Starling at the school, cool name by the way." Sitting back down, she clicks at her keyboard again. A printer starts to whir before she hands me a packet with some papers and a hotel-style key card. "Okay, so your room is in Collinwood House, suite five, which is all the way over on the far side of campus. Orientation is at nine a.m. tomorrow where you can pick up your schedule and get an itinerary for all the freshmen activities. Give this"—she hands me a small card with my name and Collinwood House suite five on it—"to one of the cart drivers and they'll take you and all your luggage over to the west quad to get your student ID and then to your house. If you have any problems or any questions, the number for student liaison services is in your pack. Also the annual welcome-freshmen party is tomorrow night, in the woods behind the gymnasium. It's huge and all the freshmen go. I've marked it on your map, you don't want to miss it. Welcome to Kingsacre, Starling."

With a polite nod, I grab my case and make my way to the golf carts. An older man takes my card and loads my case onto the back of the cart, before offering me his hand to help me inside. I take it, not wanting to be rude, but wonder who here needs a hand to get the twelve inches from the floor to the seat in the cart.

We stop at another set of gazebos, and he helps me out and waits while I have my photo taken for my student ID, where I again have to explain that I'm not married and that my name is not Lockwood. I hate that after all this time Sebastian has invaded my life again with this cruel joke. It can only be Evan who did this. He's the only person I know at Kingsacre, and the only one here who knows about my short-lived, life-altering interlude with the Lockwood heir apparent.

I wish I knew why he was doing this now. I'm not a part of his or his dad's life, I've never visited his house, or tried to cash in on the Morris name. As far as I'm concerned, Harry is my mom's new husband and Evan is his son, and that's it. I'm happy that she's happy, but given how strained my and my mom's relationship is, I have no interest in being part of her world. I'd hoped that I could remain distantly civil with my new stepbrother. Perhaps a nod in passing, but this instant attack the moment I walk through the gates, suggests that perhaps just pretending we have no idea who the other is might be a better idea.

The website shows pictures of the campus housing, but until now I haven't seen it in person. I never had any intention of going here, so I didn't see the point in coming to take a tour. Apparently the photo gallery didn't do the place any justice, because the houses are nothing like I was expecting. The housing starts at about five minutes' drive from the campus buildings with a mini suburb made up of rows of town houses. After that there's a tiny village of ranch-style homes, then a grouping of craftsman bungalows with each of the houses in the little mini village getting increasingly larger the farther away from the campus site we get. By the time the cart slows to a stop, the houses are huge and spread out, with giant gated driveways, some even appear to have pools. Collinswood house is a massive Queen Ann Victorian-style home complete with a turret, spindle work and a wraparound porch. It's gorgeous, and imposing and it can't be the place my scholarship funding is allowing me to stay.

"This must be the wrong place," I tell the driver when he climbs out of the cart and reaches for my case. "No, wait. I need to call student services, because I'm on a scholarship, there's no way that pays for me to stay in this place. There's been a mix-up with my name, so this must be where whoever my file got confused with is supposed to live. I don't want to unpack only to have to pack up and move when the person who's supposed to be living here figures out the mistake." Pulling my cell from my pocket, I open the packet, find the student liaison number and call it.

Ten minutes later, I step uncertainly up to the front door and slide my key card into the scanner. The man in student services assured me that this is where I'm living for the next four years and that there's no mistake—despite the mix-up with my name, which keeps reverting back to Lockwood on the file, even though he changed it to Kennedy twice while we were on the call.

After protests that it must be wrong, I was passed over to a manager who seemed surprised that I'd been roomed in Collinswood, because apparently scholarship kids are normally put in the town houses closest to campus. When I asked to be moved to one of those, she laughed, asked me if I was serious, then told me all the housing was full and Collinwood House was the only room available if I wanted to stay on campus.

The sound of a clock ticking greets me as I step inside the palatial home. My eyes quickly roam over the space as I inhale the scent of furniture polish and lemon cleaner. Dark wood and Gothic grandeur surround me and for the hundredth time in the last thirty seconds, I consider running away and back to the comfort of mine and my dad's apartment. As I step inside, the front door closes shut behind me and I startle, jumping forward and nearly tripping over my case beside me.

Not wanting to invade private space, I step forward and glance into the rooms off the main entrance hall. There's a living room, with comfortable-looking couches and a large TV. A formal dining room that I doubt ever gets used in a houseful of college kids, a massive kitchen with a glass-fronted refrigerator full of beer, and an honest to goodness library with a real fireplace and wingback chairs.

Climbing the stairs, dragging my case behind me, I find suites one and two on the first floor and three, four and five on the second. There's a scanner lock on each door, the same as the one on the front door, and I slide my card into the lock on the room marked with a number five. It beeps and the sound of a lock disengaging fills the silence.

Pushing it open, I find another set of stairs instead of the bedroom I was expecting. Groaning at the thought of carrying my case any farther, I grit my teeth and start to climb. My room is located in the turret you can see at the front of the house, it's a vaguely hexagonal shape with a metal-framed bed and dark wood furniture that looks great against the walls that are painted a pale-blue color. Wallpaper has been hung in panels on some of the walls, and two doors lead off the room into what I'm assuming are a closet and a bathroom.

Leaving my case in the doorway, I step toward the window and stare out at the view. From this high up, I can see the neighboring couple of houses and the campus off in the distance. I might not feel like I should be living in this huge, expensive house, but there's no way I'm going to complain about this room; it's stunning.

Opening the first door, I find a huge closet with more space than I could fill in a lifetime, let alone with the single case I've brought to school with me. The second door reveals a bathroom, with teal-blue walls, white tile and a claw-foot tub.

A smile spreads across my lips. This might not have been

my first choice school, Evan might have tried to mess with me today, and I might be living in a house with kids rich enough that I'm sure they'll hate me on sight. But this room makes it all worthwhile. This place will be my sanctuary.

Grabbing my case from beside the door, I lift it onto the bed and unzip it. All of the housing at Kingsacre comes fully furnished and with a maid service, so the bed is already made up with beautiful, soft, duck-egg-blue cotton sheets. In comparison, my case looks ratty and out of place.

I lift my things out, making piles of clothes, toiletries, books and so on. By the time it's empty, the whole bed is covered. Closing my case, I lift it up, glancing around the room, searching for a place to stash it that won't be in my way. I do a double take when my gaze lands on the wallpaper. Dropping my bag to the floor I take a step closer to the wall, my heart beating double time as I lift my fingers up and run them over the images.

Bird cages, gold ornate bird cages, imprisoning tiny little brown birds. My hand shakes as I snap it back to my chest. It's the same paper that was on the wall in the bedroom at Sebastian's house. Could this be the most fucked-up coincidence in the world? Wallpaper is generic, it's not like the stuff on the walls at Sebastian's house was made specifically for him. That could easily explain it being here in my room, couldn't it?

Except this, combined with the Mrs. Starling Lockwood bullshit doesn't make it feel coincidental. It feels orchestrated. I had the audacity to run from the GAA Elites and Sebastian

Lockwood. Could they still be holding a grudge years later? And if they are, would they go to this much effort to frighten and unsettle me?

The truth is, unless I want to pack my things away in my bag and go back to Maine, there's nothing I can do other than let things play out and see what happens. There's no one left in my life for them to use against me. My wonderful, humble, sweet father has proven that he has my back, and I don't have any friends or boyfriends they can use to punish me with. I'm all alone, just like Sebastian wanted me to be. If they try to ruin college for me then I'll just leave, like I did before. I'm not above embracing a strategic retreat if that's what I need to do.

With a contingency plan in place, I shove my case beneath my bed and one pile at a time, I unpack all of my stuff into my new beautiful bedroom. The next time I get off campus I'll buy some fabric to hang over the wallpaper so I don't have to stare at tiny captive birds, but until then I'll ignore them, just the way I've ignored him and all memories of him for the last two years.

The sound of a door slamming downstairs reverberates through the house. It appears at least one of my new housemates is home. I know I should go down and introduce myself, but after the day I've had so far, all I want to do is sleep and hopefully dream about my stress-free life by the sea in Maine.

When I wake up, it's dark and my stomach is growling with hunger. I have no idea what time the cafeteria serves food until, but judging by my internal body clock, it's late, or perhaps early.

Grabbing my cell phone from where I set it to charge on the bedside cabinet, I check the time.

Two thirty a.m. Fuck, I've slept for like eleven hours, that's one hell of a nap. Blinking awake, I let my eyes roam over the unfamiliar room. There's a faint woody scent that's vaguely familiar but I can't quite place it. I'm beneath the covers, but I remember falling asleep on top of them, I must have gotten cold at some point during my epic nap and got into bed properly

My bladder protests and I slowly climb out of bed and pad to the bathroom, not bothering to turn the light on and instead just fumbling about in the dark. My clothes are clinging to me and my skin feels clammy, so I turn on the shower, quickly strip, and step beneath the warm stream of water. There's something about showering in the darkness that's oddly therapeutic and I sigh, exhaling. I don't remember my dream, but the pulsing between my thighs says it must have been a dirty one. It's a myth that women don't have wet dreams, we do, we just wake up hot and bothered, not in a puddle of our own jizz.

Deciding to relieve a little of the tension my dirty fantasy has left behind, I slip my fingers between my thighs and run them through my slippery folds. My clit is a little swollen and I shudder as I rub my fingertip over the sensitive ball of nerves. Thanks to my entanglement with Sebastian, I'm more than a little gun shy when it comes to guys, hence why I'm still a virgin at almost nineteen. That doesn't mean that I don't know how to get myself off. Pushing first one finger, then two into my sex, I slowly start to fuck myself, closing my eyes and relaxing into the pleasure I'm causing.

An unwanted image of Sebastian touching me like this flashes into my mind and I try to force it away, but instead I remember the way it felt when he pinched my nipples, rubbed my clit and made me beg him to make me come. Even years later, it's still him that makes my sex heat and pulse with desire. I've tried to push his image away, but no matter what I do, when my eyes are closed and I'm touching myself, it's only him I see.

My legs buckle and my body jerks as I come on a pained cry, feeling his touch, the heat of his lips on my neck. I've tried watching porn, tried imagining someone else in his place, but in the end the thing that tips me into ecstasy is always him.

Needing to banish him from my thoughts, I turn the water down until a torrent of freezing cold liquid douses my heated skin. I don't want him to be the thing that turns me on, when I've fought so hard to get away from him and his terrifying intensity.

When I'm chilled to the core, I turn off the water and wrap myself in a fluffy white towel, blotting the dripping liquid from my hair as I make my way over to my closet. I know I should get into pajamas and try to get back to sleep, but with my mind full of thoughts of Sebastian, I know there's no way I'll get any more peace tonight.

Dressing in fresh underwear, running shorts and a sports bra, I slide my cell phone and key card into my running armband and push my AirPods into my ears. I don't want to piss off the housemates I've not even met yet, so I carry my running sneakers in my hand as I pad barefoot down the stairs and out onto the second-floor landing,

It's dark and quiet, if my housemates were out partying last night, they either haven't come home yet, or are all passed out drunk in their beds. Either way, I try to stay as silent as I can as I make my way down to the front door and let myself out.

The cool night air surrounds me and I inhale deeply. On the one and only time I've been back to Florida since I ran, I felt like I could never get a full breath of air, like my lungs just don't work properly here. But this is where I'll be spending the next four years, so I need to get used to surviving here, and that starts with learning to breathe again.

Kingsacre is still a complete unknown to me, after texting my dad to tell him I'd made it here safe, I glanced at my campus map for less than five minutes before I fell asleep. Now I'm standing in the front yard, trying to remember if the golf cart had approached the house from the left or the right?

Opening up my maps app on my cell, I add a pin on my current location, this way if I do get completely lost then I can use the pin to figure out how to get back to the house. Huge gates block the entrance to the driveway and as I approach them, I try to see if there's a button to press or something, but as soon as I'm within about twenty feet of them, they slowly start to open as if they're on a sensor.

While I wait, I lift first one foot, then the other up behind me, stretching my muscles. Once the gap in the gates is wide enough, I walk through it and down the asphalt road that meanders through the campus housing.

The feeling of being watched washes over me and I still, letting my eyes wander from side to side before I turn and look back at the house. It's in darkness, there're no lights on in any of the bedrooms. Shaking my head, I twist my neck from one side to the next, then take off in a slow jog.

Before moving to Maine, the idea of running would have made me laugh, but when I literally ran away from my life, I was so worried and anxious that Dad suggested I try burning some of my frenetic energy away with exercise.

The first run was ridiculous, I lasted about half a mile and by the time I got home I was coated in sweat and breathing so hard I thought I might pass out. On my second run I realized that while I was concentrating on putting one foot in front of the other, my mind was blissfully silent.

Desperate for that quiet, I started running every day and now I do a few miles in the morning and sometimes in the evening as well if I'm struggling to turn off my thoughts. Some people say you can't run away from your problems, but I disagree.

Hitting play on my cell phone, music starts to play through my earphones. I don't run to heavy dance tracks or songs with a fast beat, instead I run to a soundtrack of calming rain forest sounds, thunderstorms and classical chill-out stuff. It doesn't help me run any faster or farther, but instead it calms and soothes me.

After a mile or so, I find my groove, increasing my pace and lengthening my stride. This is the best part, when your muscles are loose, your mind is empty and you're running for the sake of running. The road is lit with streetlights, and I stay out of the shadows, doing my best to be safe even though I'm stupidly running alone at nearly three in the morning.

Most of the houses are dark, except for a few where the lights are blazing and drunk kids are littered on the grass of the yards, music blaring through open doors and windows. Perhaps in another life I might have been one of those kids enjoying a party on my first night of college, but not now. The me I am now would rather run alone in the dark than be around all those people.

It's another mile before I reach the main campus buildings and I run through the quad, across the lawns and out toward the main gates I entered through yesterday. There're still people in the valet hut where I spoke to Angelo, and I wonder if the ridiculous college valet service is available twenty-four seven.

"Starling?" a voice calls out as I run past the hut, planning to head out onto the road.

Startled to hear my name being called, I slow to a stop and turn around, finding Angelo half hanging out of the hut. "Starling, is that you, girl?"

"Hey," I pant.

"What the hell are you doing out on your own at this time of night?" he asks.

"Running."

"It's the middle of the night," he laughs.

"I had like the world's longest nap and woke up an hour ago. I couldn't get back to sleep so I figured I'd get a run in while it was quiet and learn my way around the campus."

Angelo shakes his head and sighs. "Girl, you take the bus to get here, walk your ass through the gates, and now you're running on your own in the middle of the night. It might seem like it should be safe on a campus with kids this rich, but it's not. These people think that the laws don't apply to them, you need to use that pretty little head of yours."

"I'm more than aware of how the type of kids that go here think," I say, bitterness lacing my tone. "I appreciate your concern, but I'm fine."

"Well, I kind of have to disagree, you're heading out onto the street in the dark, without a light in dark colors. You're an invisible target."

Dropping my gaze down to my black bra and shorts, I shrug a little sheepishly. "Yeah, that's probably not a great idea. No worries, I'll head around the buildings and do a circuit back to my house."

"Where's your suite?"

"Collinwood."

His eyes widen and he jolts back a little. "Collinwood?"

"Yep, I asked if it was a mistake too. There's been a bit of confusion over my name and I'm still pretty much convinced

I'm in the wrong room, but student services insist I'm not. Anyway, I should get moving before I cramp up. Thanks for stopping me from ending up as roadkill," I say, smiling as I wave and set off.

Traversing the admin buildings and the gymnasium, I do a loop around the library and science block and end up panting and gasping for a drink in front of the cafeteria. The kitchens are in darkness, but the vending machines are working and I grab myself a bottle of water, loving that my key card can be used as a cashless payment card as well.

Checking my smartwatch, I'm impressed to find that I've already done five miles and my legs still feel fresh, or at least strong enough to get me home again. Opening the water, I take an eager pull, moaning in pleasure when the cool liquid soothes my throat and quenches my thirst. The feeling of being watched again prickles across my skin and I lower my drink and slowly look around, trying to find the identity of the voyeur, but just like at the house, I'm alone.

Being this close to Green Acres must be messing with my mind, add in Evan's unwarranted trick with my name, and apparently paranoia is my new best friend. Shaking away the feeling, I take another pull from my water and then push off back toward the house as the sun starts to rise.

I get a little lost on the way back and by the time I press my card against the small foot gate I hadn't noticed at the side of the huge double gates, I've run nearly twelve miles. My legs are heavy and my breathing is labored, but my mind is clear and I'm smiling. Until I started running, I'd always scoffed at those annoying athletic people who say you get endorphins from exercise, but it's true. After a run I'm always happy and even here in this school I don't want to attend, with my stepbrother who is apparently still holding a grudge, I'm still excited for the rest of the day and the start of my college experience.

There's no sign of life from the other people in the house when I step through the front door, but it's barely five a.m. and most normal people are still asleep at this hour. Slipping my sneakers from my feet, I pad into the kitchen, pour myself a glass of water and then silently make my way back to my room.

I know I'll be tired later if I don't get any more sleep, but I don't want to go to bed and lose this buzz I'm feeling right now. Deciding to shower and get ready for my first day, I waste the next hour nervously primping, then decide I'll take a slow walk back to the cafeteria which opens for breakfast at seven.

The sun is high in the sky when I walk out of the gate again, my backpack slung over my shoulders. I glance down at my outfit and decide there's nothing wrong with my denim shorts and cropped tank top. It's casual, and came from the only outlet mall near my dad's place, but it fits nicely and shows off my toned stomach and legs.

Dad's day starts about three a.m., so I know he'll be up as I dial his number and lift my cell to my ear. "Hey honey, are you excited for your first day?"

GEMMA WEIR

"Hi, Dad, I'm not exactly excited, but I got a good run in this morning and I'm feeling more optimistic than I was yesterday."

"How's your dorm room? And your housemates?"

"When I got here, they had me registered under Mrs. Starling Lockwood."

"Lockwood," Dad says, "isn't that…" he trails off.

"Sebastian's surname, yep. I'm guessing it's Evan's attempt at a fucked-up joke. But I got it sorted out. My room is ridiculous. The scholarship kids normally live in the town houses that are on the website, but my room is in the turret of this enormous Victorian mansion. I'm pretty sure I've been put there by mistake, but when I asked to be moved to one of the town houses they said they're full, so it's either stay where I am or move off campus."

"Could Harry or your mom have paid for a better room for you?" Dad asks, his voice laced with concern.

"I guess they could have, I hadn't thought of that, but it makes sense, wouldn't look good for Harry Morris's stepdaughter to be slumming it in the cheap rooms," I mock derisively.

"What about your housemates?"

"I haven't met them yet. There're five rooms in the house and judging by the refrigerator full of beer, I'm going to guess that at least one of them is a guy. But there was no one there when I got there yesterday, and then I fell asleep and pretty much slept from yesterday afternoon until this morning."

"Well I'm sure you'll get a chance to meet them this

afternoon after your classes."

"There's no classes today, it's all meet and greet orientation stuff, then there's a big party tonight to welcome all the freshmen."

"Sounds fun, but be careful if you're going to a party. Don't take a drink from anyone, always make your own and¾"

"I know, Daddy, I've seen all the teen movies where girls get their drinks spiked, and I have those Rohypnol testers you gave me. I have no intention of going tonight anyway, you know parties aren't my thing," I assure him.

"Honey," he sighs.

"I should go, you need to get back to work and I need to eat, I slept through dinner last night and I'm starving."

"Okay, have a good day and call me later."

"I will. Love you, Daddy."

"I love you too, honey."

After ending the call, I feel both better and worse. I miss him already. He's become my safe haven and being this far away from him and knowing I won't see him again for months has me on the verge of a panic attack. Inhaling sharply, I concentrate on walking and will the rising tide of anxiety to fade.

Rationally, I know that the short two and a half months I spent with hurricane Sebastian shouldn't have had as big an impact on my life as they did. He didn't rape me, or really physically hurt me. But in an instant, he took over my life completely and it scared the shit out of me. He refused to acknowledge my wants or desires unless he could use them to manipulate me into doing what he wanted and what was worse is that no one questioned him. Not my mom or my friend, not his parents or the kids at school. No one ever considered that I wouldn't want him, so the idea that I was unhappy and overwhelmed never even crossed their minds.

I hate him for destroying my trust in people, because that experience fundamentally changed me and I'll never get to be the person I was before him ever again.

Despite the early hour, there're still plenty of other kids spilling from the houses as I pass, some look hungover, but others have an air of excitement over a new school, or new year.

"Morning," a gleeful-looking girl says, sideling up beside me with her hands holding on to the straps of her backpack.

"Morning," I reply, not wanting to be rude, but wishing I'd already put my AirPods in so I could pretend not to hear her speaking to me.

"I'm glad I'm not the only person up this early. I was so excited I just couldn't sleep. I've been up since five trying to decide what to wear. Do I look alright? I didn't want to go too preppy, but then I was worried I'd look like I was trying too hard if I wore anything dressy or like a slob if I wore anything too casual."

"You look fine," I say, taking a cursory glance down at her white tennis-style pleated skirt and pale-blue polo shirt. She looks incredibly preppy, but I don't say anything.

"I'm Samantha, but most people call me Sammy."

"Starling."

"Wow, that's such a cute name. My first college friend is a girl with a cute name, how cool is that?"

Forcing a smile to my lips I offer it in her direction, not slowing my pace, despite the fact that I can see she's having to walk quicker than she's comfortable with to keep up with me.

"What are your housemates like? There's six other people in my house, three girls and three guys, they're all couples. It's odd, but okay. I heard a lot of sex noises last night," she chirps.

"I haven't met mine yet."

"How come?"

"No one was there when I got here yesterday and I crashed pretty much as soon as I unpacked. They were still asleep when I left this morning." I say with a shrug.

"That's a shame, I bet they were all excited to meet you."

Not speaking, I wait for her to walk away, but instead she stays at my side, carrying the conversation without me needing to speak as she prattles on about everything she's excited about. When we reach the cafeteria and I grab a tray, she's at my side, then we're sitting at a table and I haven't said a word in more than ten minutes, but I'm not sure she's noticed.

"Shall I come to your place tonight, or do you want to come to mine?" she says and then pauses, smiling widely.

"What?" I splutter.

"For the party?"

"I'm not going to any party."

Her lips part and her mouth falls open. "You have to go to the freshmen welcome party, everyone goes."

"No thanks," I say dismissively, cutting off a piece of French toast and lifting it to my lips.

Sammy's talking but I'm not paying any attention as the feeling of being watched hits me again. That's the third time since I got here yesterday that I've gotten the feeling of being observed and it's starting to freak me out.

"Hey," I interrupt.

"Oh, I'm sorry, I know I talk too much. I'm sorry, it's just that I'm so nervous and excited," she says, talking at a million miles a minute.

"Is there anyone looking over here?" I ask, interrupting her again.

"Like who?"

"I don't know. I keep having this feeling like someone is watching me."

"Oh I hate that," she says, carefully glancing around the room. "I can't see anyone, but it's getting pretty busy in here now."

For the first time since she appeared at my side, Sammy falls silent and I take a moment to actually look at her. Her hair is a rich black color, pinned up on top of her head in a high ponytail that swishes across her shoulders. She's classically pretty, with warm-brown eyes and a smile that screams nice. She's the type of person who I would probably have made friends with when I was younger, but now I feel too jaded and shuttered to be around her.

"I appreciate the invite, but I don't like parties; truthfully I'm not really a big fan of people in general. I'm a loner without all the emo melancholy," I say, trying to explain why I'm going to get up and leave in a minute and then never speak to her again. There's a pang of longing for a friend in my chest, but I shut it down. Court was my ride or die, until she wasn't, she threw me over for popularity and I'm still hurt by it. I have no interest in befriending a stranger.

"Well that's okay, we don't have to go to the party, we could just hang out instead," Sammy suggests hopefully.

"That's sweet of you, but you should go to the party, meet people, make friends, find a guy and hook up. Don't waste your time on me, I'll only drag you down." Picking up my still mostly full tray I stand up and leave, keeping my coffee, but dumping my food in the trash before walking out of the cafeteria, never once glancing at the kind girl who wanted to be my friend.

Wandering for a few minutes, I end up in the quad where the orientation is being held. The lawn is perfectly cut, the meandering paths clean and full of students. Finding a tree, I sit down at its base, resting my back up against the trunk and slide in my AirPods, watching the world go by as the dulcet tones of Adele fill my ears. I know I'm a walking cliché—wounded girl listening to angsty love songs alone after having just walked away from the chance of a new friendship—but honestly I don't care. Maybe I am actually a loner with all the emo angst, all I know is that I'd rather be alone, it's safer that way. There's no one to lose if there's no one there in the first place.

Orientation is boring, the excited energy that seems to bounce around the congregated kids slides off me like water off a waxed car. All of the happiness I'd found after my run has faded and I'm ready to go back to Collinswood and sleep for the rest of the day. Classes officially start tomorrow and I join the line to collect my schedule, wondering why in this day and age they can't just email it to me.

"Name?" the guy at the desk asks.

"Starling Kennedy."

His fingers move across the keys. "Starling Lockwood?"

"Nope Kennedy, the surname is a screwup in the offices, they keep changing it to Kennedy and it changes right back to Lockwood," I say, hating that I'm having to explain I'm not a Lockwood again. Evan is an asshole for doing this. Maybe the first time it was amusing to him, and hurtful to me, now it's just annoying.

"I'll have to call student liaison services to double-check, we don't want you attending the wrong classes he says with a sigh."

"Go ahead, speak to Brenda, she's the one who's changed it the twice it's happened already," I say, rubbing at my temples with my fingers.

Desk guy pulls his cell out and proceeds to have the same conversation with Brenda that the registration and ID people did.

"Starling."

Spinning around at the sound of my name, my mouth falls open when I find Courtney standing behind me, flanked on either side by two beautiful preppy-looking girls. All three of them have matching sneering smiles plastered across their faces.

"What the hell are you doing at Kingsacre?"

The hostility in her voice surprises me. I mean, I wasn't expecting a hug, but I've literally never done anything but be a good friend to Courtney. She's the one who abandoned me, not the other way around.

"Hey, Court, I er, I didn't know you were coming to this school. What happened to Princeton?"

Her brow furrows and she scoffs. "Princeton is for ugly, rich geeks and poor people, do you even know how many nobodies go there? Kingsacre is exclusive, which is why I'm wondering what the hell you're doing here."

"I'm beginning to ask myself that exact question," I reply.

"Okay, Starling, Brenda confirmed that for some reason your records keep changing back to Mrs. Starling Lockwood no matter how many times we amend them," the orientation guy says, sliding back into his seat behind his table.

"Lockwood," Courtney scoffs. "Are you seriously trying to use Bastian's name to get ahead?"

"Nope, just Evan's idea of a joke," I say quietly.

"Evan's a darling, although they all are really. We had quite the reunion when they all came back this summer, it was just like old times."

"Fun," I say through gritted teeth, as I'm reminded all over again that she gave me up for them so easily.

"I always have fun with Bastian, we have so much in common, our parents play golf and we're practically neighbors. Our children will be unstoppable," she tells me with triumph in her tone.

"I'm sure they'll be delightful," I offer dryly.

"God, you're such a bitch. I have no idea how someone so low class can think so highly of themselves. Just because your mom sucked Evan's dad's dick and got a ring on her finger doesn't make you anything but a gold-digging whore's daughter. He offered you the world and you threw it back in his face. But just because you're back, don't get any ideas about trying to claw your way back into his bed. He's mine now."

Smirking, I try to swallow the laugh that bubbles up from my throat, but I just can't contain it and I throw my head back and bark out a loud laugh that probably makes me sound like a crazy person. Courtney and her friends eye me like I'm insane, and maybe I am, but the idea that I might actively seek Sebastian out is ridiculous. "Oh my god, I needed that. Thanks, Court, it's been so fucking great seeing you again."

Rolling her eyes dramatically, she looks me up and down and

then purses her lips as though she smells something unpleasant. "Whatever, bitch, just stay away from all of them, especially Bastian."

Saluting her sarcastically, I turn my back on her. "Well okay then," the guy behind the table who just listened to her call my mom a gold-digging whore and me a bitch says. "Here's your schedule," he says, sliding a printed piece of paper and a map across the table toward me. "So we are here," he marks an X on the map showing the quad we're standing in. "You're mostly taking required courses this semester so your English, history and humanities-based courses are in this building." He highlights the courses on my schedule in pink and then circles a building on the map in the same color. "Your math, politics and eco are in this building, he does the same with these classes in blue. Here is the cafeteria, gymnasium and pool and all of the administration offices are over here."

By the time he's finished, my schedule and map look like a three-year-old went to town on it with a box of highlighters, but I don't want to be here longer than I need to be so I just pick up the papers, nod, thank him and leave.

It's only a little after eleven a.m., but with no classes today and no real interest in meeting new people, signing up for any clubs or societies or running into Courtney again, I grab a couple of prepacked sandwiches and three bottles of water from the cafeteria and start to walk back to the house.

"Hello, little sister," a voice says from behind me a moment before a heavy arm lands across my shoulders.

Freezing, I snap my head around and find myself looking up at Evan, a smug smirk etched across his face.

"Jesus, it's like blast-from-the-past hell," I mutter. "Hello, Evan."

"Got to say, sis, I'm disappointed you haven't come to say hi, we are family after all."

Shrugging, I dislodge his arm and then step to the side and out of his reach. "We're not family, our parents just got married, that doesn't make *us*"—I motion between us—"anything."

"Harsh," Evan laughs. "Your mom is my mom now, that makes us siblings."

"Stepsiblings at best, and it hardly counts when we live in different states and don't spend any time together. You're my mom's new stepson, and we're just people who went to the same high school for a few months."

A look, that if I didn't know better I'd say was hurt, flashes across his face. "She misses you."

"Who?"

"Your mom. She misses you."

"She chose not to speak to me for a year, not me."

"You left."

"I don't want to discuss this with you. It's none of your business," I snap, increasing my pace and hoping he'll leave, but instead he just walks quicker, staying at my side.

"Of course it's my business, she's a good person, she didn't deserve you treating her like that."

Stopping, I spin around to face him. "I'm glad she's with your dad, I'm glad she's happy and that you and she have a good relationship. That was all made easier by me not being in the picture, so I've actually done you a favor. My relationship with my mom ended when your friend told me if I left him he'd take everyone I loved away from me. He won, he did take her away, but she let him. So this is where we are. My choice, his choice, her choice, they led me here and her to your dad. I was happy living with my dad, she was happy falling in love and getting married. Everyone's a winner."

"Starling¾"

"Look, Evan, it is what it is. We're not family, we're definitely not friends. I'm assuming my mom asked you to look out for me or something, but you don't need to. I'm never going to tell anyone you're my mom's husband's son, and you don't need to worry about me trying to cash in on your name here, because I won't, ever. So how about we just pretend like we've never met and if my mom asks, then I'll tell her we have lunch together once a week, or something."

"Starling."

"What, Evan?" I ask wearily, rubbing at the headache that's starting to form behind my eyes.

"We could be friends."

I scoff. "No, we couldn't." Forcing my feet into motion, I walk away, pushing my AirPods into my ears and turning up the volume as Eminem blasts loud and angry, fueling my steps with more vigor and my heart with enough bravado to not look back.

My head is pounding by the time I slide my key card into the scanner on the front door and stumble inside. The stairs feel insurmountable, but I'd rather struggle to get to my room, than crash in the living room and be found by the housemates I've yet to meet.

Each step makes my brain rattle, my eyes blur and the ball of tension I can feel in my neck worsen. When I finally mount the top step and spot my bed, I crawl on top of the comforter and then collapse in a heap, my backpack still over my shoulders.

"Urgh," I moan as I force myself upright, letting the bag slip from my shoulders and fall haphazardly to the floor. There's a bottle of pain meds in the bathroom, but the thought of getting up and walking there makes me feel ill, so instead I slump down onto the mattress, close my eyes and try to push all thoughts of Evan, Courtney, Green Acres, my mom and Sebastian from my mind.

"Wake up, little bird."

The softly spoken, familiar voice curls through my mind, wrapping around my brain like vines hanging from a tree. My eyes flutter open and for a moment, I swear I can see him, standing at the end of the bed, his face hidden in shadow, but then I blink and when I open my eyes a millisecond later, he's gone, an unwanted figment of my imagination.

It's twilight, the sun's starting to set, casting patterns through the window and across my room. It's pretty and I glance out of the glass, admiring the dying orange embers that are highlighting the horizon.

My head feels better, but my neck is stiff and my mouth is dry. I've slept the day away again and forgotten to eat. My stomach feels hollow when I remember the last proper meal I ate was the last dinner I shared with my dad two days ago. Rolling into a sitting position, I swing my legs over the edge of the bed and head for the bathroom, relieving my bladder before washing up and grabbing the bottle of painkillers from the counter, tipping two into my hand.

Making my way back to the bed, I grab my backpack from where I dumped it earlier and take out one of the bottles of water, using the liquid to swallow the pills before drinking the rest of the bottle. I eat half the sandwich, but the bread is dry, the salad limp and the chicken kind of mushy so I ditch the rest into the trash can.

For the first time since I got here yesterday, I can hear noise from inside the house. My housemates are downstairs and even though I really don't want to, I should go down and at least introduce myself to them. Assuming we all pass our classes, we could be living together for the next four years, so I need to make an effort to at least be on a polite, friendly basis with them.

My mouth feels disgusting, so I brush my teeth and smooth down my hair. It used to be almost to my butt, but since I moved to my dad's I had it cut off to my shoulders. I used to love my hair, now it's just long enough to tie up and apart from occasionally straightening it, I rarely fuss with it.

I glance at my outfit. It's a little rumpled from sleeping in it, but I really don't care. If these people dislike me because I'm a little creased, then it's just one more reason to stay away from them.

Grabbing my cell phone and key card, I slide my feet into flip-flops and head downstairs. The sound of music seems to be coming from the kitchen, so I slowly make my way toward it, not allowing the trepidation I'm feeling to send me running back upstairs to hide in my room. All I have to do is introduce myself, be polite for five minutes and then I can escape again.

When I step into the kitchen I spot someone leaning into the refrigerator. It looks like a guy and when he straightens, it's obvious that it's a he and he's tall.

"Er, hey, I guess you're one of my housemates," I say.

The guy turns and my mouth falls open. "Hunter?" I gasp.

His smile is soft and despite his size, he's never felt as dangerous as the others, even though I'm sure he could be. "Hello, Starling."

"What…?" I trail off.

"You didn't think we'd let you live all alone on a campus full of strangers did you, sis?" Evan says, stepping out from behind me and moving to take a bottle of beer from Hunter.

"We couldn't get you to come home, so we thought we'd bring home to you," Clay announces cheerfully as he steps past me.

"No," I murmur, shaking my head. "You don't go here."

"What, Mom never told you?" Evan taunts. "Maybe if you'd spoken to her a bit more often she'd have mentioned that we decided to finish out our junior and senior years together."

"All of us," Clay says with a wink.

My hands ball into fists at my sides and I close my eyes, trying to make this a dream, or a nightmare or anything that means it's not true. Except it is true, and no matter how tightly I squeeze my eyes shut when I open them, they're all still going to be here and so is he, because when Clay said all of them, he meant him too.

"Hello, little bird."

I want to be strong. I try to be strong but at the sound of his voice, my legs give way and I end up on my ass on the ground. Curling my legs into my chest, I scuttle across the floor until my back hits the cabinets, then I bury my face against my knees and cover my head with my hands. "No, this can't be happening, no, no, no."

ELEVEN

SEBASTIAN

She's beautiful, more so than she was the last time I was close enough to touch her. Her body has matured over the last two and a half years and instead of a girl, she's all woman. The soft curves I loved so much have gone and she's almost painfully slim and toned. Her hair is shorter, but still a pretty color, and I have to fight the urge to reach out and tug a strand, to reel her back to me.

I watch as Hunter reveals himself and she tenses, her fingers clenching into fists. When Evan announces his arrival, her back goes ramrod straight and by the time Clay steps into the room, she's shaking her head.

The moment Evan taunts her with the knowledge that we're all here I see her breath hitch. I've waited over two years for this moment, over two years to get her away from her dad and back into my world. Not that she was ever really out of my reach. If I wanted to, I could have taken her at any point, but that's not what I wanted, I wanted her to come back to me willingly. Only she didn't, not when I chased her, not when I gave her space and not when I showed her I could ruin her and take away all the people who were important to her.

All except her dad, that is. Before she went to visit him, I'd thought of him as a nonentity, not a player in the game. I was wrong, and no matter how much I've tried to influence him in the last two and a half years, nothing has worked. As much as I hate to admit it, I admire the man and his unwavering loyalty to his daughter.

"Hello, little bird," I call, stepping up behind her.

I expect her to look at me, then try to run, but instead, at the sound of my voice she drops to the floor, scuttles back until her spine is flush with the cabinet, curls into a ball and starts to rock as she chants "no, no, no," over and over again.

The others look to me, but I'm as clueless as them. This was supposed to feel victorious. I won, she's here, she's mine again, and this time I won't allow her another chance to escape. But seeing her on the floor, broken, this isn't what I want.

As I stand there staring at her, Evan rushes to her, dropping to his knees beside her and reaching out to touch her. The moment his fingers touch her, she freaks out. Her agonized scream is gut wrenching and then she's gasping for air, her head snapping up as her face goes flush and she grabs at her throat, a wheezing, wretched sound coming from her that's barely human.

"She's having a panic attack," Hunter says, opening the drawers and rooting through until he finds a paper bag and rushes over to her. "Starling," he says softly, drawing her attention to him, while her lips turn slightly blue and choked noises fall from her parted lips. "You need to breathe into the bag. Slow, easy breaths, okay? I'm not going to touch you unless you need me to hold the bag."

Shaking her head she grabs the paper from him, screwing the top of the bag up in her hands and holding it to her mouth.

"Slow and easy," Hunter says calmly. "Breathe in time with me. In and out." He does exaggerated breathing, kneeling just far enough away that he's not touching her, but close enough to pull her attention completely onto him. "That's it, good girl, in and out."

After what feels like an hour, but is probably only ten or so minutes, Hunter rests back onto his heels and the tension releases from his body. "How are you feeling? Better?"

Her eyes are wide and watery, the bag still covering her mouth, but she nods.

"Good, keep breathing in and out and I'll grab you a bottle of water." Standing, he moves slowly, taking a bottle of water from the refrigerator and then sliding back down onto the floor, holding it out to her.

Tentatively she reaches out and takes it, her eyes moving

from him, to Evan and Clay and then to me. I hate that what's in her eyes when she looks at me isn't lust or want, it's fear. She's scared of me, she's scared of all of us, but she was upright until I spoke to her.

Hunter reaches out and she flinches, jolting away from him as if she's expecting him to strike her. "I'm not going to hurt you. I promise, I just want to check your pulse that's all. I need to see if we need to take you to the emergency room."

"I'm fine," she says, her voice croaky and weak.

"Little bird, you're not fine. I'll call Dr. Harris."

"No," she shrieks, shuffling farther away from me and scrambling to her feet.

Hunter sends a glare in my direction, but his expression softens when he looks back to her. She never knew they watched her for the year before I claimed her. My friends were almost as angry as I was when she didn't come back from her dad's. She left all of us, she just had no idea they would be hurt by that. "Starling, all I need to touch is your wrist. My two fingers on your wrist, that's all, I promise I won't touch you anywhere else."

Her eyes flash to me and then around the kitchen before she shuffles along the counter to the right, moving behind Hunter and positioning him so he's between me and her. From this angle, I can only see half of her as she cautiously lifts her wrist and offers it to my friend. Just like he promised, he takes her pulse, then immediately lifts his hand away and steps back, giving her some space.

"Your pulse is still high, but your breathing seems steadier and the blue tinge has gone from your lips. I think we should take you to the hospital, just to have you checked out."

She shakes her head. "There's no point, Dad took me the first few times I had them and all they do is keep me under observation for a night, charge me thousands of dollars then send me home and tell me to try and reduce my stress and anxiety," she tells him, her voice barely more than a whisper.

I knew she'd had panic attacks when she first moved to Maine, but I assumed when there were no more hospital visits that they'd stopped, it never occurred to me that she just stopped going to the doctors.

"You're going to the hospital," I demand.

"Bastian," Evan says, shocking me.

"She needs to go to the fucking hospital, her fucking lips were blue ten fucking minutes ago," I shout.

"Bro," Clay says.

"No, this is bullshit, if your woman couldn't breathe and was turning fucking blue we'd be on the way to the damn hospital by now, no questions asked."

While I've been ranting, Starling has moved to the other side of the kitchen island, putting a whole expanse of counter between us, like she needs a physical barrier to stop me from getting closer to her.

"Look at her, Bastian," Hunter says quietly. "She's fucking terrified."

"Why are you here?" she asks, surprising me.

"Where else would I be?"

"Harvard," she whispers, then coughs, the sound raspy enough that I take a step forward, the urge to drag her to me almost overwhelming. "Mom enjoyed telling me about how successful you've been there."

There's a hint of derision in her tone that reminds me of the way she used to sound when she enjoyed fighting with me, playing with me.

"Cassidy is proud of all of us, she calls us her surrogate sons," I tell her, smirking. "We're all like one big happy family now she's a Morris, she really relied on us after you abandoned her."

"So I've heard, I'm glad she has a support network," she says quietly. "Why are you here, Sebastian?"

"Because you're here, where else would I be?"

Exhaling shakily, her lips pinch together and she smiles sadly. "Haven't you done enough to me? We dated for a couple of months over two years ago. It wasn't serious, we never had sex or declared our undying love for one another. You never even asked me if it was something I wanted, you just declared that I was yours and took over my life. I rejected you, so you single-handedly destroyed my relationship with my mother and took my best friend from me. Isn't that enough? Surely your ego wasn't that badly bruised by my not wanting you that you're still looking for revenge all these years later? You win, okay?

If you want me to leave, I'll go. If you want me to cut all ties with my mom, then fine, I'll do it, we have no relationship now anyway. Just tell me what you want because I don't want to play these messed-up games with you again." She's trying to sound strong and confident, but her body is literally vibrating, tremors racking her limbs.

"You," I say simply.

"What?"

"I want you."

"Why? Is it just because I don't want you? Surely I'm not the only girl who's said she's not interested?"

"You're mine, Starling, you're my little bird and you always have been, since the moment I laid eyes on you on your first day at GAA. I waited a year to even find out your name, then as soon as you were a sophomore, I made you mine. You might have run from me and I might have allowed it, but you've never been free, little bird. I've kept you tethered the last two years, let you think you could fly away, but you couldn't, the only place I'll ever let you fly is back to me where you belong."

"I don't understand."

"Ever had that feeling like you're being watched?"

She visibly tenses despite her trembling, and I smile.

"That was your security detail. Since the moment you left Green Acres and boarded a plane to Maine for Christmas, there's been a team of men following you. Every thing you've done, every place you've gone, every person you've spoken to, it's been reported back to me."

"No," she gasps.

"All the days you waited for your dad to go out on his boat before you cried yourself to sleep, I knew about. All the times you've been asked out on dates or to parties I knew about. When the doctor offered to put you on birth control and tried to get you to take anti-anxiety medication, I knew about it."

She shakes her head as a single tear rolls down her cheek.

"I knew every school you applied to, so I'd know which admissions officers I needed to bribe into rejecting you. I made sure Kingsacre was your only option, I even awarded you the Lockwood scholarship so you'd feel obliged to come here rather than let your father take out a second mortgage to pay for school for you, just in case you were accepted elsewhere."

Tears flow freely down her cheeks now, and I have to restrain myself from hauling her to me and licking them off her skin.

"Every step you've taken it's been controlled by me, orchestrated to get you exactly where I wanted you to be. Here in this house, under my roof, under my control, mine."

TWELVE

STARLING

It can't be true, it can't be. He's a kid, a rich kid but still just a kid. He doesn't have access to a security team and even if he did, why the hell would he have them following me around? What would be the point?

"Why?" I ask.

"Because you're destined to be mine."

"But I don't want you, I don't want any of it. Pick a new toy to obsess over, one who wants you back."

"You do want me, Starling."

I shake my head. "I don't, Sebastian. I don't want you. I don't want to be yours. I don't want a present or a future with you, all I want is for you to forget I exist."

"Did you know you say my name in your sleep, you dream

about me," he tells me casually like I haven't just told him I want nothing to do with him.

"They're nightmares, not dreams. You stalk me, stealing every bit of sunshine in my life until I'm suffocating in the darkness and then I die, begging you to leave me alone," I confess, not bothering to try and sugarcoat how he haunts my subconscious.

His eyes fall closed for a second and when he opens them again, they're harder, and full of steely determination. "I'll make you want me again."

Grimacing, I force a pained smile to my lips. "I never wanted you, Sebastian."

"Then you'll learn to fucking pretend," he yells, stalking toward me, and grabbing my upper arms in an unyielding grip as he leans down and kisses me.

His lips slam against mine and he forces his tongue into my mouth, kissing me with a punishing force that I loathe but which ignites something inside of me that's been dormant since the last time he touched me.

My body threatens to wilt into him, but I force myself to stay ramrod straight, not lifting my hands to reach for him, or reacting to him at all. His growl of frustration is almost gratifying enough to make me smile, but I keep my lips flat and unmoving, not wanting him to think he's done something to warrant my happiness.

"Kiss me back," he growls.

Staying still I let him kiss me, but give him nothing in return. I want him to know that he might be able to take from me, but I won't willingly give him anything.

Pulling away from me, he runs soft fingers over the skin at the back of my neck and I fight back a whimper. "I preferred your hair when it was long; when I could wrap my hand around it and tug on it," he says, gripping a thick strand of hair and pulling until I whimper.

"I like it short," I whisper.

The room is silent except for me and Sebastian but I can still feel the other guys' presence, they're still here, watching this all go down.

"You all live here, in this house?"

"Our families own it," Clay says.

"Of course they do," I nod, exhaling.

"I should go." Before I can complete a single step, Sebastian tightens his hold on my hair and yanks me back to him.

"Go to *our* room." He smiles, his gritted teeth not hidden by the composed front he's trying to exude.

"No."

"Little bird, you either go to our room, or you stay locked in your own room until I decide you can come out."

I glance up at him for a minute, then nod. "I'll take prison, I've become accustomed to loneliness and isolation the last couple of years."

With a sharp tug, I yank my hair free of his hold, trying

to hide the grimace of pain from my expression as I pad out of the kitchen. I manage to walk slowly until I'm out of sight, then I practically sprint out the front door, not caring about my belongings, just needing to be away from here, away from them, him. There's nothing here that I'm not willing to abandon for my freedom. Reaching the foot gate, I place my key card against the scanner but nothing happens. Snapping my head to the side, I glance around nervously, knowing they'll be following me soon, but the gate remains closed as I tap my card against it again and again.

"I've deactivated your card for the external gates and I've turned the motion sensor on the main gates off too," Sebastian says calmly.

My shoulders slump as I slowly turn around to find him standing at the door, his hands casually placed in his pockets.

"So I'm not going to be allowed to go to class?"

"You can go to class, you'll just be escorted there and back with either me or one of the guys."

"Why do you want me so much? Is it the rejection that turns you on?" I ask as I give the gate and my escape one last glance before turning and stomping toward the house.

"I like to own things, now I own you. It doesn't matter what you think you feel right now, eventually you'll admit you want me just as much as I want you, until then your cage will just get smaller and smaller until you do as you're told."

The smile on his face is bright and warm and in complete

contrast with the cold and menacing nature of his words, he's crazy, completely insane and the next time I run from him, it needs to be much farther away than just Maine.

He doesn't try to stop me when I barge past him and climb the stairs, not slowing down until I'm in my bedroom. The beautiful room suddenly feels much smaller than it did when I left it less than an hour ago. How in such a short space of time can my world have gone from tentatively hopeful to desolate? Sebastian threatened to lock me in here, but he must be bullshitting me. He's crazy, but surely he's not that crazy? Rushing back down the stairs, I pull on the door, but nothing happens, it's locked. He actually locked me in here.

Panic threatens to overwhelm me again, when my cell beeps with a text, distracting me. Dad hates texts, he says his fingers are too big and that it takes him too long to type out a message he could say in seconds during a phone call, so it's unlikely that it's him. It could be Mom, but we really only have a birthday and Christmas kind of relationship these days, I don't remember the last time she texted me.

Walking slowly back up to my room, I consider calling my dad and telling him about Sebastian, but if I do, he'll get on a plane and come here and I have no idea what Sebastian will do to him if he does. He's clearly unhinged and until I can figure out a way to run from him, there's no point allowing my dad to get within his firing range.

There's an unread text on my cell and I click into it.

Bastian
Dinner is in twenty minutes.

A hysterical laugh falls from my lips. Of course his number is now saved in my cell. He's stalked me for the last two years, manipulated my life, orchestrated things so I'm living with him, locked me in my bedroom and now he's texting me when dinner's going to be ready, like it's a normal meal and nothing out of the ordinary has happened.

He's insane, like certifiably insane and I'm stuck here, being controlled by his whims until I can get away from him. For a moment I wonder if the guys will help me, then laugh as the ridiculousness of that thought hits me. They must have known what he had planned, they must have helped him, or else why would they all be here too? My stepbrother is condoning his friend keeping me prisoner and no one in this house will help me, no matter what he does to me.

Maybe I just need to play along. I've run from him before and it didn't work, apparently it didn't even dent his desire for me. If anything, me leaving might have made his infatuation more intense. Perhaps if I give him what he wants he'll get bored. I'm the one that got away, the great white whale and everyone knows that not having something you desire always makes it feel more special and it's not until you have it that you realize it's not as good as you thought it was.

Resolved, I decide it's time to fight fire with fire. He wants his little bird, I'll give him a fucking flamingo. Stripping out of my clothes, I change my underwear for a pretty matching set my mom sent me as a gift last Christmas, fluff up my hair and coat my lips in sparkly red gloss. I look like a girl ready to get fucked, but this is what he wants, isn't it? Me willing and ready.

Pulling out my cell, I type out a message.

Me
What are we eating? I'm starving.

His reply is instantaneous.

Bastian
Pasta. I was expectin you to refuseto eat with us.

Me
Lemons, lemonade, I'm hungry and I hate cooking.

I wait for him to reply, but when nothing comes through, I climb off the bed, walk down the stairs and push at the door. It swings open and I inhale, then force a smile to my lips as I step out onto the landing in nothing but my bra and panties. Not pausing to give myself a moment to run back to the relative safety of my room, I add an extra bit of sway to my hips as I descend the stairs and sashay into the kitchen.

There's a sharp inhale of breath from someone as I stride into the room, prance over to the table where all of the guys except Clay are sitting, and plop my ass down into Hunter's lap.

"What the fuck?" Sebastian growls, taking hold of my wrist and dragging me off his friend's lap.

"Oh something smells good," I hum, not reacting to the

painful hold he has on me, or the horrified look on the other boys' faces.

"Where the hell are your clothes?"

"Upstairs," I grin. "Didn't seem much point putting on clean stuff, especially as I figured I'd be fucking at least one of you before the end of the night. This way I don't even have to get undressed, you can just pull my panties to the side."

Hunter chokes on air, his eyes going wide with shock as he tries not to look anywhere but at my face.

"Starling," Sebastian barks, lifting me onto my feet as he stands up, tugging his shirt off and dropping it over my head. "Cover yourself up."

"Why?" I ask, furrowing my brow exaggeratedly, pushing my arms through the sleeves and covering my bra, then pushing my panties off my hips and bending over in front of Sebastian's face as I slip them off my feet. "Sebastian always said I smelled good, what do you think, bro?" I ask, throwing my balled-up panties at Evan, hitting him square in the face.

"Starling," Sebastian shouts, grabbing me and actually shaking me violently.

"This is what you want isn't it?" I demand, sliding my hand up the back of my shirt and unclasping my bra, before I rip the shirt and bra over my head and drop them to the floor. "The four of you have me here, I'm a prisoner to all of you, I might as well be naked, that way you can all see if I'm worth the effort of holding me hostage. I've been told I give a good blow job, and that my pussy's nice and tight, but if you take turns I imagine by the time whoever goes last slides in I'll be pretty stretched out," I say with a smirk.

"Get some fucking clothes on," Sebastian demands.

"No."

"Now," he snaps.

"Why? This is what you want, so here I am, naked and waiting, but if I get to pick, I think I want Hunter to go first, he was nice to me earlier and I think I hate him the least out of the four of you. Is there going to be a rotation? Will it be one day each and then orgies Friday and Saturday and I get the day off on Sundays?"

Yanking my arm out of Sebastian's grip, I straddle Hunter's lap and kiss his shocked lips before he has a moment to protest about the naked girl sitting on him. Seeing me kissing his friend must be making Sebastian absolutely crazy, he's as possessive as they come and I think it stands a chance that he might never speak to Hunter again because my pussy has been pressed against his thighs, my tits against his chest and my tongue in his mouth. I know how much he'll hate the fact that I just said I wanted anyone but him to fuck me first, that I chose his friend instead of him.

Good, I hope it haunts him, that when he goes to sleep tonight all he can see when he closes his eyes is the girl he's obsessed with, naked with someone else.

When I'm dragged from Hunter's lap, it's with so much

force it feels like my shoulder is being ripped from the socket. I hit the floor with a thud, tumbling onto my ass before I fall backward and my head bounces off the hardwood.

"Get out, all of you, get the fuck out," Sebastian screams.

"Bastian," Evan says, his voice placating.

"Get out."

"Dude, you need to¾"

"Do not tell me what I need to do with my fucking woman," Sebastian growls, interrupting Evan, his eyes hard and burning with anger and fury as he glares down at me on the floor at his feet.

"You'll hate yourself if you hurt her," Hunter warns quietly.

"Oh I'm going to hurt her," Sebastian threatens, leaning down and lifting me up off the floor as if I weigh nothing before slinging me over his shoulder. "I'm going to hurt her and she's going to fucking beg for it."

My stomach hurts as I bounce against his shoulder as he sprints up the stairs until we reach the door beside my own. It's not locked and he pushes inside, closing it behind us, before he lowers me to the floor and then takes a step back.

"Do you think it's funny to rub your naked cunt all over my friend?"

I can't help it, some of his crazy must have infected me because I smile. "I think it's fucking hilarious, because once you've done whatever you plan to do to punish me and you go back downstairs to your friend, you won't see him, all you'll see is me, completely naked, willingly grinding on his hard dick while I tongue fucked his mouth, and you'll know that the only way I'll do it to you is if you force me." I have no idea where my words are coming from. I have literally never spoken like this in my life, but I'm so angry and scared and out of control that all I want to do is have him experience just a glimpse of the pain he's caused me.

Bracing myself for his violence, I'm not expecting soft hands to lift me off the floor and gently place me on the bed. I'm too shocked to fight before he's climbing down on top of me, his hand pressed between my breasts with enough force to immobilize me as he pushes his hand between my thighs and thrusts two fingers into my pussy.

I scream, grunting with pain at the intrusion, I'm angry, not turned on, and his fingers feel thick and full as he pulls them all the way out of me, spits onto them and then slams them back into me again, his saliva only making my body accept them fractionally easier.

I scream and thrash beneath him, but he doesn't even pause long enough to allow me to adjust, he fucks me slowly, forcing his fingers up to the knuckle then pulling them all the way out, before thrusting them back into me again. Without uttering a word, he roughly slams his lips against mine and kisses me animalistically, and I hate myself when I feel my body start to react to his touch.

I hate him, I hate him so much and yet my pussy becomes

slick the more aggressively he fucks his fingers in and out in time with his tongue in my mouth. It doesn't take long before my body heats and tenses for an impending orgasm, but as I'm on the edge, he pulls his fingers free and abruptly stops kissing me.

A groan of frustration slips past my lips and he smirks, running his tongue along the length of my neck before he nips at my earlobe. I expect him to release me, but instead his hand slips between my thighs again, only instead of filling me he seeks out my clit, circling it with the tip of his finger. He rubs slowly until I'm panting and arching my hips, seeking out his touch, then when I'm on the precipice of coming he pulls his finger away and I cry out in frustration.

A sly grin slides onto his mouth as he blinks, looking down at me like a predator does when it knows it has its prey completely at his mercy. I cry out when his thick fingers fill me again, pushing me to the edge and refusing to let me fall. Over and over he works me up, then stops until tears are running down my face and I'm writhing beneath his impenetrable hold, my chest tight and feeling bruised from how hard he's pinning me down.

"Please, no, please," I beg as his thumb leaves my clit and I cry out. The sound that falls from my mouth is desperate, almost a mewl as I try to lift my hips off the bed, following him as he leans away, begging him to allow me to come.

"You don't want me. You want Hunter. You want to rub *my*

cunt all over my brother."

"Please," I choke out.

"Please what?"

"Don't stop."

"Ask me," he orders

"Make me come."

"Ask nicely."

"Please, please, please," I chant.

"The only way you get to come is on my dick."

Two fingers fill me again and I almost splinter, just at the feeling of fullness. My body is so worked up, my muscles are itching and burning with the need to release some of the tension he's built with this awful game of tease and deny.

"Your muscles are so fucking tight I can barely move," he taunts.

"Please," I pant.

"I'll give you a choice, little bird, you can go back to your room and sleep, but you don't get to come or you can take my dick and earn as many orgasms as you can before you pass out from pleasure."

A better girl would run while she had the chance, but right now there's nothing but want consuming my body. No matter how much I hate him, I can't deny that my thighs are slick with my arousal and my skin is so hot and taut I feel ready to explode if I don't get some release soon.

"Please," I whine, releasing my hold on his hand that's still pinning me down.

"Do you want me to fuck you, little bird? Do you want my cock in you so deep you can taste my cum at the back of your throat?"

I nod and his smile is wicked.

"Arms above your head, hold on to the headboard."

I do as I'm told, lacing my fingers through the slatted wooden headboard and gripping tightly. Shuffling backward, Sebastian climbs off the bed and slips off his jeans and boxers, his dick popping free and bouncing up to hit his stomach. He's big, bigger than I remember, the head red and dripping precum as he climbs back onto the bed and crawls between my parted thighs.

"Condom," I croak as the wide head touches my entrance.

"No," he says, pushing forward and letting the tip of his cock slide into my soaked core.

"I'm a virgin," I cry, fear making me tense and grip down on the head.

"I know," he smirks, slamming forward and breaking through my virginity with a brutal thrust.

I scream in pain, the searing burn so much more intense than I imagined. Without even pausing, he moves, fucking me viciously as his hands hold my hips tight enough to bruise. The pain barely has a chance to fade before his thumb is on my clit and he's forcing me into an orgasm, my body exploding, my muscles jerking and twitching.

"Good girl, now I want you to come on my cock," he snarls, tilting my hips and reigniting the sparks his fingers had ignited earlier. I come again with a cry, but he just keeps on fucking me until the pleasure and pain become one and my eyes start to roll back in my head. "Another one, little bird," he orders, working my clit until a third, agonizing orgasm splinters, leaving sharp shards of bliss in its wake.

My body goes lax, too exhausted to do anything but lie there as he holds me up, his hard dick slamming mercilessly into me again and again.

"You're not done yet, Starling, you either come again with my cock in your cunt or I'll shove it into your ass and you can learn what it's like to have your tight little asshole fucked raw."

"I can't," I moan.

"You can and you fucking will," he growls, sliding his dick from me a moment before he flips me onto my stomach, drags my ass into the air and forces his dick back into me again.

A pained whimper falls from my lips as his dick fills me, feeling even bigger and harder from this angle.

"That's it," he groans, slowly pulling almost all the way out, then slamming back in again with so much force my stomach slides farther up the bed with each thrust. When his fingers find my nipples, pulling and tugging, I come with an agonized cry, the orgasm so painful that I whimper with each shudder of pleasure.

His thrusts become erratic and he groans a deep masculine

sound as he shudders and fills me, hot bursts of cum coating my sex. For an agonizingly long moment neither of us speaks or moves. Eventually, he slides his dick from inside of me and I slump down onto the bed, too exhausted to do anything but pant for breath. Lifting my hips, he slides a pillow beneath me, propping me up as he moves to the end of the bed.

"Fuck, little bird, your cunt is swollen and gaping, with my cum dripping out of it," he says tauntingly, as I glance over my shoulder and find him kneeling between my legs, his phone out and aimed at my sex.

"Sebastian," I gasp, trying to roll to the side and hide myself.

"Don't fucking move," he warns, gripping my hip and keeping me in place as he aims the cell between my thighs again. "I want to remember this moment, my cum, mixed with your virgin blood." Probing fingers stroke between my folds, then slowly push inside of my tender channel. "You'll take all of my cum from now on, Starling, it's all for you. Your cunt, your ass or your mouth, I won't lose a drop, all of it will end up inside of you. You'll be my wife and my cum slut, I'll worship the ground you walk on and then pin you to our bed and force my dick into your cunt while you snarl and fight. I'm going to fuck you so often my cum's going to be dripping out of you all day every day. Your panties are going to be permanently soaked with a mixture of our arousal so you're always wet and ready for me to take."

Tears escape my eyes and coat my cheeks. I'm angry that

instead of pissing him off and hurting him with my behavior tonight, I ended up naked in his bed just like he wanted. My body is humming with the pleasure that he's wrung from me and as much as I hate it, I love it in equal measure.

I'm sore and yet weirdly relaxed, it's not a sensation I've ever experienced before and I don't really know how to feel about it. The bed dips to the side of me, then an arm curls around my waist, pulling me back into Sebastian's firm body.

"I won't let you go, Starling, I couldn't two years ago and I never will, not now I know how it feels to be inside you."

"I'm on birth control, although you already know that, don't you?"

"Not anymore, I removed them from your luggage earlier."

"You can't decide that. I'm eighteen, I'm not even sure I want kids and I definitely don't want any now."

"I want a houseful of babies that look just like you, so we might as well get started now."

"What about what I want?" I ask quietly.

"The moment you ran away from me years ago, what you want stopped being important. I gave you a chance to come back to me, to be worshipped and adored, but you didn't. Now you'll do as you're told and perhaps I'll let you earn back some of the freedom that's under my control, eventually."

THIRTEEN

SEBASTIAN

Even though she's naked, in my bed, my cum dripping out of her cunt, it still feels like she's too far away. I've gone over two years without touching her, and now that she's here I won't ever let her go again, even if she hates me for it.

Since she ran from Florida and me, it doesn't feel like I've taken a full breath, not being able to see her, to control her, to own her was like being a prisoner in my own psyche. I hadn't realized how much I needed to have complete control of her until it was ripped away from me and now, I'll do whatever it takes to never have to be without her again.

Somewhere in the back of my head I thought she'd be happy to see me, that she'd fall in with my plans for us without question. The rocking, crying and panic attack I wasn't expecting. She's not the same sweet, quiet girl she was when she left GAA, she's different, but I don't want her any less. In some ways she's broken, in others she's stronger than ever and despite her reluctance, I want her more than I ever did before.

My arms are wrapped around her, probably a little tighter than they should be, but it feels as if I give her an inch of space, she'll hide herself behind her wall of hurt and I won't allow her to put distance between us. I don't regret taking her virginity, it was always mine, it has been since she was fifteen, but a part of me wishes it hadn't been in anger.

The moment she strode into the kitchen in nothing but tiny panties and a bra, the night was always going to end with my dick rammed inside of her, but when she took off her clothes and kissed Hunter, my sanity dissolved and I became nothing more than fury and fire.

Perhaps tomorrow when bruises mar her flawless skin, I'll feel some remorse, but I doubt it. I like the idea of marking her, I did it in high school to punish her and tell everyone that she was mine and now my dick has been in her cunt I want to plant a flag in her womb and fill it with my kid.

I've never not used a condom before now and it was fucking glorious. I don't care what she wants, now I've felt her wrapped around my cock, there's no way I'll ever put anything between us. Until now she's been on an oral birth control, but I took the supply of pills from her room when I was in there yesterday, and I won't be allowing her to renew it. Her medical records show it was only prescribed to stop her from getting pregnant, not for anything else so she'll be fine without it.

Her fingers touch my hand around her waist and I smile to myself, until she starts to try to lift my arm. "What are you doing?"

"I need to pee and then go back to my room."

"This is your room now."

Her sigh is weary, and there's a shakiness to the sound that warns she's close to tears again. "Does it matter that I like my room and don't particularly want to share with you?"

"No." I chuckle, I know this isn't a funny moment, but I can't help but be amused by her.

"If you're keeping me here, the least you can do is let me pee so I don't get a UTI, and then feed me, I really am hungry."

"If you hadn't decided to try to use Hunter as a pole, we'd have eaten the dinner Clay cooked for us by now."

Her own laughter rattles through her chest, as she chuckles lightly.

"You think it's funny?" I snarl.

"Tragically so."

Fury races through my body and my muscles tense so quickly I swear I feel them become so taut I'm worried they'll snap. "If my brothers ever see you naked again, I'll bend you over and fuck you right there in front of them. I'll fill your pussy, your ass and your mouth with my cum and I'll let them watch so they know that you're mine, that you'll only ever be mine."

"I hate you," she whispers.

"That's okay, hate me all you want, but it won't change anything. You'll still be mine, my girl, my cum slut, my little bird."

"I'm not a slut, I was a virgin until you stole it. And if I'm a bird, what does that make you? Am I the prey and you the predator? Now you've captured me and taken what you want, why don't you let me go?"

"I'm your cage, Starling. I was always going to catch you, but I'm keeping you too."

"I hate you," she says again.

"Didn't seem much like hate when you were coming all over my cock," I say arrogantly, reluctantly sliding my arm from around her waist and sitting up. "Go pee."

The moment she's free, she jumps up from the bed and rushes to the bathroom. I've already removed the lock from the door, just in case she tries to hide from me in there. I considered taking the door off completely, but I'm hoping she'll learn sooner rather than later to just accept that we're together.

There's a soft gasp of pain, then the sound of her peeing, and I can't help the smile that spreads across my lips. I wasn't gentle, she's going to be sore, but I can't seem to find it in me to regret that. She's sore because I pushed my dick through her hymen and claimed her pussy for the very first time. Like a caveman I want to beat my chest with pride. Her security detail were under strict instructions to make sure no guys got close enough to think they even had a chance at taking what's mine, but in the last two and a half years they haven't had to intervene even once.

She ran from her home, her mother, her friend and started over somewhere new, but apart from her relationship with her father she's barely made any attempt to get close to anyone else. I went to see her in Maine more than once, the last time I told her if she didn't come home I'd take away all the people who were important to her. I was angry, furious even, and I did what I promised I would.

Removing Courtney from her life had been almost too easy. She'd jumped ship at the first hint of popularity and a place on the arm of one of The Elite. I'd assumed Cassidy would be harder, sadly it hadn't been difficult to persuade her that offering Starling an ultimatum was the way to go. It just never occurred to me that Starling wouldn't back down.

I destroyed her relationship with her mother and it's my only regret in this whole sordid mess. Cassidy is still heartbroken and Starling is a shell of the sweet, caring girl I became obsessed with. Now that I have her back, I'll fix it, I'll give her back her mother and the guys can be her friends, I'll wrap her so tightly into our group that she'll never want to run again.

The bathroom door opens and Starling emerges wrapped in a towel, her perfect body hidden from my view. Jumping up from the bed, I prowl toward her. She flinches and backs away, but I snap my arm out and grab the towel, ripping it from around her as I drag her to me, pressing her naked breasts against my chest as I reach down and force my hands between her legs. "Did you try to clean all my cum out of you?" I growl.

"There was blood," she gasps, a fine tremor running across her skin, leaving goose bumps in its wake.

Pushing two fingers into her cunt, I smile at how slick she is. "Are you sore?"

"Yes," she grimaces.

"Good." Lifting her off the floor, I grip one of her thighs and wrap it around my waist, walking us backward until I can sit down on the edge of the bed.

"Sebastian," she argues.

"All my cum is going inside you, little bird. It doesn't matter how sore you are, or how many times I've taken you already that day. My little cum slut gets it all, so spread your legs and I'll be as gentle as I can. If you fight me, I'll make it hurt."

For a moment she does nothing, just stares at me, a mix of hurt, hate and desire flashing through her eyes. Then almost imperceptibly, she spreads her legs. It's barely an inch, but it doesn't matter, she's done what I told her to, she made a choice and now I'll reward her.

"Good girl," I coo, smoothing my palm up her spine, caressing her skin as my lips find her neck, kissing her gently. Lifting her, I use my free hand to guide my cock to her entrance, then I slowly lower her down onto my length.

"It hurts," she whimpers.

"I'll make the pain feel so good," I promise when I'm fully seated inside of her. Using my finger, I lift her chin and lock our gazes together. "I fucking love you, Starling, I have since the moment I laid eyes on you."

Swallowing visibly, I don't wait for her to respond, leaning forward and kissing her roughly. I expect her to fight, but instead she kisses me back, her tongue tentatively tangling with mine.

"Such a good girl," I praise, loving it when her cunt clenches around me. Using one arm, I start to lift her up and down my length slowly, pushing my other hand between us and finding her clit.

"Your cunt is gripping me so tight. You're so fucking perfect," I tell her as I work her clit, lifting her up and down until her arousal coats me and her hips roll on their own, her body learning how to take me. "Good girl," I praise again, and she moans softly. She likes it when I praise her. "You're such a beautiful little bird, you feel perfect, I love being inside of you, I love you."

The more I tell her how perfect she is, how good she is, the more her hips move, her fingers gripping me tightly as her breath turns ragged and she seeks out my lips with her own, kissing me.

"Come for me, baby, come on my cock and soak me in your sweetness."

"Sebastian," she gasps, pushing up with her hips and then dropping back down, riding my cock as she chases her own release, my name on her lips.

"That's it, don't stop," I encourage. Rubbing at her clit, I clench my teeth and deny my orgasm until her cunt clamps down on me so tightly, I think she might strangle my cock. She comes on a wailing cry, throwing her head back and gasping my name. I fuck her through her orgasm and follow her over the edge, filling her with my cum again, branding her from the inside out. "My good girl, so good, so perfect," I coo, kissing and sucking at her neck as she calms, her body melting into mine, her head falling exhausted to my shoulder.

We stay like that for a long time, my dick inside of her and my arms wrapped around her, while her head is rested against my shoulder. Her stomach growls and chuckling, I lift her off my dick and lower her onto shaking legs. "You okay?"

Silently she nods.

Pushing up from the bed, I look down between her thighs to where her legs are wet and my dick gets hard again. "Fuck, little bird, I want you again."

"Sebastian," she whimpers.

"Don't worry, as long as you behave I'll keep my dick in my pants. You need to be able to walk in the morning."

FOURTEEN

STARLING

My body clenches with fucked-up arousal at his words. I shouldn't want him to touch me and I certainly shouldn't want to have sex with him. My pussy is pulsing so hard it could probably register on the Richter scale, but even though I should, I don't hate the idea of him fucking me again.

Tiny tremors of pleasure are still vibrating through me and I'm not sure if I want to smile or cry, or just curl into a ball and rock like a mental patient. My body is confused and I don't know what to do or feel.

I'm naked, but I'm too exhausted to care, so I just stand while he opens a large wooden dresser and pulls something out. Crossing to the closet, he grabs a shirt and heads back over to me, shocking me when he sinks to his knees at my feet, holding out a familiar pair of panties. Dumbstruck, I stare down at him, until he taps one of my ankles.

"Lift your foot, baby."

I do as he asks and once both feet are through, he pulls my panties up my thighs.

"I need to go clean up."

"No you don't," he smiles, pulling the panties over my hips, then sliding his hand over the fabric between my thighs, pressing it into the mess that's between my legs. "I'm going to fuck you so often your panties will always be soaked, I'll make you so desperate for me that your pussy will cream just at the sound of my voice when I tell you it's time to be my good little bird and take my cock."

I shudder at his words. I don't know what it is about him calling me good girl, or good little bird that makes me want to part my thighs and offer myself up to him. I hate him, I really do, but when he says those words to me, his breath heating my skin, I forget all about loathing him and all I can feel is want.

Soft jersey fabric drops over my head, the shirt long enough to cover me to midthigh. Pushing my arms through the sleeve, I glance down at the Kingsacre crest on the front.

"You look good in my clothes, little bird. Let's go eat."

At some point he must have pulled on sweatpants, but his feet are bare and so is his torso. There's a tattoo over his heart that I hadn't noticed and as he waits for me to move, I take a closer look, then suck in a sharp gasp.

"When did you get that?" I ask, shakily pointing to the ornate cage with the beautiful bird inside that's inked into his flesh.

"After you left."

It's beautiful, the cage so gorgeous and real it feels like I could reach out and touch metal, but it's the heart-shaped lock that draws my eye. "Why?" I ask, reaching out a trembling finger and running it over the lock.

"Because I was always going to bring you back to me and I promised myself when I did, I'd lock your cage so you can never run from me again."

Closing my eyes, I squeeze them tightly and drag in a shuddering breath.

"Come on, baby, I need to feed you," he says, ushering me from the room with a hand on the base of my spine.

I let him guide me down the stairs, too shell-shocked to protest until he's sitting in a chair and placing me in his lap. It takes me a moment to realize the others are all in the room too, the plates still lying on the table.

Without saying anything, Clay gets up from his seat and bustles around the kitchen, pulling a pan from the oven and placing it in the center of the table before removing the foil from the top, revealing a steaming pile of pasta coated in what looks like tomato sauce and cheese.

My stomach lets out a loud growl and all of the guys chuckle.

"We worked up an appetite," Sebastian says loud enough

that I feel my cheeks heat and I want to melt into the floor where I don't have to see my stepbrother and his friends snickering and smirking.

"And now suddenly I'm not hungry anymore," I hiss, standing from Sebastian's lap, only to be dragged back down, his arm suddenly an iron bar keeping me in place.

"Sit. Eat," he orders.

His anger reignites the fear and anguish I'd managed to push to the back of my mind and I just want to curl into a ball and cry again. My emotions are all over the place. One minute I'm desolate, the next rebellious, the next horny, but this is what he's always done to me. He overwhelms me until I can't even trust my own instincts.

"Beer, water, soda, juice?" Evan asks, dragging my attention from my internal freak-out.

"Water's fine, thanks."

Getting up from the table, he crosses to the huge built-in drinks cooler and takes out four beers and a bottle of water, then hands them out, giving me mine first. His eyes seem to be raking over me, his brows furrowed lightly.

"Are you okay?" he asks cautiously.

"Well, I'm a prisoner, the guy I moved halfway across the country to get away from apparently wants to lock me in a cage and I just let him take my virginity because he worked me up so hard I forgot that I hate him," I word vomit, laughing hysterically.

Evan's eyes widen and he looks from me to Sebastian behind me.

"You're not a prisoner," Sebastian says quietly.

"Aren't I? Can I get up and leave, pack my stuff and go home?"

"No."

"Then let's call a spade a spade. I'm a prisoner."

The guys all stare at me, like they have no idea what to say, like me calling them on their bullshit is completely unexpected.

"Little bird," Sebastian growls in warning.

"There's no point sugarcoating it, is there? You wanted me here, so here I am. None of this was my choice and you know it's not what I want. But like you've already told me, what I want isn't important, this is all about you, because I had the audacity to not fall in for your plans for me when I was sixteen."

"Starling." His voice is icy, but really, what else can he do to me now that he hasn't already?

"What do you want from me, huh? I'm not going to pretend that I'm happy about this situation just to make you feel better about it. The four of you are holding me captive; I'm a prisoner and this is my cage," I say, throwing my arms in the air and scoffing.

Hunter, Evan and Clay all shuffle uncomfortably in their seats and I can't help the smirk that spreads across my lips. "What's up, boys? Not enjoying your role as jailer as much as you thought you would. At least Sebastian gets to fuck me. I'll still hate him for it, but he's getting his dick wet. What are you three getting? I don't hate you quite as much as I despise him, but make no mistake, I hate you all too."

"We¾" Clay starts.

"You what?" I interrupt him. "You what?"

"We don't want you to hate us," Hunter says quietly, his intense eyes boring into me.

"Awww, well that sucks for you then doesn't it," I say sardonically, ignoring the plate of food in front of me and reaching over to grab a roll from the bowl in the center of the table. Sebastian's hold on me loosens marginally, so I take the opportunity to stand up. "Now if you'll excuse me, I'll take my prisoner's ration of bread and water back upstairs to my cell." Turning to Sebastian, I smile widely. "Now am I in solitary confinement in my own bed, or am I being shackled to yours?"

"We'll be sleeping in our bed," he says tersely.

"Yes, warden, sir," I say, offering him a mock salute before turning and marching to the door, pausing and spinning around to face the guys. "All prisoners get exercise time in the yard, I run at five a.m. and as I'm not allowed out without one of my guards, I'll let you decide which one of you gets to accompany me."

My Bravado lasts until my fingers wrap around the door handle for my door and it doesn't open. As much as I can throw sass at the guys and pretend like I'm just full of anger when I'm around them, as soon as I'm alone, the sadness and fear take over. Stumbling into Sebastian's room, I rush into the bathroom and turn on all the faucets, letting the sound of running water cover the sound of me breaking down. Reality hits me like a wrecking ball and my legs collapse beneath me as I sink to the floor and sob into my hands for the life I should have had and the reality I'm being forced to live.

I'm not sure how long I cry for, long enough for the water to heat and for the room to fill with steam. Pushing the plug into place I let the tub fill with water and then climb into it fully clothed, ignoring the burning sensation as the water scalds my skin. When the stinging fades, my body goes numb and I lean my head back into the water and close my eyes, steadying my breathing as I listen to the sound of the water moving around me.

I feel it the moment he opens the door and steps into the bathroom, but I don't open my eyes, or make any attempt to speak to him. After a moment, he leaves again and I exhale a breath I hadn't known I was holding. When the water goes cold, I get out, shrugging his sopping-wet shirt and my panties to the floor before wrapping myself in a fluffy towel.

His frenetic energy pulses between us when I step into the room, but I don't speak and neither does he. I can feel his gaze following me around as I open the closet and take out another of his shirts, pulling it on.

My stomach's empty, but I ignore it, lifting the edge of his rumpled sheet and climbing into his bed. Rolling to my side I turn my back on him, but he doesn't speak as he turns out the light, climbs in behind me and curls an arm around my waist.

I'm not sure what time it is when I blink awake, it's dark out, but my body clock is so out of whack it could be midnight or five in the morning. There's heat at my back. Sebastian. Everything comes back to me in a rush. This is his bed, I'm his captive and there's nothing I can do about it.

His hand is between my thighs, fingers slowly stroking me. I could fight, but what's the point? I'm not entirely sure he'd stop if I really didn't want his touch, but the truth is as much as I wish I did, I don't hate the way it feels when he makes me come.

That's always been the most confusing thing about how I feel when I'm around him. I'm scared of him, of the way he feels, of the way he takes over and disregards my wants, but the moment he touches me, or kisses me I'm lost to him. From the very first time that he manipulated me into stripping naked for him in my bedroom, my body has reacted to him, like he's my very own brand of narcotic.

In real life I despise him, but in the quiet moments, when it's just us, I can't deny the way he disarms me. Sure fingers part my folds and he slides two into me, not moving, just filling me.

"Spread your legs." His voice is rough with sleep, low and gruff.

Pushing my legs apart I bite down on my lower lip with my teeth, determined to stay quiet. I'll allow him to touch me, allow him to give me pleasure, but I'll be damned if I let him see me enjoy it. He doesn't deserve it and I'm ashamed to let him know how much I like the way he plays with my body.

"Good girl, you're so wet. Even though your cunt is swollen from my cock it's still dripping for me."

I swallow back my moan and he continues his ministrations, not moving the fingers that are buried inside of me as his other hand finds my clit, circling it and pinching, gradually increasing the pressure until my hips are moving of their own accord, needing more.

"Roll onto your stomach, knees up beneath you."

He doesn't remove his fingers as I move, keeping the pressure on my clit until I'm face down on the bed, my knees curled up beneath me, my ass and pussy in the air.

"Such a pretty little cunt, so tight and hot. Are you sore? Does it hurt?"

Clasping my hand across my mouth, I stifle my moans, not making a sound.

"Huh, you've got nothing to say? You had no problem talking earlier. How about we play a little game instead? Use my fingers, fuck them like you would my dick, if you can stay quiet you can sleep in your own room for the rest of the night, if not then you'll ride my dick until you're screaming my name loud enough for the entire house to hear, then we're going to a party."

Even knowing that playing with Sebastian is a fool's errand, I can't help myself. His fingers are inside me and no matter how much I pretend otherwise, it feels good and my body is screaming at me to move, to give myself the friction I need.

Rolling my hips experimentally, my sex moves up and down his fingers and a pulse of tingling sensation sparks to life at my core. He doesn't move, and I roll my hips again, biting on my bottom lip to stay quiet.

"Don't stop, little bird, fuck my hand like getting off would be the key to your freedom," he growls angrily. "My cock's bigger than two fingers so maybe you need a third."

My pussy stretches painfully as he pushes a third huge finger inside of me. It hurts, the burning sensation blocking out the pleasure I'd been feeling before. Maybe that would be good, if it hurt I could stay quiet and win. Half a night in my own bed might not be such a huge victory, but he'd hate it and that would make it all the sweeter.

Starting slowly, I push back onto him, forcing his digits in deeper, then rolling forward, allowing them to slide almost all the way out, before pushing back again. Impaling myself deep I embrace the pain, taking it in and using it to patch up the holes the pleasure has caused in my mental walls.

"Harder," he demands and I comply, moving faster as the pain slowly changes, morphing into an unrecognizable burn that hurts in the best way possible. My hips move of their own accord, my body's instincts taking over, pushing away logic and rational thought and replacing it with primal need.

By the time the first moan of bliss slips from my lips, all thoughts of winning have dissolved from my head. Me, him, the game, none of it matters when all I need is to come, to splinter and claim the pleasure my body is chasing. Just as the torrent of sensation is about to topple, his fingers are ripped from me and my pussy is empty and pulsing.

"No," I cry.

Seconds later his hands are beneath me, lifting me, holding me over him, positioning me. He impales me onto his cock in one devastating move. I'm more full than I've ever been in my life. My legs are either side of his, my pussy stretched wide around his girth and it feels like the head of his cock is battering my stomach every time he roughly lifts me up, then slams me back down onto him.

My first orgasm takes me by surprise, exploding with no warning and making me clamp down so hard on Sebastian's cock he actually growls.

"Fuck, little bird, your cunt is like a vise, but you didn't scream my name." His thumb finds my clit and within moments I'm coming again. This time, I do scream, gasping his name when he leans up and bites my nipple, sending an aftershock of bliss rolling through my muscles.

"That's it, milk my dick, take every drop of my cum."

My core is still fluttering when I'm lifted and spun around like I weigh less than a rag doll, his dick is inches from my face, shiny and wet with a mixture of both of us.

"Suck me clean, little bird," he demands, sliding his fingers into me again.

I pause, and his palm lands on my ass, spreading my cheeks. "It's either your mouth or your ass, I'll let you choose."

My ass tightens on instinct at his threat and I part my lips and slowly suck him into my mouth.

"Fuck, little bird, fuck your mouth feels amazing."

I brace for the unpleasant taste, but the salty tang isn't as disgusting as I was expecting and there's a sweetness that I can only assume is me? Licking and sucking, I clean all of our arousal from him, enjoying the feeling of being in control, until his hand tangles in my hair and he pulls me off him. "Enough, my dick needs a minute to recover," he chuckles.

"What time is it?" I ask, wiggling and trying to move from my awkward position.

"Almost midnight."

"You want to go to a party now?"

His hold on my hair tightens, dragging my head back. "Yes, get up, there's a dress for you in the closet."

"I'm tired."

"You lost, get your ass up before I fuck you again."

Dragging my sore, aching body from the bed, I pad into the bathroom and turn on the shower, but his arm snakes around me turning the water off. "I need to shower."

"No you don't, I want everyone to smell me on you. To know you're owned and freshly fucked."

"You're an asshole, I'm not going anywhere smelling like stale sex and self-hatred."

His hand tangles in my hair and he yanks my head back so hard a shriek of pain startles from my lips. "You'll go where I tell you to go, wear what I tell you to wear and do whatever the fuck I tell you to do."

"Prisoner 101," I nod. "And they say kids don't learn anything in college these days."

His laugh is low and rough against my ear. "Cute. Now go get dressed."

He loosens his hold on my hair enough for me to turn and leave the bathroom. My flight instinct has me eyeing the door, but I know running right now isn't my path to freedom, so instead I make my way to the closet and open the door. The space is huge and one side is filled with men's clothes, the other with women's. Tags are still hanging from the array of dresses, pants, shirts and other stuff. It's more clothes than I currently own, more clothes than I'll ever need.

"This one," Sebastian says, stepping past me and into the vast space, plucking a gold dress from the rod and handing it to me.

"I can't wear this."

"Why?"

"Because you need tits and ass for a dress like this, I don't have either."

"I agree you need to gain some weight, but try it on for me anyway."

I'm naked, but I don't bother putting on underwear and

instead just pull the dress over my head. It falls like a potato sack to midthigh, shapeless and awful.

"Take it off," he orders.

Pushing the straps from my shoulders, the dress falls to my feet and I step out of it, bending down to pick it up.

"Leave it," he orders, picking the dress up and throwing it into the corner.

"That's a thousand-dollar dress," I gasp.

"Forget the dress. Pick something to wear."

"If I have to go to this party, I'd rather wear my own clothes."

"All you own is denim shorts and athletic wear," he says derisively. "Pick something appropriate."

"There's nothing wrong with my clothes," I hiss through gritted teeth.

"When you don't want male attention, I completely agree. But you're mine and I just got you back, I want the entire school to see you and know who you belong to. So either pick something, or you can try on everything in here until I find something I like."

Narrowing my eyes, I glare at him, but instead of backing down he just smiles. Shaking my head I step forward and start to root through the clothes, finding a pair of ripped jeans and pulling them on. They're so tight they might as well be painted on, but they give me the illusion of curves that I can't help admiring in the floor-length mirror. Spotting a pretty satin bralette in a deep-burgundy-red color, I free it from the hanger and pull it over my head, positioning it to cover my modest tits. I slide my feet into black leather pumps that I don't need to see the red sole to know are absurdly expensive and likely impossible to walk in.

"Fuck, little bird, I wanted to show you off, but now I'm not sure I want to share you," he rasps, moving behind me and wrapping his arm around my waist, his face appearing in the reflection of the mirror.

Fisting my hair, he drags it to one side and presses a kiss to the back of my neck. He softly nuzzles for a moment until his teeth clamp down and pain shoots through me as he marks me the same way he did when we were in high school.

"Sebastian," I cry, fighting to free myself when his arm bands around my waist, keeping me in place as he brands my skin.

"Perfect," he whispers when he finally releases me, admiring his work. "Put your hair up, I want to be able to see my mark on you."

Thirty minutes later, Sebastian half guides me, half drags me through the gates and into a waiting golf cart. I'm not sure where they were being kept but apparently, they belong to the house. Hunter, Evan and Clay keep eyeing me warily, but I have no interest in speaking to them, so I keep my gaze fixed on the passing trees and pointedly ignore all of their attempts to bring me into their conversation.

The sound of the party hits us ten minutes before we actually reach the woods where it's being held. Instead of having to hike down the path, Hunter drives the cart to the edge of the crowd and parks in a spot that almost seems to have been kept vacant just for them. Sebastian halts me when I try to climb out. "You're with one of us at all times, you don't take drinks from anyone else."

"Whatever," I say childishly, but I just don't care anymore.

"I'm fucking serious, Starling, if you try to run, I'll find you and when I do, I'll lock you down so fucking tight what you're feeling right now will seem like flying."

"Yeah, yeah. I promise not to try and escape tonight, warden. I'll be a good little inmate, Scout's honor."

He scowls at my tone, but really, what else can he do to me that he hasn't already done? Taking my hand tightly in his, he climbs out of the cart first, then pulls me out, dragging me into his side and wrapping a hand firmly around the back of my neck. It's a proprietary move and I hate that I like it, almost as much as I loathe it.

"What do you want to drink?" Evan asks me.

Ignoring him, I force my face into a bored expression and glance at the party raging around us.

"Starling, can we please just try to be friends?" Clay asks.

Turning my attention back to the three men standing in front of me, I blink slowly. "No."

"This is so fucked up," Hunter growls angrily.

"She'll come around," Sebastian says, his grip on me tightening.

I laugh dryly and shake my head. "Give me one good reason why I'd want to be friends with any of you after you've done this to me?"

"Because we're all you've got," Clay murmurs quietly.

I laugh again, the sound bitter and angry. "I have plenty of practice at being alone, I'd rather have no one than any of you."

The three of them look... hurt? But why? It's not like we've ever been close, I'd never even spoken to any of them before Sebastian bulldozed my life and destroyed it.

Evan scowls, then turns and marches away. "This is so fucked."

Pulling my cell from my pocket, I tap at the screen and open up the book I started reading on the plane.

"What are you doing?" Sebastian demands.

"Reading."

"We're at a party."

"So?"

"So, you don't fucking read at your first college party. Tell me what you want to do. Drink? Dance?"

"You wanted me here, so here I am. You can force me to be somewhere, but you can't force me to enjoy it."

"You're in college, you should be ten shots in, making friends with perky blondes or some shit."

"You want me to make friends," I scoff. "Why? So you can use them to punish me when I piss you off? Yeah, I learned my lesson, I'm good. I'm not going to run, so go do what you need to do and I'll read my book, you can come find me when you're ready to go."

His brow furrows and he looks genuinely baffled by me, like he has no idea what to do.

"Here," Evan says, returning with five bottles of beer in his hands.

"I'm good," I say, not lifting my gaze from my cell.

"You want something else? I'm pretty sure they had wine coolers and some tequila."

"Nope," I pop the *p* sound.

"Take the damn beer," Sebastian snarls.

Reaching out, I take the bottle and immediately tip it, letting the contents fall to the ground beside me. "Thanks, that was delicious," I deadpan.

"Fucking hell," Sebastian curses. "Come on, let's go, I want to make sure everyone sees her with me."

"Will I get to leave quicker if I ask people to form a circle and then just bend over? You can fuck me, shouting mine, mine, mine, then everyone will know," I snark.

"Shut the fuck up, Starling."

Miming zipping my lips, I focus my attention back on my cell and start to read, or at least I pretend to read while Sebastian guides me with his tight territorial grip on the back of my neck.

People stop us every few steps, greeting the guys like they're the prodigal sons, returned to save the world. Sebastian introduces me to each person, but I don't bother to engage with more than a tip of my chin, or a distracted "Hey" before I focus my attention back to my cell.

I know people are wondering who I am and why Sebastian is giving me so much attention, when I'm making it obvious I don't want to be at the party or with these boys, but just like in high school, no one questions them. The guys bring me more drinks, but I tip them all away without taking a sip and in the end, they give up, staring at me with sad eyes and forlorn expressions.

All of a sudden, Sebastian's grip on me loosens as a girl barrels into him, throwing her arms around his neck and kissing him passionately. "Bastian, baby, I missed you, I missed all you guys," Courtney says, in a breathy, lusty tone that makes me snort derisively.

"Courtney," Sebastian says coolly, removing the limpet from his body and setting her down a few steps from us, before reaching for me and wrapping his palm back possessively around my nape.

"Starling, I'm surprised to see you here," Court says tersely.

"Hmmm," I agree noncommittally.

"Boys, you should come back to Harrington House with me, we could have fun, like we used to."

"We're good," Hunter tells her dismissively.

Courtney scowls, then her gaze swings back to me. "It didn't take you long to crawl back, you know they like to share, don't you? Did you offer to whore yourself out for all of them?

They won't keep you, you were only ever a toy, they'll use you, then discard you."

"Here's hoping," I say, lifting my head and smiling widely.

"Starling," Sebastian warns.

"What? You can parade me around and pretend we're all happy or what the fuck ever, and strangers might believe it, but she knows the truth. She knows I left my mom, my home and my life and ran halfway across the country just to get away from you. There's no point pretending with her. Court wants you, she'd make perfect arm candy. You could train her to be the perfect little robot you want and when you get fed up, you can pass her along to one of the others. I'm happy to step aside and leave you two lovebirds to it, in fact, I'll just go." I try to step away, but Sebastian snaps his hand out and catches my wrist, manacling it in his grip, as the others close in around us, forming a human cage around me.

"Courtney," Evan sneers. "Go away."

"Are you joking? Don't tell me you want her too?"

"She's my friend and my stepsister."

"She hates you," her gaze travels over all four boys. "All of you, she always has. I thought she was just playing hard to get back in high school, but you really don't want anything to do with them, do you?" she laughs gleefully.

"No, I don't."

"Oh, this is brilliant. The great Sebastian Lockwood can't get the girl he wants to want him back."

"Fuck off, Courtney," Sebastian warns.

"Oh I'm going, for now. But when she runs again, you'll need to come begging on your knees to get me back," she laughs. "Starling, this has been fun. I was going to threaten you again, but I don't need to warn you away from him, you don't want him anyway. Bye, babe, have a good night."

"Bye, Court," I smirk, thoroughly amused.

"She threatened you?" Clay demands.

"We had a grand reunion yesterday where she advised me she'd had you all and that her and Sebastian were practically engaged and I shouldn't bother trying to get his attention," I giggle.

Strong hands grab me and I'm turned into Sebastian's chest. Tipping my chin back he forces me to look at him. "I never fucked her."

"I don't care if you did," I shrug.

FIFTEEN

SEBASTIAN

"I don't care if you did."

Her eyes are earnest and almost laughing at me and I fight the urge to haul her into the trees and fuck her until she's screaming my name loud enough for everyone at the party to hear. She looks beautiful, but the emptiness in her gaze pisses me off. She should care if I fucked her best friend. She should be angry, furious even, but instead she's impassive, disinterested.

Worry that I really did break her flows through me. It wasn't my intention. I just wanted to punish her, to make her come back to me, to make her confess what I knew... that she wanted me as much as I wanted her. But I think I went too far. All those years ago when I told her I'd take everyone important from her, I never meant it. But when she didn't come back, when she refused to fall in line, I was too far gone, too heartbroken that she would run from me that I acted harshly.

The friend was always going to have to go, even knowing I was with Starling, Courtney propositioned me within hours of me first publicly claiming her friend. I told the guys to play with her a little while I cemented things with my little bird, but it turns out the rich girl, who befriended the poor girl, was just a shark, setting things up to make her friend the bait when she needed it. She confessed to Evan one time that she'd seen the way I watched Starling right from the start, seen the way the others followed her and monitored her and then just bided her time, knowing it was only a matter of waiting until I staked my claim.

"Can we go?" Starling asks, bored.

"No."

Rolling her eyes, she scowls. "Fine, can we at least sit, these shoes are killing me."

I glance to Hunter, who nods, leading a path through the throngs of excited college kids to a small bonfire, with lawn chairs and huge wooden benches carved out of logs set around it. Sitting down, I pull Starling into my lap, while the guys take chairs on either side of us. Several familiar faces fill the chairs opposite and suddenly, instead of it being a party, it's a powwow for the young, rich and powerful.

Instead of keg stands and tequila shots, the talk moves to alliances, engagements and business deals and I love it. Being here, being revered by some of the most powerful families in America with Starling on my lap, is everything I've ever wanted. Of course, when we leave Kingsacre we'll change Solo cups and bonfires for boardrooms and top-shelf whiskey, but regardless of the location, my friends and I will still be the ones others seek out for approval.

I was hoping my little bird would have a drink tonight, I ache to see her relaxed and enjoying herself, but no matter what we bring her, she just pours it away. Even in my lap, she's still tense, poised to go, to run from me, and I've no doubt tomorrow she'll have bruises from how tight my grip is on her.

Letting her go isn't an option, so I need to fix what I broke. I need to make her fall in love with me, to make her see that I can make her happy. The guys are all pissed at me too, Starling is so angry at all of us, but I don't think they expected her hatred and it's eating at them, especially Evan. She's his stepsister and I know he genuinely wants a relationship with her.

"Let's go," I say, lifting her from my lap and onto her feet, holding her steady with my hands around her waist. Draping my arm across her shoulders, I press a kiss to the side of her neck as I follow Clay through the crowds and back to the cart that's parked in our spot. I might not have been at Kingsacre for the last couple of years, but the others were, and I visited my brothers enough that people already knew who I was before I officially transferred. Our status on campus is why we have a parking spot mere feet from the party, and why our cart is untouched and there's a clear path out without us having to wait for others to move. Lifting Starling onto the seat, I climb in next to her, placing a restraining hand on her thigh as Evan drives us back to the house. I'm tense until the huge metal gates close behind us and I know she's contained, unable to run from me.

It's nearly three a.m., but instead of heading upstairs I follow the guys to the kitchen, towing Starling along with me.

"I'm tired, I'm going to sleep," she says, trying to tug her hand free of my grip.

"You need to eat first," Hunter says quietly. "We've been here two days and all you've eaten is half a sandwich and a dry roll, you're practically wasting away anyway."

"I'm not hungry and how do you know what I'm eating, are you all following me?"

"There's always eyes on you," I tell her, not flinching at the accusing glare she darts in my direction.

"Please, Starling, just eat something. I'll make whatever you want," Hunter begs.

"I need to sleep," she argues.

"Eat and then you can sleep, little bird," I tell her.

"What do you fancy? Burgers, sandwiches, waffles, pancakes, French toast," he offers a little desperately.

"Prisoners don't normally get a choice," she snaps.

"You're not a prisoner," I snarl.

Her scoff is derisive and dark. "I've been a prisoner since the day you declared I was yours. You tried to wrap it up in a

267

pretty girlfriend bow, but if you take all the glitz away, I'm still here against my will. Why don't you just tell me what I've got to eat and I'll eat it, so I can go and sleep."

Hunter's shoulders slump and he moves silently around the kitchen, pulling together the ingredients for a sandwich as we all silently watch. He slides it in front of Starling and she picks it up and slowly eats, opening the bottle of water he places in front of her and drinking, until both the plate and bottle are empty.

"Can I go to bed now?" she asks.

I nod and she kicks off her shoes, bends to pick them up and leaves. I listen as she climbs the stairs, not relaxing until my cell beeps to notify me that my bedroom door has been opened.

"This is so fucked up," Clay growls.

"You need to let her go, this isn't going to work, she fucking hates you, all of us," Evan says sadly. "She's my sister, man, and she really fucking hates me. I don't... I've never had a sibling before, I don't..." he trails off, his expression defeated.

"Was she like this in Maine? This angry? What about friends? Is there anyone we could bring here, to make this easier for her?" Hunter asks.

"She didn't make any friends, it was just her and her dad. We can't bring him here, he hates me, she told him everything," I admit.

"She must have some friends, there must be someone," Clay says.

"According to the guards I had in the school, she didn't.

She went to school, did her work, but she was a loner, never engaged, never went out, never really spoke to anyone unless she absolutely had to."

"You need to let her go, get her a place at the school she wanted to go to in Maine," Evan tells me.

"No," I snarl. "She's mine."

Shoving back his chair and jumping to his feet, Evan parts his lips, ready to yell at me, but Hunter speaks first. "She's broken, we broke her. This girl isn't the same Starling we knew, this isn't the same Starling you fell in love with."

"Then we fix her," I shout.

"You need to give her space," Clay suggests.

"She'll run, she's planning her escape already, her eyes are always searching for a chance to get away. You can't stop her from going home for the holidays and once she leaves, unless you do something to fix this, she won't come back," Evan says.

"So we don't let her go," I snap. "We take her home to Green Acres for the holidays, she needs to fix things with Cassidy anyway."

"I'm not sure that's fixable," Evan sighs. "Starling only takes Cassidy's calls on her birthday and Christmas, the rest of the time she just doesn't answer. Cass cries so hard every time it goes to voice mail that my dad told her to stop calling. We destroyed their relationship and I think forcing Starling to come home will only make things worse."

"We really are the fucking monsters she thinks we are,"

Hunter laughs darkly. "We have until winter break to fix this, if we haven't, then I'll drive her to the airport myself and pay for her tuition for her new school. We ruined this girl, we did this and if we can't fix it, then none of us deserve to have her in our lives."

When Hunter storms from the room, I stay stuck in my seat, trying to process what he just said. He's right, this is all our fault, but I know I can't and won't give her up, even if I'll never deserve her. One by one, Evan then Clay leave, until it's just me sitting alone in the kitchen, considering my sins and what I can do to atone for them. By the time I push the door open to my bedroom and step inside I have a plan in my mind, a way to make her want me, to make her need me the same way I need her.

As I strip out of my clothes and climb into the bed beside her, I vow to fix this, one way or another, there's no other option.

SIXTEEN

STARLING

My eyes open a few minutes before my alarm goes off and I groan, stretching my arms and legs as sleep dissolves from my muscles, only the pain of yesterday's activities pulsing between my thighs. I can feel the heat of Sebastian's body behind me and I freeze, hoping not to wake him as I roll toward the edge of the bed.

"Where are you going?" he asks sleepily.

"For a run."

"No."

"Yes."

"It's too early, run later."

"I run at five."

"Not anymore you don't." he growls tiredly, wrapping one

arm around my waist and the other in my hair as he drags my head backward and presses his lips against mine.

Yanking my head away from him, I wince as a chunk of hair comes free, wiggling away and into a sitting position. "I need to run, Sebastian," I gasp, feeling panic start to rise into my throat.

"Hey, what the fuck? What's the matter?" he asks, sitting up in bed and staring at me, wide eyed.

"I. Need. To. Run," I say through panic-laden breaths. "It keeps me sane. I need to run."

"Calm down. You're not going on your own, you don't leave this fucking house without one of us. How far do you go? You sort of wandered last time."

"You followed me?" I pant, my chest feeling tight, my vision dimming at the sides.

"Of course I did, you got up in the middle of the night, it's fucking dangerous."

My eyes feel too large for my head, my skin tight. He's not going to let me go, I'm a prisoner, but even those in jail get to roam and have some exercise. I'm on the verge of another panic attack, I've never had two so close together, but this is what being around him does to me. My mind descends into a mental tailspin and there's nothing I can do but brace for impact and hope I'm still me on the other side.

"Fuck. Little bird, stop, just fucking breathe, I'll run with you, but if you try to leave campus there will be consequences."

Nodding rapidly, I scramble off the bed as he reaches for

me. His brow furrows as if he's surprised that I wouldn't want to be touched by him when I'm feeling this overwhelmed and vulnerable. My dad would comfort me, he'd talk me off this ledge I'm balanced precariously on, but he isn't here and Sebastian is the cause of my panic, not the resolution.

Ignoring the fact that I'm naked except for one of his shirts, I stand up and try to expand my lungs and pull in as much air as I can. Closing my eyes, I try to forget where I am and who I'm with and picture myself in my room at my dad's place. I pretend the silence is the peace of the calm existence we lived and gradually it works. When I open my eyes I'm not in the bedroom anymore, I'm in the bathroom, backed up against a cool tile wall, my hands covering my ears.

Blinking, I cough to clear my dry throat. I'm not sure how I got in here, if I walked myself, or if Sebastian carried me in here. My throat is sore and my chest is still tight, but I can breathe and the blind panic has faded to a pulsing undertone of anxiety that I know won't go away anytime soon. My hands are shaking as I reach in and turn on the shower, not waiting for it to warm before I step beneath the frosty-feeling water. The cold shocks me, but I embrace it, stripping off his shirt and ducking my hair beneath the frozen stream, dousing myself before it becomes lukewarm. I turn the water off before it gets hot and jump out of the shower, rubbing my goose bump–coated body with a towel.

When I finally lift my head, I find Sebastian standing in the doorway watching me. "Are you okay?"

Silently I nod.

He nods back, but all of the smugness has gone from his expression and in its place is a cold vacantness that terrifies me. He hated that I flinched from his touch, even back in high school, so it must be driving him crazy that I won't let him comfort me when I freak out now. Without a word he moves to the dresser and opens a drawer, pulling out panties, running shorts and a sports bra and tossing them toward me. Opening a second drawer, he pulls out clothes for himself and we dress in silence.

"My sneakers and AirPods are in my room."

"It's open, we'll move the rest of your stuff into our room once we get back."

"I'd rather keep my things in my room."

"Not your choice, I thought you understood that."

Because I'm your prisoner, I say inside my head, but I manage to keep my expression clear as I run up the stairs to my room and grab my sneakers, armband and AirPods. I could barricade myself inside and refuse to leave, but I really do need to run, so instead I descend the stairs and then calmly make my way out of the front door, hating that the electric gates open the moment they sense our presence.

The urge to run is almost overwhelming. If I had a car, if I could outrun him, if there was a chance I'd escape, I'd bolt and never stop running until I was free of him. But here and now there's nowhere to go, at least not before he caught me.

Pushing my buds into my ears, I do my usual stretches, set my run tracker, turn up my mellow running playlist and go. I don't bother to look behind me, I know he's following, I can feel the intensity of his presence but I refuse to let him infiltrate my happy place, so I ignore him and just run. After a while, the routine of putting one foot in front of the other settles into place and I lengthen my stride, enjoying the freedom of living entirely in my head from one step to the next.

I don't turn toward the main gates this time, instead I circle around the main building again, looping the entire smattering of brick-built buildings as I go. Running the same loop another three times, I reluctantly turn back toward the house, my lungs warm, my legs comfortably sore. Ignoring the vending machines I stopped at yesterday I continue straight on to the house, feeling a resigned sense of hatred for the place the moment it comes into view.

Sebastian passes me for the first time when we reach the gates, using his key card to unlock it, then motioning for me to walk through. My feet stop on the threshold, and I glance up at the house, my prison. I don't want to willingly incarcerate myself again, but I'm not sure there's another choice, at least not for the minute. I will get away from here and him, but I can't be impulsive, I need to be calm, make a plan, know where I'm going and how I'll get him to leave me alone for good the next time I run.

Stepping through the gate, I march up to the front door

and straight into the house, not pausing as I make my way to the kitchen and pull a bottle of water from the refrigerator. I suppose technically, it's not mine to drink, but I figure the least the assholes I'm living with can do is buy drinks and snacks, I am their prisoner after all.

Drinking thirstily, I gulp down the cold liquid between pants. I ran a little over ten miles and my muscles are fatigued in the way that makes me smile even though I'm coated in sweat and panting.

One of my buds is pulled from my ear and I startle, spinning around to glare at Sebastian. "Hey."

"You run ten miles every morning?"

"Sometimes at night too."

"You never used to run."

"I never did a lot of things until you invaded my life."

"Why are you pretending that I was such a fucking monster?" he demands.

Tipping my head back, I close my eyes and inhale, attempting to calm my flaring anger. "You can keep me here, you can control my life again, you can force me to sleep in your bed and have sex with you, but you don't get to know what's going on in here." I tap at my temple.

His hand wraps around my neck, gripping me tightly as he backs me against the refrigerator, the glass cold against my heated skin. My heart is racing and it's not through fear, or at least it's not all fear that's making my skin tremble and my nipples pebble. Firm lips find mine and he plunders my mouth, not touching me anywhere else other than the palm around my throat and his lips on mine.

I should fight, knee him in the balls or claw at his hold around my throat, but instead I melt into him, kissing him back as I tangle my fingers in his shirt and wrap my legs around his hips, grinding my sore pussy against his hard dick.

A moan of protest falls from my lips when he pulls away, ending the kiss.

"Looks like I'm forcing you, doesn't it, little bird? It's time to stop pretending I'm the bad guy when you want me as much as I do you."

"Enjoying sex isn't the same as wanting you," I rasp.

"You'll learn to love me the way I love you, and if I have to do that through orgasms, well that works for me. You're mine and I'll make you love me, make you want me, make you need me. Go shower and get ready for class, I'm not in until later so Clay's going to take you."

"I'm not a child, I don't need a fucking babysitter."

"Look me in the eye and tell me you won't run if I let you go out on your own."

Lifting my gaze, I try to make myself seem honest and calm, but the truth is we both know I'd be gone the moment I got a chance, and he's smiling before I've even opened my mouth.

"Exactly, you're a flight risk, Starling, so it's either a babysitter or you stay here."

"I hate you," I snarl, pushing him away from me.

His smile is sinister. "I'm okay with that."

"I need my stuff from my room."

"The door's open, but I want you to wear some of the things I bought you."

"I told you most of that won't fit, you bought clothes for someone who looks like Courtney, not for me," I snap. "I'll let her know you got her some gifts, I'm sure she'll be more than grateful."

"We'll go shopping after class and you can pick things that will fit your body until you put on some weight. I plan to make sure you eat properly from now on."

Rolling my eyes childishly, I stomp up the stairs and into my turret. Yesterday morning I was so grateful for the peaceful space, but now all the joy has been sucked out of the room. Turning on my shower, I wash and then wrap myself in a towel and open my closet door. It's empty, entirely empty, all of my meager belongings stripped from the rod and removed while I showered.

Anger barrels through me and I drop my towel to the floor and descend the stairs completely naked, the multitude of bruises Sebastian's rough treatment has given me clearly on display. Throwing open the door to his room, I find him sitting on the edge of the bed, wearing only a pair of black boxer briefs, his cock hard and straining at the fabric.

"Come here, little bird."

"No, I need to get ready for class," I protest, trying to step around him. Snapping his hand out, he grabs my wrist as I pass and hauls me back to him.

"Get on your knees."

I shake my head. "No."

"Get on your fucking knees, your cunt must be sore, but I'll fuck it if you force me to. I told you all my cum was for you, so get on your fucking knees and open your mouth."

My shocked gasp is so loud it's almost funny. "You can't do this…" I whisper.

"Who's going to stop me," he taunts. "Now get on your knees, I want to feel your lips around my dick."

A shudder ripples through me as I slowly sink to my knees between his legs. I expect him to stay seated, but instead he stands, his cock level with my face.

"Take my cock out."

My fingers shake as I reach out and push his boxers over his hips until his hard dick bobs free, precum dripping from the tip.

"Lick the head," he orders.

Tentatively, I push out my tongue and lick over the swollen head, the taste of the clear salty liquid filling my mouth. I feel a tear leak from my eye and roll down my cheek. He catches it with his thumb, bringing it to his lips and sucking it into his mouth.

Soft fingers stroke over my hair as he caresses me. "Eyes on me, little bird, I want to watch. Look how hard I am. It's all for you, my dick's only ever gotten hard for you since the moment I saw you."

"Sebastian," I whisper, but I'm not sure what I want. Most of me wants to get up, to run away and hide, but a small part of me wants to lick him, to tease him and taste him and make him come. I want to make him feel as out of control as he makes me, I want to take back some of the power he's wielding over me.

"Get to it, little bird, show me how much you want my dick. I want to feel the back of your throat, show me how much of a good girl you can be."

More tears fall from my eyes and I close them, hiding from him in the only way I can.

"Open your eyes, no hiding," he demands as if he can read my thoughts.

Leaning forward, I part my lips, my eyes locked on him as I engulf the head with my mouth. His skin is warm, almost hot, and a wave of something that feels a lot like desire washes over me.

"Jesus fuck, your mouth feels amazing," he rasps, his fingers tightening in my hair until pain laces across my scalp.

I suck on the head until his hips start to move, pushing his length farther into my mouth. "That's it, little bird, all the way in, show me how good a cock sucker you can be. I'm going to take your mouth every fucking day, so you need to learn how to get me off."

Trying to move, I start to withdraw my mouth, letting his dick slide out, but he doesn't allow it, holding my head firmly in place and pushing his cock down my throat until I gag. I slap at his legs, but he doesn't release me. His fingers tangled in my hair, he holds me in place, my nose pressed against his groin for a long second, until eventually he lets me pull back and I gasp for air the moment my throat isn't full of his dick.

I've barely got my breath before he's pushing back into my throat again, only this time he doesn't hold me there, allowing me to set the pace and depth as he groans words of encouragement.

"Fuck, little bird, that's good, so fucking good."

"Don't stop, god, don't fucking stop."

By the time my jaw begins to ache, I'm enjoying myself, it's not the act necessarily, but the power I feel as I'm doing it. His dick is in my mouth, one clamp of my teeth and I could literally bite his cock in half. Right now he's at my mercy, his pleasure completely dependent on me.

"I'm coming, baby, swallow it all, don't lose any of it," he growls animalistically, holding my hair tightly and keeping me in place as he comes in my mouth in thick spurts that hit the back of my throat, forcing me to swallow instinctively.

When his hips stop jerking and his cock starts to soften, he drags my head away and smiles down at me with a look of… awe on his face? Grabbing me beneath my arms, he pulls me from the floor, holding me to his chest as he kisses me almost reverently. I know I'm not the first person to suck his cock, but for whatever reason, he seems ecstatically happy with me right now.

"Fuck, little bird, you're perfect, so fucking perfect. I love you so damn much," he praises, before his lips find mine and he kisses me again, not caring that his cum was in my mouth only moments ago.

I melt into his embrace, then remind myself that I'm his prisoner and force myself to pull away and stiffen. "I have class."

"You could stay home," he cajoles, his smile charming and compelling.

"It's the first day."

"Fine," he sighs dramatically, flinging himself down onto the bed to watch me get dressed.

My meager belongings have been added to the row of new clothes in the closet, looking shabby and cheap beside the expensive designer offerings he's bought. No matter how nice the clothes are, I don't want anything from him, so I ignore all of the beautiful things in favor of my ratty denim shorts and a plain tank top I bought at Target.

"Keep the shorts, but change the top," he remarks when I step out of the closet fully dressed.

"I like this tank."

"I can see your nipples."

"No you can't, I have a bralette on."

"Starling, change the shirt. Now."

With a scowl, I turn and head back into the closet, stripping the tank over my head and replacing it with one of the things he got me. It's a cropped shirt, with armholes that are wide enough you can see all of my white lace bralette from the sides.

"No," he snarls.

Smirking, I spread my arms wide. "You picked this shirt."

"I didn't know it'd be that sexy."

"That's sounds like a you problem, not a me problem," I shrug. "Now I need to go, or I'll be late for class. Did you say Clay's my prison guard today?"

"Little bird, you're fucking pushing it with that attitude. Now your ass isn't leaving this room wearing that shirt, go change to something that covers what's mine."

"You've had a problem with the last two shirts, why don't you just go pick something so I can leave."

Lips pressed together into a hard line, he climbs up off the bed, tucks his still semihard dick into his boxer briefs and storms past me and into the closet. The sound of his muttering filters into the bedroom and I cross my arms over my chest and wait impatiently, tapping my foot against the wooden flooring.

"Here, put this on," he says, stomping out of the closet and holding out one of his T-shirts for me to wear.

"Fine, whatever," I say, pulling the tank over my head and replacing it with his shirt. It's huge on my much smaller frame, so I quickly roll the hem up and tie it in a knot at my hip, then fold the sleeves over so they fit a little better.

Perhaps another girl would be bothered that they're wearing a huge guy's shirt, but I really don't care what I wear. Instead of fighting with him, which would mean exchanging more words than I want to, I just grab my backpack, cell phone, AirPods and Chucks and leave the room without a single glance back in his direction.

I find the other guys all in the kitchen. Hunter is flipping pancakes on a griddle, while Evan is sitting at the dining table and Clay is leaning against the counter.

"Inmate Kennedy, reporting, sir," I drawl sarcastically to Clay.

"You need to eat, I made you breakfast," Hunter says, flashing me a soft smile.

"No, thanks."

"You need to eat, you ran miles this morning," Evan agrees.

"The asshole upstairs already made me change my shirt three times, I'm late, I'm ready to leave."

"Starling, can we please just call a truce?" Evan begs.

"I'll wait outside, if I'm late you can explain the reason why," I say, ignoring Evan and speaking directly to Clay. Turning my back on all of them, I march out the front door, inhaling deeply and trying to find that elusive, full breath that's eluded me since I came back to Florida.

"Here," Clay says, appearing beside me, holding out a banana and a bottle of water.

The moment the gates slide open wide enough for me to fit through, I stride away, trying to figure out a way to escape without him realizing. Pushing my AirPods into my ears, I drown out the sound of him with some old-school '90s angry-girl music. The dulcet tones of Alanis Morrisette fill my ears and I manage to block out all thoughts of Elite, Collinwood House and anything else that's related to Sebastian Lockwood. Instead, I focus on the crescendo that the music is building inside of me. I try not to think about the fact that my mom calls this album the sound of her puberty, or that it was her who told me to listen to it one day when I was filled with teenage hormone-induced rage. By the time I reach the building my very first college class is being held in, I'm angry and empowered. I am woman hear me roar.

"I'll be here when your class finishes," Clay tells me.

"Fantastic, I can hardly wait," I deadpan, flashing him my middle finger as I open the door to my classroom and walk inside. Intro to economics is quite possibly the most boring class I've ever taken, but as I have no idea what I want to major in, I figure I might as well get as many of my required general ed classes out of the way in my first semester.

After two years of avoiding people and friendships, I've got becoming invisible down to a fine art. Most people think that sitting at the back of a class makes you unapproachable, but that's where they have it wrong, you actually need to be a row or two away from the front. No one likes the people who sit on the front row, but they never notice the mediocre middle people, so that's who I've become. Two rows from the front, two-thirds of the way along the row, I'm in the perfect position to be completely unremarkable. Or at least that's what I'd be if the beautiful Clay Jansen wasn't waiting right outside the classroom doors for me the moment the bell rings to signal the end of class.

He's the type of attractive that it's impossible to ignore, so all my hard work to blend into the crowd is destroyed when everyone watches him smile widely at me. Ignoring him, I pass him as if he's a complete stranger, but he races to catch up with me and slings his arm over my shoulders. "Your next class isn't for an hour, I thought we could go grab a coffee and maybe something to eat."

"No thanks."

"Okay, so what do you want to do for the next hour?"

"I don't really care what you do, but I plan to go sit my ass down under that tree over there and read," I say tersely, walking to a tree and sliding down the trunk until my ass is rested against the roots in the grass.

I ignore Clay as he paces in front of me, obviously at a loss for what to do. Eventually, he sinks to the ground beside me and sighs dramatically. "We're trying to fix things," he says after an interminably long silence.

I try to ignore him, engaging with any of them is futile, but I find myself eager to understand them, at least in this. Lowering my cell to my lap, I exhale, lift my head and stare at him. "Why?"

"Because we don't want you to hate us."

I'm disappointed by his answer, I'm not sure what I was expecting, but I wanted, no needed something more than just that lame, surface-level explanation.

"What does it matter if I hate you? We're not friends, we never have been. I'd never spoken a single word to any of you before the day Sebastian took over my life. He didn't ruin our relationship, we never had one. So be honest, just be fucking honest, what difference does it make if I hate you all?"

His eyes flash with hurt, but what does he have to be hurt about?

"Did Bastian tell you that he spotted you on your very first day at GAA?"

"Probably, he's said a lot of bullshit, I try not to listen."

Clay laughs a little brittlely. "Well, he did. He saw you in the group of new freshmen and he literally stumbled over his own feet just at the sight of you. For him it was instant. Love at first sight or whatever you want to call it. But he knew he couldn't approach you. You were a freshman, freshmen are untouchable, even to The Elite."

"This is a cute story and all, but what does this have to do with you?"

"We followed you."

"Excuse me?"

"He wanted you to be safe, so we followed you. Me, Evan and Hunter, we followed you, learned everything we could about you, because he loved you."

"I was barely fifteen and he was what? Sixteen, almost seventeen? Did none of you ever just put his want for me down as a childish crush? Normal people don't obsess over a girl they've never spoken to, they don't have them followed, stalked. They walk up to them and say, hey."

Clay smiles a soft, aw-shucks smile. "Our families make alliances. We don't marry for love, we marry to create bonds with other rich families, it's old fashioned, but it's how the rich stay rich and powerful. If Bastian had been older when he saw you, he wouldn't have been able to pursue you, because his family would already have had someone lined up for him to marry. Claiming you when he did, before he even knew your name is the only way his parents would have even allowed him to take you out on a date."

"So you, Evan and Hunter already have fiancées?" I ask skeptically.

"My parents are in talks with the La Mar family, there's been talk about Hunter and the Hollins girl and Evan was expected to marry Bunny Lawrence, but your mom is putting up some resistance about an arranged marriage that Harry is indulging at the minute."

I'm shocked by how calmly he's talking about marrying a girl he doesn't care for, like it's a business arrangement, which I suppose it is. "This still doesn't explain why you care if I hate you."

He sighs, wearily. "Because for a whole year we got to know you, we watched you work too hard, watched you with Courtney, with your mom, we felt like we knew you, like you were one of us. You are one of us. Bastian is my brother, so that makes you my sister. I've never had a sibling before, but I want us to be friends, for you to rely on us."

His words and his expression are earnest, almost hopeful, but instead of feeling sympathy, I'm outraged.

"You think of me like a sister?" I ask, needing to see if I'm understanding what he's saying.

"Yes," he nods eagerly.

"If I were your sister, would you want my life to be completely controlled by a man?"

His eyes cloud, but I don't stop. "As your sister, would you want me to be in a powerless relationship where I was being held against my will, where in a fit of anger a man isolated me, removed all the meaningful relationships in my life until all I had left was him? Would you want your sister to be held captive by that man, forced to have sex with that man and used for his pleasure without thought for if that was something she wanted?"

He fidgets uncomfortably from his spot on the floor. "It's¾"

I interrupt him. "Are you going to say it's not like that? Because from where I'm sitting, it's exactly like that. Sebastian strolled into my life when I was barely sixteen years old and declared I was his. When I was so unhappy and lonely that I ran to the other side of the country to get away from him, he threw a tantrum and destroyed my relationship with my mother. Years later, he orchestrated a situation that has left me yet again vulnerable and isolated, only this time, he took my virginity and is literally holding me captive in a very expensive cage."

Clay swallows thickly. "Did he." He pauses, swallows again and then speaks. "Did he rape you?"

I laugh and the sound is dark and hollow. "Does it matter?"

He nods. "Yes, it does."

"And what if he did? What would you do if I told you that he raped me?"

"I'd take you to the police and I'd make sure he got what he deserved."

"So, stalking and imprisonment is okay, but you draw the line at rape?" I scoff. "I'll have to remember that."

"Oh fuck, he raped you, didn't he? Jesus, fuck, I didn't, I didn't... Let's go, I'll take you now, we'll go to the police, now. Did he, er did he hurt you, I mean other than that? Oh fuck," Clay's rambling, his words coming out in an almost indistinguishable rush as he jumps up from the grass and holds out his hand for me to take, then immediately drops it to his side again. "I'm sorry, of course you don't want me to touch you, I let him... fuck."

"He didn't rape me." I could have said he did, I could have used this as a way to get my revenge, to get away from them once and for all, but it would be a lie. As much as I wish everything he'd done to me had been taken, the moment he touches me, I'm more than willing.

"He, he didn't?"

"No, although it's nice to know you do have a conscience in

there somewhere."

"I would never, not knowingly."

"But you didn't know, did you? You let him force me to sleep in his bed, not knowing or really caring what he'd do to me, or if I'd be okay with it. Is that any different really?" I ask.

His hands are shaking as he runs them through his hair, pressing his lips together in a firm line. I swear there are tears in his eyes, but before I have a chance to ask him, he shakes his head. "You're right, it's no better." Then he turns and walks away, leaving me alone, sitting on the grass, watching him go.

SEVENTEEN

SEBASTIAN

Clay's face is tight and pale when he throws open the front door and storms into the kitchen. "Did you rape her?"

"What?"

"Did you rape her?"

"No, of course I fucking didn't, I love her. Where the fuck is she?"

"When I left her she was sitting beneath a tree. But that's not important, I want you to look me in the eye and promise on *her* life that you didn't fucking rape her."

Standing, I cross the room to where one of my best friends is looking at me like I'm a fucking monster and stop when I'm only inches from him. Then I lock eyes with his. "I didn't rape her."

He nods, then steps back and rubs at his face with his hands. "Did she tell you I did?"

Laughing, he shakes his head, his eyes glassy. "No, she said you didn't rape her, but she did make me see things a little more from her fucking side. We can't do this. We can't keep her here. I know you call her little bird, but she's a human and she doesn't want this. I won't be her jailer anymore."

"Me either," Evan says, appearing in the doorway. "And I know Hunter doesn't want this either. It's wrong, bro. She's so fucking different, so fucking broken and we did that to her. You need to leave her alone and pay for some fucking therapy for all the damage we've done to her."

"I can't let her go," I confess.

"This Starling isn't the girl you fell in love with. She's fundamentally different, the shit we've put her through, it changed her and the truth is, bro, you don't know her, not really. You know stuff about her, but you don't know *her*," Evan tells me.

"I love her."

"I know," he says sadly. "But she doesn't love you. She doesn't even like you. She hates all of us and she should."

"I can't just let her go, I can't."

"Even if you'll know she was never with you by choice, that she'll never feel anything but hatred for you?" Clay asks.

"She wants me."

"Bro, we're a walking fucking example that you don't need

to have feelings for someone to have sex with them. Lust is a hormone; it doesn't mean anything. Sex is just sex."

"She's mine," I say, the words sounding so right on my lips.

"Is she? Or are you just hers?" Clay asks quietly.

EIGHTEEN

STARLING

As I watch Clay disappear from sight, I wonder if this is all some elaborate trick Sebastian has come up with to test me to see if I'll run. It's the type of thing he'd do, allow me a long enough chain to hang myself with and then enjoy punishing me for trying to get away from him.

For a moment I think about just leaving, walking out of the gates and not looking back, but what's the point if he'll just go back to having people watching me twenty-four seven? I might as well be here and getting a good college degree. I'm a prisoner either way, because I was never free of him, even when I thought I was.

I wait for Clay to come back, or for Sebastian to hunt me down, but no one comes and in the end, I decide to just go to class. If he really does have eyes on me then he'll know where I am. My English class is a little more interesting than econ, and my sociology class even has me sitting forward in my seat as I listen to the professor speak passionately about the study of people and the things we're going to be looking at.

When no one is waiting for me at the end of the period, I make my way over to the cafeteria and pick some food, choosing to take it to an empty table in the courtyard, rather than share with other students.

Sammy, the girl who followed me to freshmen orientation, spots me, shouting my name as she makes a beeline across the courtyard. Dropping her tray to the table, she plops down into the seat opposite me. "We should exchange cell numbers, that way we could arrange to meet for lunch when we can," she says enthusiastically.

"Er, yeah I'm not sure of my schedule yet," I tell her, considering just dumping my lunch like I had the day she decided to join me for breakfast. But I'm hungry, except for the sandwich Hunter made me and Sebastian forced me to eat, I don't actually remember the last time I had a proper meal. My stomach feels hollow and empty, and the burger I've picked smells amazing, so instead of leaving, I ignore her and eat while she has a completely one-sided conversation, telling me all about her first two classes and her sex-crazed housemates.

"I swear all they've done is have sex since the moment we got here, I found the six of them all doing it at the same time in the living room the other day. My house is like a permanent orgy, which is fine, more power to them, but I don't want to touch anything, just in case there's fluid or something on it. I spoke to student housing, but they said there're no rooms in any of the other houses on campus at the minute and I either have to just deal with it till someone moves out, or rent a place off campus."

Instead of paying attention, I zone her out and daydream about Sebastian fucking me in the kitchen or the living room and the guys walking in on us. The thought is kind of hot. None of the others are remotely sexually attractive to me, although they're all beautiful men, but the idea of them watching Sebastian fuck me, is much more appealing than it should be.

My body starts to heat as I imagine him bending me over the kitchen counter, his dick pounding into me while Hunter, Clay and Evan watch him play my body until I'm nothing but need and sensation, begging the man I hate to make me scream in the way only he knows how.

"Starling. Starling," Sammy calls, dragging me from my dirty daydream and forcing me back to the present.

"Sorry, what?"

"I was asking if you fancied doing something tonight? We could go out for drinks or just hang out at your house. Which house are you in again?"

"Collinwood," I tell her, instantly regretting it.

"Collinwood is one of the private houses, is your family alumni?"

"Er, no, but my mom's new husband's family is. I'm here on a scholarship, but I'm assuming he pulled strings to have me put in the house rather than the normal scholarship housing."

"But that house is owned by…" she trails off. "What did you say your surname was?"

Shoving the last bite of my burger into my mouth, I stand abruptly, grabbing my tray. "Sorry, I have plans tonight." Dumping the remaining food into the trash, I hoist my backpack onto both shoulders and walk away.

I only have one more class today, so I head straight over to the gym for the university-required PE course I have to take. Luckily, the class description said it was a free-form exercise requirement, with no grades, just mandatory attendance. Signing in on the sheet, I follow the other people into a huge gymnasium and take a seat in the bleachers. A few minutes later, an instructor arrives and hands out a sheet listing all the exercise classes that are available, as well as use of the indoor running track, weight gym and swimming pool. All we have to do to pass is spend an hour and a half here twice a week. After that we all head for the changing rooms and I switch out my clothes for a sports bra and a pair of running shorts and head for the yoga class that's on today's list.

There're only a handful of other attendees, but by the time the class has ended I feel calm and relaxed.

"Hey," a male voice says as I make my way out of the yoga studio and over to the running track, intending to do a couple of laps just to warm down.

"Hey," I say, barely acknowledging him.

"I'm Chase."

"Starling."

"Do you wanna run together?" he asks hopefully.

"I'm just going to do a couple of laps to warm down."

"That's okay, I'll use it as my warm-up," he smiles. He's tall, but not as tall as Sebastian, broad like a football player maybe, or at least athletic.

Not saying anything else, I walk to the edge of the track and then break into a light jog. He keeps pace at my side for the first half of a lap.

"Are you a freshman? I don't think I've seen you around here before."

"Yep."

"Cool, I'm a sophomore."

I nod, but don't speak. Another half a lap passes before he speaks again.

"You're making me feel a little pathetic here," he laughs.

"Hmm," I say, not agreeing or disagreeing.

"So pretty loyal to your high school boyfriend?" he smiles.

"Nope, just not interested."

"Harsh," he laughs. "I'm on the football team if that makes a difference?"

"None."

"Wow. Friends then?"

"I'm good, thanks. Enjoy the rest of your run." Then I jog off the edge of the track and over to the changing rooms. Not bothering to shower or change, I stuff my clothes into my backpack and sign out before exiting the gym and turn to walk back to my beautiful prison.

The entire journey back to the house, I'm on edge, waiting for Sebastian to jump out on me, to drag me back to my cage and refuse to let me go again. By the time I push open the front door, I'm practically vibrating with nerves. He'll know I was speaking to that guy and sitting with Sammy at lunch, he'll know I was interested in my sociology class and somehow, he'll find a way to use it against me.

The house is quiet as I step inside, but not empty, I can feel the intensity of his presence.

"Starling," he calls from the living room that I've yet to step inside.

"What?"

"Come here please."

It's on the tip of my tongue to tell him to go fuck himself, but he's got me so paranoid, so tense and worried that all of this is one of his fucked-up games, that I find myself walking into the living room. Instead of waiting to pounce, he's sitting in a chair, his hair unusually disheveled, his expression sad, pained almost. The others are in here too, slumped into their seats and all wearing matching forlorn expressions.

"What's going on?" I ask.

"Would you join us please?" Sebastian asks, pointing to one of the empty chairs.

"I'd rather not."

"Please," Evan says, imploringly.

I sit down on the edge of the chair, bracing myself for whatever fucked-up thing is going to come out of their mouths.

"I'm sorry," Sebastian utters.

"Okay," I say slowly.

"I'm so fucking sorry. I love you, I love you more than anything, but this was wrong, it was all so fucking wrong and I'm just. I'm sorry."

"Is this some kind of joke? Because honestly, it's not funny."

"Jesus," he hisses. "Look, you're free to go, the doors and gates will all open, I won't stop you from leaving and no one will follow you, at least not like before. I'm not sure I'll ever be able to go without knowing you're at least safe, but I promise they won't ever tell me where you are or what you're doing and they'll never intervene unless you're in danger. You'll never have to see me again; I'll stay away from any event where we would both be expected to attend. I'll even tell Cassidy the truth, if that's what you want."

"I don't understand," I whisper.

"I shouldn't have brought you here, I shouldn't have said or done the things I've done since I got you back. I'm sorry about your mom, I never thought things would go this far, I thought you'd come back, I thought you'd fall out for a couple of weeks and then you'd make up. I know you won't believe me, but I never wanted to destroy your relationship with her, I just wanted to punish you for leaving me."

A dry, brittle laugh bursts from me. "So you're telling me that last night, when you told me what I wanted didn't matter and I should just do as I'm told from the cage you created for me, has suddenly changed to, go be free? I'm sorry," I scoff. "You'll have to excuse me if I call bullshit."

"We don't want you to leave," Evan says. "But we understand if you want to. There's an open plane ticket on your bed that can be exchanged for a ticket to anywhere in the world. If you choose to go, none of us will stop you."

"If I choose to leave?"

"You could stay," Sebastian says hopefully.

"With you?"

"No." His voice is sad, but resigned. "But Kingsacre is one of the best private universities in the country. Your tuition is covered, as is your room here and your meal plan."

"What's the catch? There's always a catch with you. Let me guess, I can stay, but in your bed, or to be at your beck and call whenever you want your dick sucked? Or maybe you want to marry me, so you don't have to allow your parents to arrange a political marriage for you?"

"No catch, no loopholes."

"I don't believe you. Why go to all the trouble of arranging to get me here and then less than a week after you capture me, let me go?"

"Because contrary to what you believe, I'm not a monster, or at least I don't want to be." He swallows thickly. "I don't want you to think of me as nothing more than a monster."

"So if I walk outside, the gate will open for me?" I ask dubiously.

"Yes."

"And if I keep on walking, straight out the entrance gates and onto a bus, you won't stop me?"

"I'd prefer it if you'd let one of us call you a cab, but no, no one will stop you."

Getting up, I walk away from them, not believing what he's saying and needing to see it for myself. Opening the front door, I stride outside, gasping when the gates start to swing open the moment I approach them. Cautiously I step forward, glancing over my shoulder, waiting for the moment that he chases me, but the door stays closed and no one comes.

What the hell is going on? This has to be a game, it's the only thing that makes sense. Spinning around, I march back into the house and straight into the living room, where all four guys are still sitting. "The gate opened."

Sebastian nods, his hands clenched together and rested on his knees, his head lowered.

"I don't understand this game."

"It's not a game. I'm going to fix things between you and your mom. I'll leave you alone, or I'll try to. I can go. If you want to stay and you don't want me here, I'll leave."

"Leave my mom alone," I snap.

"I'm going to tell her everything, that it's my fault."

"No you won't. My mom's an adult, she could have believed me, like my dad did, but she chose not to. I'm not interested in her being sorry only after you tell her she should be."

"Starling, she misses you," Evan says, a pleading tone in his voice.

"I can't help that."

"All of your belongings are back in your room, as well as all the things I bought for you. You can keep them, sell them or give them away, they're yours to do whatever you want with. If you decide to leave, let me know which school you want to attend and I'll ensure you receive the acceptance you would have gotten had I not intervened and of course, I'll cover your tuition."

"Just like that? You pull all this shit to get me here and under your thumb and just like that you're giving up and setting me free? Was this all just about sex? What, now you've had me I've lost the appeal?" My brows are knitted together and I can feel anger building in me, ready to explode.

"Little bird, if you tell me that you want me, this, that you think you can forgive all the shit I've done, that there's even the faintest hope that you could love me the way I love you then I'll lock the door and keep you tied to me for the rest of eternity. Is that the case? Do you want to be with me?"

"No," I say a little too quick.

Nodding, he stands and starts to leave. Pausing beside me, he grabs my chin in gently shaking fingers and kisses me reverently. "I love you, little bird." Then he strides quickly away, the sound of his heavy footsteps filling the silence until the crash of his bedroom door slamming shut ricochets through the house.

"We're all sorry, Starling, we were all complicit in what's happened to you, but I promise you we won't mess with you or your life anymore. I know you don't care but we'd like you to stay, this is a great school, better than the others you applied to. Use us and this opportunity, take back a little of what we took from you," Evan says solemnly as one by one, the three remaining boys stand and exit the room, until I'm alone wondering what the fuck just happened.

It takes me fifteen minutes before the shell shock wears off and I'm capable of moving. Slowly I climb the stairs to my room in the turret, testing the door several times before I'm confident that I'm not locked inside.

All of my belongings have been replaced in the spots I unpacked them into, my tiny selection of clothes mixed with the closetful of expensive designer things Sebastian bought for me. Dragging my case from beneath the bed, my hands shake as I begin pulling things from the rod and shoving them inside. It isn't until I'm zipping the bag closed that I start to wonder if I'm doing the right thing.

Two years ago I fled from Sebastian, but really, what good

did that do me? I'm older now, but all running got me was a broken soul and a laundry list of mental health issues. Will running again make things any better? In the back of my head, I've always questioned what would have happened if I'd just stood my ground and fought back, would he have backed down?

I'm not sure what prompted his change of heart today, maybe it was my conversation with Clay, or the multiple emotional meltdowns I've had since he stepped back into my orbit. But whatever it was, maybe this time I don't have to run to be free of him.

This could all still just be a game, but the open plane ticket voucher is here, just where they said it would be. It can be my emergency backup plan, my escape. Evan told me to use them, use this opportunity and perhaps I should. Could I stay here? Live in this house, with them, him?

Thoughts of revenge taste sweet on my tongue as I consider it, but would that make me as fucked up as them? Maybe getting on with my life here could be the biggest revenge I could gain. Sebastian has always thrived on his control over me, even when I wasn't even in the same state as him. Being here, right under his nose but outside of his control, would be torture for him.

The more I think about it, the more I like the idea. I could make friends, date, test his control over and over again until he cracks, then I'll leave and when I do, it won't be because I'm running away, it'll be because I'll have taken everything I can, everything I need. Then I'll have the sweetest revenge ever, by moving on and never thinking about him ever again.

NINETEEN

SEBASTIAN

Two weeks. That's how long I've been forced to see her, smell her, watch her, but not touch her. It's pure, raw torture and I hate it. I expected her to run. I thought she'd be gone by the next morning, but instead she shocked us all by staying, sashaying out of her room at five in the morning in her running gear and heading out the door, like it was the most normal thing in the world for her to do.

My eyes never left the tracking app for a second of the hour she was gone, and the only reason I stopped myself from following her was because her security team tracked her progress through the cameras I had installed on every inch of the route we ran together.

She hasn't uttered a single word to any of us, not even a

grunt in acknowledgment of our existence. But now that the gates and doors always open for her whenever she leaves, she's starting to relax, at least when I'm not around.

My body aches for her. Knowing she's here, knowing how she feels and tastes and sounds but not being able to touch is like a physical pain that only seems to be getting worse with every moment that passes without her. She was mine for a day, but in that short space of time, I gave her my soul and without it I'm hardly more than a shell.

She watches me when she thinks I'm not looking. I can feel her eyes on me, and I spend hours watching back the footage from the security cameras in the shared spaces of the house to see her staring at me. There're cameras in her room too, but I made Clay promise to never let me view them no matter how much I beg or threaten him. Of course, I can access them if I really want to, but no one but me knows that.

She's wary of me and I know a part of her is still waiting for me to drop the facade and reclaim what will always be mine. But there's also heat in her glares, a spark of want hidden beneath all the hatred. She might despise me, but she enjoys the passion that flares between us the moment we touch.

If only she knew all the things I want to do to her. How I fantasize about tying her to my bed and locking the door, kissing her and fucking her until she's so drunk from all the orgasms I've given her that she'll forget why she hates me and falls in love with me. I dream about plucking her off the path when she runs in the dark and kidnapping her, keeping her my prisoner in an actual golden cage made just for her.

My fantasies are becoming more and more disturbing with every moment that passes when she's not mine.

I'm still following her.

I'm not sure I'll ever stop, but I stay at a distance, not letting her feel my presence like I did during her first couple of days on campus. Back then I wanted her to know she was being watched, now I just simply can't look away.

She made a friend. The same girl who latched onto my little bird on her way to freshmen orientation. Samantha Hartley is a freshman too, her family is old money, rich, but not as wealthy as they used to be. She lives in Alistern House with six other people who appear to be three sets of open-minded couples. According to Clay's research, the six of them rarely attend classes and instead use their time to vigorously attempt to impregnate each other in every part of the house.

The three girls are the Attingham triplets, whose family is on the verge of bankruptcy. It appears that the girls are aware that they need to secure wealthy spouses and instead of an education, they're using Kingsacre as husband-hunting ground. Considering one out of the three sisters is already pregnant and it's only the third week of the school year, their plan seems to be coming together. Their unwitting victims are Tim Grimes, Nicholas Farris and Chris Morgan-Baraclough. All relatively new money and seemingly unaware of their latest fuck buddies' financial precariousness.

Sammy isn't a bad choice of a friend for my little bird, I might have promised to stay out of my girl's life, but that was never going to happen. There's no way I'll allow anyone around her who's going to hurt her. Clay has made it his mission to befriend Starling, even though she's rebuffed all of his attempts so far. Evan is desperately trying to use the stepbrother card to force a relationship with her and Hunter is determined to feed her.

None of it is working, she still hates us.

It's been two weeks since I told her I was sorry, that I promised her I'd leave her alone.

I lied.

She's mine and I can't let her go, not even if I wanted to. The game has changed, but the result will still be the same, she'll be mine. Only this time she'll think it's her choice.

The front door opens and I know it's her before she even steps into the house. My skin buzzes with awareness the moment she's close, like every atom in me knows when she's in my orbit. I want to grab her by the throat, pin her to the wall and rip her clothes from her until she's naked and wet and begging for my cock.

I miss the feeling of being inside of her. I promised her all my cum was for her, that from now on whenever I came it would be in her or on her, but after two weeks, my balls are bluer than fucking Papa Smurf. I've had much longer dry spells, the two and a half years she was in Maine were hell, but once you've had perfection, everything else pales in comparison. If I can't be inside her, I'd rather keep my dick in my pants. At least back then I had my hand. Whacking off isn't exactly my first choice, but it was still a release, now I don't even have that. The moment she's back in my arms, I'm going to fuck her so hard and so often my cum will be dripping out of her constantly for at least the first six months.

During the two years I spent at Harvard before I transferred to Kingsacre, I almost killed myself with a heavy class load, knowing that once I got here with her, I wouldn't want to be too busy with schoolwork to focus on her. If I wanted to, I have enough credits to graduate this year, but instead I'm just taking a couple of courses and the rest of my time is all about her.

All the air seems to evaporate from the room the moment she steps into the kitchen, freezing midstep when she sees me sitting at the table. Of course I'm only here because I'm waiting for her, but I don't say that. Instead I let sadness fill my eyes and allow my shoulders to curl forward. I'm the image of a kicked puppy. Sad, alone and rejected.

After a second, she starts to move again, dashing to the refrigerator and opening the door to peek inside. We all have a meal plan to eat three meals a day in the cafeteria, but Hunter and Clay love to cook, so we keep a fully stocked pantry of fresh ingredients. I also make sure there's a constant supply of the snacks my little bird likes to eat.

No matter how many times the guys offer, she always refuses to eat with us, but she's not above taking snacks to eat in her room. Reaching in, she pulls out an apple and the jar of peanut butter. It goes rock hard and almost impossible to spread if you keep it in the refrigerator, but she likes it like that so that's where we leave it.

Getting up, I cross to the drinks cooler and pull out a bottle of beer. "Beer?" I ask her, deliberately not making eye contact.

She jolts like I've hit her, but I try not to react, taking out a second bottle and offering it to her as I walk back to the table, fighting the urge to brush up against her. She takes the bottle from me then stares down at it, like she's not sure how it got into her hand.

"How are you finding your classes so far?" I ask, twisting the top off the beer and bringing it to my lips. The liquid is cold and I take a long pull before lowering it down to the table.

"I never took you for a beer drinker."

I stifle a smile, forcing my eyes to stay downcast and pathetic. "No? What kind of drinker did you take me for?"

Her eyes widen, like she's shocked herself by speaking to me. The truth is, no matter how much she thinks she hates me and my obsession with her, it's become omnipresent in her life. I was the big bad wolf, hiding in the shadows, a constant in her world and without me, she's adrift, lost.

I want to say her name, to force her to speak, to answer me, but I can't, so instead I wait, pretending that it doesn't kill me to not be able to control her.

"Whiskey, or maybe a mixed drink," she says after so long I'd almost given up on her answering.

"I do enjoy a good single malt," I say, smirking at the table where my elbows are resting.

Out of the corner of my eye I watch her look at the bottle warily, then carefully twist the top off and take a tentative sip, grimacing as she swallows.

"Oh my god that's disgusting," she chokes.

A chuckle slips from my lips, but I still keep my eyes from hers, standing and crossing to the cooler. Pulling down one of the strawberry wine coolers I bought for her, I offer it out to her. "Here, try this." She doesn't move so I take the beer from her hands, and swap it for the cooler, then slide back into my seat.

To her, I hopefully look calm and distant, which is exactly what I want her to see. Inside I'm roiling with the urge to tackle her to the ground, pin her with my body and sink my cock into her so deep she can taste my cum in the back of her throat. I want to breed her, own her, brand her. I want to dominate every aspect of her life until she can't even breathe without looking at me for permission. A part of me knows that my thoughts have gone from primal to fucking psychopathic, but I just don't seem to be able to do anything about it.

Not speaking, I ignore my own beer and instead lift hers to my lips and drink. I swear I can taste her sweet breath on the rim and I close my eyes and exhale happily, content for a second just from sharing something she's had on her lips.

The twist of the metal top crunching fills the silence, then the hiss of carbonation as she lifts the bottle to her lips and drinks. "Mmm," she hums.

"Better?"

"Much. Strawberry is my favorite."

"I know."

"Oh," she says quietly. "Did you? Did you buy these for me?" It sounds like it pains her to ask, like it hurts her that I would know she'd like something and buy it for her, but I've always been generous with her, even when she didn't want me to be.

"Yes," I nod.

"Oh."

She shuffles from foot to foot, like she wants to run from me, but also wants to stay. This is what I need. Even an inch of hesitation is enough for me to start to wheedle my way back into her life again. "I didn't force you, did I?" I pose it like a question, but I know I didn't. She might hate me, but that's never stopped her body from responding to me, craving me.

The bottle slips from her hands, but somehow I reach out in time to stop it from crashing to the floor. Suddenly, I'm next to her, only a handful of inches between us.

"Tell me the truth," I whisper, leaning imperceptibly into her body and waiting for her to react.

"No, you didn't. You didn't force me," she whispers back,

her pupils dilating at my nearness, her breathing becoming audible. I need to be careful not to push her, if I take too much now, she'll only put up stronger walls next time. I've lost control for the moment, but I'll get it back. I can't take it from her like I did when she was barely sixteen, this time I'm going to have to seduce it from her. Letting her feel like she holds the power while I ensnare her in my web again. I'm still her cage, only this time she'll be the one locking herself in, not me.

"Hunter's making pasta tonight, you should join us," I say, taking a step back and loving how her body drifts toward me even as I pull away. She's never had to deal with me being the one to back away before, and I enjoy how discombobulated it's making her.

"Oh, I¾"

"It's only dinner, housemates eating together, nothing more. I know you don't want to be their friends, but perhaps this could be a first step toward tolerant cordiality."

"Tolerant cordiality," she smiles. "I'm not sure that's ever been something to work toward, but okay, dinner."

"Do you still have Hunter's cell phone number? You could text him, or I could if you'd prefer?"

"You can let him know. I have homework to get on with."

"Sure," I say dismissively, sliding back into my seat and lifting my beer to my lips without even glancing her way. Her surprise and possibly annoyance follow her all the way out of the room and upstairs.

I hold back my smile until I hear the door to her room close. "You'll be mine again soon, little bird."

TWENTY

STARLING

What the actual fuck?

Sebastian Lockwood is an asshole.

Today is the first time we've spoken since the day he apologized and set me free. This boy has stalked me for years. Years, and yet only two weeks after he told me he loved me, that he didn't want me to think of him as a monster, he's absolutely fine, like we've never been more than passing acquaintances.

Fine. How can he be fine? I'm not fine. I should be, but I'm not. After that day when I made the decision to stay, to use this opportunity to get a great education on their dime and a little revenge at the same time by showing him just how little I cared about him, I spent the first three days in full-blown panic mode. Constantly looking over my shoulder. I jumped at the slightest noise. I slept at the bottom of the stairs to my room, with my foot in the door, making sure I wasn't going to end up locked in.

It took a week before it sank in that it might be real. No eyes on me, no one watching me, nothing. The others have all reached out to me. Evan wants to be my brother, Clay my friend, Hunter my personal chef. But Sebastian hasn't done anything. He hasn't tried to talk to me, to see me, to dominate me. Nothing.

How does someone go from obsession to disinterest so instantaneously?

I wish I could be like him. I wish I could just switch everything off inside of me, but I can't. Something changed the moment he told me I was free. I don't know what it was, but instead of pushing him from my thoughts, my psyche has become consumed by him.

He's all I can think about, all I dream about. Him giving up his obsession has created an obsession in me and I hate it. I want to forget him, but he's always there at the back of my mind. I know I should leave, that being here in this house is only fueling my madness, but leaving now feels impossible.

When I was trapped here all I wanted was to escape, but now I'm free, I just don't seem to be able to walk away.

How dare he be so disinterested that he can't even be bothered to look in my direction. He ruined me, haunted my waking and sleeping hours and now I'm not worth a single glance. A fucking bottle of beer is more interesting. Then there was that moment when he stopped my bottle from hitting the ground and he was so close to me. Close enough that I could feel the heat of his breath on my cheek. I thought he would kiss me, that he'd do what he always does and overwhelm my body with his touch, but instead he stepped back. He was inches from me and instead of putting his hands on me, he treated me like I was a stranger he was offering his seat to on the bus.

He stepped back. Just moved, like being that close to me didn't bother him at all. I want to scream, to stomp back downstairs and punch him in his stupid beautiful face, because how dare he ruin me and now not even care?

Agreeing to have dinner with them all is reckless, but the smell of the food Hunter has been cooking each night has been driving me a little crazy after eating the tasteless collection of food they serve in the cafeteria. The burgers and sandwiches aren't too bad, but the evening meals are just so damn bland I'm at risk of dehydrating from all the salt I'm having to douse my food in. You'd think at a school where the tuition fees are more than the average American makes in five years, the food would be practically Michelin starred, but apparently cafeteria food is cafeteria food no matter where it's made.

My skin feels tight as I strip out of my jeans and tank and step under the cold water of my shower. I'm crazy, he's making me feel crazy and I hate it. The need to run claws at my throat, so I haphazardly blot the water from my skin, pull on my tight running shorts and a sports bra, then grab my sneakers and armband before stomping downstairs and out of the front door.

Sitting on the front step, I slide my feet into my shoes and tie the laces, attach the armband and then stretch while the gate slowly opens. I barely give my muscles a chance to get warm before I'm sprinting. I race across campus to the outdoor track I found when I was avoiding returning to the house one afternoon.

Setting a blistering pace that I know I won't be able to maintain for long, I stride onto the track and pump my arms, racing along the lane like the devil himself is chasing me. I'm not sure how long I last but by the time I collapse to a heap in the grass beside the track, my lungs are burning and my legs feel like Jell-O.

Gasping for air, I lift my weak, sweat-soaked arms over my face and just breathe. The familiar quiet that always finds me when I run settles over me and I close my eyes, basking in the desperately needed numbness.

"Here, you look like you could use this," a male voice says from above me.

Opening my eyes, I blink up at a familiar-looking guy hovering over me, a bottle of water in his outstretched hand.

"Er," I say dumbly.

"Chase, we met at the gym a couple weeks ago."

"The football player," I say through my rasping breaths.

"You remembered," he laughs, folding himself down to a seated position beside me. "Here." He offers me the water again. "It's sealed."

Smiling, I take the bottle from him and open it, cracking the seal and drinking thirstily. "Thanks."

"So are you running from something, or training for a comp?"

"I'm definitely not a competitor," I laugh as my breathing starts to normalize.

"So should I be keeping an eye out for a dude in a mask with a machete or something?"

"No," I smile. "Just trying to outrun my personal demons, not real ones; you know how it is."

His expression sobers, and something that I don't recognize flashes through his eyes. "Ah, personal demons, I have a few of those myself. You know what helps?"

"What?"

"Sex. Those bastard demons are allergic, sends them running. Want to try it out?"

My eyes widen and for a brief moment I look at him and consider it. Chase is attractive, tall, good-looking, muscled but not in a meathead way. Sebastian might be the only man I've had sex with, but that doesn't mean that I can't be with anyone else. I could kiss him. I could let him touch me, touch him in return. I could go back to his room and let him fuck me. Only the thought literally does nothing for me. My stomach doesn't curl with anticipation, my sex doesn't pulse with heat and desire, my brain doesn't spark with how wrong it is but how right it feels, like it did when I was with Sebastian. All I feel with this boy is nothingness.

"Interesting offer, but no thanks. I'm pretty fast, I don't need to scare the demons off when I can just outrun them." Rolling to my feet, I smile. "Thanks for the water, see you later."

"Let me know if you change your mind."

"I won't," I reply quickly, lifting my bottle in salute to him as I turn and walk away, glad that my legs are solid enough that I don't stumble as I head back toward the house.

The sounds of the guys are coming from the kitchen when I drag my tired ass through the door, but I head straight upstairs, showering the sweat from my skin and then redressing in soft short shorts and the tank with the wide armholes that flashes my bralette. The memory of the way Sebastian looked at me when he growled and insisted I changed—refusing to let me leave the house in something this revealing—fills my head.

Brushing out my wet hair, I leave it loose, not bothering to try to blot the water dripping from the ends and making the fabric of my shirt almost opaque. I couldn't one-hundred-percent say that I haven't dressed specifically for the purpose of provoking Sebastian, though I'll never admit it out loud. Something inside of me needs to prove that he still gives a crap, but I don't understand why. What does it matter if he still wants me or not? I don't want to be the object of his obsession. I just want to know that he can't get over me so easily, that his impact on me and my life was more than just a passing fancy he can forget about the moment he loses interest.

My phone beeps with a text and I immediately expect it to

be him, only when I glance at the screen, it's not, and I force down the wave of disappointment that sweeps through me.

Evan

Hey sis, Bastian said you're having dinner with us ☺ that's awesome. Come down, Hunter says it'll be ready in five minutes.

My stomach churns uncomfortably at Evan calling me sis, I know technically I am his stepsister now our parents are married, but it feels alarmingly similar to Clay saying I felt like their sister because I was Sebastian's and he was their brother. He said they felt protective of me, because they'd watched me, which I suppose is kind of sweet; or as sweet as stalking gets anyway.

When I pass the full-length mirror on my way to the stairs, I take a moment to inspect my reflection. Long toned legs, tiny shorts that cling to my ass, a glimpse of my stomach, the loose tank that shows the hot-pink bralette beneath. My cheeks are rosy and my skin is beginning to tan from the Florida sun, my eyes look wide and alive for the first time in too long to remember.

My mind refuses to think about why I look different, why I feel more awake, more animated than I have in years. It can't be him. Sebastian Lockwood is the cause of all my misery and pain, he can't be the reason why I'm finally coming back to life.

Pushing the disturbing thoughts to the back of my mind, I ruffle my wet hair until it resembles more beach tousled rather than drowned rat, and then head downstairs, ignoring the butterflies that burst to life in my stomach.

"Starling," Clay says excitedly the moment I step into the kitchen, the rich smell of garlic surrounding me as Hunter stirs a pan on the stove.

"Hey."

"Come, sit," Evan says enthusiastically, like an overeager puppy.

My eyes search the room for my nemesis, but he's not here and I'm disappointed. What the hell is wrong with me? I can't be disappointed that Sebastian's not here, there's no way that's possible. I'm wary, that's all it is. Years of paranoid conditioning has me looking for him, nothing more.

"Er, is there anything I can do to help?" I ask, feeling like I need to be on my best behavior.

"Hunter's fine, come and sit," Clay grins, reaching for me and then stopping himself at the last minute.

"Thank you for offering, but it's only pasta, as soon as Bastian gets down here, I'll plate up," Hunter says, his voice soft. Weirdly, Hunter is the one I'm the least angry with, maybe it's the fact that he's always appeared to feel bad about the things Sebastian did? He never did anything to stop it, but I think on some level he felt how wrong it was.

"Is he?" I swallow. "He's eating too? I wasn't sure."

"We can ask him not to," Evan offers.

"No," I reply a little too quickly. "No, it's fine, I just wasn't sure if he had class or whatever," I trail off lamely.

All of the air is sucked from the room when he walks in. His chest is bare and his hair is still wet. He must have just gotten out of the shower and all he's wearing is a pair of loose basketball shorts, even his feet are bare. I can't look away.

How can I hate this man so much and still react to him so strongly? I live with three other incredibly hot guys, and today a cute football player suggested we have sex and my body was tied down tighter than a submissive in a BDSM book. But apparently the moment my tormentor, my jailer, the man who is the cause of all of the absolute worst times in my life steps into the room, I'm practically flooded with arousal.

My panties are damp and I know without looking that my nipples have tightened and pebbled in reaction to his nearness. Every single orgasm I've had in the last two and a half years has either been given by him, or was a direct result of fantasizing about him.

But while I'm creating a lake between my legs, he has barely glanced in my direction. He's unaffected, completely disinterested. He knows I'm here, I saw him look at me and then look away as if I'm not worth even a second glance.

Two weeks ago his cock was inside of me, tearing through my virginity and using me in a way no one has ever done before. The things he said to me that night—that I was his, that my cunt, my mouth, my ass all belonged to him, that l was his cum slut, that all his seed was for me—and now I'm nothing.

Nothing.

Maybe I am nothing to him now. I'm sure I'm not the first girl to lose her virginity to the oh-so-great Sebastian Lockwood. But no, he said I was his obsession, told me over and over that I was his, that I belonged to him. If that was true, how can he be so disinterested?

"Someone grab drinks," Hunter says, pulling me from my angry internal rant.

"I'll get them, what does everyone want?" I ask.

There's a chorus of, "Beer please," from them all so I pad to the drinks cooler and take out four beers and a bottle of the strawberry wine cooler I had earlier.

"Jesus, sis, got to say, as your brother I am not loving those shorts, your ass is hanging out of them," Evan laughs.

"It's a good thing you're not really my brother and that I don't care what you think of my clothes," I snark back, putting the drinks on the table and taking the empty seat between Clay and Evan, directly opposite Sebastian.

My gaze finds his, expecting to see his anger over Evan's comment about my ass, or the fact that his friends have seen me in these tiny shorts that are incredibly small and tight, but his expression is completely bland and his lack of reaction makes me furious.

TWENTY ONE

SEBASTIAN

Not punching Evan in the face and dragging *my* little bird back upstairs to rip those fucking shorts off her and spank her ass until it's hot and red and she knows never to put herself on display for other men's eyes ever again, is the hardest thing I've ever had to do.

My eye is twitching with the concentration I'm having to exert to keep my expression neutral and disinterested, to not stare at her with all the anger and frustration and need I'm actually feeling from being this close to her.

My brothers keep checking on me, waiting for me to lose my shit, but I won't. They all believe what I told her, that I'm sorry; that she's free, that I'll stay away. I needed them to believe. After all, if I can sell this bullshit to them, my closest, my family, then I can convince her it's true too.

I understand why they buckled, why they turned on me and urged me to release my little bird. A part of me actually appreciates how they stood against me and defended her, but if they really thought I could walk away, that I could let her live her life without me in it, then they're idiots.

Starling Kennedy is mine and nothing, not them, or their guilt, or even her can change that.

She's wearing the shirt that I bought her, the one I made her take off because it showed more of her tits than it actually covered. It's the first time she's worn anything from the closetful of clothes I picked for her. That's how I know she's dressed just for me. She's wearing those ridiculous booty shorts and that shirt to provoke a reaction from me.

I saw the way she reacted to my dismissal earlier. She may hate me, but she loathes being ignored by me even more. If I really was leaving her alone like I promised I would, I'd have to leave, or make her leave. There's no way I could be around her and not have her be mine.

But this outfit tonight, her having dinner with us, it's her joining the game. Those shorts, that shirt, it's her taking the first shot, detonating the first bomb. It's game on and I'm playing to win, because she's the prize and this time, once I have her, I'll never let go.

TWENTY TWO

STARLING

I hate him.

I really hate him, more than I hated him when he took over my life when we were in high school. More than when he manipulated our families and ruined my and my mom's relationship. More than when he revealed he'd orchestrated me being here in this house, under his thumb.

Somehow, being ignored by him makes me hate him a thousand times harder than ever before and I hate that more than anything else.

The day after we all had dinner together, I ate breakfast in the kitchen, taking Hunter up on his offer to make pancakes. Sebastian came into the room, lifted his chin in greeting and then proceeded to text on his cell phone for the entire length of time it took him to eat, then he left without uttering another word or looking at me again.

Two days later, I came downstairs wearing nothing but a towel and then proceeded to stretch up to the highest cabinet to reach down a glass I didn't need, but instead of fuming over my near nakedness, by the time I turned around he had his cell to his ear speaking to someone on the other end as he left the room.

He's made it clear that whatever he thought he felt for me, he doesn't feel anymore and instead of being relieved, I'm livid.

How dare he be finished with me? How dare he make me all twisted up inside, while he goes on with his life without a care in the world? Dr. Google seems to think I'm suffering from Stockholm syndrome, which is basically when a captive falls in love with their captor, and I think that might be it. Only it's not love, it's lust; animal, primal lust.

I don't love Sebastian, that's impossible, but I'm starting to accept that I do want him. My body craves him, or at least the things he can do for me. He thinks he's done with me, but I have a different plan. I refuse to believe that he can just get over years' worth of infatuation in an instant and to prove it, I plan to torment him, until he breaks down and fucks me.

What exactly I'll do after that, I don't really know, but right now all I can think about is being beneath him again, having his huge dick inside of me, quelling the itch that only he can scratch.

It's Friday night and for the first time ever, I'm willingly going to a party. Sammy has proved quite the little stalker herself, so instead of fighting to push her away, I think we've actually become friends. At the back of my mind, I know that Sebastian will take her from me if I let her get too close, but a periphery friend will be okay, as long as I don't allow myself to get attached to her.

This party was Sammy's idea, apparently there're parties every weekend out in the woods where the freshmen welcome party was held. Although she doesn't know who hosts them, just that it's an open invite to all students. When she first suggested we should go together I balked and refused, but now I'm actively trying to piss Sebastian off, what better way to do it than to get dressed up, go out, drink and dance without him?

My closet is still full of all the sexy dresses and outfits he bought for me, although I've only worn a couple of the shirts until now. Flipping through the hangers, I discard all the dresses that need more T & A than I currently have, and pull out all the ones that should fit.

I don't know if he actually chose these things himself, or if he paid a personal shopper to select them for me, because there's a wide selection ranging from slinky satin minidresses to cute tea dresses, and even a couple of maxi dresses that are super pretty and feminine. Even though I told him these things were more Courtney's style than my own, now that I'm looking at them more closely, it's clear that they were picked for me.

The colors are all mostly warm to complement my skin tone,

with a few bright pieces dotted in here and there, and the styles are sexy, but not too risqué or slutty. Slipping a deep-red silky dress over my head, I sigh as the cool fabric clings to my skin, hugging my meager curves and fitting like it was designed just for me. The hem ends midthigh, but the loose halter neck closes at the base of my neck, leaving my entire back tantalizingly bare.

I feel unbelievably sexy, but I force myself to take it off and swap it for a black dress with cap sleeves and lace panels that offer a glimpse at my cleavage, and a cute A-line skirt that swirls around my thighs. They're both beautiful, but when I drop the white dress over my head and smooth it down, I know I've found the one.

The bandage-style dress conforms to my body like a second skin, curving upward over my stomach toward a cutout on one side that reveals my skin from my hip to just beneath my breast, with just a hint of underboob visible. The soft fabric feels bonded to my breasts, wrapping tightly around my torso until it splits off into a single asymmetric strap that curves around my collarbone until it meets the fabric at the back.

Something about the way I'm both covered and revealed at the same time makes me feel powerful, and even staring at myself in the mirror I can't help but pull my shoulders back and stand a little straighter. This dress makes me feel like a fighter, not the weak mouse I've been since I ran away.

Adding salt spray to my hair, I tease it into tousled mermaid waves, slide my feet into strappy black sandals —another one of Sebastian's purchases—and add another coat of mascara to my smoky-eye makeup. Sliding a tube of gloss, my cell phone and key card into a tiny gold purse that has a strap so it hangs from my wrist, I blow myself a kiss in the mirror and head for the door.

If even a tiny part of Sebastian still thinks of me as his, then seeing me in this dress and knowing I'm going to a party without him will push him over the edge. If it doesn't… then, well, I'm not sure what I'll do, probably pack up and leave, because even though I shouldn't, now I don't have his attention, his eyes, his brand of crazy focused on me, I want it. Fluffing my hair one last time, I pull in a deep breath and then march down the stairs, pushing open my door and striding out onto the landing like I'm in *Dynasty* and in the middle of a slow-mo entrance scene.

"Hey Starling, are you expecting someone, because there's a chick at the door asking for you," Clay shouts up the stairs, loud enough for the entire house to hear.

"Yes, let her in and keep your hands to yourself, she's my friend and off-limits to you guys," I shout back.

With my hand on the banister to steady myself in my heels I descend the stairs and stride confidently into the foyer where Sammy is standing with all four guys looming around her.

"Starling," she cries, her lips splitting into a wide grin when she sees me.

"Hey, Sammy, do you want to grab a drink here first, or just head straight over to the party?" I ask, ignoring the incredulous looks I'm getting from all but one of my housemates.

"You're going to a party?" Evan asks slowly, like he thinks he misheard me or something.

"Yep," I nod, grabbing Sammy's arm and dragging her away from the guys and into the kitchen. Opening the refrigerator door, I pull out a couple of wine coolers and pass one to her. "You look amazing," I tell her, taking in her tight leopard-print miniskirt and simple tight black cami, tucked in to show off her impressive breasts and flat stomach. It's a hell of a change from her usual preppy style, but I love it.

"Thanks. My parents prefer me to wear conservative clothes, but I've managed to do a little college shopping online since I got here. You look unbelievable by the way, I'm totally straight, but you in that dress is kind of making me question it."

We both burst out laughing just as Evan, Clay and Hunter storm into the kitchen.

"Who's the friend, sis?" Evan asks. "And which party are you going to?"

"Sis?" Sammy questions.

Rolling my eyes I shake my head. "Ignore him, we're not related. This is Evan, he is my mom's new husband's son. Then this is Clay and Hunter," I point to them each in turn. "Guys, this is Sammy, she and I met on our way to orientation."

"Harsh, sis, you couldn't have just called me your stepbrother?" Evan smirks.

"No, I couldn't."

"So which party did you say it was?" Hunter asks, trying to sound nonchalant.

Sammy opens her mouth to tell them, but I interrupt. "Just some party some people in our history class invited us to."

"And you're wearing that?" Clay asks, waving his hand up and down, motioning to my dress.

The prickle of unbidden tears sparks to life in my eyes, but I blink them away. It shouldn't be Clay asking about my dress in a disapproving tone, it should be Sebastian. He wouldn't let me wear a white tank because he thought other guys would see my nipples through it, yet I'm here in a dress so tight my thong might as well be dental floss it's so tiny, and he hasn't said a word. He's not even here, because he doesn't care.

"Don't worry, you can borrow it another night," I snap, finishing my bottle off and then looking expectantly at Sammy. "You ready?"

"Sure," she nods, a hint of confusion in her expression. Without asking me what's going on, she finishes her own drink, then takes my hand and walks with me over to the front door, ignoring the three shocked guys following us.

"Have a good night," I call behind me, dismissing the guys as we step out of the door and toward the gate. I stop breathing altogether when the gate doesn't move as we approach it, and a warmth floods my chest, instantly freezing to ice when the huge metal gates slowly begin to part.

He let me go. He saw my dress, heard I was going to a party and then just let me go.

I shouldn't care, but I do. Maybe I've been testing him, seeing if this was all an act, if I actually am free. He passed and I doubt there's a shrink anywhere in the entire country who could explain why my heart feels like it's breaking.

"Starling, are you okay?" Sammy asks as we climb into her golf cart and start to drive away.

Shaking my head, I bring my hand to my lips and cover the whimpering sound that's fighting to get free.

"Oh my god, what's the matter?" she asks, pulling the cart into the driveway for one of the other houses and turning all of her attention to me.

"I'm an idiot. He did everything. I hate him, but he let me go," I half sob, half ramble. I know I'm not making any sense, but my thoughts are so jumbled that I can't make my mouth form the words to explain.

"Wow, okay," Sammy says, taking my hand and squeezing it. "I don't really know what any of that means, but I'm guessing it's to do with a guy?"

I nod.

"It isn't your stepbrother is it, because I'm going to be honest, if it is that's so freaking hot."

I shake my head, blinking away the tears that are threatening to fall. "His name is Sebastian, we went to the same high school for a while."

"Lockwood? Sebastian Lockwood?" she asks slowly, her eyes widening.

For a moment I wonder if I'm making the best decision by telling her the truth. Could she use it against me somehow? Then I just decide to do it anyway. If I really have faded from his notice then I'm not sure I'll stay here anyway, so what harm can it do to tell her the whole sordid truth? So I do, I tell her about him deciding I was his the first day of sophomore year, I tell her about him manipulating my mom and best friend. I tell her about running to my dad's and being so overwhelmed by the idea of him, that I never came back. Then I tell her about him warning me that there would be consequences for leaving him. About the way he stole my mom from me. By the time I explain about having no idea he was at Kingsacre until they ambushed me in the kitchen, her eyes are so wide they're like saucers and her mouth is literally hanging open.

"So let me get this right. He got you here, had you basically under house arrest, sleeping in his bed, having sex with him and then he just apologized, told you, you were free and now he's not bothered?" Sammy exclaims.

The scoff that falls from my lips is bitter and angry. "Pretty much," I shrug. "It's been a couple of weeks now and he's barely even glanced in my direction. At first I thought it was just another one of his games. He's always enjoyed letting me think I've got the upper hand, then showing me he was already six steps ahead. But he really just doesn't care."

"Given everything you've just told me, aren't you pleased that he's lost interest?"

Groaning, I let my head flop back until I'm staring up at the roof of the cart. "I am pleased. I hate him, but I'm also pissed. This boy has haunted me day and night for the last two and a half years and now he's just lost interest, like I was a toy that he got bored of, or a game that he was obsessed with until something new came along."

"I mean I kind of get it," she offers noncommittally.

"Do you, because I don't. I should have packed my bags and gone the moment I had the chance, but instead I'm still here, living in a house with him, in the room literally next door to him. I'm free, but I feel more caged now than I did when he was the constant monster beneath the bed."

"You like him," Sammy gasps dramatically.

"I really don't think I do. He's been the cause of so much misery. But…" I trail off.

"How was the sex?" she whisper-shouts.

"I don't have anything to compare it to, but if it was bad, then I think good would kill me."

Giggling, she slaps her hand over her mouth. "You want to fuck your stalker."

"It's not fair that he gets to just say that it's over. I want to fuck him up, I want him to feel some of the pain and misery he's caused me. I want my revenge, but none of that is going to happen when he doesn't care anymore."

"Maybe he's just playing it cool," she suggests, turning the cart around and heading back down the road toward the party.

"Sebastian doesn't understand the concept of playing it cool, he's completely single minded, a total control freak. If he still thought of me as his, I wouldn't be sitting here wearing this dress."

"What? Why? You look hot as hell in that dress."

"It's not the dress, he bought it for me, it's me in the dress going to a party around other guys. He's more than just standard jealous and possessive, he's, lock me in the house, fuck me until I'm comatose and his cum is dripping out of me, then make me wear the dress and go to the party so everyone will see and smell that I belonged to him."

"Wow," Sammy says, elongating the word.

"Yep. I wore these tiny booty shorts and a shirt that barely covered anything to dinner the other night around his friends and he never said a word. I was practically climbing the counters in nothing but a towel and he was too busy texting to notice. He had an entire team of security guys following me around and reporting my every move to him for two years while I was in Maine, but the other day, I went for a run, then sat, chatted and got propositioned by a guy and nothing."

"Starling, I hate to say it, but you seem to be putting in an awful lot of effort into getting back a guy you said you hate."

"I can't help it," I groan. "It's like he exorcised his own obsession with me, and it immediately took root in me for him."

"The best way to get over someone, is to get under someone else, so that's what you need to do. Let's do a little drinking, a little dancing and then we can find you a target for the night. Even if all you do is grind against him and let him kiss you, it's a step in the right direction."

I nod, agreeing. "Thank you for not giving up on me when I was an emo bitch to you. My ex-bestie turned out to be a real POS and I haven't tried to make any friends since, because I was always worried Sebastian would find a way to use them against me. You could have just walked away and never spoken to me again, but I'm so glad that you didn't."

Waving her hand around, she smiles. "I'm a stage-five clinger, you'll never get rid of me now. Plus, I live in a permanent live-sex show, I need you more than you need me."

Her giggle is enough to make me smile and I settle back into my seat and resolve to not think about Sebastian again tonight. Maybe she's right, maybe instead of thinking about him and how good the sex was, I need to focus on how amazing it will be with someone else. Perhaps it's always that good? I mean, people wouldn't be as obsessed with it as they are if it didn't make you feel good.

I'm giving him all this credit and more than likely it's just that sex feels good, orgasms make you feel epic and together we had a lot of them. But I can find someone else to make me feel just as good without the mindfuck that Sebastian brings to the table.

Unlike the last party, there isn't a parking space conveniently empty and waiting for us, so we abandon the cart at the back of a huge pile of carts and then proceed to make our way through the woods on foot.

Heels and hidden tree roots don't really mix, but eventually we emerge from the path and into hedonistic chaos. I never went to any high school parties, so I don't know if this is usual party behavior, but this is nothing like the college parties I've seen in films.

The freshmen welcome party had a chilled bonfire vibe, this is nothing like that. Instead of fires with lawn chairs, there're glass heaters full of dancing flames, dotted between the trees that have been wrapped with LED strips that pulse and flash along with the heady music.

At the last party I refused to drink, so I never really considered where the various drinks the guys were fetching me were coming from, but tonight there's proper bars set up with bartenders mixing cocktails.

The music is so loud the bass feels like it's pulsing in my chest and I immediately start to move to the beat. Sammy grabs my hand and tows me over to one of the bars, ordering us Long Island iced teas and two tequila shots each.

"For courage," she smiles, leaning forward and speaking into my ear to be heard over the noise of the music and crowds of people. Lifting her glass, she throws back the first, then second shot and I follow her lead, swallowing the disgusting liquor and trying to hold back a grimace.

"Tastes awful, but it works," she says with a wink, dropping a twenty into the bartender's tip jar and handing me another drink in a tall plastic cup. I take a sip and sigh when it's sweet and doesn't burn all the way down to my stomach.

Sammy reaches her hand back and grabs mine, leading us both onto the makeshift dance floor. She immediately starts to dance, so I do the same, sipping at my drink as the pulse of the music drags me under its hypnotic beat.

For a while we dance together, ignoring anybody who approaches us, but as my glass gets emptier, my confidence increases and when a cute redheaded guy with freckles and serious guns curls his arm around my waist and dances in rhythm with me, I don't push him away.

TWENTY THREE

SEBASTIAN

Allowing her to leave the house, wearing that dress, was a lesson in control. Her long legs and toned body were wrapped in the tight white fabric and it took all of my resolve not to drag her back to our bed by her hair.

She was waiting for me to react. The dress, the hair, the party, it was all for me, she's testing me, seeing how long it'll take me to break. She's been seeing how far I'll allow her to push me all week and tonight I almost hit my limit, until I saw her face when the gates opened to allow her to leave.

She was hurt. For all the times that she's told me she hates me and wants me to leave her alone, now she's sad that I'm not following. We're both still playing a game, only I'm not sure who's winning anymore.

The moment the girls drive away in the cart, Evan, Clay and Hunter barge into my room. "Did you see what she was wearing?" Evan growls. "Are you seriously just going to let her go off to a party on her own looking like that?

"She's not mine," I answer, hating the way the lie sounds on my lips.

"How long are you going to carry on with this bullshit?" Hunter asks, his eyes narrowing as he dares me to lie to him.

"You all told me what we were doing was wrong, that I needed to let her go, to set her free. What did you think her freedom was going to look like? Did you seriously think she'd want to spend all of her free time locked up in the house with you guys? She was always going to make friends, go to parties, move on. This is what we agreed."

"Her security detail will stop anyone from approaching her," Clay says, like he's reassuring himself.

"She doesn't have a security detail on campus," I lie again. There isn't a moment when she's out of my sight that she doesn't have eyes on her.

"Get dressed, we're going to that fucking party, the two of them are like a walking target. I don't believe any of this nonchalant shit you're trying to sell, she's yours, your little bird, there's no way you'd let another guy near her," Evan snarls, stomping into my closet, pulling a shirt from the rod and throwing it at me.

Snickering to myself, I don't move until all of my brothers

have left my room to go and get changed. I don't really need to go tonight, I have seven guys watching her every move with strict instructions to remove any man but me who tries to touch her, but after seeing her face, I know she needs me. She needs to be reminded of why I'm the only man who will ever own her, the only person she'll ever choose to belong to.

Throwing the white shirt over my head, I roll the sleeves up to my elbows and change my sweats for fitted shorts. I look like the rich, preppy asshole that I am, but I don't care. Sliding my feet into white sneakers, I grab my cell and my key card and then leave my room, unlocking Starling's room with the app on my cell and climbing the stairs. Her scent hits me the moment I enter her space and I groan as my dick instantly hardens. I've missed the way she smells. Not being able to be close enough to touch her has been torture, but it needed to happen.

The next time I touch her, there'll be no way she'll be able to deny how much she wants me. Her attempts to gain my attention this week have been cute. Those tiny fucking shorts, prancing about in nothing but a towel. She thinks I wasn't interested enough to pay attention, but I've watched the security footage of her ass playing peekaboo out the bottom of that towel as she reached for a glass she didn't need more than a hundred times already.

When I reclaim her, it'll be because she begs to be mine again, but there's no reason why I can't give her a taste of what it's like to belong to me. If she asks nicely, of course.

Both calmed and aroused by being in her space, I run my fingers over her comforter, moving around her room and touching her ancient laptop that's sitting on her desk. Several of the dresses I bought her lie discarded on the bed and her pajamas are balled up on the chair. Stepping into the bathroom, my dick hardens even further when I think about her naked and wet and suddenly the urge to mark her is too strong to fight. Before I can question what I'm doing, her body wash is in one hand, my hard cock free of my pants in the other. Gripping myself tightly I stroke up and down the length of my cock, imagining her tight nipples pebbled from the cold, her pussy wet and smooth, ready to be licked. It doesn't take long until my balls are pulling tight and I'm spilling my release into the bottle, my cum mixing with the soap. Releasing my spent cock, I tuck it back into my shorts and replace the lid on the bottle, shaking it to make sure its thoroughly mixed. I promised her all of my cum was for her, and this load might not be inside her, but she'll be rubbing it into her skin every time she has a shower from now on.

Exhaling happily, I exit her room, engaging the lock again and sauntering downstairs to find the guys all impatiently waiting for me in the foyer.

"Finally, get your fucking ass moving, this is your woman who's at risk here," Evan snaps aggravatedly as he throws open the door and stomps over to the golf cart.

"Are you really prepared to let her hook up with some asshole at a party, just to make a point," Clay asks.

"What point am I making?" I ask, annoyed that two weeks ago they were all telling me I needed to let her go and now they're telling me to get her back again. "She doesn't want me, you all agreed that I needed to leave her alone. What the fuck do you expect me to do?" I think a part of me thinks I should feel bad for lying to them, but I need them on board once she does come back to me. I can't have them telling me I have to give her up every time she gets pissed at me or them. It feels like I'm almost playing with them as much as I am her, but they forced me to set her free. If they hadn't, she wouldn't be at this party right now, she'd be bouncing on my cock, locked in her gilded cage.

"She wants you," Hunter tells me quietly. "She was worried and unsure the first couple of weeks, but this week she's been angry. Starling wants your attention, that's why she's been provoking you, although I'm not sure you've even noticed, you've been so determined not to pay any attention to her."

"You guys just need to fuck it out or something, I'm getting sick of seeing my sister's ass," Evan laughs.

Inside I'm smirking, but on the outside I keep my expression neutral and shrug. "I'm not sure, I think maybe we missed our chance. Mom and Dad have mentioned how advantageous an alliance with the Eadberht Corporation would be. They have a daughter, she's just turned eighteen, if I'd never met Starling I'd probably already be engaged by now, so..." I trail off deliberately. Of course it's all utter bullshit, the Eadberht's do have a daughter, but even though they only knew Starling for a short time, my mom and dad are still fully intending to have her for a daughter-in-law; they'd never suggest I sacrificed love for a political marriage.

"No," Hunter growls in his quiet, purposeful way. "You'd make that poor girl miserable because it will only ever be Starling for you. You fucked up with her, I think if maybe you'd have acted like a normal seventeen-year-old when you first met and not some megalomaniac millionaire, she would have liked you for you. You pushed too hard and she ran, then you fucked up again bringing her here the way you did. But she wants you, maybe not the way you want her yet, but if she was completely lost to you, she would have left and she didn't, she stayed. This is your chance, don't give her a reason to run again."

Hunter is usually quiet, so when he has something to say, we listen. Of course I already know everything he just spelled out so eloquently, but it's nice to know he's exactly where I want him to be, which is firmly on team make Starling fall in love with me.

"He's right," Clay agrees, as Evan nods. "You need to figure out how to win her back, you love her, you can't just walk away from that."

I take a moment, forcing a pensive look to my face as if I'm carefully thinking about what they're saying, then I nod. "I love her." It's the first honest, true thing I've said since we started this conversation. I love Starling and it's more than just my obsession with her, she's everything. I want to be her north, but she's the needle on the compass, without her, all directions are meaningless.

A hint of guilt permeates into me, I shouldn't be manipulating my friends, the men I consider my brothers, but I need them on board with helping me do whatever I need to do to tether my little bird to me again.

"Any idea how I can get the ball rolling?" I ask.

TWENTY FOUR

STARLING

The feeling of the tequila humming through my veins makes the music seem louder and more all-consuming, and I love it. My hands are in the air, while my ass is pressed up against the front of a very aroused guy, his arm curled around my waist.

With my eyes closed, I try really hard not to notice how wrong it is to have some random guy's hard-on pushing into me. I want to be able to embrace this moment, my first real college party—the first party the guys dragged me to doesn't count. But even though I'm doing all the right things, it just feels so wrong.

The guy, whose name I don't even know is slightly behind the rhythm, his arm around my waist is floppy and neither claiming or supportive it's just sort of hanging there. I can feel his hardness pressing into me, but I'm not feeling even an ounce of arousal and I think I'm supposed to be. Isn't that the purpose of dancing like this, to simulate sex, to see how well you'd fit together? If it is, then the answer with this guy is not that well.

I want to push him off, but I don't know the etiquette. Is it really insulting if I ask him to remove his limp arm and his underwhelming-sized cock away from me? It feels rude, so instead I just go with it, throwing back what's left of my drink and trying not to cringe when the guy nuzzles into my neck.

Sammy is immediately across from me, apparently she has the etiquette down, because her tongue is down the throat of a pretty blond boy with messy surfer-style hair, her hands groping his toned chest beneath his unbuttoned shirt.

Pulling free of the guy—whose name I really wish I knew, if only so I didn't keep having to refer to him as *the guy* in my head—I smile and wave my empty cup at him, signaling in the general direction of the bar. Nodding, he smiles, but thankfully doesn't offer to come with. Pushing my way through the throng of people, I join the back of the line, exhaling slowly and watching the people around me who all seem so much more comfortable than me. I'm used to being alone, but even when I was in Maine I felt Sebastian's phantom eyes on me, even though I knew he was hours away in a different state. Knowing he doesn't care enough to watch anymore makes me feel bereft.

Stepping up to the bar I order myself another Long Island iced tea. Whoever organized this party made it a free bar, but I push a tip into the jar and then move off to the side, standing on the edge of the dance floor with the shadowy trees behind me.

A prickle of awareness washes over me and I tense, suddenly feeling like I'm being watched, but there's no way Sebastian is here. If he cared enough to come, he'd already be laying claim to me, making sure everyone around knew who I belonged to.

"Where's your friend?"

Gasping, I turn toward the sound and find Sebastian standing placidly at my side, his hands in his pockets.

"She's dancing," I tell him.

"I meant your male friend." His face the picture of unassuming placidity.

"Oh." Sudden panic floods me, but why am I worried he might have seen me dancing with another guy, I'm not his and he is most definitely not mine. "I needed another drink." I lift my glass and he smiles.

"I see, he didn't really strike me as your type."

"My type? What would that be exactly?"

"Someone who provokes a reaction a little stronger than confusion and discomfort from you," he replies, leaning in so I can hear him over the volume of the music and the roar of the party going on around us.

"Maybe I'm just not used to dancing with strangers at parties, I'm not exactly a social butterfly."

"Hmm, maybe. Or maybe he just didn't do anything for you."

I nod noncommittally. "You're right, redheads aren't what

I'm craving, I'll try a brunette next time."

His laugh sounds menacing even through the volume of the music and the sounds of the party going on around us.

"By all means, don't let me stop you." Lifting his arm, he gestures to the mass of dancers.

I don't want to go back out there, dancing with Sammy was fun, but allowing guys to touch me feels… wrong. I've avoided all human contact for so long and now that there's no little voice warning me he'll find out, I can't stand the thought of anyone's hands on me but his. But I don't want him to think I'm stopping myself because of him, so I lift my glass into the air and offer him a silent toast, forging forward into the crowd until I find Sammy. She and her friend have come up for air, now he's curled around her back, grinding to the dirty bass line while he nibbles on her neck.

"Starling, where did you go?" she asks, her voice a little slurred.

"To get a drink, you were busy or else I'd have gotten you one."

Smiling drunkenly, she waves me off. "It's fine, Rob." She stops, and glances over her shoulder to the guy who's dry humping her butt. "Rob?"

"Ross," he smiles.

Laughing, she turns back to me. "Ross is going to get us drinks."

When Ross detaches himself from her, she throws her arms

around my neck and hugs me tightly. When she leans back, she leaves one arm curled around me and starts to grind with me in the way that girls do when they want guys to look at them.

Not wanting to push her away I go with it, but having her hands on me feels almost as weird as the redheaded guy's hands did. I'm relieved when Ross gets back and she enthusiastically launches herself at him, locking her lips with his and kissing him passionately.

My body sparks to life a moment before a familiar arm encircles my waist. "She's an affectionate drunk, isn't she?" Sebastian asks.

"She's definitely friendly," I say, holding myself stiffly against his hold, not wanting to give in to my craving and relax into his touch.

"I'd like us to be friends," he breathes against my ear.

My feet stop moving and I freeze to the spot. His arm falls away and I slowly spin around, narrowing my eyes the moment I'm standing in front of him. "What did you say?"

"I'd like us to be friends." The small shrug he offers me is the thing that pushes me over the edge and before I can even think about what I'm doing, my hand is in the air and slapping against his cheek.

His eyes widen in shock and I swear there's an audible gasp from the people around us, but I don't stick around long enough to see how they react. Pushing my way through the crowd, I text Sammy as I go to let her know I'm leaving and ask her to text me when she gets home.

"Asshole," I mutter, my gaze focused on the ground, trying to watch where I'm going and not trip over a tree root. "Friends, fucking friends."

I'm so focused on not falling and angrily ranting about Sebastian that I don't notice someone's following me until I'm plucked off the ground, dragged off the path and pressed back against a tree.

"Calm down, Starling, it's only me," Sebastian says as I'm parting my lips to scream. The sound dies in my throat and the fear that has turned my blood cold all morphs into unrestrained anger.

"What the fuck are you doing? I thought you were attacking me, you fucking asshole."

"I called your name several times, I've been following you since you stormed off, but you were too busy calling me an asshole to notice," he says calmly.

"You are an asshole," I shout into his obnoxiously beautiful face.

"I know," he smirks.

"Stop smiling."

"I'm sorry, I just forgot how cute you are when you're angry."

"Why are you here?" I ask.

"Because it's Friday night and there's a party."

"No, I mean here, now," I clarify.

"Because you stormed off upset, I wasn't sure how you were planning to get back to the house."

"I hate you so much," I snarl.

His lips twitch a moment before he leans forward and breathes against my ear. "You don't hate me."

My lungs stop working, my heart stills and my sex perks up in excitement at how close he is to me right now. Leaning back, he pulls his full lower lip between his teeth and watches me, waiting for something, but right this second, I have no idea what.

"I think you wish you hated me, but you can't, because I'm the only one who makes you feel."

I try to shake my head to deny his words, but the only noise I can make is a pathetic whimper.

"Do you need it?" he asks, his voice a whiskey-tinged rasp that makes me swallow down a moan of desperation.

"Need what?" I practically pant.

"To feel."

I try to shake my head, to say no, but I don't. I can't. I want him and it's not some animalistic urge, it's a need, a want, a choice. My body isn't overruling my head, I'm not unaware of what's happening here, even though a part of me wishes I could use that as an excuse for what he makes me feel. I'm angry at him, furious that he has the audacity to suggest we be friends, but I want him. I need him and I hate it, or maybe I just hate that I don't hate it.

For weeks I've yearned to feel the way he makes me feel. I tried to replicate it with rebellion, but it didn't work. I sought it out from others, but I stayed cold in the face of replacing his touch with someone else's.

"I need it too," he confesses on a whisper.

My lips part as I lift my gaze to his. He's so beautiful, his face regal and austere, sometimes almost sinister with how perfect he is.

"You can have anything you want, all you have to do is reach out and take it," he taunts.

My eyes fall down to my hands that are gripping the fabric of his shirt tightly. I assumed he was holding me in place, imprisoning me like he usually does. But he's not touching me, his arms are hanging loosely at his sides. I'm the one keeping him here, the one holding him captive.

"You're usually the one who takes whatever you please," I say breathily.

"I know. I took too much, now I'll only take what's offered freely."

Swallowing thickly I glance guiltily around us, but we're alone, everyone else is busy at the party. Relinquishing my hold on his shirt I lift my left hand and place it on his right arm, slowly sliding it down until I reach his hand. My skin feels alive, tingles of power and sensation building until I feel like I'm vibrating with nerves and excitement. Slowly I lift his hand up, guiding it to my breast.

"Just for tonight," I tremble.

"Spell it out for me, Starling, I want to hear you say exactly what you think this is."

"Make me feel, Sebastian. Just for tonight, I'm…" I pause, then inhale. "I'm offering myself to you."

For the longest moment of my life, he just looks at me, his palm still pressed against my breast. Then he lurches forward and collars my throat while his lips plunder my mouth. In an instant my body comes to life, exploding with need and want and desire. The night is both brighter and more immersive, lighting up the world around me even as the darkness presses in on us.

His lips devour mine, his tongue forcing mine to submit as his fingers squeeze just enough around my throat to remind me that each breath I take is because he's allowing it. I want more. I want his hands on me, his fingers in me. I want him to make me come and then force me to do it again and again. I want him to take away my choice and make me accept whatever he wants to give me, and I want it all right now.

Blindly reaching for his hand that's not around my neck, I try to drag it downward, needing him between my legs, but instead of doing what I'm silently asking, he tenses his arm, making it immovable as he grips my neck, then releases me, stepping back and assessing me coolly.

"What? Why are you stopping?" I gasp.

"I'm not sure this is a good idea," he admits, rubbing a hand over his hair.

"What?" I snap. "Are you serious?"

"I'm not sure you're thinking straight, you've been drinking."

"I've had two shots and one and a half cocktails, I'm more than capable of making my own decisions."

"And you want this?" he questions, his expression mostly calm with a hint of something I can't quite identify.

"I want you, Sebastian, I need you and I'm offering you me. So what are you waiting for?" I taunt him.

A second later my feet leave the ground and my back hits the trunk of a tree as the skirt of my dress is shoved up and he rips my thong clean off me. Two thick fingers slam into me and I let out a long, low moan of pleasure as he pumps them in and out. I'm so wet I can hear the sound of my own arousal and feel the way it coats my thighs.

"This is going to be fast and quick; I'll take my time on round two," he smirks a second before his fingers are replaced with his rock hard and much bigger than I remember cock.

I open my mouth to scream, but Sebastian shoves my thong between my lips, gagging me with the underwear that he just tore off me. The taste of my own arousal fills my mouth, but I don't have a chance to decide how I feel about that before he starts to fuck me.

My legs are curled around his hips and I lock my ankles at his back, holding on to his shoulders while he slams his cock in and out of me, not giving me a second to get used to his sheer size.

Unadulterated bliss hits me when I combust; an orgasm wrenched from me as I scream around my panties, feeling the sound in the back of my throat even if nothing more than a muffled cry escapes my lips. I'm barely moving, simply holding on while he fucks the ever-loving shit out of me against a tree no more than fifty yards from where a college party with hundreds of guests is raging. It's hot and dirty and brutal and I love it. I'm on the verge of coming again when he pulls out of me, spins me around and then slams into my pussy again from behind as I struggle to find purchase on the tree I'm now facing.

Delivering a sharp slap to my ass, he sets a frantic pace as he drills me from behind, his hold on my hips tight enough to bruise and I want it to. We barely had a day together before he freed me, but not until he gave me a glimpse of what it means to be truly owned by him. In that twenty-four-hour period he gave me more pleasure than I've ever known and then it was gone, and I've been craving it ever since.

A sense of loathing hits almost in unison with my second orgasm, but Sebastian doesn't even pause, fucking me as I scream and writhe. His thrusts become deeper, harder until he grips my hips to the point of pain and comes deep inside of me.

For a moment, neither of us moves. My cheek is pressed against the tree I'm holding, my legs are spread wide, my dress bunched at my waist, Sebastian's cock still inside of me. We could be discovered at any moment, but neither of us tries to move. Somehow the sounds of our panting breaths are louder than the raucous noise of the party behind us.

Sebastian loosens his grip on my hips and I whine in protest when his dick slides out of me, the heat of his cum dripping out of my sex. Lifting my head, I glance over my shoulder and find Sebastian with his cell in his hand, the camera focused between my thighs.

"Seriously?" I croak, pulling the fabric from my mouth.

His eyes lift to mine and he smirks, completely unrepentant. "Let's go."

"Go where?"

"Don't you remember? I already told you this was only the first round. You didn't think this was it, did you?"

I push my dress down, covering myself, and he scowls.

"I'm not done with you yet, Starling. You gave yourself to me for the night, so you're mine until the sun comes up. Now let's go."

Wrapping his fingers in a tight grip around my wrist, he drags me back onto the path until we reach the same spot we parked our cart in for the first party. Smiling, he lifts me off the ground and places me into the front of the cart, following me in and immediately pulling away.

"Won't the others need the cart?" I ask, glancing back toward the woods that we're speeding away from.

"They'll be fine, I texted them to let them know we were

leaving and to ask them to keep an eye on your friend."

"What? When?"

"While you were running away."

"Presumptuous much?" I snip.

"Get your head out of the gutter, sweetheart. I just wasn't about to let you wander about on your own at night." His palm is resting on my bare thigh and as we get closer to the house, he inches his fingers higher until he's playing with my folds, massaging his cum that's still coating my thighs into my skin.

The gates open for us the moment we reach the house and instead of parking the cart around the side, he abandons it right in front of the entrance. I expect him to drag me inside, but instead he turns me to my side, and slides me along the seat until my legs are dangling outside and I'm lying along the bench.

Parting my legs, Sebastian pushes my dress up until I'm bared for him, naked from the waist down, my panties gripped tightly in my hand.

"You've got the prettiest pussy I've ever seen," he murmurs, parting my lips with his finger and thumb as he stares down at me. "So pink and wet and perfect."

Keeping me spread wide, he pushes two fingers into me then pulls them all the way out. He does it again, dipping into me then withdrawing and again until I'm squirming on the seat as he fucks me with his fingers in the open where anyone could see.

"I wonder if I can make you squirt for me?" he muses,

adding a third finger and curling them upward until he finds my G-spot, and I moan wantonly in pleasure.

"We only have tonight, just fuck me. I want you to fuck me again," I beg.

Laughing, he lifts his eyes and smiles at me. "Don't worry, after I play for a little while I'm going to fuck you until you scream. But first I want to see if I can make you come so hard you cover me in your arousal the way your cunt's coated in mine."

His fingers start to move again and I see stars as he circles my clit with his thumb while he works my G-spot with his talented fingers. I come almost immediately, screaming out my release while he continues to work my pussy, fucking me with his fingers until a pressure unlike a normal orgasm starts to build. "Sebastian," I say cautiously.

"That's it, sweetheart, come again for me, how does it feel?"

"Like I want to pee, in a really, really good way," I whine, the thong I'd been gripping in my hand forgotten as I writhe against the bench seat, my fingers clenching tightly to the leather.

"Perfect, baby, fucking perfect. Come for me, just let go and I promise it'll feel so fucking good."

I try to hold it back, horrified that I might pee when I come, but his fingers are relentless and when I can't hold on anymore, I orgasm, and it's not like anything I've ever experienced before. The orgasm implodes inside of me, but it's more than just coming, it's like a full-body release as all the pressure he's built up inside of me squirts out of me.

"Fuck, that is the hottest thing I've ever fucking seen. I'm soaked, Starling, you gushed all over me."

My eyes fall closed and I let my head drop onto the seat beneath me, my arms flopping to the side.

"Oh hell no, we're not done. My dick has never been so hard."

Scooping me off the seat, Sebastian flings me over his shoulder, marches into the house and up the three flights of stairs to the floor we share. I expect him to take me to his room, but instead he pulls my key card from my purse, opens my door and carries me upstairs.

Lowering me to my feet, he unzips my dress and shoves it to the floor, his wet shirt and pants follow suit and then we're both naked.

"I want you to ride my dick while I suck on your nipples," he says, sitting on the edge of the bed and pulling me down into his lap. Stradling him, I grab his cock and guide him into my soaked sex. I'm literally dripping with a mixture of his cum and my own and his dick slides easily into me until I'm full of him and my ass is pressed against his thighs.

"Offer me your tits, sweetheart," he orders, but right now I'll do whatever the fuck he wants, so I lift my breasts with my hands and lean toward his mouth. Capturing them in his hands, he sucks first one nipple, then the other into his mouth, rolling the tip with his tongue. "Ride my cock, baby, make us both come, else I'll pin you face down over the end of your bed and drill your pussy until you're begging me to stop."

For the first time, possibly ever, I'm not scared of him, or his threats. He won't hurt me, not in a way I won't enjoy, and knowing that is freeing and powerful. Moving slowly to start off with, I slide myself up and down his cock, teasing him with shallow glides that feel nice but won't lead to us screaming with ecstasy.

"Faster," he chides, scraping his teeth over my swollen nipple as I moan. I lift almost all the way off him, before sliding him all the way to the hilt, getting deeper with each thrust.

It almost feels like I'm in control, like I'm using him for my pleasure, but he's definitely topping from the bottom, caressing and lapping at my breasts when I'm doing what he's telling me to do, punishing me with nips and bites when I'm not.

When I finally do come, it's a hot burn that starts in my toes and moves steadily upward until my sex is clenching his dick so hard I can barely move.

"Motherfucker," Sebastian growls from behind gritted teeth, gripping my waist and lifting me up and down his length, forcing my pussy to milk him until we're both panting and covered in sweat.

After our breathing has slowed, he carries me to the shower and washes me. Then he pulls the showerhead from the wall, messes with the flow by twisting the top and forces it between my legs.

The heat and pressure of the water startles a low moan of shocked sensation from me. I knew that you could use a showerhead to get yourself off, I've just never tried it until now. Why have I never tried it? Teasing me, he uses the jet on my clit, never allowing me to focus on his probing fingers against my tight asshole while the water is like a hundred tiny hands massaging me all at once. And when I come again, it's with the water spraying directly onto my clit, and two of his fingers filling my ass.

TWENTY FIVE

SEBASTIAN

Rolling off Starling, I flop into a boneless heap on the mattress beside her. My dick actually feels chaffed from the amount of sex we've had tonight, but I don't care. She offered herself to me for the night. She gave herself to me, because no matter what she says, or how hard she fights, she's mine, and no one will ever make her feel or react the way I do.

After I got her off in the shower, I ate her pussy for nearly an hour, making her come again and again until she begged for my cock. When I finally gave it to her, it was with her face to the comforter, her hair in my fist and her ass in the air. After the fourth or fifth round, she fell asleep and I woke her up with my dick, rolling her to the side and lifting one leg while I fucked her. I haven't let her clean up since and right now her pussy is a sopping mess of my cum. I've lost count of how many pictures I've taken of her cunt overflowing with me.

She hasn't mentioned us using condoms, but we haven't been careful, I love seeing the mess I've made of her too much to ever use anything. Twisting to the side, I take in her ravished appearance. Her neck and breasts are coated in bite marks and hickeys. Her nipples are swollen and red from me sucking on them and her cunt is puffy and so fucking well used she's going to feel me for days.

I want her again, but honestly, I'm not sure I can get another erection even if I wanted to. Her eyes are closed and her chest is moving rhythmically up and down, I've fucked her into an exhausted stupor. Grabbing my cell, I turn on my camera and take a picture of her, naked, well used and fucked beyond exhaustion. Switching to video, I pan it up and down her body, zooming in on her kiss-swollen lips, her nipples, the hickeys on the inside of her thighs and finally her cunt and tight asshole.

Like this, ravished and exhausted, she's utter perfection and now all I need is for her to open her eyes and tell me she loves me. She's not there yet, but tonight has pushed her a massive step closer to my ultimate goal.

The sun is just starting to peek over the horizon as I grab my clothes and force myself to slip from her bed. I don't want to leave. I want to take her to my room, slide my cock into her and chain her to me, but I tried that and it didn't work. I need her to wake up alone. I need her to question why I'm not there, to feel sad, to crave me and my touch, my cock and my attention. Her body will remind her of me with every step, but I want her thoughts to be consumed by me too.

I know it's an asshole move but as I lean down and press a kiss against her lips, I make a silent promise that once she's mine, like she's always meant to be, I'll never let her wake up without me again. That I'll never let her question how I feel about her, how much I want her, how I don't want to exist without her.

"I love you, little bird," I murmur against her lips then I leave, hating each step that takes me away from her. "Give yourself back to me soon."

TWENTY SIX

STARLING

My body slowly comes to life and I groan as my muscles protest against the movement. Taking stock of what hurts I realize it's all of me. I feel weak and yet it's not a bad pain, more of an exhausted bliss.

Blinking my eyes open, I stare up at the vaulted ceiling above me. There're tiny stars painted into the rafters that sparkle in the sunlight. Twisting my head to the right I expect to find Sebastian, peaceful and almost soft in sleep, only the bed is empty. I'm alone. Reaching out I touch the sheets beside me, they're cold he's been gone a while.

He left.

He fucked me all night, waking me up with his dick every time I fell asleep and then he just left. I rack my brain, trying to decide if he woke me up to say goodbye, but the last thing I remember is him draping my legs over his shoulders and fucking me. He held me immobile, not able to do anything but take him pounding into me over and over until I screamed my release. I must have passed out after that and instead of sleeping beside me, he left.

Sitting up, the sheet I must have pulled over myself at some point slips to my waist and I see the remnants of our night all over my skin. My nipples are swollen and red, not their usual pink, there're bite marks and hickeys all over me and from the tenderness in my neck, it's received the same treatment.

There's dry cum on my stomach and as I lift the sheet my thighs are covered in it too. I'm honestly not sure how many times we had sex last night, but it must be at least nine, or ten. Curling my legs upward, there's a pull between them that I know will linger for at least the rest of the day, maybe longer.

My bladder protests, so I carefully climb out of the bed and pad slowly to the bathroom. When I'm done, I wash my hands and stare at my reflection in the mirror. I look well and truly fucked. Ridden hard and put away wet. Ravished. But instead of basking in the afterglow of amazing sex, I feel hollow and empty.

I expected him to be here, I expected to have to deal with his domineering ways, to have to kick him out and remind him that what happened between us was just a one-off. But instead I'm alone. He didn't even care long enough for the sheets to cool before he was grabbing his clothes and any other evidence of him being here and leaving me like I was nothing more than a girl he met at a party and spent the night screwing.

Is that what I am? Am I a one-night stand? Is that what last night was? From the moment he tore into my life and smashed it to pieces he's called me little bird, but last night he never used the pet name even once. Should I have known I wasn't special to him anymore?

Tears fill my eyes and instead of trying to fight them, I let them fall. I cry for myself, for an amazing night that's been ruined by his absence, and I cry because as much as I hate it, I wish he was here. I wish I was fighting with him; I wish he was here so I could tell him he was an asshole and that he doesn't own me. But he's not and I hate it.

More tears roll down my cheeks and I'm not sure why. I don't want to care about him, but the moment he put his hands on me last night, all the unanswered questions I've been asking myself over and over again didn't seem to matter, because he was the answer to them all.

The boy who blew my world to pieces, is the only person who can put me together again, but I gave myself to him last night and this morning he was gone. He's spent years chasing me but the moment I stop running he turns and calmly walks in the opposite direction.

My own confusion wars with the anger Sebastian always seems to provoke in me. Half of me wants to storm downstairs and kick him in the balls for leaving, the other half refuses to ever chase him.

A beeping sound calls me back into my bedroom and I flop onto the bed, grabbing my cell from where I apparently put it on charge last night. There're three texts from Sammy and a missed called from my dad.

I feel too ragged to speak to my dad right now. He knows Sebastian is here. I didn't tell him that he orchestrated me being here too or why he did it, I just told him that Harry had arranged for me to be in the same house as Evan and that the others had all decided to transfer here to be together for their junior and senior years. Dad was furious, he tried to get me to leave, to come home to Maine, I refused. That was a week ago and both of us have been too stubborn to contact the other until now.

Clicking into my messages, I promise myself that I'll call Dad later.

Sammy
Where did you go?

Sammy
Clay (OMG how hot is he!!!) Sebastian took you home. AHHHHHHHHH I really hope he's fucking you into the matress right now. I want to hear ALL the dirty details tomorrow.

Sammy
Are you alive? Did he wear your pussy out???

A bark of laughter falls from my lips and I type out a reply.

Me

I'm alive, not so sure about my pussy.

She replies almost instantly.

Sammy

YES GIRL!!!! So are you and the stalker back together?? Is that what you want?

Me

He was gone when i woke up.

Sammy

WTF what a douche!!! Want to go get breakfast off campus? We can drink mimosas and bitch about beautiful boys.

Me

Do you have a car?

Sammy

Of course. Get dressed I'll come grab you in our cart?

Me

KK see you soon.

I try to jump up from the bed, but my limbs protest and I groan, pushing my hand between my thighs and gripping my battered pussy. Rolling more sedately off the mattress, I head back to the bathroom for a much-needed shower. When I've washed all the dried cum off my body, I get dressed in a pretty pale-blue sundress and then use concealer to cover the worst of the visible hickeys Sebastian gave me. I'm pretty sure I left some on him too, so it won't take a genius to figure out what happened between us last night.

When I'm as presentable as I'm going to get this morning and walking as tenderly as I can, I descend the stairs hoping to avoid my housemates—especially Sebastian—until I can decide what to do about him.

"Morning, sis," Evan says, walking out of his bedroom door just as I hit his landing. "Rough night?" he asks with a wink.

"Urgh," I groan, "You'd have thought with as much money as your families have, they'd invest in some soundproofing."

"All the bedrooms are soundproofed, all except yours. Normally I'd be totally down for a free porn soundtrack to fall asleep to, but then just as I was drifting off you'd go again and again and again. If I'm honest I'm impressed with both of y'alls stamina. I'm actually surprised you can walk at all today."

"Oh my god, Evan," I cringe, punching him in the arm as we walk down the stairs side by side. "Did you even consider just not telling me you heard me having sex last night?"

He wrinkles his brow for a second as he thinks, then he turns and smirks. "No."

"God, I hate you."

Dropping his arm across my shoulders he pulls me into the kitchen. "Having a sister is fun," he laughs, only releasing me when Clay and Hunter both jump up from their chairs, turn their attention to me and start to clap.

"Fuck you," I hiss, rolling my eyes as I flip them the bird, ignoring them as I grab a bottle of water from the drink cooler.

"Where's Bastian?" Clay asks.

I shrug. "No clue."

"Has he seen how short that dress is?" Hunter asks with a raised brow.

"He bought it, so I'm going to go with yes, but as he'd gone before I woke up this morning I'm also going to suggest he wouldn't care either way." I have no idea why I'm telling them this. We're not friends and they're firmly team Sebastian, they've proved that over and over. But a part of me wants to know what they think. If they're as shocked as I am that he ghosted me this morning, or if this is standard operating procedure for him.

"What do you mean?" Evan asks, walking to stand beside me.

"I mean, we fucked, then I fell asleep with him in the bed and woke up alone."

"Did he leave a note? Maybe he went to get coffee or breakfast or something," Clay suggests, but I can tell by the expression on his face that he doesn't believe it.

"No note, and he'd been gone a while. I mean, it doesn't matter, we agreed it was just for the night, he honored that. Suppose there's a first time for everything."

"Wait, so you guys didn't make up? You're not back together?" Evan asks.

"No," I shake my head. "No, we didn't even... No. Last night was just about sex."

"Do you want to get back together with him?" Hunter asks, in that quiet way of his.

I shrug, avoiding any of their eyes, because the truth is I really don't know how I feel about Sebastian. "You can't get back together with someone you never agreed to be with in the first place."

The sound of a golf cart horn beeping from outside breaks the strained moment between me and Sebastian's friends, and I shake off the weirdness of discussing this stuff with them. "That's Sammy, see you later."

"Where are you going?" Clay asks.

"Off campus to get breakfast."

"Take my car, don't ride the bus," Evan says, holding his keys out for me to take.

"Oh, I can't drive."

"But you have your permit," Clay says.

"Having a permit and knowing how to drive are two different things. Mom can't drive either, we planned to learn together, but then… well you know what happened and I left. But it's fine, Sammy has a car. Bye."

All three guys stare at me a little shocked, but I don't ask them what the problem is, I just leave, eager to get some space and some time away from campus for the first time since I got here.

"Morning, girl, you look surprisingly fresh for someone who was being fucked all night," she says in greeting.

"You don't look too perky. What happened with Ross?"

"Who?" she grimaces.

"The guy you were making out with?"

"Wasn't his name Rob?"

"No," I laugh.

"Oh. Well your housemates are serious cockblockers. After I got your text to say you were leaving, they decided to come play security to me. They scared Rob off."

"Ross."

"Yeah, him. They scared him off and then kept giving every guy who came near me death stares until they left. My lady balls were so blue by the time they dropped me off at home that I had to bring out my BOB to save the day."

"If you weren't up all night having sex, why do you look so tired?"

She grimaces. "Because my orgy-loving roomies were. I walked in on a full-blown sex show. The triplets. Did I tell you the girls were identical triplets?"

"Er, no," I laugh.

"Yep Amie, Amelia and Anastasia Attingham. They're either nymphos or they are looking to get knocked up before the end of the first semester. We've only been here a few weeks and Amie is already engaged and pregnant. I assumed that might make her and Tim take a step back from the constant orgies, but no, now she's jumping from cock to cock, warming them up for her sisters. I really, really need to move out, I've got to the point where I'm frightened to touch anything in case it has someone's fluids on it."

"Ewww that is gross. I wish we had a spare room in our house, I'd love another girl to balance out the testosterone in that place."

We chat away until we reach one of the valet stations and a familiar face steps out. "Starling," Angelo says with a bright smile. "How you doing?"

"Hi, Angelo, I'm good thanks, this is my friend Sammy."

"Hey, Sammy," he nods, glancing at her briefly then turning back to me. "I haven't seen you around, I thought you might come visit me."

"Er, yeah, it's been a hectic few weeks, settling into school, making friends." I shrug.

"Yeah, that's cool. Maybe you'd let me take you out some time?" he asks.

"Ohhh, er."

"Ahh someone snapped you up already, didn't they?"

"No, I don't have a boyfriend, it's just." Wrinkling my brow I try to decide what to say. "Er, it's complicated."

Angelo nods, his smile dimming. "I get it. But if things uncomplicate themselves, or you change your mind, you let me know."

"I will," I nod, offering him a small smile.

Another valet arrives with Sammy's car and I climb into the passenger seat, not glancing in Angelo's direction as she pulls away from the curb.

"He was cute, why did you say no?"

"I don't know, he is cute, but he doesn't really do anything for me."

"Hmm," she says, smirking knowingly at me as we drive through the entrance gates and onto the road.

"This is the first time I've left campus since I got here."

"What?" she gasps. "How come?"

"I don't have a car and the closest bus stop is like twenty minutes' walk from here."

"You ride the bus?" she asks appalled.

For the first time in years, I remember how ignorant of the real world the wealthy and entitled are. "Yeah, that's how normal folk get places when they don't have a car."

"Wow, I sound like a stuck-up bitch, don't I? I'm sorry, there's just no way my parents would let me take a bus anywhere, they think I'm too young to even be in school, they wanted me to defer my place at Kingsacre and stay home for another year."

"It's fine, it's just been a few years since I was around the überwealthy. The tiny town we lived in, in Maine was just full of fisherman and their families, the nicest car in town was the shiny new school bus."

"But your mom married Daddy Warbucks, so you're like rich now too. Also, fuck you very much for not telling me exactly who your stalker and your housemates were. The Lockwoods, Morrises, Rossbergs and Jansens are like American royalty, they're not just rich, they're next level rich and insanely powerful. To be honest, if I'd known you're basically a Morris I think I'd have been too intimidated to speak to you that first day."

"I'm not a Morris. I'm a Kennedy, just the plain old normal daughter of a fisherman from Maine, Starling Kennedy. My mom married into all that, not me."

Sammy mouths "Ohh," then falls silent for a few minutes until we reach a small row of shops, bars and restaurants.

"I literally had no idea this was here," I admit.

"Have you been eating on campus this whole time too?"

"Mainly. The last couple of weeks since I started trying to piss Sebastian off, I've been eating more at home, the guys like to cook, which I find odd, but the refrigerator is always stocked and the food in the cafeteria at night is truly awful."

Sammy parks the car and we climb out. She heads toward a cute restaurant with comfy-looking sofas out front in beachy pinks and oranges. We sit and a waitress takes our orders.

"Has he texted you yet?" she asks.

"He hadn't before we left. I'm not sure he will, he's not the wait three days type, he's the slide an engagement ring onto your finger while you sleep kind of a guy."

"Oh my god, I love him. You make him sound like such an asshole."

"He's the biggest asshole."

"With the biggest dick by the looks of it, don't think I

haven't notice how you're walking this morning."

"I'm actually in pain, my thighs are chaffed and I think I might need to take some Tylenol, my pussy has a pulse."

"Oh my god," she cackles. "Tell me everything, how did it even happen? Last thing I remember was you dancing with a sexy ginger, then we danced, then you were gone."

"Urgh, I don't even know. He said he wanted to be friends."

"Friends?"

"Exactly, I mean what the fuck? So I got really angry and I just wanted to leave, so I texted you and then he followed me and caught up to me, and the next thing I know we're fucking against a tree."

Her mouth falls open and then twists into a grin. "Just like that? He suggests friends, you suggest some alfresco sex?"

"It's all a bit of a blur, he did his Sebastian Jedi mind trick shit and said he wouldn't take anything from me anymore, said that I had to offer; and oh my god, I think I kind of begged him." Covering my face with my hands I groan.

"You like him, don't you?" Sammy asks, her tone serious now.

"I hate him."

"Okay, just for a minute, take away all the stuff from the past and just think about what's happened since you got to Kingsacre. You like him."

"The problem is I can't discount the stuff that happened, it shaped me and fundamentally changed me as a person. I might and it's a really big question mark, like *this* version of Sebastian, but how can I forget everything he's done to me?"

Our waitress arrives with our food and I fall silent, thanking her as I lift my mimosa to my lips. "Why didn't she ask for ID?"

"None of the bars along this strip bother asking for ID from the Kingsacre students," she says, waving my concern away. "Okay, so let's take it one offense at a time. You guys met in high school?"

"Met probably isn't accurate, I never spoke to him before the day he announced I was his. But yeah, according to him and the others, he saw me when I was a freshman and decided I belonged to him."

"That's when Clay, Evan and Hunter started watching you for him? This is the bit I don't understand, why didn't he just come say hi?"

"GAA, the school we went to, has these weird rules. Every freshman has a year to prove who they are, and that means for the first year they don't really interact with the older kids and the older kids aren't allowed to mess with them. It's supposed to give you a year to find your place or some shit."

"And Sebastian and the others were like prefects?"

"The Elite, yeah. There's a tradition that the graduating Elite seniors pick their replacements from the juniors, but the guys were picked as freshmen. It was a whole thing, but basically it meant they were royalty, they were Elites for three years, not just one, and their word was law."

"So they were the kings and Sebastian wanted to make you his queen, but he didn't make his move until your sophomore year?"

A bitter laugh falls from my lips. "Yeah, it was the first day of classes and I had a shift at the diner I worked at straight after school. By the time I had my uniform on, they were sitting in a booth in my section. I was so scared, I thought they were there to tell me I was getting kicked out of school, but instead Sebastian told me I was his and that I had to quit my job. Clay went and spoke to my boss and came back with my final paycheck. I'm not entirely sure what they threatened him with, but he told me not to bother coming back."

"Wow."

"Oh that's not even the worst thing they did that day. They forced me to get into their car and then he just started telling me I was his. God, I think he even mentioned us getting engaged. I freaked the fuck out and must have passed out, because when I woke up I was in a bedroom at his house. He had a doctor there for me and he called my mom out and she stayed the night. I still don't know how he managed to convince everyone that I was there willingly, but no one ever questioned it."

"Your mom never thought it was weird?"

"No. Mom drank the Kool-Aid from day one, she loves Sebastian, I told her what he was doing and she just brushed it off as teenage drama. When I went to Maine I had a complete fucking meltdown. I told my dad everything and he never questioned it. He hates Sebastian, well all of them really."

"But apart from that first few days, Sebastian hasn't been a total psycho, right?"

I exhale slowly. "No, not really. He scared the crap out of me that first day, he said all this shit about cages and clipping my wings and loads of other fucked-up stuff, but then he just changed his mind and set me free."

"Wow," she says again.

"Half of me thinks he's still fucking with me, but I just don't know anymore. I want to walk away, to leave and forget about him, but it's like he's infected my thoughts. He's been the monster under the bed for so long now, I just don't think I can just pretend he's not a part of my life."

"And the sex?"

"Well I've got nothing else to compare it to, but it was phenomenal, completely out of this world. I came so many times I actually thought about asking him to stop making me orgasm at one point. I don't know what it is about being with him, our past is so toxic and even when he's not messing with me, it still feels like he's messing with me. Last night when I was dancing with that guy, all I could think about was that it felt wrong, him touching me. I got asked out a couple of days ago and I felt nothing but an icky guilt, like if I agreed I'd be cheating. When Sebastian touches me, even after all our fucked-up history, it feels right."

"Oh my god, this is some next level messed up," Sammy laughs.

"Tell me about it. I've never even kissed anyone but him."

"We need to change that. You can't make an informed decision about Sebastian if you've never experienced anything else. There's a block party tonight at Bufford Row in the town houses, we're going to go and you're going to find a cute guy to kiss. If it's good then great, you can explore what boys are like away from Sebastian and his mind fuckery. If it's bad, or it feels wrong, then maybe as messed up as he is, Sebastian is the one, and you need to figure out a way to forget the past and move forward."

TWENTY SEVEN

SEBASTIAN

It's been hours since I left her room and I can still smell her on me. I need to shower, but the thought of washing her off my skin is repellant. My cell is at my side, I half expected her to text me this morning, but she didn't, instead her and her friend went out to breakfast and haven't been back since.

When her security team advised me that she left campus I almost followed and dragged her back. I'm happy to allow her the illusion of freedom in the confines of Kingsacre, but if she tries to actually leave me, I won't be able to allow her to go.

As hard as it was to leave her this morning, I'm confident it was the right thing to do. I know she was confused and a little pissed, she even spoke to the guys about it, but making her mad is completely worth it if it forces her to deal with the way I know she feels about me.

My dick starts to harden the moment I let myself think about how it was between us last night. I never forced her the first time we had sex, but there was definitely some coercion, manipulation and heated emotions that fueled it. Last night was all about want and need. She offered herself to me and that gift made everything better.

For me there're several types of sex. There's sex for sex's sake, no emotions, not repeats, just the fun of shoving your dick in someone until you get off. Then there's fucking, usually fun, sweaty and enthusiastic, sometimes repeated, but never taken too seriously. What Starling and I have done is angry fucking. Hot, intense, insanely good sex that you want to do again the moment you finish. It's the kind of sex that you never forget, that changes you and bonds you to the other person for the rest of forever because it's fueled by emotions that are so strong they may fade, but they'll never go away.

Last night changed things for us. We're still playing this game we've been playing since the first time I saw her, only now we're in the final round with only a handful of turns left to take, winner gets it all. She doesn't know it yet but I only ever play games I know I can win. I want her back in my bed by the end of the week and my ring on her finger by the end of the month. The best thing is that she'll come to me willingly, admitting that it'll only ever be us and that her future doesn't exist without me in it.

My cell beeps and I grab it hoping it's from her, but it's from her security team.

Sec 1
Just returned to campus.

They're more discrete now, watching her from a distance, but no matter what I told her and the guys, there's always eyes on her when she's not with me. I wait on tenterhooks for her to get back to the house, but thirty minutes later she's not back so I contact them again, asking for her location.

Me
Location?

Sec 1
Alistern House.

She's at her friend's house. I don't like it, but it's not as if I can go and retrieve her without confessing that she's being followed, so instead I head downstairs and find the guys playing Xbox in the living room. "Hey," I say, sliding onto the couch next to Clay.

"Hey," Evan says, not looking away from the TV screen and the game he's playing.

"What's up with you and Starling? Her room's not soundproofed, we could hear you making her scream all fucking night long," Hunter growls.

I smirk. "Yeah, sorry about that. You hearing I mean, not me fucking her all night long."

"She told us you bailed before she woke up?" Evan asks, a

challenging gleam in his eyes.

"We agreed it was just for the night, so I booked before the sun came up and I broke her rules," I shrug, feigning nonchalance.

"I thought you were gonna try and work things out with her. How is fucking her, then making her feel like shit by ditching her before she wakes up fixing things?" Clay asks accusingly.

"Hey I'm trying to make things right, I stayed away until she came to me. Last night I asked her if we could start over, try to be friends and she suggested we fuck. It was her idea; she made the rules, I'm just trying to follow them," I say, holding my hands up like I'm surrendering.

"She was upset that you weren't there," Hunter offers.

"You hoping to see her tonight? Maybe you could ask her out on a date or something?" Evan suggests.

"Nah, I'm going to give her some space, respect those boundaries she's always saying I cross. We live in the same house, it's not like we're not going to see each other," I tell them with a shrug, forcing my expression to stay neutral while I spew bullshit to my best friends.

I spend the next few hours playing Xbox and resisting the urge to text Starling and demand she get her ass home. But by the time the pizza we order for dinner arrives, I'm starting to get more than pissed. Pulling my cell from my pocket I text her security team again.

Me

Location?

Sec 1
Party - Bufford Row.

Me
Who?

Sec 1
Starling, Sammy and three unknown males.

Me
Have they touched her?

Sec 1
Negative. Shall we intervene?

Me
No, I'm on my way.

Sec 1
Copy.

"I don't want to stay in tonight, this is our junior year and since Starling got here I've been a moody motherfucker. Anyone know any parties happening tonight? Let's go be social and get some beers," I suggest.

"Bound to be a party somewhere, let me send a few texts," Evan says, pulling his cell out.

Resting my hand on my knee to stop my foot tapping impatiently, I force myself to eat while I wait for one of my friends to tell me there's a party at Bufford Row.

"Chad says there's a lacrosse party down on the field," Hunter says.

"There's a block party at Bufford Row," Evan offers.

"Is that the town houses closest to campus?" I ask, already knowing exactly where it is.

"Yeah, I forgot about it, they always throw a party a few weeks into the semester. Everyone in the row opens up their houses and chips in for a few kegs. They have the party in the street outside and each house has like a different theme. Last year they picked retro video games. One house was Pacman and they dressed up in these homemade costumes, it was awesome." Evan laughs.

"Sounds good to me, my balls are fucking blue, I need to find me some pussy tonight," Clay laughs.

Smiling to myself, I take another bite of my pizza, imagining all the things I'm going to do to my little bird when I get her into my bed tonight.

TWENTY EIGHT

STARLING

Sammy wasn't lying when she said her house was like a permanent orgy. When we got here, she steered me straight up the stairs to her room, but not before I spotted not one, but two couples going at it in the living room. When I reached out to put my hand on the banister, she slapped it, taking my hand in hers and pulling me to the middle of the stairs. "Fluids, don't touch anything out here."

Cringing, I pull my free hand to my chest and cautiously follow her to the first floor, so glad that I never offered to take my shoes off when I came inside. When we reach her door, she unlocks it and we both step inside.

"Wow, are they seriously like that all the time? When do they go to class?"

"I'm honestly not sure that they do. The one that's pregnant and her guy leave occasionally now, but the other four are at it like rabbits twenty-four seven," Sammy says with a disgusted grimace. "I'm all for having a lot of sex and living your life with your own set of rules, but it's common space and they don't ever come up for air long enough to clean. The cleaning service refuses to come in because they keep walking in on them fucking. I had to pay one of the cleaners extra and then escort her to my room to get her to clean my bathroom."

"Oh my god," I laugh.

"It's not funny," she insists, "If my parents find out I'm living with six nymphos, they'll drag my ass back home and I'll be doomed to church on Sundays and knee-length tea dresses for the rest of eternity."

"There's space in my room to add another double bed if you want to move in with me," I suggest.

"Considering you had a fuckfest with your hot psycho ex last night, staying with you would probably be jumping out of the frying pan and into the fire."

I roll my eyes, then shrug, conceding she might have a point. Sammy convinces me to borrow something out of her closet to wear to the party so I don't have to go home and run the gauntlet of my nosy, overprotective housemates.

The shorts I borrow are khaki green with big gold buttons. They look sexy paired with the cropped tank she thrusts into my arms. Our feet are the same size so I slide on the strappy gold

sandals she insists look amazing and pray that I don't fall over
and break my neck in heels this high.

Twisting my hair up into messy space buns on the top of
my head, I keep my makeup light and add a bright-red lip. By
the time we're outside her house and dousing our hands in
liquid sanitizer, I've almost forgotten about Sebastian and how
conflicting my feelings are for him.

Hooking her arm through mine, Sammy leads me around
the side of the house to where she parked the cart earlier when
we got back. "Best thing about having housemates who never
go anywhere is never having to share the cart."

Climbing in, she backs out of the space and pulls away
from her house, chatting nonsensically about boys and kissing
and other stuff that I don't pay attention to. Instead, I take the
time to psych myself up to find someone to kiss tonight. Sammy
is right, how can I justify whatever my feelings for Sebastian
might be if I've never experienced anything different?

Having a random guy at a party with his hands all over me
felt all kinds of wrong, but that doesn't necessarily mean that all
guys are wrong for me. Maybe he was a creeper or something
and my body unconsciously figured that out when his hands
were on me.

Five minutes later, I hear the first signs of the party as the
dull thud of heavy bass hits my ears. There're so many more
people at this party than the one in the woods and the throng has
a tension-filled vibe that sets my nerves on edge. Sammy parks

the cart at the end of the row and we climb out, holding hands so the dense crowd doesn't separate us when we push into it.

The smell of body odor and weed fills the air and I wrinkle my nose. You'd think with this many rich kids in one area they'd be able to afford to buy decent deodorant, but apparently money doesn't equal personal hygiene. Trying really hard not to touch anyone, I follow Sammy through the mass of people until we reach a row of kegs where a huge guy who looks more like he should be a bouncer rather than a student is standing with his arms crossed.

"Evening, ladies, cups are ten dollars each, you can refill as many times as you like, but if you lose your cup you have to buy a new one."

Sammy and I shrug, then pull out money and hand it to the guy, who passes us each blue plastic cups with the Kingsacre logo on them.

"Kegs are tapped, always pump your own, don't take a drink unless you fetched it yourself," he warns.

"We will, thanks," I say, offering him a smile for the safety talk, but not wanting to think about why he feels like he needs to warn us.

As we fill our cups, I feel like I'm at a real college party. The party in the woods with its cocktails and bartenders felt too rich kid to be a real college experience, but drinking beer from a plastic cup I just paid for feels much more authentic.

"Dancing or checking out the houses first?" Sammy asks.

"The houses all decorate to a theme, this year it's Hawaii so expect some sand, grass skirts and coconut bras."

"Let's dance a little first, get a few drinks into us, then we can check out the houses with a bit of a buzz," I suggest.

Sammy smiles brightly then lifts her cup into the air, I tap mine against hers and we throw the foul beer back, turn and fill our cups again before making our way into the crowd to dance.

An hour later, I'm a little drunk and loving life. My hands are in the air and I'm dancing like I don't have a care in the world. Sebastian has barely managed to enter my thoughts at all since that first beer.

"Shots time," Sammy shouts, pulling a flask from her purse and waving it in the air giggling. Unscrewing the top she lifts it to her lips and takes a drink, grimacing slightly before handing it to me. I take a drink too, gagging when the sour hit of tequila coats my throat.

Some guys approach us and we're all dancing when a large body moves behind me, not quite touching me but close enough that I can feel them. Glancing over my shoulder, I'm surprised to find Chase smiling at me.

"I thought it was you, you look seriously hot," he says with a wink.

"Hey, Chase, yeah this is probably better than the drowned rat look I was wearing at the track," I laugh.

He laughs too, dancing behind me without making a move to get any closer. Turning my head back to Sammy she shimmies closer to me, leaning in until her mouth is pressed against my ear. "He's hot."

"That's the guy who asked me out the other day," I confess.

"Perfect, you know he's interested, kiss him and see how it feels," she urges.

Shrugging I try to imagine leaning in and pressing my lips against Chase's lips, but the moment I start to think about it, Sebastian's face replaces Chase's and my body starts to heat.

No. This isn't about Sebastian, I know my body reacts to him. Kissing another guy is about figuring out how it reacts to someone else, and to do that I need to pretend that Sebastian doesn't exist.

We all dance for a bit longer, then I feel Chase move closer, tentatively placing his hands on my hips. When I don't push him away, he moves closer still until my ass is practically sitting in his groin, our bodies moving as one to the beat of the music.

"Let's go check out the houses," Sammy shouts. The group of guys that I'm now realizing must be Chase's buddies all agree and we move as a group, topping up our cups on the way. This is the first time I've been in Bufford House, the place I would have been living if Sebastian hadn't manipulated things to get me where he wanted me.

The row of houses are all connected by a long hallway with doors opening off into each house and the living space beyond. The floor of the hall is covered in sand and my heels instantly sink into it. Stopping, I pull my sandals off and carry them as we walk as a group to the end house and enter into it. The living room has been decorated with plastic palm leaves and we're offered flower leis as the sound of tropical music greets us. A hula contest is in full swing and we shuffle past it and into the kitchen area, where a row of guys are being soaked in water for a wet-Hawaiian-shirt contest.

"Hell yes," Sammy hoots, and three of the attractive athletic guys grin at her.

We spend a little time in the house, joining the other girls to judge the wet shirt contest, by stepping up to feel the pecs and abs of each guy in turn until a winner is crowned.

The next house is underwater themed, with snorkels being used as funnels to down tropical punch. In the third house, Chase and the other guys all dart forward to take part in a limbo competition, and I'm laughing my ass off when Bruce, one of Chase's friends, shuffles along the floor like a crab to get under the limbo stick.

The crowds are even thicker in the fourth house, and Sammy and I lose hold of each other as we shuffle toward the kitchen where some kind of competition is happening. I try to keep sight of her, but there're so many people and without my heels I can't even see over the shoulders of people ahead of me.

"Don't worry, I can see them, just hold on to me and I'll get us back to them," Chase says, offering me his hand.

Nodding, I take his hand and let him push through the crowd, creating a path for me to walk along. Meandering in and out of

OBSESSION

people, it seems to take forever, but we finally reach the wall, only instead of being at the door that will take us to the kitchen, we're at the doors that lead to the ground floor bedrooms. This is wrong. Chase said he'd get me back to Sammy and the others, but instead he's led me away from them and toward bedrooms. Panic seizes me, but before I have a chance to scream or run, Chase's hand closes over my mouth, his arm banding around my waist like a steel bar as he drags me kicking and screaming into a bedroom, closing and locking the door behind us.

"That's better, just the two of us alone at last," Chase says with a sinister smile.

"What are you doing, Chase? We need to go and find Sammy and the others," I say, trying to stay calm.

Tilting his head to the side, he takes in my appearance, letting his eyes scan over me, rubbing his thumb over his bottom lip. "No, I don't think so,"

"I want to leave," I say, moving to unlock the door.

I'm not expecting the brutal backhand that explodes on my cheek, knocking me to the floor. "Do you know who I am?" he asks, a manic gleam flashing in his eyes.

"We have gym together," I say, clutching my cheek.

"I'm Chase fucking Lawrence. I'm the starting quarterback for the Kingsacre Royals, I'm going to the NFL. Pussy lies down and spreads itself in front of me and you... You," he shouts, "You say no to me. No one says no to Chase Lawrence."

Shuffling away from him, I glance behind me, trying to find

an escape route. I'm trapped. Other than a window on the other side of the room, and the bathroom that I'd have to get past him to lock myself inside, there's nowhere to hide.

"You're just like all the other rich bitches who think they're too good for the guys here on a football scholarship, but I'm a god, on the brink of becoming a legend. You don't get to say no to me, you're nothing but a cunt to be used and I'm going to teach you a lesson. So be a good fucking bitch and take your clothes off and maybe I'll go easy on you," he snarls, spit flying from his mouth with each angry word.

TWENTY NINE

SEBASTIAN

The sheer quantity of people at this party is unbelievable. There're probably twice as many people here as there was at the party in the woods last night and unlike last night, there's no bar or bartender, just kegs lined up on the floor with a guy taking money for a cup to drink from. It's like the great unwashed came to Kingsacre overnight and all decided to congregate here, dancing to terrible music.

I expected to be able to find Starling straight away, to be able to "bump" into her and then mindfuck her into coming home with me again, but instead I'm pushing my way through the crowd aimlessly, trying not to lose my shit and start picking people up and throwing them out of my way until I find her.

My little bird is tiny, if she's in the middle of this crowd and gets pushed, she could end up being trampled. Pulling my cell from my pocket, I text her security team.

Me

Location?

I expect an immediate response back, but two minutes later I still have nothing. Evan, Clay and Hunter are all here with me, but they look as pissed off as I am about having to push through the hoard of people. I text again.

Me

Location?

Again, I receive nothing in reply. I'd call but the music is so loud I can barely hear myself think, so there's no way I'd be able to hear anything they say to me.

Me

Where the fuck is she?

When I finally receive a response, it makes my heart stop beating and panic surge potently through my gut.

Sec 1

Location unkown. She entered the 4th house in Bufford Row with Sammy and a group of four men. We had eyes on her until they got seperated in the crowd. Sammy and three men are in the house's kitchen, Starling's location is still unkown. We have backup heading to the area.

My emotions collide in a mixture of fear and anger. This is the first time in over two years that I don't know where she is and what she's doing. She could be in danger; she could be fucking that guy that she's with. I did this, I pushed her too far again, expecting her to act in the way I anticipated she would, always feeling like I know when to zig to her zag.

I can't let this happen. She's mine and I refuse to let another man touch what always has and always will belong to me. Stopping, I turn to look to my friends, letting them see the panic on my face.

"What's up?" Clay shouts.

"Starling is here."

"Cool, let's find her," Evan smiles.

"Her security lost her, they know she went into one of the houses with Sammy and a group of guys, but the group got separated and they don't know what happened to her and one of the guys."

"You still have a security team on her?" Hunter growls angrily. "You told her, and us, that you told them to stop watching her."

"I lied," I confess.

"What the fuck, bro?" Clay says angrily.

"I know, okay? I know I'm an asshole and you can punch me or do whatever the fuck you need to do after we find her."

"Who is the guy?" Evan asks.

"I don't know," I say, pulling at my hair agitatedly.

"Are you worried because you think she's going to fuck this guy, or because you think she might be in danger?" Hunter asks.

"Both. I can't. She's mine."

"Her tracker," Evan yells, his eyes almost as panicked as mine.

"Fuck," Clay hisses, shaking his head and spinning slowly in a circle.

I consider it for a minute, before opening the app on my cell phone that has the ability to show me the location for the trackers all of us have implanted in the skin at the back of our neck. None of them have ever been activated, including Starling's. I select her icon and change the tracker status to active and wait as a red dot appears on the screen, then I quickly move forward as the app advises the distance to the tracker's location.

It feels like it takes forever to push our way through the throng and into the hallway that runs along the front of all six houses in the row. According to the map, she's still in the fourth house, and I angrily barge past people, shoving them out of the way as her location counts down.

Five hundred meters

One hundred meters

Fifty.

Thirty.

Twenty.

When it reaches ten meters, we're standing outside a row of doors that lead to bedrooms and I see red. Lifting my foot up, I kick in the first door, finding the room empty. I do the same to the second door, not caring about the gasps from the people still partying in the house that are now watching me. It's empty too. When I reach the third door, I can hear muffled sounds. Wasting no time I kick open the door, only to find Starling on the floor beneath a huge guy. She's kicking and screaming, frantically trying to push him off her as he rips at her clothes.

Blackness engulfs the edges of my vision and all I see is her face and the terror that's etched into her beautiful features. I don't realize I've moved until I've ripped him away from her, pinning him beneath me as I'm slamming my fist into his face over and over.

"Sebastian."

The sound of her voice pulls me from my murderous rage and I stop, my knuckles split and covered in a mixture of his blood and my own. His face is a mess, his hands lifted, trying to protect himself from my fists.

"Sebastian," she calls again, her voice cracking.

Pushing off him, I turn toward her, moving a step closer, watching her intently, not wanting to scare her. Scrambling off the floor she runs to me, launching herself into my arms as gulping, broken sobs burst from her shaking body.

The next hour is a blur. Starling refuses to release me, even as the police take her statement and she tells them how he dragged her into his bedroom and attempted to rape her using the party noise to cover the sounds of her screams.

The moment I tell them who I am, the police barely question why Chase Lawrence's face looks like hamburger meat. With

Starling's statement, the bruise on her cheek from where he hit her and the video from the camera he'd set up to record him raping my girl, it's a pretty open and shut case for the cops who haul him away handcuffed to the stretcher in the back of an ambulance.

Sammy, Evan, Clay and Hunter are all standing around us, watching as Starling clings to me. "Let's go home," I whisper into her neck, supporting her weight with my hands beneath her ass as I stand up and carry her out of the now-empty house.

The others follow us out, but no one speaks as we make our way back to the carts. I climb into ours with Evan and Hunter, While Clay gets into Sammy's with her.

"Bring her back to ours, she can stay the night in case Starling needs her," I tell Clay, who nods.

No one speaks as we drive back to the house until I unlock the front door and step inside. "Little bird, do you want Sammy to help you get cleaned up?" I ask.

"No," Starling says, her face buried in my shoulder.

"Will you let me help you?" I ask quietly.

I feel rather than see her nod, glancing at the others before I slowly climb the stairs to the third floor. Pushing the door open to my room, I carry her straight into the bathroom and turn on the shower.

"I need to put you down so you can shower, okay?"

"No, don't leave me," she begs.

"I'll stay in here if that's what you want."

"Get in with me."

Nodding, I lower her to the floor and carefully help her remove her clothes. "Get rid of them, I never want to see them again," she says, her lower lip trembling.

My own clothes are covered in blood so I quickly strip and then throw both her and my clothes onto the landing to deal with later, before rushing back to her.

She's still standing where I left her, her arms wrapped around her naked breasts, her eyes closed.

"What do you need me to do?" I ask, completely at a loss as to how to make this better.

"Help me wash his touch off."

Nodding, I slowly approach her, carefully rubbing my thumb over the darkening bruise on her cheek. I expect her to flinch, but instead she leans into my touch, a silent sob breaking from her lips.

Lifting her, I help her beneath the water and between us, we wash her skin, until she's pink and her sobs have changed into soft tremors. Once she's clean, I grab a cloth and get all of the blood from me, then turn off the shower and grab a towel for her, wrapping it around her as I lift her out, placing her on the floor.

Wrapping a towel around my own waist, I carefully dry her skin while she stands still and just allows me to take care of her. If this wasn't the most fucked-up situation ever, I'd be loving the way she's giving her trust to me.

When we're dry, I grab one of my T-shirts for her and pull it over her head while she pushes her arms into it. It falls to her knees, but I still grab her a pair of my boxers and offer them to her. She shakes her head, sitting down on the edge of the bed.

"I don't know what to do," I admit, feeling useless.

"I'll be okay, he scared the shit out of me, but he didn't actually do anything before you found me."

Exhaling a slow breath, I try to stay calm and not let the rage that's still simmering below the surface boil over.

"How did you find me, Sebastian?"

Exhaling slowly, I think about what to do. I could lie to her, tell her that it was all just chance. I could use this to my advantage, twist this awful night into another game, but that doesn't feel right. I love her and tonight she was almost hurt, almost raped because I played games with her and sent her spiraling into the arms of a rapist. I don't deserve her, I never have. It's time to tell her the truth and then actually let her go, it's the only way I can stop hurting her.

"I lied when I told you I called off your security detail. I didn't."

"What?" she asks.

"I lied. There's been someone following you all the time since you got here, they never stopped, even though I told you they had."

"Why?" she breathes.

"Because I couldn't bear giving up that control over you,"

I confess.

"So they found me?"

I shake my head, "No, they had eyes on you when you first went into the house, then when you split from Sammy, they lost you."

"Then?" she trails off.

This is it, this is the moment I make her hate me forever. "Can I touch you?"

She nods and I reach for her hand and then bend down, placing her fingers on the back of my neck right at the base of my hairline. "Do you feel that?" I ask, moving her finger back and forth over the microchip about the size of a grain of rice beneath my skin.

"What is that?"

"When I was a kid someone tried to kidnap me, Evan, Clay and Hunter. They knew our families were close and that we traveled to school together every day, so they planned to hijack our car, take us, then ransom us back to our families."

"Oh my god," she gasps.

"Somehow, our families found out and the person was stopped, but afterward, a doctor came to the house and injected tracking devices into us. We all have them, our parents too."

"Okay," she says slowly.

Lifting her hand, I take it from my neck and curl it around, placing it on the back of her own neck, positioning her finger over her own tracker.

"How?" she pants.

I don't want to, but I let go of her hand and exhale as I prepare to tell her everything. "The day we came to you at the diner, you passed out in the car on the way home. I had our family doctor come to check on you. He gave you some water to drink that I had him lace with a sedative. While you were asleep, I had him implant that into your neck."

Her hand trembles as she lifts it to cover her mouth.

"I swear to you that I have never activated it, not before tonight, but when you went missing and your security didn't know where you were I freaked out. I'm not sorry that I did this to you, because it got me there in time to protect you, but I am sorry for how I went about having it fitted in the first place."

Her eyes are wide and she's looking at me like she has no idea who I am, like I'm as big a monster as the man who had her pinned to the floor tonight, and maybe I am.

"I've never felt anything like the obsession that consumed me the day I saw you for the first time. I'm not saying that to excuse everything that I've done, I'm just trying to explain it maybe. Being an only child and coming from the family I do, I'm used to being spoiled, it doesn't hurt that I look the way I do. Until you, I've never met anyone who didn't fall at my feet and agree to do whatever I wanted just to please me. As conceited as it sounds, it really never even crossed my mind that you wouldn't want to be my girlfriend."

Swallowing thickly I look at her, knowing that after tonight she'll never be mine again, but knowing that I need to tell her anyway.

"I thought you were playing hard to get, that the push and pull was all just a game. And then you ran. When I first assigned the security team to you, it was out of hurt pride. If I couldn't be happy with you, then I wouldn't let you be happy with anyone else either. It wasn't until I got you here that I saw the damage I've done to you. A part of me wants to lie and say that I'm sorry, that I wish I could go back and stop myself from falling in love with you on the first day of your freshmen year. But I don't. I will never regret loving you, because even though you were barely mine for a few weeks, they were still the best days of my life. I lied when I told you I was setting you free after you got to Kingsacre, I never intended to leave you alone. I told myself it was just another game to let you think you were free, so when you did come back to me, it would be willingly. But I fucked up and because I'm an asshole I pushed you toward that guy. I'm so fucking sorry, Starling. You got hurt, you were nearly raped because I'm an asshole who can't deal with the woman I love not loving me back. But I promise, I fucking promise that I'll leave you alone from now on. I'm gonna pack a case and tomorrow, I'm going to transfer back to Harvard. I'll make this right."

THIRTY

STARLING

Sebastian starts to stand and I reach out and grab his arm, halting his movements. He's thrown so much information at me in the last five minutes that I barely know where to start to work through it all, but the thing that sticks out the most is that he loves me.

"You love me?" I question. It's not the first time he's told me, but it's the first time I actually believe him.

"More than anything else in the world, more than I realized it was possible to love another person."

"I have a tracker in my neck?"

"I can arrange for it to be removed, there's normally a tiny scar, but I can get a plastic surgeon to make sure you can't see anything."

"Why are you so obsessed with me, Sebastian?" I ask. "I need more than you seeing me and knowing I was meant to be yours."

His laugh is low and sad. "It started because you were beautiful, but then you said no to me. It was like you lit a match against a tinder, you fought, you bartered, you challenged me and I love it. And now it's because I broke you and you came back fighting. You are singularly the strongest, most stubborn, resilient, beautiful person I have ever met. You refuse to do as I say, ignore my rules, flout my threats and laugh at my ultimatums. You make me fight you, for everything, and I have never needed anyone the way I need you. In the world we live in, all I have to do is say my name and problems just fall away. I beat the shit out of that guy tonight and if I were anyone else, I'd have been arrested, but as soon as I told them who I was they were shutting up their little notepads and walking away. I love you, because you don't give a crap who I am. I love you because the moment I touch you it feels like my skin is set on fire. I love you because you are the only person I know I'll never ever get bored of."

"So you love me because I'm a pain in your ass?" I laugh.

A soft chuckle reaches my ears and I can't help but stare at him. "You are everything I'll never deserve."

"You took over my life in high school."

"I know."

"You turned my best friend against me."

"In my defense, she confessed really early on that she was only friends with you because she saw me watching you and she thought you might help her get to me and the others."

"You destroyed my relationship with my mom."

"I know," he says, bowing his head.

"You stalked me."

"I did," he nods.

"You sabotaged my college plans to get me here."

He silently agrees.

"You had a tracker implanted in my neck and had a security team follow my every move?"

"Yes."

As I list his crimes, I feel a smile start to form on my lips. Nothing about what he's done is funny, but I can't help it and by the time I'm finished, I'm giggling. This boy, this man has put me through so much. But he's also protected me in his own fucked-up way. He's cared for me, made me feel more than I realized was possible.

He orchestrated the destruction of my relationship with my mom, but if I'm honest with myself, wasn't it fractured before he came into my life? Before Sebastian I was more of the parent than she was. I worried about and paid the bills, I did the grocery shopping and cooked our meals. I was the adult, while she hid from the world behind her keyboard and the worlds within her books. Sebastian might have hammered the final nail in the coffin, but I can finally admit that what happened between me and her wasn't solely his fault.

I was numb until he brought me here and jump-started me again. Now I'm living, with a new friend and possibilities. His love is a hurricane that hurts and destroys but when you're in the eye of the storm with him, it's calming, peaceful and beautiful.

For the very first time, I allow myself to be honest about how I feel about him. I don't disguise my feelings with hurt or anger, I just let them flow out and think about how I'd feel if he was gone.

"I love you too," I blurt.

"What?" he gasps, leaning into me, crowding me, before he inhales sharply and leans back, putting space between us again.

"I'm in love with you," I say, trying the words out on my tongue and liking the way they feel.

"No you're not. You hate me, you should hate me."

"I do, and you're right I should hate you. I don't really understand why, but I love you too, no matter how fucked up it is."

With the words out there, I exhale and relax. Saying it out loud is like taking a weight I hadn't realized I was carrying around off my shoulders. "I love you," I say it again.

"You can't love me," he says, shrugging with that austere look he gets that makes me want to slap him.

"I can't?" I question.

"No, you can't. I'm an asshole, I've done terrible things to you, ruined your life, ruined you. You hate me, you don't love me."

Scoffing, I crawl across the bed and into his lap, straddling his legs until my butt is sitting on his thighs. "Sebastian," I whisper against his lips.

"Yeah," he gasps, his hands curled into fists at his sides as he tries to stop himself from touching me.

"Shut up and kiss me."

The End

EPILOGUE

Since the attack and me confessing my feelings for him, everything and nothing has changed between us. He insisted that I hated him and couldn't possibly love him after everything he'd done and I agreed, then I stripped naked and convinced him that I could both love and hate him in equal measures. After that I think he decided not to look a gift horse in the mouth and just accept that I want him in spite of our tumultuous past.

For the first two weeks he was on his best behavior, not demanding anything from me and waiting for me to offer whatever I decided to give him, but after two weeks of taunting and torturing him, it got old and I found I actually missed his over-the-top, crazy, jealous, obsessed, stalkerish ways.

When I confessed this to him, he refused to believe it. He

was absolutely convinced that I was playing with him, getting revenge for all the mind-fucking he's done to me over the years. I can kind of understand why he felt like it could all be a cruel joke, and I'll admit seeing him insecure and unsure of himself was an incredibly gratifying experience, but as much as I might be tempted to, I've never played those kind of mind games with him.

It wasn't until I went deliberately AWOL that he lost his shit and the real Sebastian finally came out to play. After he tracked me down and fucked me so hard I screamed loud enough to make my voice hoarse, we sat down and talked about which of his stalker behaviors I could tolerate and which were hard limits for me. Then he spent the whole night forcing orgasm after orgasm on me, to try and get me to agree to things I told him were deal breakers.

No matter how normal Sebastian pretends to be, I know that his obsession with me is as potent and out of control now as it was the day he decided I was his. And a month down the line I've discovered I enjoy pushing his buttons until he loses control and turns into the snarling, angry, threatening man he was the day he revealed he was my cage and that he'd never let me go.

I know I still have a full-time security team following me around, but I've never seen them and most of the time I forget they're even there. As much as Sebastian likes to pretend he doesn't want to keep me locked up, he confessed that he would struggle to not know where I was at all times and I came to the conclusion I could tolerate being followed as long as I didn't have to see it, or feel the eyes on me.

The tracking device is still beneath the skin in my neck, but he promised he's never activated it unless I was actually in danger. He did activate his though and from the app he installed on my phone, I can know exactly where he is at all times, not that I've ever thought to look.

The messed-up history we share hasn't just disappeared since we admitted our feelings for each other, and it'll be a long time before my dad will ever accept that Sebastian and I are together. He doesn't understand how I could possibly forgive him for everything he's done to me, and I get it, some days I'm not sure I'll ever be able to totally forgive him completely either. But what my dad is starting to understand is that even with all the awful things that have happened between us, we love each other, and sometimes love doesn't make sense and it isn't always kind. I'm hoping at some point in the future they can become tolerantly cordial toward each other, and possibly, eventually Dad could maybe learn to like him. My mom is over the moon that Sebastian and I are trying to work things out, she even turned up at Kingsacre thinking that mine and her relationship would be instantly fixed too. Just like my dad isn't willing to forget Sebastian's sins, I'm not ready to pretend that my mom didn't abandon me when I needed her the most. Perhaps we can reclaim some semblance of a friendship in the future, but for right now I'm still keeping her at a distance.

Mine and Sebastian's relationship is our own special brand of fucked up and even though it shouldn't, it works for us. I do whatever I want and he fights me on it, trying to get his own way. Sometimes I win, other times he manipulates me until I give in and give him what he wants. It's probably not healthy and it's definitely not normal, but it is us. It's love and hate and complete, out of control, beautiful obsession.

ACKNOWLEDGMENTS

Wow, this book didn't want to end!

I've really enjoyed being able to explore a new world and add a darker twist on a sexy story. Sebastian is all kinds of fucked up, but I really fell for his unapologetically psycho behavior.

When I was asked to be a part of the Filthy Elites Anthology, I saw the lineup of other authors and instantly thought I'd been invited by mistake. My next thought was to say yes before they figured out I was the wrong person LOL. Impostor syndrome is a real thing and this was probably the first time I've really experienced it, but no matter how I got here, I'm so thrilled to have my book be in a set with such outstanding authors.

The last few years have been all kinds of messed up (thanks, COVID), and I think more than ever we've needed the escapism of a good book, so I really hope you've enjoyed this chance to step out of your own life and into my characters.

I'm really hoping my wonderful editor Sarah Goodman likes Sebastian, I have a sneaking suspicion she will.

Like always, my bestie Sarah gets a mention, because I love her and she rocks.

My wonderful fellow author and friend Sybil Bartel, this book has an ending because you listened to the ten thousand messages I sent you and helped me end the book that just wouldn't end. You inspired me to write in the first place and you're always there when I need you, thank you.

To the wonderful team at Hudson Indie Ink, you guys rock, thank you for having my back.

Finally to all the fabulous people who've read this story, I hope you enjoyed it and I have lots of other OTT JP heroes to read if you want more.

ABOUT THE AUTHOR

Gemma Weir is a half crazed stay at home mom to three kids, one man child and a hell hound. She has lived in the midlands, in the UK her whole life and has wanted to write a book since she was a child. Gemma has a ridiculously dirty mind and loves her book boyfriends to be big, tattooed alpha males. She's a reader first and foremost and she loves her romance to come with a happy ending and lots of sexy sex.

For updates on future releases check out my social media links.

ALSO BY GEMMA WEIR

The Archers Creek Series

Echo (Archer's Creek #1)

Daisy (Archer's Creek #2)

Blade (Archer's Creek #3)

Echo & Liv (Archer's Creek #3.5)

Park (Archer's Creek #4)

Smoke (Archer's Creek #5)

*

The Scions Series

Hidden (The Scions #1)

Found (The Scions #2)

Wings & Roots (The Scions #3)

*

The Kings & Queens of St Augustus Series

The Spare - Part One

(The Kings & Queens of St Augustus #1)

The Spare - Part Two

(The Kings & Queens of St Augustus #2)

The Heir - Part One

(The Kings & Queens of St Augustus #3)

The Heir - Part Two

(The Kings & Queens of St Augustus #4)

*

The Montanna Mountain Men

Property the Mountain Man

Owned by the Mountain Man

Kept by the Mountain Man

Claimed by the Mountain Man

Saved by the Mountain Man

OTHER AUTHORS AT HUDSON INDIE INK

Paranormal Romance/Urban Fantasy

Stephanie Hudson

Sloane Murphy

Xen Randell

Sorcha Dawn

C L Monoghan

Sci-Fi/Fantasy

Devin Hanson

Crime/Action

Blake Hudson

Mike Gomes

Contemporary Romance

Gemma Weir

OBSESSION

Lightning Source UK Ltd.
Milton Keynes UK
UKHW011827190622
404644UK00001B/14

9 781913 904265